RELATED MATTERS

Other Books By William Hatfield

LGBT Fiction

TNT Series
Menu for Murder
Blown Choices
Bare Soles
Cheating Deaths
Deadly Views
Related Matters

LGBTQ Key West Romance

Diane Isis Bar & Girl Series
The Glare at Dusk

Science Fiction

Fists of Earth Series
Captive Audience
Duel Roles
Tough Crowd

Pawns of the Blade Series
Emperer's Blade

Short Story Collections
Key Notes

William Hatfield

Published by William Hatfield

RELATED MATTERS, Copyright 2021 by William Hatfield

All rights reserved. No part of this book may be reproduced, stored in a retrieval system or transmitted in any form or by any means without the prior written permission of the publisher, except by a reviewer who may quote brief passages in a review to be printed in a newspaper, magazine, journal, or online venue, such as blogs, websites, social media, or on toilet paper.

ISBN-13 979-8-5364-8897-3

This book is a work of fiction.

The characters, incidents, and dialogue are drawn from the author's quirky imagination and are not to be construed as real. Any resemblance to actual events or persons, living, dead, or undead, human or alien, is entirely coincidental.

Cover Design and Illustration by Jim Harrison/MetaVisual
Interior Design and Layout by Symes Design

First and foremost, I would like to thank my wife, Karen Hatfield, for her patience with my writing addiction. During certain portions of the writing process, I become quite obsessed and single-minded.

I would also like to thank my beta readers that find so many of my "whoopsies" and occasional inconsistencies. For "Related Matters", I would like to thank A.J. Wilcox, Dena K. Bovee, and Bruce E. Goll in particular for this project. Sometimes life intrudes, but their ability to juggle life and editing for the last six months were a godsend. I look forward to the return of the rest of "Bill's Betas" for the next project.

"Related Matters" is the last book in this storyline before the emergence of Covid-19. In fact, I hint and plant a foreshadowing of the year to come. The next TNT book will be slammed full of action with a struggle between factions you may remember from earlier books in the series. It will also stay true to the timeline of 2020, including Key West actually closing up for a month, and restricting access for at least that long.

So, enjoy this mostly light-hearted holiday season story, knowing that bullets, germs, and bodies will be flying about the oldtown in the next.

Before I forget, thank you to everyone that gambles a few dollars and hours of their time to read my books. I hope you enjoy reading them even a portion as much as I enjoy writing them.

Chapter One

He entered through the back entrance, walked past the pool tables, and went to the bar. There were several stools open. He planted himself on one and ordered a bottled beer, ignoring the "Tequila Tuesday" signs posted in the bar area. He casually looked around the room, saw a few couples out on the dance floor, more at tables.

As he watched, two women came in the front door, holding hands. He ignored them, and focused on the male couples, searching for unattached men. There were several at the end of the bar, but they were in a group, and all clearly knew each other. He looked up at the tables and booths on the second floor overlooking the dance floor and the small stage up against the front windows.

All he saw were more couples, or groups of either men or women, socializing, talking and laughing, obviously friends or more.

He put some money on the bar and walked back to the pool tables, looking intently at the players and kibitzers. Again, mostly couples or friends.

He wondered if there was such a thing as a family gay bar. If so, this establishment would probably be the poster child. Even the college age young men seemed either in couples, or in a group of friends that knew each other well. He felt eyes on him, probably from couples at the nearby tables, judging him.

What the hell did they know?

He downed his Bud Light, and tossed the bottle in a trash can as he walked out.

Too risky.

♦ ♦ ♦ ♦ ♦

Tess decided it was nice enough to sit out in the courtyard to eat her lunch. Her morning classes at the Key West School of Massage had been interesting and informative, and the time had flown by. She was afraid this afternoon was going to be less enjoyable.

All the students in her class were grouped in pairs. Her partner was Katrina, a pushy Russian woman about five years older than her. She'd made no secret of her desire for them to develop a "friendship with benefits", and repeatedly told her she had too much clothing on, was too uptight, and that it was okay to enjoy the sensuality of a good massage.

Tess had reminded her time and again, over the past couple months, that none of that was in her plans. She wasn't interested in anything more than passing her tests and fulfilling all the requirements to graduate in March with her license to practice massage therapy.

Not for the first time, she considered telling Skipper Gainey, the lead instructor and head of the school that she'd like a different partner.

Each time, she thought about how close March was, and surely she could fend off the woman for that long. All things considered, she knew she could.

But the woman used such gross stinky oil, Tess felt the necessity of rushing home and furiously scrubbing herself afterwards.

She took a bite of her sandwich, and speed dialed her Tue Bear. Her girl had the day off, which meant this morning Tuesday had run her usual mini-marathon at sprinter pace, swum the equivalent of the English Channel, and should be back from her Wednesday late morning class at the women's gym they used. She would lift weights, maybe spar with one of the other women for a few minutes, and be introduced to a new martial arts move she'd never tried before.

All under the intense scrutiny of Marisela Little, one of the owners. Mari, as everyone called her, was a black belt in Taekwondo and Aikido. She'd also mentioned something called Krav Maga, but Tess had no idea what that was.

Tuesday answered on the second ring.

"Hey, Babe, how's school?" her lover said in a laconic voice.

"This morning was very helpful," Tess said, trying to sound positive. "This afternoon, we're working on the arms and wrists, so I'm hoping for an afternoon without Katrina's hands drifting too far off target."

"Do you want me to talk to her?" Tuesday said brusquely, and Tess winced. She knew that tone.

"No, Hon, I got this." Tess tried to sound both firm and positive. "Friday is the last class this year, and we don't pick up again until after New Year's. Anyway, this is Wednesday, which means you should be focusing on tonight's softball game."

"For the season," Tuesday said, and Tess smiled as she heard both excitement and a little wistfulness in her voice.

Her team, the Amazons, had already won the regular season championship, and now were playing the last night of the season-ending tournament for the championship. That was exciting, but it also meant there wouldn't be any more games until late January.

What will we do with our Wednesday nights, Tess asked herself and smirked. She was pretty sure they'd think of something. Certainly for the next two. Christmas Day in a week, and New Year's Day a week later. Or, as Tuesday called it, Football Bowling Day.

"Did you spar?" she asked, more to take her girl's mind off the team than actually caring.

"Uh, yeah, I sparred with Oshba," Tuesday admitted, and Tess winced.

"How bad was it?" Tess asked hesitantly. She knew how proud and defensive her girl could be about things like this. It wasn't like it was her fault she was only five foot one, *if* she was wearing thickly soled shoes, Tess thought irreverently. And Oshba *was* a trained bodyguard, as well as ex-terrorist and assassin.

Tess didn't know that last part for a fact, but Oshba's girlfriend Phoebe had alluded to it, as had her boss, Yasmin, Nathan's girlfriend.

Oshba didn't talk much about her past.

"I held my own," Tuesday said firmly, and Tess smiled, translating her words. Oshba had pretty much had her way with Tuesday. Although about the same size as Tess, at five foot six inches, where Tess had long, sinewy dancer muscles, and worked out to be limber and graceful, Oshba had at least twenty or more pounds on her, all muscle. When you saw her without outer clothes on, it was very impressive.

Especially her stomach.

Oshba was the first girl Tess had ever seen that had a six-pack. Tuesday said that Diane, one of the owners of the restaurant that sponsored the Amazons had an even more impressive one, but she'd never actually noticed it.

Tess found that hard to believe. Diane was an older woman. She had to be nearly forty.

"I'll be home a little after four, so we won't have to rush to the game," Tess said.

"The game isn't until seven, so I'll have time to scrub that stinky oil Katrina uses off you," Tuesday said, and Tess smiled at the hopeful tone in her lover's voice.

"Save your strength for the game, Tue Bear," she said in a scolding tone. "Time for that later tonight."

She smiled as she ended the call. She pictured Tuesday sitting out by the pool, wearing her Gators visor and a smile, and her breathing got a little heavier.

I am so going to marry that girl.

Phoebe whistled under her breath as she worked her way down the line of jet skis, carefully topping off each machine's gas tank. Aurora had the last tour on the water now, and had eighteen machines out. She was due back in about twenty minutes, but would immediately need to board Freedom Wind for the sunset cruise.

She finished and gave the machines a critical eye. They were clean, fueled, critical parts, such as spark plugs, had been checked and were fine. They were in neat rows, leaving room for the last batch to fit on the dock platforms.

Phoebe felt her biceps and thought they seemed a little firmer than before she started working here. She knew her legs were stronger, as well as her back. She would always be lean, with long, ropy muscles rather than bulky ones, but she was fine with that.

Phoebe felt something and froze in her tracks. She closed her eyes for a moment, and then they popped open in shock. She whirled around to see Grandma Emily and Mother Grace standing on the dock next to the hut.

They were living proof she would never have a bulky musculature. Both were about her height, and lean, just like her.

Grandma Emily was sixty-nine years old, and her thick hair was a mix of different shades of grey and white. Oddly enough, she had one thick strand of black hair that defied the ages, and hadn't greyed. It ran from near the top of her head, down her left side to just cover her breast. She wore a skirt that hung to her ankles, with broad swathes of color in bands around her, and an Indian cotton shirt that hung to her hips. She controlled her hair with an orange cloth belt tied around her head like a headband.

Mother Grace would be fifty, next year. Her hair was a curious mix of black, grey and white. She kept it a little longer than shoulder length. She wore loose harem pants with bands of print and patterns around each leg, as well as artistic renditions of stately elephants. On top she had a light material cut like a serape, with patterns of rich, full, color combinations that shouted to catch the eye. She wore a man's fedora that Phoebe didn't recognize.

Phoebe started walking towards them, and felt her pace pick up until she ran the last ten feet and wrapped her arms around both of them.

"Mother, Grandma Emily, what are you doing here?" Phoebe hugged them enthusiastically. She alternated between hugging each of them individually, then impulsively did it again.

They looked at each other, then at her.

"Are you taking your herbal supplements? Your aura is quite different from the last time we saw you," her mother said, and Phoebe frowned at her.

"Mother, my being happy doesn't mean I'm sick or crazy," she said. She watched her mother look her over closely, which was nothing new, but a little annoying at this point in her life. Especially when her concern was that Phoebe was unnaturally cheerful.

"Are you being careful with your skin, daughter?" she asked. "Those shorts and that golf shirt are exposing you to a lot of sun."

"I improved on your level fifty sunscreen to create my Level Adamantium sunscreen that won't let me burn. I use it every day, and apply more as needed through the day. And they're called polos now. Nobody calls them golf shirts anymore."

Phoebe suppressed a sigh. Her mother's concerns were valid and she was right. But her assuming Phoebe was ignoring her ultra-pale skin was insulting. Phoebe had learned at a very early age that her skin was defenseless against the Florida sun. Which was why she'd developed such an interest in chemistry and sunscreen.

"Give me a little credit, Mother."

Grandma Emily tried to cushion Phoebe from Grace, which she appreciated, but at this point in her life, it was annoying that it was necessary.

"So this is where you work?" Grandma Emily asked and looked at the hut. "This looks nice."

"In the summer and early fall, it's extremely hot, but we have an air conditioner," Phoebe said with a smile as she went inside and held up Tess's little fan. "If we get another one, we'll have stereo A.C."

Both women looked at her curiously. Phoebe sighed and nodded. "Yes, sometimes I make jokes. No, I never have the urge to do myself in. Yes, I am happy. No, I'm not doing drugs or drinking in excess." She paused at that, and tempered her comment. "I probably could stand to have one less glass of wine or frozen drink, now and then."

"Where is everyone?" her mother asked, looking around their pier and the dock area. "Do they leave you all alone here? Is it safe?"

Phoebe gestured to the pier, and the two schooners, three catamarans, and the ferry currently tied up. "The tall ships and catamarans will do a

Related Matters

sunset tour, and the crew are either grabbing dinner, or a snack, or working onboard. The ferry doesn't go out every night, and is tied down and locked until the weekend. We have eighteen jet skis touring around Key West right now. One of my new roommates, Aurora, is leading the tour, and they will be back in about fifteen minutes. Or less. I'll introduce you to her. She won't be able to talk long, because she's crewing on one of the tall ships, the Freedom Wind, for the sunset champagne cruise."

Phoebe got an idea.

"The ship isn't full yet, and I don't think we'll have any more customers show up. Would you like to go out on it? They'll have free wine and sparkling wine they pretend is champagne. The quality is iffy, but you can have as much as you like."

"We're here to see you, Phoebe," her mother said firmly, but Grandma Emily looked at the two tall ships.

"What will you be doing during that time, granddaughter?" she asked, and Phoebe smiled at her.

"I'll be servicing, washing, and gassing up the jet skis Aurora is bringing in, and doing the end of day accounting chores, make up the deposit, that sort of thing. I really won't be able to talk with you much until later anyway." She had an idea.

"After we close, I'm going to Diane Isis Bar & Girl, both for dinner, and to celebrate with the girls on the softball team they sponsor. The Amazons should win their tournament tonight."

"I like the name," Grandma Emily said, and Grace nodded reluctantly. She looked at Phoebe.

"Your roommate's name is Aurora?" she asked. "The Roman Goddess of Dawn."

"She *is* Italian," Phoebe said neutrally, thinking about how much fun or how totally uncomfortable the next six hours might end up being. "Why don't you take the sunset cruise, and then I'll be off work, and they'll have food set out for the celebration. Most of my friends will be there."

Her last comment got her funny looks from both women.

"How much is the cruise?" her mother asked, and *her* mother made a face at her.

"It'll be free," Phoebe said. "I'm an employee, you are family. You ride for free, as long as there's space, and there is." She had a frightening thought.

"Where are you staying?" she asked nervously.

Grandma Emily was watching her face and started laughing. Her mother gave her a sardonic look. "Why, we're staying with you, Phoebe.

Is your bed big enough for three?"

"I don't know," Phoebe admitted. "Two is the most I've had in it. That was fine. C'mon, I'll show you the boats, introduce you to the Captains."

She purposefully walked fast enough they had to hustle to keep up. She knew that last comment was going to generate some questions.

"Phoebe, I think you have a customer," her mother called out to her, and Phoebe sighed and turned around to see Oshba standing next to the hut. She grinned and ran to her, jumping up at the last moment.

Oshba caught her easily, and Phoebe wrapped her legs around her lover's waist, her arms around her neck and shoulders. They exchanged a long, very satisfactory kiss in that position.

"Your timing is perfect, Hubibi," she whispered, and Oshba looked at the two women curiously. She still held Phoebe by her butt cheeks, easily holding her in place. "You better put me down for a moment."

Oshba lifted her away and Phoebe lowered her legs until her feet touched the dock. She turned around, facing her mother and grandmother, her arm slipping around Oshba's waist. Without hesitation, Oshba put her own arm around Phoebe's thin shoulders, and as always, Phoebe felt safe from anything the world could throw at her.

"Mother Grace, Grandma Emily, this is Oshba Salehi, the love of my life," Phoebe said and watched both women size her up.

Without realizing it, Oshba had dressed perfectly for making a good first impression on both women. She wore harem pants much like Mother Grace's, only Oshba's were hip huggers. Her top was a brilliant yellow and bunched at the top of her shoulders and a little less than halfway down her biceps. The combination left her stomach uncovered, and Phoebe bit back a smile as she watched both women stare at her lover's abdominal muscles. Her brown skin contrasted attractively against the bright yellow top.

"Oshba, this is my mother, Grace Stark, and her mother, my grandmother, Emily Stark," Phoebe finished the introductions and heard the sound of the jet skis approaching. She looked at her family. "You might want to watch this, it's kind of cool. Aurora is bringing in the tour."

They all looked past the bow of the huge cruise ship in the next facility, and saw one girl, wearing a bright red bikini, her hair flying out behind her lead a large group of jet skis past. They disappeared behind the cruise ship, and reappeared a minute later, rounding the stern of the ship.

Aurora saw them on the dock, and waved merrily as she slowed down and let her jet ski slip up onto the wooden ramp. She immediately turned around and directed everyone into a semblance of order as they docked their machines.

The customers all seemed very cheery, and were laughing and talking, both with each other, and with Aurora. Several times she pointed at the large glass jar firmly attached to the railing they had to pass to get to the dock.

Phoebe saw several people look at her, then at the hut, and walked towards it. She turned to the others. "I have to work for a minute."

She strode to the hut, answered a couple questions, and sold a combo pack of her shampoo, conditioner, two bars of key lime soap, and skin moisturizer. She could feel her mother and Grandma Emily come closer to watch as she sold a few more items, including two bottles of her Level Adamantium sunscreen.

The crowd finally moved on, and Phoebe turned back to her family. Oshba had told Aurora who Grace and Emily were, and they'd exchanged introductions. Aurora seemed in no hurry to change into the standard crew uniform of khaki shorts and Freedom Seas polo, and Phoebe finally caught Aurora's eye.

"Are you crewing tonight?" she asked, and Aurora nodded. "You know Captain Jeff won't let you work in a bikini. Scoot. We'll see you when you get back. We're taking them to Diane Isis for dinner and upstairs."

"Oh good," Aurora said, and smiled at the women. "My boss is telling me to quit flirting and get to work, so I must go. The high seas call me. Hopefully, it's mermaids and not sharks."

She grabbed her bag from behind the counter and ran down to the shed to change. They all watched until she disappeared into the bathroom.

"That is a beautiful woman," her mother said.

"No, that is a very dangerous woman," Grandma Emily corrected her. She glanced over at Phoebe. "Watch out for that one, Phoebe."

"She and I have already discussed that," Phoebe admitted. "Since we are housemates and will be spending time together regularly, I thought it prudent to tell her I was not available. She told me she'd already decided that I was safe from her wiles. She has no intention of trying to seduce me."

"She did not think you are beautiful enough to seduce?" Oshba asked very quietly. Phoebe laughed and hugged her close.

"No, you silly old alsaqr sharisa, she knows your skills and has no desire to experience them." Phoebe laughed, thinking about their conversation.

Oshba smiled at her tenderly, and put her arm around her as they turned together to face the older women.

8

"Are you going to go on the sunset cruise, Mother and Grandmother Stark?" Oshba asked them, and Phoebe loved her even more for her attempt to socialize with them. It wasn't one of her strong points.

"Why, are you waiting for us to go so you can make out?" her mother asked, and Grandma Emily laughed.

"No, mother. When your cruise leaves port, I will do all those chores I told you about." Phoebe smirked, which startled both women. "That will leave me between twenty and twenty-five minutes before the ships start returning. *That* is when we will make out."

Grandma Emily stepped close to Oshba and gave her a hug. She hesitantly returned it. The older woman held her by the shoulders, and although her eyes widened as she clearly felt the hardness of the muscles beneath, she didn't let it distract her.

"I hope you and Phoebe have a wonderful relationship, and may Mother Earth Gaia bless you both." She glanced at Phoebe, and then turned back to Oshba. "I don't believe I've ever seen her so happy. And as cool as Key West is, that alone wouldn't have transformed her so." She released Oshba, but couldn't resist pushing against her bicep with a finger.

"It sure didn't the first ten months she was here," Mother Grace said pointedly. She looked at Oshba. "May Gaia bless you both and your union, er, I mean, relationship."

Oshba looked thoughtful, and turned to look at Phoebe. "Did your mother just try and marry us?"

"Not intentionally, I don't think," Phoebe said, and couldn't resist giving both women food for thought. "You're a little ahead of yourself, Mother. We probably won't get married until next year."

"Come along, Gracie dear, and pull your jaw up," Grandma Emily said, and pulled her daughter along by the hand. "We have a boat to catch."

Phoebe quickly printed out two tickets under employee purchases and handed them to her grandmother. The two women headed down the dock towards where they could see Aurora working on the deck of one of the ships.

Phoebe felt her lover's arms close around her from behind, and sank back against her.

"I feel so safe when you hold me," she said softly.

"I would happily hold you the rest of our lives, Phoebe, my love," Oshba whispered in her ear. "Did you mean what you just told them about next year?"

"I did. Although it would depend on some things," Phoebe admitted.

"Really? Such as what?" Oshba asked, her tone a little cautious.

"Well, one of us will have to ask the other to marry them, and I would rather it was you that did the asking," Phoebe said, and squirmed around so they were facing, her still in Oshba's arms.

"I will happily ask you," Oshba said. "Why do you not wish to ask me?"

"Because, silly falcon, I want to be able to say yes," Phoebe said, and stretched up to kiss her lips. "And then to run around like a chicken with her head cut off, screaming and telling everyone you finally asked me to marry you. And I said yes."

Oshba looked into her eyes and smiled tenderly. "And when would you like this to occur?" she asked curiously.

"I'll let you know," Phoebe said, and laid her head against Oshba's shoulder. "Let's find out what your lady intends, and make our plans then."

She sighed.

"I just signed a year's lease. I don't see us waiting that long, but I also have a hard time imagining my moving into Yasmin's home, or you moving in with the three of us." She shrugged. "If one of them needed to move, we could probably make that work."

She pulled away from Oshba, hard as that was to do. "Right now, I have work to do. We'll talk and smooch when I get that done."

"I can wait," Oshba said, smiling.

A few hours later, they walked into the Diane Isis Bar & Girl. The team had just arrived a few minutes earlier. She could hear them on the roof as they approached the building.

Phoebe watched her mother and grandmother slowly walk around the restaurant area, looking at all the paintings, reliefs, sculptures, and what looked like a ship's figurehead of a warrior woman, with sword raised and pointed straight ahead. It started flush with the wall behind the bar and stretched forward well above the bar to thrust a sword straight ahead, as if charging into battle. Other than a silver winged helmet, the woman was totally nude, to below her waistline, where her body merged with the wall.

"There's so much to look at," Grandma Emily said, staring at the figurehead. She looked at Phoebe in awe. "They must have taken years to acquire all this art, from all over the world."

"Actually, almost all the art was done by one of the owners, Diane Sparks," Phoebe said, wanting to impress them. It worked. Her mother slowly shuffled down the bar, looking at the various paintings on the back wall. She stopped at one that showed the bar from across the road. Two attractive women waved from the roof, obviously naked. The heavy piping guardrail along the edge of the roof conveniently covered their naughty bits. "She only paints, draws or sculpts nude women, and if the subject is a real person, she will only do them after seeing them nude."

"Can't argue with her tastes," her mother said slowly, breaking into a grin as she rounded the corner of the bar, and saw the ancient Wonder Woman jukebox in the gaming area to the back, by the pool tables.

"Come upstairs, and let me introduce you to some people," Phoebe said, and led them out the back door and up the stairs. "All this will still be here later, when we come back down."

The roof was fairly full, and Phoebe saw Izzy talking with Tess, and a few other women. Everyone had already removed their shirts, and Shanda was slipping between players, topless, getting drink orders, joking, talking about the game.

Emily and Grace stopped dead at the top of the stairs and stared around the roof. Emily noticed the row of women archer statues, bows bent, ready to release their arrows, and she oohed and stepped over to look at them. Then she saw the centerpiece of the roof, the statue of the two women preparing to have oral sex. She knelt next to it and looked at it in awe.

"Izzy, this is my mother Grace," Phoebe said, and they shook hands. Izzy was tall, several inches shy of six feet, voluptuous, long black hair flowing down over her shoulders. She looked every bit a Roman goddess. "That woman about to go down on the statue is my Grandmother Emily."

"I heard that, young lady," she said, and looked at Phoebe, then at Oshba, speculatively.

"Yes, we have, and that's enough on *that* subject," Phoebe said crisply, and her grandmother grinned and nodded her head. She stood up and looked around.

"So, why has everyone taken their shirts off?" she asked, and Grace nodded.

"I was just going to ask that."

"After a game, most of the ladies are soaking wet with sweat, and the shirts are icky and uncomfortable," Izzy said, and shuddered. "And hugging them in cold clammy stinky shirts is gross. So they strip them off, and everyone gets to show their bras off."

Shanda picked that moment to slide between them, carrying four buckets of longneck beers. She was an inch or two taller than Phoebe, but her muscles were lean and hard. She made carrying two buckets of five beers packed with ice in each hand look effortless. Her breasts were practically nonexistent, except for obscenely protruding nipples. "Vanilla and chocolate, ladies," she said, shaking her shoulders to make them wave, and kept going.

"Shanda says she doesn't own a bra because why would she?" Izzy admitted. "And you can't argue with the truth."

Phoebe took a deep breath and pulled her polo off, revealing a new bra Oshba had bought for her. It was black and pushed her small breasts upward, giving her some semblance of cleavage.

Oshba followed suit, showing an identical bra, except it was brilliant yellow, same as her shirt. It made her own modest breasts look bigger and also allowed viewers to see her layers of muscles on her torso, as well as her zero body fat content. It also showed off her numerous scars on her back, as well as several on her sides and stomach.

Grandma Emily made a sound of distress and reached out towards the thin lines that crisscrossed her back. Without seeming to notice her, Oshba casually shifted around back next to Phoebe, turning so her back was out of reach.

"Grandma Emily, Oshba is very private where her scars are concerned," Phoebe said quietly, and her grandmother nodded slowly.

"I'm very sorry if I intruded on your personal space, Oshba," she said, tearing her eyes away from staring at Oshba's torso. "I didn't mean to offend you."

"I am not at all offended, Grandma Stark," Oshba said immediately. "I understand your curiosity, but they are from a time and circumstances in my life that I wish to leave buried."

Phoebe watched her grandma nod slowly,

Aurora pulled her shirt off, and she had a similar style bra. She was bosomy and, as Tuesday once said, looking at her without a top simply caused brain freeze. Phoebe and Oshba laid their shirts on a table, neatly folded, and Oshba looked at Phoebe.

"What would you like, little bird?" she asked, and Phoebe smiled.

"Either a Barbie or a Penis Colossus," she said. "Surprise me."

Oshba tried to flag Shanda down and Phoebe turned back to her family to see her mother pulling her serape off. She folded it neatly and set it on top of Phoebe's polo.

"Blend in with the natives, I always say," she said smiling, and called out to Oshba. "Would you tell that girl with the delightful nipples I'd like to order a bucket of beer?"

"Here, this will hold you until it gets here," Diane Sparks said, offering her a longneck Corona out of a bucket on a nearby table. She was Izzy's wife, an inch shorter, but probably at least thirty pounds heavier, all of it muscle, well proportioned, and very defined. Phoebe was proud of how fit Oshba was, and her stomach was lined with muscles. But Diane's muscles were defined and firm, from neck to toe.

"Thank you," she said, and sized Diane up. Phoebe recognized the routine and hurriedly interceded.

"Mother, this is Diane Sparks, the artist that did most of the artwork in and on this building. And, Izzy's wife. Diane, this is Grace Stark, my mother."

Phoebe turned to see her grandma looking quizzically at the people around the roof. She turned to Phoebe. "I didn't wear a bra," she said.

Phoebe opened her mouth to tell her that was okay, and not mandatory, but her grandma unbuttoned her cotton blouse, removed it, and placed it on top of the rest.

Phoebe wasn't really surprised. She knew both women's comfort levels with nudity. She smiled as Izzy saw and thought her grandma felt pressured to take her shirt off.

Izzy told her she didn't have to remove her shirt.

"Oh, that's fine, dear," Grandma Emily said, smiling at her. She gestured at some of the players, and their baseball pants. "Don't the girls ever find that their pants or shorts are chafing, and have clay all over them?"

Izzy was sipping her red wine and snorted some of it up her nose, she laughed so quickly.

"Don't get choked up on me now, young lady," Grandma Emily said, and looked at Izzy's bra. And, Phoebe assumed, the breasts they partially hid. "That's a very pretty bra you're wearing, Izzy. It looks like it's coaching your girls up nicely."

Izzy stared at her, then over at Phoebe, and started grinning.

"I think I should introduce you to my wife, Diane," she said, and put her arm around Emily's waist. "She's the artist that did these statues, and a lot of the ones downstairs, as well as the paintings."

Phoebe decided there was plenty of time to introduce them to some of her other friends. She was ready to relax for a few minutes, holding hands with Oshba.

"I believe you need this," Oshba spoke into her ear, as she handed her a frozen drink. "I got you a Barbie. Up here, tonight, anything penis related seems like a poor choice."

One of the blond twins on the softball team happened to be walking past. Phoebe knew both of them were straight, much to the dismay of the rest of the team. She leaned forward and whispered in a conspiratorial voice.

"They grow on you."

Phoebe snorted her drink and Oshba hurried to find napkins.

Chapter Two

Lawrence Farrell secured his tray and handed his empty plastic cup to the flight attendant. He looked out the window and watched the ground grow nearer. The skyline of Atlanta was briefly visible as the jet swung into its final approach.

He didn't have to look at his watch or iPhone to know the flight was on time, and that he had more than sufficient time to make his connection to Dallas-Fort Worth. Fortunately, for the work portion of his trip, he was going as his blue-collar, butch dyke Luanne Johnson persona, and it wouldn't take any time to change into it before he had to board. As usual, he had no checked baggage.

He'd reserved his seat in the front of the plane, just before the first class partition, and made it off the plane quickly. He only had his small carryon suitcase and his laptop bag, and a heavier jacket that he strapped to his bag.

He saw a men's restroom ahead, and went inside and locked himself into the handicapped stall. He quickly took his solid blue sweatshirt off and unrolled a padded bra from his socks and underwear, in his carryon suitcase. It only took a moment to put it on, replace her sweatshirt with a grey Mavericks t-shirt, spike her hair with some hair gel, run a safety razor over her face, removing any hint of an afternoon shadow, and put just a hint of mascara and lipstick on. She slipped into a gun-metal grey hoodie, and repacked her carryon, complete with the heavier jacket, now neatly folded inside.

Luanne pulled the hood up to cover her hair, stared at herself for moment, and gave a slight leer.

"What are you looking at, bitch?"

No one paid her any attention as she exited the stall, and the restroom. Her connection was only six gates away. In her casual jeans, t-shirt and hoodie, hood now down, she attracted no attention, except for an interested stare from the fem in a lesbian couple that thankfully ended up seated near the rear of the plane.

A couple hours later, she was leaving the Dallas/Fort Worth International Airport in a taxi, bound for the American Airlines Center, home of the Dallas Mavericks. Her carryon and her laptop case were stashed in a locker that reminded her there was a four-hour limit. That was fine. She'd be back here in half that time, getting ready to board the last flight back to Atlanta.

Her hood was down, and she noticed that people's eyes automatically gravitated to her hair, hardly looking at her features. She wasn't really busty enough for anyone to pay much attention to her body, except for that one fem on the plane. Her jeans were loose, so the fact that she hadn't bothered strapping her male organs out of obvious sight didn't matter.

Unless someone tried to grab her crotch, no one would be able to tell she was carrying extra equipment.

She had no trouble using her digital ticket on her phone and found a woman's restroom. She sighed when she saw the line, and looked longingly at the almost deserted men's restroom nearby. But she waited patiently, pretending to read the news on her phone to discourage idle conversation.

When she finally was in a stall, she carefully opened the little pillbox and slipped the silver ring on, making sure the little pearl ball was firmly in place. She slipped it on her left fourth finger, flushed the toilet for appearances' sake, washed her hands and left.

Luanne made her way to the gates giving access to section 107. She walked down the steps until she saw her mark, seated with a couple other men, watching the teams warm up.

The Mavericks were playing the Celtics tonight, and there was a lot of verbal abuse happening between the fans of the two teams. Luanne nodded to herself, verified that her target would use the same gate she had if he went to get a beer or use the john.

She showed an usher her ticket, and he pointed at an open seat four spots from the aisle, which she already knew. She made her way to her seat, ignoring her neighbors, from either team, and proceeded to pretend to watch the game, reacting as a home fan would.

She thought about the target, Mark Durham, and was satisfied this should be a stress-free, uneventful contract. At some point, he would either get thirsty, or have to pee. And then she would have him. If she had to, she could wait until he left, but she didn't want to cut the timing so close to make her flight back to Atlanta, later tonight.

Mark Durham was an ICE agent and worked border patrol. He was in Dallas for a couple days to catch the game and, if he stuck to his usual routine, hit the titty bars with his buddies. The men with him were all ICE agents, but none of them were in on his side business.

None of them were traffickers in children, and routinely sold immigrant children to some very bad men in El Paso. Durham may or may not have known that many of these children ended up victims of a prolific sex trade in children, and Luanne didn't care.

Whether he knew or not, he *should* have, and tonight he would pay the price. And she would get paid for doing something she would have happily done for free.

Durham and his buddies stayed put for most of the first half, and Luanne was beginning to get restless. She was eager to do the job, and be on her way. She'd already had a couple women notice her as they passed on the steps, and give her interested gazes. When the two from the flight from Atlanta passed by, they both noticed her. The fem gave her a smile, which her partner caught, of course, and her glare was immediate.

It transferred to Luanne far too quickly. The last thing she wanted, was to attract attention by having to kick some jealous woman's ass. But the fem pulled her arm, and the butch dyke let herself be led off to wherever they were going.

A few minutes later, Durham and one of his friends got up, and headed up the steps. They were carrying empty plastic beer cups, and she suspected the arena had some sort of cheaper refill choice they were going to take advantage of. She gave him a minute and then a little more, before she got up, made her way past the people in the seats of her row and headed after Durham.

She'd done her homework, and knew where the closest beer stand was, sure enough, there he was. There was a good-sized crowd in line, all of them thinking they were beating the half-time crush. The lines weren't well defined, and Luanne felt herself smile as she turned the ring around on her finger so the pearl was inside her fist.

As she got close, she twisted the pearl and pulled it off, revealing a needle as fine as thread. She walked past him to another part of the line, and gave him a quick pat on his lower back. He had a nylon jersey on, and the needle easily penetrated the material.

As the needle pierced his skin, the ring gave a static shock, and they both gasped. Luanne carefully replaced the pearl and clicked it into place.

Durham turned around, an annoyed expression on his face.

"What the fu…?" he started, and Luanne interrupted him, shaking her hand, as if she'd been bitten.

"Wow, talk about static electricity," she gasped, and stared at him. "If you were a girl, I'd take it as an omen. But not when it's an old…"

"Aw, shut the hell up, lezzie bitch," he snarled. His initial look of interested speculation changed to anger and embarrassment. He tried to rub his back where he'd felt the charge, but it was just high enough to be difficult to reach. He stopped trying, and looked like he was going to say something more, but Luanne didn't give him the chance.

"Screw you, old man," she sneered, and kept going. She listened but he didn't follow her. His friend made a comment, and his focus shifted to him.

Luanne walked out of the arena and walked until she saw a taxi. She waved him down, and an hour later, she was sitting at her gate, waiting for her flight back to Atlanta.

The Mexican cartel had wanted him to suffer in his death, but wanted no connection back to them that would cause an investigation into Durham's activities. Since they were taking over his network, attention was the last thing they wanted.

A concentrated burst of brown recluse venom, as well as several other less obvious fast-acting poisons that were almost undetectable after they reached the bloodstream would cause a painful death, and not lead anyone to check a connection to the cartel.

Lori Lynn walked up the stairs to the roof of Diane Isis and saw a very wild scene. She took a sip of her whiskey sour and watched the camaraderie. Of course, everyone had removed their shirt, and it appeared that at least one of the women, in addition to the wiry black girl with the afro, hadn't worn a bra, because she was topless.

She looks pretty good for an old broad, Lori Lynn thought, and hid her grin. She looked for a place to put her top, and saw a stack of shirts neatly piled next to Phoebe. She decided that would work.

Lori Lynn was wearing Capri styled leggings that looked like jeans, and a floral peasant blouse with a gathered neckline and voluminous long sleeves, gathered at the wrist.

She was lean, almost six feet tall, very fit. Her breasts were full, if not huge, and with her build, drew almost everyone's eyes. Lori Lynn took a deep breath and pulled her blouse off, and was very self-conscious about the bra she'd chosen. It was new and this was the first time she'd worn it.

It was a pale blue Gilly Hicks crochet lace unlined balconette bra, and was very comfortable. The material was also very thin, with just enough lace pattern to keep it from being sheer. Her girls filled it nicely. She would never wear it to work, but it felt very liberating, not only wearing it, but knowing everyone could see it.

Except for her temporary partner, Sergeant Nico Skourellos, of course. She wasn't going to torture the poor man that way. He was such a gentleman, not to mention shy as anyone she'd ever known.

He was also very sweet. Today, he'd told her to forget about driving to Diane Isis. He would take her there and find things to do until she called him to come get her. Having to go back for her car the next morning was getting old for both of them.

"Looking good, Lieutenant," Shanda said as she passed. "I don't have to be a detective to know nice girls when I see them."

"Thanks," Lori Lynn said dryly. S*mart ass.*

Lori Lynn saw Yasmin talking to several women. Nadezhda, one of her bodyguards, stood discreetly off to the side, always watching, but so subtly, most of the woman on the roof didn't even notice her. Of course, to Lori Lynn, the detective, the Arab woman screamed danger, and with good reason. She was a couple inches shorter than Lori Lynn, but was clearly a workout fanatic, and had the muscles to prove it. Between that and her rugged face, with a strong nose that had clearly been broken a couple times, she looked as tough as any woman Lori Lynn knew.

Well, except for Mari Little, a city cop that taught martial arts classes in the women's gym she owned. Mari was in a class all her own, with multiple black belts and decades of training.

She knew Yasmin's lover, Nathan, was playing a set with Dr. Leek's Prime Rib Veggies at Eddie's tonight, as he always did when the blues band played there. When Nathan sat in with them, they did nothing but classic rock, and the combination of talent was easily the best cover band she'd ever heard.

Even as she had the thought, Yasmin looked at Nadezhda, who nodded. They began to work their way toward the stairs. She had once told Lori Lynn she went to every one of Nathan's gigs, and the band started playing in about half an hour.

Not for the first time, Lori Lynn caught herself staring at the young Arab girl. She was only twenty-one, and drop dead beautiful. She looked like she belonged either in a Miss Universe pageant, or on a runway, modeling slinky dresses for the stars. Tall and slender, long thick straight black hair down to her buttocks, it was easy to see how she'd caught Nathan's interest initially. They'd known each other less than three months, but Yasmin had just bought a beautiful house in Key West, and made it clear that she was here to stay.

And he was the reason.

"We will be back after my Nathan finishes playing," Yasmin told Izzy, who nodded knowingly. "I'm sure he will find something to occupy his time for an hour or so."

Nathan knew Yasmin's routine, and since Diane Isis's roof was off limits to all men, he would have dinner at Smokin' Tuna. Hanging out with his cute little bartender best friend, Lori Lynn thought, and decided she was being catty. Nathan and Sarah were good friends, and nothing more. Even so, Lori Lynn had noticed he was very protective of her as if she was his sister or daughter.

Or lover.

Izzy saw her and came over and admired her Gilly Hicks, joking about how Wednesday nights allowed her to shop. She was wearing a tasteful light blue thinly layered bra that teased with transparency, but never quite delivered.

"Do you think Ashley is coming tonight?" Lori Lynn asked, and Izzy grinned at her. "She's a friend," she added lamely.

"I get it. Safety in numbers," Izzy laughed. "I know you like men, Lori Lynn, and I've seen you with Sergeant Nico enough times to know which man in particular."

"We work together," Lori Lynn began, and Izzy raised her hand.

"I get it. And you outrank him, you're probably his boss," Izzy said sympathetically. "And with the Monroe County Sheriff's Department, that's a no no. I get it."

Lori Lynn started to try and tell her that she meant they were just friends, but could see Izzy wasn't going to buy it and gave up.

"I worked with him for a couple years before I realized what a great guy he is," Lori Lynn admitted.

"I know," Izzy nodded, looking pensive, and maybe even a little sad. "We've known Nico since he was a brand new rookie. I met him the day Diane and I reconnected here in Key West, fifteen years ago. He was partnered with Richard Carlson, who'd taken Diane under his wing, even if she didn't know it yet."

"I loved Richard," Lori Lynn said, and felt sad. "I could go and talk with him about anything. You know, he kept rescuing runaways, up to the day he…" She stopped, looking sad.

"Yeah, we both miss him. He was like a surrogate father to us," Izzy said, and something in her voice made Lori Lynn look at her sharply. "Hell, we miss both of them. You know, Nico's first date with his ex-wife was at Diane's first art show here in Key West. Of course, when they got together, she pulled him into her world, at the expense of his own personal circle of friends. It went from seeing him every week, sometimes a couple times, to maybe seeing him at holidays or special occasions."

"Really?" Lori Lynn looked at her curiously. "We haven't really talked about her at all. But he did mention he missed the old days and some really good friendships." Lori smiled, remembering a day in particular that they'd sat on her boat, pretending to fish, for the entire day, just talking. "We talked about so many things that day, but he wasn't very specific about that point in his life. Sometimes, something will remind him, and he gets this sappy, kinda sad puppy dog look on his face. He'll make a few comments, then change the subject."

"Sometimes it's the oddest things that bring back old memories. For Diane and me, it's those crazy TNT kids," Izzy said softly. "They're a mess, but the cutest, nicest mess I've ever seen. They bring back memories of an old friend or two." Her voice sounded pained, and Lori Lynn was concerned.

"You want to talk about it?" Lori Lynn asked, and Izzy shook her head.

"No, well, I mean, I'd love to sit down and chat with you more often, and talking about those days would probably be therapeutic." Izzy sighed and glanced over to the far corner of the roof. "But not tonight. This night is already too schizoid. We just won the last game, running our championship string to four, but one of our players lost her brother yesterday."

"Oh, I'm sorry," Lori Lynn was startled. "She played tonight?"

"We didn't expect her, but she showed up, and said she needed to play. To take her mind off how her brother could die of either the flu or pneumonia, living in Key West, Florida."

"That's weird," Lori Lynn frowned. "The weather hasn't been bad. Which did it turn out to be?"

"They're not even sure that's what it was. The doctor finally called it the flu, but the symptoms didn't really match up quite right."

"Weird," Lori Lynn repeated, and they both jumped as a roar rose from the women around them.

"I think Ashley Tanner just arrived," Izzy said, smiling at Lori Lynn wanly.

"It sounds more like she just took her shirt off," Lori Lynn said, trying to bring a smile to the woman's face.

"Wardrobe malfunction, maybe?" Izzy asked and they both grinned.

"Enquiring minds need to know," Lori Lynn said and they worked their way through the crowd.

Ashley was a statuesque five feet ten inches tall, athletic, yet volup-

Related Matters

tuous. She had firm full breasts, a high school graduation present from her parents, twelve years ago. They stuck straight out like pop-up headlights from an ancient classic car.

Ashley pulled her tube top off, showing a bra that reinforced her monumental breasts from beneath, but did a very inadequate job of covering their fronts.

They both clapped and cheered with the rest of the women. Lori Lynn watched Tess give Ashley a hug, and giggle, pretending to struggle with her breasts to get close enough to kiss her cheek.

Tess saw Lori Lynn and came across the roof to hug her. She looked down at Lori Lynn's breasts and said they reminded her of her Tue Bear's boobies. Firm and leading the way. Lori Lynn snickered.

"My Tue Bear's boobies are perkier, but your level of perkosity is impressive," Tess said with a totally deadpan face. It took Lori Lynn a moment before she realized the girl was feeling her drinks. She said that, and Tess giggled, and held up her frozen drink.

"I'm feeling my Barbies," she said, and took a sip. She saw Lori Lynn's expression and held the drink out for her to try. Lori Lynn tried to remember the last time she tried someone else's drink and couldn't. As a law officer, she could never do that. That was a rule encased in stone.

She took a sip.

"Oh, a frozen daiquiri," Lori Lynn said, and thought it tasted awfully good. She looked at her depleted whiskey sour and debated in her head. Tess correctly read her thoughts and started giggling again.

"How can you two be so terminally cute?" she asked, smiling at Tess. The girl got a thoughtful look on her face, and finally nodded decisively.

"I think it's because we're cute," she said, and started giggling again.

Ashley Tanner found them right about then, as did Tuesday.

"Lieutenant Lori Lynn Buffington, imagine seeing you here," she said, smiling as she gave her a hug. As always, Lori Lynn was a little stunned by how solid those bludgeoning rams were. Yet they seemed to flow in motion when she moved, and molded right around her own breasts when they hugged. Ashley had told her they were a graduation present from her parents, and she decided Ashley's parents were quite different from hers.

"What you drinking girl?" Ashley asked, looking at the empty glass in her hand.

"Well..." Lori Lynn began, but Tess spoke up.

"We're drinking Barbies around here," Tess said firmly. "No Kens allowed."

Ashley looked at Tess with a grin, and then at Lori Lynn inquiringly, who shrugged.

"Barbies, it is," Ashley said and called out. "Shanda, two Barbies, please."

"Let's get some food into you, Babe," Tuesday said, appearing at Tess's side. She gave them both a quick hug, then led Tess over to the overflowing table of snacks and appetizers.

Ashley Tanner was engaged to Wally Wilson, the owner of Freedom Seas, where Tess, Tuesday, and Phoebe all worked. She also ran one of Wally's B&Bs, and had just gotten her realtor's license. She knew everyone around town and managed to sell a couple modestly priced houses.

Then Yasmin came to town, apparently fell in love with Nathan, Key West, and maybe Tess as well, from what Lori Lynn could see. She had just found out Ashley was a realtor when she decided Key West was the home she'd been searching for. She bought a three-million dollar house on the corner of Whitehead and United. Even splitting the commission, Ashley would break into a grin every time it was mentioned.

Shanda handed her a Barbie, and Ashley hooked her arm in hers, and turned her towards the milling ladies.

"You're not at work, Lori Lynn. Let's go tease the lezzies on what they can't have."

Lori Lynn couldn't help but grin as she let herself be dragged over to the group gathered around the topless older woman.

Just before midnight, Lori Lynn carefully texted a message for Nico to come pick her up. The response was immediate.

I'm downstairs.

"Oh, Nico is downstairs," she said, and Grace and Emily clapped and cheered her on. She hugged them both, blinking when she did Emily. She didn't think she'd ever hugged a topless woman before.

Lori Lynn got her things and said goodbye to Izzy and Diane. She walked down the stairs and through the restaurant, which had maybe a dozen people either eating or drinking at the bar. She finished her Barbie and set the empty cup on the bar as she walked by.

Several customers raised their glasses to her. She wondered if she knew them, nodding back amiably.

Nico was just turning away from Shanda and putting his wallet away. He saw her and grinned, but got ahead of her and held the door.

"Thank you, good sir," she said and saw his car parked across the road. She got in, tossed her things on the dash, and fastened her seatbelt.

Nico started the car and as he pulled out, glanced over at her.

"Did you have fun?" he asked.

"Oh yeah, the place was packed and everyone was in weird moods. Speaking of weird, Phoebe Stark's mother and grandmother were there, and they're a hoot. Her grandmother wasn't wearing a bra, but she still took her shirt off and went topless all night."

"I could tell you were having a good time," Nico said. Lori Lynn looked at him suspiciously.

"How?" she finally asked.

He pulled up to a stop sign, opened his phone and handed it to her. She read her text to him.

Ken U come peck me up!

"Well crap," she said, and he chuckled.

"What were you drinking?" he asked.

"I started out with my usual whiskey sour, but Tess introduced me to Barbies, and I ended up drinking those the rest of the night."

"Hmm," Nico said, and his grin widened. "What exactly *are* Barbies?"

"Frozen lime daiquiris," she admitted. "You know, the exclamation mark is right next to the question mark on the iPhone keypad," she said, and shrugged. "It was probably the light on the roof. It's a little dark up there."

"Right," Nico said, and started laughing. "So when did you want me to "peck you up"? And where exactly?"

Lori Lynn sighed and shook her head.

"Don't start," she said firmly. "I ate dinner, and I spaced my Barbies out over the evening."

"But what is Ken going to say?" Nico said, and she saw he was grinning widely.

"Don't try and imply I was drunk," she said, frowning at him. She blinked her eyes hard a couple times to clear them.

"Okay, just tell me this," he said, and she looked at him. "What is that in your shirt pocket?"

"This shirt doesn't have a…oh, crap!" she said, looking down at her pretty, new Gilly Hicks crochet lace unlined balconette bra, light blue. She looked up on the dash and saw her blouse with her little purse.

She stared straight ahead, and exhaled noisily. She could feel Nico laughing next to her, but didn't look.

"Great bra, by the way," he noted.

"Aw, shaddap," she muttered, and he laughed harder.

◆ ◆ ◆ ◆ ◆

"Last night was the best time I've had in years," Grandma Emily announced, and Grace nodded her head in agreement.

Phoebe resisted the urge to sigh. The first time she'd said that, half an hour ago, it had been gratifying. The second time, kind of cute. The half dozen or so times since, not so much. Emily and Grace, as Phoebe always thought of her grandmother and mother, had shown up a little after nine, at the hut, to thank her profusely for taking them to Diane Isis last night.

"You told me that, at least four times last night," Phoebe reminded them. "That and all the times this morning already, I think you just hit a baker's dozen." Which reminded her. "Did you two have anything for breakfast? I know a few places that are kind of reasonably priced."

"The bed and breakfast had a very nice continental breakfast with a lot of fruit, cold cereal, and the best fruit bread I've had in years," Grace said, and Emily nodded. "No, I think we'll probably wander up Duval Street and maybe do a little shopping."

"I think your girlfriend is very nice, Phoebe," Emily said, and looked at her closely. "She's quiet, but clearly madly in love with you. I must read her palm and her cards. How did you meet, again?"

"Her employer, Yasmin, is Nathan's girlfriend," Phoebe said, and waited for the inevitable.

"We met Yasmin last night. And Nathan is…?" Grace asked.

Phoebe sighed.

"Nathan is Tess and Tuesday's roommate," Phoebe said patiently. "He's an exceptional singer and musician, and does mostly rock and folk from the late sixties, early seventies, with a few newer songs tossed in. You two really should take notes."

"We met a lot of people last night, Phoebe," Grace said pointedly. "And what exactly does Oshba *do* for Yasmin? Is she some kind of companion, like a nurse, or a maid?"

"If she is, she's the most muscular nurse I've ever seen," Emily muttered, clearly reliving when she hugged Oshba and felt her muscles. "You could bounce quarters off those abs, like a marine making his bed. The other woman, Nadi, I believed everyone called her. Now that one is muscular, but in a bulky, barroom bouncer way."

Grace nodded, and Phoebe wondered what the heck her grandmother was talking about, with the reference to quarters and beds. She debated how much to tell them about Oshba and Yasmin, and mentally shrugged. They were going to find out pretty fast anyway. Especially if she and Oshba were getting married.

The thought took her breath away for a moment and she felt weak-kneed.

"Are you okay, dear?" Emily asked immediately. "You suddenly looked a little woozy."

"I was remembering last night, after I told you we were going to marry," Phoebe admitted. "Oshba said she will ask me as soon as I tell her it's time. Oshba, and the other employee, Nadezhdah, or Nadi, as you heard, are Yasmin's bodyguards. She's from the royal family of Abu Dhabi, and kind of exiled, for her refusal to commit to what they think is a normal lifestyle and for refusing to marry some old sheik."

Emily and Grace looked at each other.

"Where to start?" Grace mused, and nodded to herself. She gave Phoebe a piercing look. "Are you two really serious about getting married next year? Next year is less than two weeks away. And you've barely met. And she's really the first person you've ever had a romantic relationship with."

"I was her first as well," Phoebe admitted. "She says she made out with a couple girls and boys when she was a teenager, but it didn't get far. Her childhood was very rough, and romance never entered in."

"She's older than you," Grace said, and Phoebe nodded again.

"She'll be thirty next summer," Phoebe said. "I'll be twenty-two then." She stared at both of them. "I hope you both become comfortable with the idea, because it *will* be happening. I know Oshba would love to have both your approvals. She was an orphan, and the closest thing she ever had to a family before Key West, was a terrorist cell of the Houthi in Yemen. But either way, she and I *will* marry next year."

Both of them stared at Phoebe. A smile tugged at Emily's lips. She glanced over at her daughter.

"It looks like our Phoebe is finally beginning to become a Stark woman," she said, and Phoebe was relieved to see pride in her grandmother's face. "It shows in your aura, and even your voice resonates more. In fact, yesterday, the way you took charge with the young Italian girl, I was beginning to wonder if you were a manager already."

"No, but I know what needs to be done, and I'm no longer the newest hire," Phoebe admitted. "Tess is the real boss, after the owner, Wally. That reminds me, Nathan plays happy hour this evening, and then he sits in with the band that follows him for a set. They do all that music you went to Woodstock to hear, back in the day, Grandma Emily."

"Is he any good?" Grace asked, and Phoebe smiled.

"He's pretty good," she said, intentionally understating the truth.

"Tess is going to grab a bite to eat, and then go listen to Nathan for an hour or so. By then we'll be closed up here and Tuesday, Oshba and I will be going there for the first set with the band, unless Oshba's working tonight. Then she'll be with Yasmin, and they'll be there from when he starts until he's done for the night. Tess said she'd love to have you join her for dinner at Captain Eddie's."

The two women looked at each other, and shrugged.

"That sounds fine, dear," Emily said. "Should we come back here?"

"Around five?" Phoebe suggested and they both nodded. She sighed in relief. Finding babysitters for watching her mother and grandmother could be a challenge.

Related Matters

Chapter Three

Tess watched Emily and Grace glance at both sides of the laminated menu for Amigos Tortilla Bar. They'd been lucky and gotten seats at the long bar that ran across the front of the restaurant, facing Greene Street. It was open air seating, and unseasonably nice for December. The breeze off the water a couple blocks away was modest, and not chilly.

A waitress stood on the sidewalk, facing them across the bar counter.

"Can I get you drinks while you decide?" she asked, and both women ordered Coronas. Tess debated and decided to hold off on the liquor.

"Just water for me," she said, and the woman nodded and was gone.

"What's good, here?" Grace asked, and Tess smiled.

"Everything we've tried, so far," she said, and pointed at the burrito bowls. "Those are good. The square Tacos are my personal favorite."

"Square tacos?" Emily asked, and Tess smiled and nodded.

"In Key West, everyone has their own personal stamp on things, to make them stand out," Tess admitted.

"Smart," Emily said, and all three of them started as the waitress put their drinks in front of them. "Goodness, you're quick, girl."

"Do you need a couple more minutes?" she asked, and all three of them shook their heads.

"I'd like your Veggies Burrito Bowl," Grace said, and Emily leaned back to look at Tess behind her daughter's back. She smiled mischievously.

"I'll try these square tacos with grilled fish," Emily said, and Grace frowned in disapproval.

"What kind of fish is it?" she asked suspiciously. "It's not tilapia, is it? You know they…"

"Are you eating them, daughter?" Emily asked mildly, and looked at the waitress. "I'll take the platter."

"You got it, and it is Mahi Mahi, by the way," she said, glancing at Grace cautiously.

"That'll be fine, dear," Emily assured her. "What about you, Tess?"

"I'll get two tacos, one Carnitas, and one Chorizo Potatoes," Tess said, and the woman nodded her approval and was gone.

"That girl is fast," Grace muttered, and Emily winked at Tess.

"Maybe, but she probably already has a boyfriend or girlfriend," she said, and Tess smiled.

"You two are funny," Tess said and looked at them both curiously. "Phoebe is so different. She's always so solemn and self-deprecating. At times, when I first met her, I thought she seemed very depressed. I think I was right. Well, she *was* depressed," she qualified her words.

"Oshba?" Emily asked, knowingly, and Tess nodded.

"Oshba," she agreed.

"So tell us how she is now, and the nitty gritty on Oshba," Grace asked, and ignored a nudge from her mother.

Tess sighed, knowing resistance was futile.

"She's one of Yasmin's bodyguards and, I don't know, lady in waiting? Maid?" Tess didn't quite know how to describe it. But they both nodded, and she realized Phoebe must have told them at least a little about them.

"I think this is Oshba's story, and either she or Phoebe should be the ones to tell you any personal details. But I know she had a very harsh childhood. Everyone in her village was wiped out except some of the youngest children. They were taken by the terrorists, and raised in youth training camps. I think she was four. But I'll leave the rest for them to tell you. I don't really know that much more about her, except that she's crazy about Phoebe."

She could tell both of them were debating whether they could grill her for more details, but the waitress showed up with their food, and she sighed in relief.

Tess watched them try their dishes, and not try and hide their approval. For at least a few minutes, she was spared the grilling as they all dug in and ate like there was no tomorrow.

After a few minutes, they all slowed down, and Grace looked at her speculatively. Tess felt misgivings, but was relieved to see they'd tabled any further questions. For the moment, at least.

"I'm surprised you're so chipper today," she said, smiling a little at Tess. "It looked like the frozen daiquiris were hitting you pretty hard last night. How did you feel this morning?"

Tess blushed and laughed, a little self-consciously.

"I hadn't eaten anything except a very light lunch, and frozen drinks always hit me harder than anything else," she admitted, embarrassed at their first impression of her. "I'm not a lush or anything, but it's been a long year. It's kind of nice to get to the end of it. I felt fine this morning. And I'm sure 2020 is going to be a much better year than 2019 was."

"I'm not so certain," Grandma Stark said slowly. "I've gotten very mixed messages in the portends. Of course election years are always stressful."

"No politics," Grace said firmly, and her mother nodded her agreement reluctantly. They both looked at Tess, and their apparent thinking and acting in unison unnerved her. "So, Phoebe tells me after the owner, you're the big boss in charge at Freedom Seas. We didn't see you at the docks when we were there. I suppose there are business offices somewhere?"

"Phoebe said that?" Tess asked, touched that her friend gave her such high kudos. She shook her head. "Wally, the owner, has me do a lot of the detail work and some of the bookkeeping. I minored in accounting at the University of Florida. We do have a business office, but I was at the Key West School of Massage. Tomorrow is the last day of classes for the year."

"You're a masseuse?" Grandma Stark asked, her eyes lighting up. "Do you teach there?"

"No, I'm a student," Tess said, laughing with self-deprecation. "My major was in education, and teaching jobs are few and far between around here. I had Phoebe's job until early October. In fact, I hired her to replace me on the schedule. My intention was a career move to give me more flexibility over my work schedule, as well as a secure income. But Wally keeps finding things for me to do. And he lets me set my own hours, so I still get a paycheck." She winced. "Which is good, because massage school is expensive."

Tess was embarrassed talking about herself and tried to shift the focus of the conversation.

"So, your first day in Key West. What did you do today?" Tess asked. Her heart sank as both women grinned and looked at each other.

"Nice segue, young lady," Grandma Stark said and winked at her. "All these skills and shy as well."

They all laughed, although Tess thought hers sounded a little weak.

"We went shopping on Duval for a while, had a snack for lunch, and then found a delightful place to work on our tans," Grandma Stark said, and raised an eyebrow as she looked at her daughter. "I believe Grace may have still been shopping for *something*, although I think she faces long odds."

"Hush, Mother," Grace said, and looked at Tess, shaking her head. "It's not like *she* was ignoring the siren's call last night at Diane Isis."

"Working on your tan," Tess said thoughtfully, and then got it and grinned at them. "You found the Garden of Eden, up on the roof above The Bull."

"We did," Grandma Stark agreed. "And my poor lust-starved daughter found the lovely bartender."

"Nadine?" Tess asked, wondering if Nadine qualified as a lovely bartender. She had to be in her forties, although she was holding up well for an older lady. She looked again at the mother and daughter and realized her perspective might not match well with the two women. She knew from Phoebe that Grace was at least fifty, and Emily was sixty-eight or nine. She tried to remember if Nadine had a girlfriend or partner. "She seems very sweet. I've only talked to her a couple times, but I like her."

"She's tough, and I like that in a woman," Grace said, her eyes staring off into space, clearly picturing the bartender. "I'm amazed her breasts are still so firm and not stretched out, considering she goes topless at work every day." Her face colored a bit. "At least, that's what she said."

"I've never seen her wear a top," Tess admitted. The Garden of Eden was a clothing optional bar on the roof of a two-story building a few blocks away, on Duval. The main floor was The Bull, an open bar that featured live entertainment of every sort. The second floor had the Whistle Bar, with balconies overlooking Duval and some pool tables inside. "Of course, I don't really hang out there. Nathan goes every Monday afternoon, and plays Scrabble with Marilyn. He knows Nadine much better than either Tuesday or I do."

"Does he play in the nude?" Grandma Stark asked, looking intrigued. "And who is Marilyn? I thought he was with the Arab girl."

"Oh, he is," Tess rushed to clarify. "Marilyn is a couple years older than you, Grandma Stark. When Nathan first moved to Key West, she had a room for rent. He didn't want to live with her because she kept making moves on him. We rescued him when we asked him to be our roommate. She still flirts with him, but we think it's more habit than any serious intention of getting him into her bed."

"She sounds fun," Grandma Stark said, and frowned in mock disapproval at Tess. "And please, I only have one granddaughter. Call me Emily."

"Okay, Emily," Tess said, smiling at her, and looked questioningly at Phoebe's mother.

She snorted.

"Grace suits me just fine," she said, and looked slyly at her mother. "I only have one daughter, although it looks like I may soon have a daughter-in-law."

Grandma Stark, no, Emily, looked startled, then thoughtful.

"That's right," she said, looking pensive. "It would be nice to have another woman in the family."

"I doubt she's a witch, though," Grace said regretfully, and Emily nodded her agreement.

Tess bit her lip. They were right, but on the other hand, Oshba was far more complicated than they had any idea.

"What is it, Tess?" Emily asked, looking at her shrewdly. "You know something we don't?"

"I probably do," Tess admitted, stalling to figure out how to avoid giving up too much information about Oshba that wasn't hers to share. "I don't think she's a witch, but she does love Phoebe very much. And I think that relationship is very good for both of them."

"Phoebe says you're her best friend," Emily said slowly, watching Tess's face curiously. "She also says you're the kindest person she's ever met."

"She said that?" Tess asked, touched. She blinked at the tears that threatened to appear. "That's very sweet of her to say."

"Let's finish up here and go meet your roommate, Nathan," Grace said gruffly, and Tess saw her mother hide her amusement. "Everyone says he's so good, we have to hear for ourselves."

Tess smiled and said nothing.

Tess led Emily and Grace into Captain Eddie's and smiled at Nathan. They heard him finish a Jim Croce song, "I Got a Name," as they walked in.

Nathan smiled back at Tess, and glanced at the other two women curiously. He gave them a friendly nod, and broke into "Eight Days a Week" by the Beatles. Emily and Grace stared at him a moment and then looked at each other, nodding their approval.

Tess saw that, as expected, Yasmin was seated with Nadezhda, and had an excellent view of Nathan. With a slight shift of her chair, she would have as good a view of the stage the band would be playing from. They had a line of tables pulled together that they shared with some men from Eldamar, the all-gay community Tess, Tuesday, and Nathan lived in.

Nathan was the only heterosexual living in the block of seven historical homes that had been converted into apartments. Tess and Tuesday were the only females. The owner, Philip Leblanc, had been very strict in adhering to his unspoken, unwritten rule of male gays only, until Tess and her Tue Bear moved to Key West. Tess's mentor at the University of

Florida had turned out to be an old flame of Philip's, and he'd let them move in. Almost a year later, Nathan became their roommate to help cover the rent. At that point, he'd only been in Key West a couple weeks, had been sleeping in his car, and showering in the rinse shower at the Garden of Eden.

The bar was filling fast, and both of the older women sat down across the table from Yasmin and Nadi. Tess settled into the chair next to Yasmin, and the girl's hand automatically crept into hers.

Melanie set a glass of Chardonnay in front of her, and took Emily and Grace's drink orders. She didn't linger and Tess suspected she was covering a lot of tables.

Tess watched Emily and Grace scope out Captain Eddie's with amusement. She smiled at Yasmin, who smiled back.

"Yasmin, Nadi, you met Emily and Grace last night, right?" Tess asked, and Yasmin nodded, looking at them with ill-disguised amusement.

"Phoebe's grandmother and mother," she said, nodding to each as she spoke. "Ladies, it is good to see you again so soon. Phoebe has become a very important part of our little family, and we must thank you for raising such an interesting young woman. Right, Nadi?"

Nadi was startled to be included in the conversation, and nodded slowly. She eyed the two women curiously. She looked startled as she realized they were both appraising her, as if she were a potential date or love interest. Tess watched with amusement and realized she was seeing a very rare sight.

Nadi looked nervous, and unsure of how to act towards Emily and Grace.

"Oshba is my little sister in every way except blood, and it is good to see that she and Phoebe make each other so happy," she finally said. When Emily leaned forward, as if entranced by her words, she hurried to continue. "My lover, that is, my *boyfriend*, Carlos and I, were glad to see them find such happiness when they met."

Tess tried to hide her grin as she saw Yasmin's head swivel to look at her senior employee. She felt Tess's eyes on her, and her face had an expression of surprise and almost wonder.

"When you said it was becoming more than strictly physical, I did not realize he had attained the rank of boyfriend," the Arab girl said.

"We haven't really discussed it," Nadezhda admitted. "But remember, I told you a few days ago that our interest in each other *might* be expanding to more than just physical, and such a relationship is the next logical step."

"So you did," Yasmin actually purred. "I simply enjoy getting you to admit it out loud."

She turned back to Emily and Grace as Nadi made a face.

"It is so good when I see my grumpy older sisters finally begin to have a personal life, and find someone they care for."

"You're related?" Grace asked, sounding startled. She looked at the two of them, and Tess could almost see the thought balloon above her head as she pictured Oshba, and tried to find any physical traits in common.

"In spirit only, I am afraid," Yasmin admitted. "Technically, they are my employees and protectors, but I have come to love them both very much."

"Protectors." Emily looked thoughtful. "So they are your bodyguards?"

"That and so much more," Yasmin said, looking at Nadezhda fondly. "Nadi also takes care of any business transactions or other day to day logistical needs that may arise. Oshba does much of the actual legwork, as well as any advance work when we are traveling or spending any significant time in public." She smiled cynically. "Oshba can look very daunting, but she can also be invisible, for all intents and purposes. When she wishes it, people do not seem to notice her."

"We look forward to getting to know her better," Grace said, and leaned forward a little. "What can you tell us about her past, and what she's like?" Emily winced and shook her head in consternation.

"The story of Oshba is for her, or Phoebe to tell you," Yasmin said gently. She'd clearly been anticipating questions, and was ready to rebuff them. Tess had watched Nadi tense up at the question, and it looked like she'd been about to interrupt her lady, but she sat back in relief at Yasmin's words. "I *will* tell you she had nearly no childhood, as such, and has never displayed any tendency or ability to make friends or engage in casual conversation with anyone other than Nadi. At least I have never seen her do so."

Nadi closed her eyes and sighed in frustration. Yasmin bit her lip, and smiled ruefully at Tess and the two ladies.

"And that, I believe, is the signal for me to refrain from adding any detail."

Emily chuckled and shrugged her shoulders in mock resignation.

"I could have told my daughter she would not be getting any gossip out of either of you," she said, and glanced at Tess. "Or Tess, for that matter."

They all looked over at Nathan as he finished a James Taylor song called "Every Day."

He was doing his usual mix of songs, bouncing from the Beatles, Elton John, Billy Joel mix to Steely Dan, Chicago, and other artists, showing his versatility with his voice.

"He does an amazing job playing and singing classic rock, for someone his age," Emily said, and Grace nodded her agreement.

"His age or any other age," Yasmin said firmly, and Tess bit her lip to keep from smiling. When it came to almost anything regarding Nathan, she was fiercely loyal and protective.

"When we met him, he said his parents are huge classic rock fans, and his mother is a musician, and teaches music," Tess said, remembering. "He says they have an amazing collection of vinyl, cds, and even cassettes and 8-tracks. As a little kid, he would listen to them constantly. Of course, he can also find almost anything on YouTube as well."

Nathan went right into "Oh, Very Young" by Cat Stevens, and both Stark women nodded their approval and listened intently, nodding their heads in rhythm. Tess saw Yasmin doing the same, and she realized she was, as well.

"He is very good at adjusting his voice to sound like the original artists," Emily said, and nodded her head as Nathan reached the bridge of the song. "He has a very discerning ear."

"He's as good as everyone implied, if not better," Grace reluctantly admitted. "His Cat Stevens is inspired."

Tess glanced around the table when the song ended, and saw that it was apparently couples' night, as far as the gay men of Eldamar were concerned. She turned to Grace and Emily, gesturing towards the men.

"Ladies, these gentlemen live in our community and are more family than friends and neighbors," Tess said, smiling at Marvin briefly, before letting her eyes swing around the table, acknowledging the eight men there so far. "We have Marvin and Simon, Mohsen and Gerald, Walter and Tommy, and Leon and Richard. Gentlemen, this is Phoebe's mother, Grace, and her grandmother, Emily."

Tess was glad to see both women were fast on the uptake and immediately understood the men were couples. She knew from last night that they liked women, but since both had borne at least one child, she assumed they were bisexual.

And they both seemed to be on the prowl. Their attention went back to Nathan, even as Melanie dropped off their Coronas without slowing as she passed.

Tess decided this was going to be an interesting evening.

Both ladies had to test the waters for themselves to be convinced that all the men of Eldamar were gay, not bisexual. Then Emily flirted with Melanie briefly, but the waitress had no trouble with setting them straight.

"Ladies, I've been living with my old man for over twenty years. I am a confirmed heterosexual. I appreciate the attention, but if I was going to experiment with women, I would have tried that years ago."

Melanie had continued on about her rotation of tables without further comment, and it wasn't until she was well out of distance, that Yasmin leaned forward, a troubled look on her face. She looked from Emily to Grace to finally settle her gaze on Tess.

"When she says 'old man', she does not mean her father, does she?" Yasmin made a face. "I have seen children in movies and on television channels use this expression in that way."

Tess laughed involuntarily, and looked at the Arab girl apologetically.

"I'm sorry, Yasmin," she said contritely. "I didn't mean to laugh…"

"It can also mean the man she's living with," Grace said, grinning despite her obvious attempt not to. "It probably means he's at least a couple years older than she is, and they might not be married."

"You do see kids call their dads their 'old man'," Emily agreed with Yasmin. "But in this context, it means the man she lives with. Her partner. And that she is almost certainly from a blue-collar or redneck family background."

"For all my open-mindedness when it comes to sex, that would be, as they say, a bridge too far," Yasmin said, wrinkling her nose. "Trying to picture my father in my bed…" She visibly shuddered.

Nadezhda snorted as she tried to suppress a laugh. Yasmin turned to give her a mock glare that Tess didn't think had much heat to it.

"Not being able to imagine that is a good thing," Tess said, wondering if Yasmin was play-acting. She got her answer sooner than she would have preferred.

"Oh, I can imagine that lecherous man wanting to climb into my bed all too easily," Yasmin muttered as she suppressed another shudder. "Not as easy as my brothers trying to, but certainly something I have no trouble believing. When my sense of my sexuality began, all of them struggled between outrage, pity, disgust, and lust. As well as envy," she finished, no humor in her voice or face as she drained her glass.

She reached for the bottle, but Nadezhda beat her to it. A half glass of the champagne finished the bottle, and the Arab woman winced and looked at her lady questioningly. Yasmin nodded without speaking, her eyes focused on something other than the room around her.

As if on cue, Nathan began playing another Cat Stevens song, "Sad Lisa", and Yasmin pulled herself together and turned to face him, watching him intently. As Tess watched, her face relaxed, and her expression softened.

She seemed to feel Tess's eyes, and turned back to face her.

"Worry not, dear Tess, I am fine," she said quietly, and looked at her questioningly. "Would you like to dance? Even though this is a sad song, it is one of my favorites, and Nathan does it so well."

Tess was surprised. They had fast danced together before, but never a slow song.

"You swing both ways, Yasmin?" Emily asked shrewdly, and Tess could see the gears start rolling in her head.

"I have enjoyed sexual encounters with both sexes, more times than I know," Yasmin admitted. "But Tess and I have a friendship that is strong and caring. Both Tuesday and my Nathan know our dancing together would not be of a sexual nature. They have a strong monogamous relationship, and my Nathan and I have made commitments to each other. As far as other partners for sex goes, my memories will have to serve."

Nadezhda was in the act of raising the empty Dom bottle to signal Melanie, and she froze, staring at her lady, looking stunned.

Tess stood and held her hand out to Yasmin, hoping she didn't look as dazed as Nadi did. As they embraced and began drifting slowly across the dance floor together, Tess was surprised at how strange it felt to dance with someone taller than herself. The last time had been with a man, almost five years ago, long before she knew she was gay. She was also feeling bemused at Yasmin's words regarding her and Nathan. Not to mention the fact that as they danced, she realized the Arab girl was leading.

"Did my words shock you, dear Tess?" Yasmin whispered in her ear, and Tess gave a little laugh.

"Not as much as they did poor Nadi."

"Yes, I feared one of us would need to apply CPR to her," Yasmin said lightly, and her voice grew serious. "I found out much about myself during my little trip to Finland. I can be very selfish and self-centered. But my Nathan means more to me than anything I can imagine. The thought of losing him because I could not give up the right to take anyone I please to my bed, whenever I wish, made me examine myself a little closer. *Much* closer, in fact."

"So it would seem," Tess said, stalling as she thought through the younger girl's words. As they slowly circled the dance floor, she saw Tuesday enter, pretending to waltz.

She saw them dancing and waved. She pretended she was about to give her usual sloppy licking kiss to Nathan, but missed him completely, and kept right on going to the table.

Melanie arrived about the same time with another bottle of Dom for Yasmin and a plastic cup of Chardonnay for her Tue Bear. Her girl looked at the bottle with yearning and Melanie laughed, said something, and put the bottle in the bucket of ice water, taking the empty away.

Tuesday sighed visibly, and Tess felt Yasmin giggle.

"Has she been good today?" she asked mischievously, and Tess shrugged, smiling at the thought.

"For her, I guess she has," Tess admitted, and Yasmin made a production of sighing.

"I guess I will have to share with her, then," she said in mock despair, and they both sighed as the song ended. Yasmin tightened her hold into a hug, and looked at her as they released. "This was fun. We need to do it more often. It gives us a chance to talk, just us two. And Nathan doesn't really enjoy dancing very much."

"That's true," Tess said, remembering a conversation she'd had with him last summer. "He says he's always been the entertainer, and feels very self-conscious when he dances, as if everyone is watching him."

"He told me the same thing, in Mexico, the night we met," Yasmin admitted. "I must admit, I didn't really believe him at the time, but that is so a Nathan thing for him to think."

Tess smiled.

"It is," she agreed. They reached the table and she happily submitted to Tuesday's wraparound hug. Over her girl's shoulder, she saw Phoebe, Oshba, and Aurora greet everyone. They'd walked well behind Tuesday as they entered, in case she had any sort of special entrance planned. With her, you could never be certain. Tess hid a smile as she saw Aurora sit next to Emily and immediately engage her in conversation.

"Miss me?" Tuesday asked, and Tess kissed her lips gently.

"Do you even have to ask?"

Tess idly wondered what song the band was going to end with. The bar was packed, with standing room only. Melanie had a helper and they'd both been buzzing around nonstop, taking drink orders, delivering them, busing the tables.

It looked like Steve and Ted hadn't expected such a full house tonight, because they didn't have Gunther, the big black bartender from Jamaica, working. This meant Ted at the bar, usually more than able to handle a Thursday night crowd, was being pushed to his limit to keep up with a very thirsty crowd.

Steve, his older brother, and the manager of Captain Eddie's Saloon, was clearing tables, jumping behind the bar to make drinks, ringing up the orders, and even with that help, they were barely able to handle the crush.

Early on, Emily had watched them working, and Tess had to admit, it was impressive, even though she'd seen both of them in action before. She saw Emily admiring them, and felt obliged to mention they were the owners of the bar, and both married. She also said there was a good chance that Betsy, Ted's wife, was either already somewhere in the room, or would be there shortly.

Sure enough, Tess saw her clearing tables, wiping them down, gracefully slipping through the crowd, time and time again, with empty bottles, cups, soaked napkins, some empty pizza boxes, using her dancing skills and agility to somehow make her way through the packed people without spilling anything. She was deceptively fast, and Tess had been impressed. In the year and a half they'd been coming here, she couldn't ever remember Betsy helping out.

She and Steve's wife, Mari, were co-owners of a women's gym, and she worked there five or six days a week. She led aerobics classes, and did every single routine, without pausing, even as she called out to the patrons, guiding them, correcting them on form, encouraging them to keep going.

Tess knew for a fact she led at least five classes every weekday, and at least three intensive, high impact classes on Saturdays. So when she would joke about leaving all her strength in the gym, no one ever questioned her watching her husband and his brother work their tails off, without offering to pitch in.

But tonight, she was zipping around the bar, at light speed, helping them keep the crowd satisfied.

Mari was a Key West uniformed cop, and also taught martial arts classes at the gym in her off time from her shifts on the streets.

Steve and Ted were both six and a half feet tall, and their tight t-shirts left no doubt as to their physical fitness. Ted was an Army Ranger, and had done multiple tours in Iraq and Afghanistan. Steve was a SEAL, and had done the same number of tours as Ted, plus one.

When Tess told Emily that Mari was the only person in Key West, or in the keys in general, for that matter, that anyone thought might be able to beat either of them in a fight, despite giving up a foot's height to both of them, she'd sighed and nodded her understanding.

A little later, when Tess was slow dancing with Tuesday, her girl had whispered that there was one other person in Key West that might be able to match up with them.

Tess thought Tuesday waiting to say this was unusual, and thought about it for a moment. She nodded her understanding.

"Oshba?" she asked.

"Oshba," Tuesday confirmed and smirked. "She's about that good, and we both know she'd use knives."

Tess laughed, despite her abhorrence of violence. She knew both Nadi and Oshba were extremely well-trained, but Oshba's upbringing brought a wildcard to the mix. She had a sneaking feeling that Phoebe's girlfriend was still struggling with understanding the moral issues, and the basic concept of right and wrong.

Tuesday put it succinctly.

"If she saw either of us in danger, she would jump right in and save us," her girl said, and Tess smiled in relief. She knew Oshba had never been presented with recognizing a code of conduct until she was in her twenties.

Tuesday's next words made the hair on Tess's arm stand up.

"Of course, thirty seconds later, if Yasmin told her to kill us both, she would."

Tess shivered and finally whispered back. "I don't think we should tell this to Emily and Grace."

"Yeah, probably not their first choice of behavioral issues they want to see in their future daughter-in-law," Tuesday said, and popped her gum.

Tess pulled her thoughts away from that line of thinking, remembering how effusive both Stark women had been about Nathan, as he finished up his happy hour solo gig with "And When I Die," by Blood, Sweat & Tears.

Grace had leaned forward after the first verse, staring at her.

"He nails the voice of every single lead singer he does," she said, awe present in her voice.

"That's our Nate-boy," Tuesday said, glancing over at Nathan for a moment before returning her attention to Grace. "It's amazing how his issues with multiple personalities help him in his entertainment career."

Both Stark women stared at Tuesday uncertainly. Finally, Emily allowed a grudging smile to appear.

"Okay, I admit it," she said, and laughed. "You have the best deadpan face I've ever seen."

"Ah, thanks," Tuesday said, bobbing her head a little in cheerful reaction. Then her expression changed to a questioning one. "What do you mean?"

Tess laughed. "Tue Bear, don't frighten the nice witches, or they'll turn you into a newt."

Grace snorted and shook her head in disapproval.

"Now there you go, making stereotypical jokes about witches. I'm sure Phoebe has impressed upon you that we take our duties as Wiccan Witches very seriously."

"That is true," Emily mused, keeping her lips from curling up in humor. "Newts are so last millennium. In this day and age, here in Florida, we turn you into those little lizards that cats are always biting the tails off of."

Tuesday sniffed and shrugged.

"That gizzard would have the perkiest boobies you ever saw," she said, and Tess laughed out loud.

Yasmin leaned forward.

"My Nathan has a wonderfully nice personality. In fact, I believe he is the second nicest person I've ever met," she said, and smiled. "The nicest person I've ever met, or ever hope to, is my best friend forever, Tess. She is undoubtedly the sweetest person in Key West, or anywhere else, for that matter."

Emily and Grace glanced at each other, looking bemused.

"That *does* seem to be the common sentiment," Emily admitted, and Grace nodded her agreement.

Tess felt her face heat up, and was relieved to hear Nathan finish the song, and thank everyone for showing up, and to stay around. The band, Dr. Leek and the Prime Rib Veggies, would be starting to play at nine, and he'd be joining them for their first set.

She covered her embarrassment by jumping up and going to help Nathan pack up. Even so, Tuesday beat her to it, and was unplugging the speakers. She handed the end of the speaker cord to Tess, picked up the speaker, and headed for the stage.

"Good sets, Nathan," Tess said and gave him a kiss on his cheek. She began coiling the cords loosely, as Nathan had shown her, so they wouldn't kink up. It only took them a couple minutes to get everything packed and stored under the stage. Nathan used the band's keyboards when he sat in with them, to save time.

Tess had, on several occasions, heard Nathan say their toys were better than his. With all the gear packed, Nathan went over to give Yasmin a hug and kiss. Nadi vacated the chair next to her, and casually wandered towards the bar, looking the crowd over for any potential problems that might affect Yasmin's safety.

Of course, there were none.

Tess saw Nathan hadn't picked up his plastic beer pitcher tip jar yet. It sat on a barstool, and a customer was standing nearby, looking at the stool longingly, but polite enough to not touch the packed pitcher. She smiled at the man, picked up Nathan's backpack that was on the floor, leaning against the stool. She carefully lowered the tip pitcher into the backpack, keeping it upright, and zipped it up.

Tess nodded to the stool, and the man thanked her, and took the stool. He eyed her as if speculating whether she was available or not. She smiled at him sympathetically, even as she shook her head. She pointed over to where Tuesday was giving Nathan a licking bath of a kiss on the cheek.

"My girlfriend is the one with the perky boobies. We're monogamous. Not to mention gay."

"I was afraid of that," the man admitted ruefully, and took it with good grace. "Sometimes, you have to take a chance to find out the possibilities. Have a good night."

"You, too," Tess said, and pointed at a table with mostly women near the center of the floor. "I think they're all straight. Be a nice guy, be sweet, and who knows, you might get lucky. Stick around for the band, and ask one of them to dance."

"Thanks for the tip," he said, looking at her curiously. He clearly hadn't expected a sympathetic rejection with an encouraging suggestion. "You two make a nice couple."

Tess had smiled as she walked back over to the tables in time to see Nathan stand up, shaking his head at Grace.

"I go by Nathan. Tuesday has never been one to conform. No reason she should start now." He shrugged good-naturedly. "So she calls me Nate boy. But to the rest of the world, I'm Nathan."

He leaned over Yasmin, and she gave his cheek a swipe with a napkin, giving a mock glare to Tuesday, who grinned at her. Then she kissed him on the lips.

"I believe this is where I should say 'Knock them dead, my dear Nathan,'" she said, and he grinned down on her.

"I'll do my best," he said, and turned to the stage.

Nathan chatted briefly with the band members, even as he got behind the keyboards, made some adjustments, and shifted his microphone slightly.

A few minutes later, they started playing, and Tess smiled as she recognized the song by the Who. It was "Won't Get Fooled Again." It was also the very first song Nathan had played with the band in public, back in June. No one had known he'd been practicing with them, and that his playing the first set whenever the band was playing at Captain Eddie's would become routine.

Tess glanced at Emily and Grace and smiled when she saw them trying to not look awed. She turned around to check, and sure enough, Ted was pulling shot glasses down from a high shelf, lining them up, scowling as the regulars at the bar began calling out that they wanted a shooter as well.

The room was jumping, but Steve got behind the bar and kept taking drink orders while Ted prepared a long line of shots of whiskey. By the time the band reached a certain point in the song, Ted had dispersed about thirty shots, by her reckoning, to patrons standing at the bar, waiting.

"What is happening at the bar?" Grace asked curiously, and Tess answered without taking her eyes off the line of drinks. Sure enough, she saw Betsy show up in front of the second one in the line, holding the glass casually, keeping it on the bar.

"Watch this," Tess answered, and watched Ted take hold of the first shot, and Steve standing next to him, take the third in line.

Nathan screamed at the appropriate point of the song, as they ended the instrumental bridge, and went into the final verse.

The moment you could hear his scream, everyone lifted their shots, drank, and slammed the empty glasses on the bar, upside down. Tess wasn't at all surprised to see that Betsy beat everyone. She always did, every single time.

Everyone watching, or shooting the whiskey, roared as Betsy raised her arms in triumph. Ted and Steve took the kidding with good graces. This certainly wasn't an unusual event.

"So that wisp of a woman just beat over two dozen big men, and a bunch of other women as well?" Emily asked, and laughed. "How often do they do this?"

"Every time the band plays a song by the Who," Tess said, turning back to the table. "Ted and Steve are huge Who fans, and they always celebrate hearing them with a shot of whiskey. It started as two brothers having the usual sibling competition thing, and then Betsy jumped in, and she always wins. But it's like waving a red flag to the regulars, and now it's become a major big deal."

Tess grinned at Tuesday.

"I think Nathan and the band keep learning Who songs, just to make them do this, at least a couple times every night Nathan sits in with them."

Tuesday nodded back at her. "And they charge customers for those drinks, so although their egos are taking a hit, it's not hurting the business any."

"So, you think they'll do it again before Nathan finishes?" Emily asked thoughtfully.

"I gar-own-tee," Tuesday drawled, and Tess nodded her agreement.

Phoebe sighed. "And so it begins," she said, and Nadi snickered.

"I think I'm going to jump in on the next one," Emily said thoughtfully, looking at the crowd packed three deep around the long, oblong bar. The vast majority of the drinkers were men, and Tess bit her lip to keep from laughing.

"Grandmama Emily, I think I will join you when you do," Aurora said thoughtfully, and Tess stared at her.

Aurora was from Italy, the great-granddaughter of Diane and Izzy's best friend in the world, Stella. She was sent to stay with the two women, supposedly to allow her to experience new things, different ways of thinking, as part of her training as a future owner and probable CEO of Stella's vast commercial empire. It spanned much of the Mediterranean Sea, or so Aurora said, and Tess couldn't quite see what Stella had in mind. What she *could* see, was Aurora breaking hearts, left and right, of a growing number of men and women by either seducing, or allowing them to seduce her, for liaisons that never seemed to last more than a week.

Aurora's current main squeeze was a very sweet girl that was a waitress at the Smokin' Tuna Bar a block away, and she'd lasted longer than any of Aurora's previous conquests. Tess wondered if Aurora was getting ready to move on, and was actually considering a woman three times her age.

"Very Harold and Maude," she muttered, and Tuesday snorted. Tess couldn't see how she could have heard her words, but she clearly did.

"More like Maude and Maude, except one of them is twenty-one, instead of seventy, Tuesday said in a low voice that didn't carry.

"I don't know whether to be impressed or grossed out," Tess whispered into her girl's ear, and Tuesday looked at her owlishly.

"Yes," she responded, and Tess sighed. Then she jumped as the crowd at the bar roared again. From the laughter and clapping, Tess didn't have to look to know Betsy had done it again.

A couple songs later, the band started playing "Soul Sacrifice" by Santana, and Aurora looked at Emily questioningly. They both stood and went out on the packed dance floor. It was a driving song with a lot of drums and bongos, and both the young woman and the aged grandmother writhed to the rhythm, dancing provocatively close together, deeply focused on each other.

"I can't take either of you anywhere," Phoebe said in an accusing voice, and Grace snorted.

"Don't look at me," she said firmly. "When Nathan is done playing, I'm going back to the Garden of Eden, and spend some time with that very attractive bartender, Nadine. I think her shift ends at eleven."

Tess felt her girl stiffen next to her, and looked over in time to see something she'd rarely, if ever, seen before.

Tuesday looked shocked.

Phoebe saw it too, and grimaced. She felt Tess's eyes on her and shook her head. "It's times like this I really suspect I may have been adopted."

Tess smiled as she thought about all the odd conversations and things that had happened during Nathan's set with the band. It was almost more entertaining than the band. When the band started playing "Eminence Front" by the Who, both Emily and Aurora had dashed over to the bar. Grace had followed at a more sedate pace. They did their shots, but to no avail.

Betsy won again.

When the band did a medley of fun, rocking Beatle songs, the entire bar seemed to be singing along. She thought the crowd's voices could probably be heard at Sloppy Joe's, a block away.

Tess focused on the band, giving Nathan a close scrutiny, He gave her no inkling of what they were going to end the set with.

Kris, the lead guitar player, and usually the lead singer, told people they were going to play one more song, and then take a break. He thanked Nathan for sitting in with them, and reminded the audience Nathan would be back, playing with them again tomorrow and Saturday nights.

He glanced at Nathan, who nodded, and with no visible cues or count, the band began the song. It was by Rare Earth, and called "I Just Want to Celebrate." Tess smiled. This was one they hadn't played before, and she was impressed by the harmonies. Emily and Aurora headed back to the dance floor, as did a lot of other people.

Grace returned from the bar, muttering to herself. She'd decided Melanie was so busy, it would be quicker if she just paid their bill at the bar. Tess thought it was funny that Melanie had appeared, as if by magic, to take her card, and take care of her, even as she dumped off a bunch of empty bottles and cups, and Ted began filling her tray with another load of orders.

"That woman works hard," Grace said, and looked impressed. "I'm heading to the Garden to see Nadine," she added, and stared at her mother, dancing very sensuously with Aurora. "Really?" she asked, glancing at Phoebe.

"Aurora just told her she was going to the Smokin' Tuna to see how Mariah is doing, and will probably stay there until she gets off work," Phoebe said tonelessly. "I guess Grandma Emily isn't getting lucky tonight."

Grace looked thoughtful, and then hopeful.

"I think her daughter might be, though," she said, and headed for the door.

Phoebe watched her leave, shook her head for perhaps the hundredth time that night.

She turned to Oshba, who had her right arm around Phoebe's shoulders, the left out of sight below the table, her hand probably on Phoebe's leg, kissed her neck gently, then gave it a nip. Phoebe smiled playfully at Tess.

"I know her granddaughter is definitely getting lucky tonight."

Oshba nodded solemnly.

"I am not a witch that can see the future, like you. But I am certain you are correct."

♦ ♦ ♦ ♦ ♦

He frowned, feeling very frustrated. The bar was crowded, and that was good. Thursday nights were Thirsty Drag Queen Thursdays. There were plenty of single men scattered between straight couples there for the sole purpose of seeing some of the weird world they'd heard about, but never experienced.

There was also a scattering of couples, both gay and lesbian, and some groups of men that appeared to be either birthday parties, or some work related event.

He could probably hone in on a guy, meet him, and eventually get him away from the crowd. But to do so would require meeting his friends or acquaintances, leaving a trail of his presence.

That was the last thing he wanted. He sat through the show, not at all interested in it. Men wearing women's clothing did nothing for him. He thought someone might see him, sitting alone at the bar, and approach him, solving the dealing with the friends issue.

One short, seriously overweight older man did offer to buy him a drink, but he refused, raising his own and saying it was his last of the night.

What he was really saying was that he thought the fat faggot was gross, and just enough older than he that the idea of even touching him, or letting the old man touch him, was repulsive. He was pretty sure the man picked up on that, and the next time the bartender checked on him, his previous pleasant manners were gone.

He decided this club was a lost cause and left, leaving change as a tip.

♦ ♦ ♦ ♦ ♦

Chapter Four

Oshba turned onto William Street, and halfway down the block, slowed and pulled into a small parallel parking space behind a compact car. Behind her, Phoebe reluctantly released her hold around her waist, and climbed off the Harley. As her girlfriend took her helmet off, Oshba put the kickstand down and climbed off herself.

The next building had a porch that spanned the entire front of the first floor of the building, as well as a second story balcony that did the same. A modest sign over the steps to the porch and front door said "Key West Bed and Breakfast." Emily sat on a white rocking chair, nursing a cup of coffee.

"Good morning, Grandma," Phoebe said, and leaned over and kissed her forehead. Oshba nodded to the older woman.

"Good morning, Grandma Stark," she said, and Phoebe's grandma made a face.

"Please, Oshba, call me Emily," she said, and Oshba nodded.

"Yes, Grandma Emily," Oshba said, and Phoebe snickered, causing her grandma to stare at her a moment.

"It's going to take me some time to get used to you doing that," she muttered, and Phoebe shrugged.

"I'm happy and in love," Phoebe stated proudly, then relented. "I do have to admit, it took a while to get used to feeling giddy. And smiling felt odd at first."

"It's a good look on you, though," her grandma said, and Phoebe was bemused at how happy that comment made her.

"Where is Mother?" Phoebe asked, looking up at the second floor. Oshba watched as the pale girl's eyes narrowed, first in puzzlement, then annoyance. "Please don't tell me…"

She stopped speaking and turned to look farther down the street to the next corner. Both Oshba and Phoebe's grandma's eyes followed hers, and

Related Matters

they watched Grace round the corner at Eaton Street, wearing the same clothes as the night before.

Grace saw them as she approached, and Oshba kept her face blank as she saw the woman make a face.

"Well, *she* certainly had a good time last night," Phoebe muttered under her breath. "Look at her aura."

"So I see," muttered her grandma, and Oshba had a hard time keeping from laughing at the envy in her voice. Phoebe clearly heard it as well, and she gave her grandma a vexed look.

"I hope you didn't wait up for me," Grace said saucily as she climbed the porch steps.

Her hair was still damp, probably from a shower, and her skin practically glowed. Phoebe submitted to a hug, and then looked at her suspiciously, and leaned forward and sniffed.

"You just used my products," she said, looking confused. "Shampoo, conditioner, and body wash for certain. Moisturizer as well?"

"All those," Grace admitted, startling Oshba with an unexpected hug. "It turns out that Nadine is a big fan of yours. Some woman at a bookstore convinced her to try the conditioner, and the rest, as they say, was history." She lifted a lock of her hair to her nose and sniffed. "I must admit, you did an excellent job with this batch. They're all superior. Even better, I think, than your grandma's. Or mine," she admitted grudgingly. "The key lime scent is inspired."

"Did you have a good time last night, daughter?" Emily asked in an innocent tone, and Grace gave an enigmatic smile.

"Yes I did, and I hope to have more of the same tonight," she began, and Oshba watched Phoebe shake her head vigorously.

"I don't need to know this, or hear about it. I have to get to work," Phoebe said, glancing at Oshba. "And Oshba has to go back to their house. She's on duty today and tonight. Will you be stopping by the dock?"

"Of course, granddaughter," Emily said, taking a sip of her coffee. "We'll get ourselves together, and come by in a couple hours. Your mother has already showered, so she's ahead of me. Although she *may* want to put on some fresh clothes. May we bring you anything?"

"Oshba made me a sandwich, and I have some yogurt," Phoebe said as she climbed on the cycle behind Oshba.

"What kind of sandwich?" Grace asked suspiciously, and Oshba concealed her amusement at Phoebe's answer.

"A good one."

50

Phoebe put her helmet on as Grace tried to push the matter. She tapped on it and said she couldn't hear her.

As Oshba slowly rolled out of the parking spot, she heard Phoebe's mother ask her grandmother.

"Where did you get the coffee?"

◆ ◆ ◆ ◆ ◆

Tess took a deep breath, and turned away from the door, and the flow of students leaving the building to have lunch. She continued to the end of the hall and slipped through the door into the administrative offices. She saw Skipper Gainey, the lead instructor and head of the school, sitting at her desk, pulling a cute little Sailor Moon insulated bag out of a drawer.

Tess suppressed a smile as she looked at the cooler, then at Dr. Gainey.

"You laughing at my Sailor Moon cooler?" she said, frowning in mock anger at Tess.

"I think it's cute," Tess admitted, and gave the older woman a frank look. "It was just...unexpected."

"Hrumph," she said, her eyes twinkling. "You should have seen me in my blue, pink, yellow and even green hair days. I loved cosplay."

"You don't love it anymore?" Tess asked, pretty sure she knew what Dr. Gainey was going to say.

"Everyone grows up, at some point," she admitted, sighing. "It's hard to convince a governing board you're serious, when you have yellow hair. But I did love Japanese Animation."

"Sailor Uranus is a bold move," Tess said, remembering some of the storylines she'd read when she was younger."

Dr. Gainey looked startled, then smiled.

"Ah, Sailor Moon cooler, blond or yellow hair, Sailor Uranus." She nodded. "Good analytical thinking, Tess."

"I did some cosplay when I was in high school, and then in college," Tess admitted. "I never did dye my hair. I did the wig thing." She winced at some of the images that came to mind. "It's also how I met the last two boys I ever got serious with. Although I don't know that anyone else would consider them serious relationships."

"Just in it for the sex, hmm?" Dr. Gainey said, and frowned. "I think that comment might have been across a line. Please forgive me if..."

Tess shook her head, grinning.

"It's your lunch time, and we're talking cosplay. I doubt lines apply."

"Hmm," Dr. Gainey said, and Tess was startled at how much that reminded her of Nathan. "Well, it *was* how I met the girl in my first serious relationship. And my husband."

"I thought you were married to a woman," Tess said, startled. "I thought I met her at the ice breaker at the beginning of the program. Deanna Sage?"

"She *is* my wife," Dr. Gainey admitted. "Her, I met in Gainesville at UF when I was working on my doctorate."

"Go Gators," Tess said automatically, and did the Gator chomp. She was startled when Dr. Gainey mirrored her actions.

"Go Gators," she said, and shook her head. "I can't believe that's still ingrained in me. Pavlov's dog has nothing on me."

"Tuesday and I don't even realize we're doing it, half the time," Tess admitted, and thought about what they'd just been talking about. "So, you're divorced from the man now? Was that because you…"

Dr. Gainey held her hand up.

"Oh, we're not divorced. I'm still married to Jason, as well as Deanna."

"You're in a threesome?" Tess blurted out, shocked, and then covered her mouth, mortified. "I'm sorry. That came out wrong." She thought for a moment. "So, your marriage is polygamous? Is that what you call it? Or a triad?"

"Any and all of those are accurate," Dr. Gainey shrugged. "We say we're in a polyamorous marriage, and all love each other as equally as we can. It helps that we're all bi."

"Your husband is bi?" Tess said, her mind automatically going to Nathan and Yasmin.

"He is, although he hasn't had a relationship or sex with a man since we got serious," she admitted. "Off and on, over the years, we've talked about looking around, and being open to making it a marriage of four, but he says he hasn't really felt he was missing anything. Deanna and I do try and keep an open mind to the possibility at some point."

"Wow, there is so much more to you than I realized," Tess breathed, staring at the woman. "It's so easy to forget that even teachers and administrators have a past, and even present, that is so different to the image most of us have of you."

"And what is your image of me?" she asked, and Tess blushed.

"I thought you were gay, with a wife, and one of the sweetest professors I've ever had," she said, and hurried to continue. "I think I got most of that right, except the gay part. And I never would have guessed that you were into cosplay."

Dr. Gainey laughed merrily.

"We all have our hidden depths and past," she said, and then leaned forward to give Tess an intent stare. "So, in the very, very recent past, you decided to stop in and see me at lunchtime. About what?"

"Oh, that's right," Tess said, and felt the heat hit her face with a fury. "I'm not sure I should even ask this. I don't want you to read any more into it than I'm saying."

"And you are saying?" Dr. Gainey encouraged her to continue. "Or asking? Which is it?"

"Is there any chance I could switch partners with someone?" Tess blurted out. "Please don't read too much into this. She hasn't done anything wrong, exactly. It's just…"

Tess stopped, trying to remember the carefully worded request she'd agonized over writing and memorizing last night.

"Has she touched you inappropriately in the daily exercises?" Dr. Gainey asked gently, and Tess shook her head quickly.

"No, not quite. But she's made it clear she would like to, and I've told her time and time again that Tue Bear and I have something special, and I don't wander, and I want her to quit pressuring me." Tess blurted that all out, and immediately felt guilty. "I'm sorry. I'm probably being…"

She stopped as Dr. Gainey raised her hand.

"Say no more, Tess," she said quietly. "I've seen some of your body language going into and coming out of, the sessions. And I've heard a few of her comments. This isn't an unknown problem. Every group, we find it necessary to do a swapping of a few partners to try and remove any discomfort from the situation. When we return after the holidays, you will have a new partner. I have several pairings that need changing, and I will try and find you a like-minded student."

"Oh, thank you, Dr. Gainey," Tess said, sagging in relief. "I'm sorry I kept you from your lunch for so long."

"Don't worry about that, Tess," she waved a hand and pulled a Publix yogurt, Jello pudding, and a couple plums out of her cooler. She surveyed her meal and sighed. "Thanksgiving was brutal, and Christmas is next week. Lunches have been very mundane this month. Deanna and I have both been on a diet all month."

Tess stood, and smiled at the woman. "Isn't Jason dieting too?"

"Jason is a chef, and the reason we both have to," Dr. Gainey said tersely, then smiled at Tess. "I look forward to your getting through the program, and you can call *me* by name. Skipper is much more personal than Dr. Gainey or ma'am."

Tess giggled, and shook her head.

"That might be harder than you think, Ma'am," she said, and

shrugged. "My Tue Bear is working on getting her Captain's license, and she'll always be my number one skipper." She remembered what Tuesday had packed into her lunch bag without her knowledge this morning, and pulled it out and set it on the desk, hand still covering it.

"From one skipper to another," she said quickly and rushed to the door. "Have a nice lunch!"

"Peeps?" Dr. Gainey exclaimed, and picked the two-pack up in wonder. "*Snowman* Peeps? Are these even from this year? No! You can't leave these with me!"

Tess was still laughing as she fled down the hall and out the door.

◆ ◆ ◆ ◆ ◆

Chapter Five

Carlos watched what he called the inner circle go into the conference room. His immediate supervisor, Hector Acevido closed the door firmly behind them, giving him a quick glance as he did so. He had no idea what the meeting was about, but from the expressions of the men on the other side of that door, it was serious.

He kept his face blank as he looked at the other men around him in the outer office. From their expressions, he realized they knew no more than he did. Senor Machado and his right arm, Eduardo Hernandez, were in the conference room, of course, leaving Eduardo's second, Jorge de la Rosa seated across from him, looking dour.

Senor Machado's oldest son, Santiago Machado was inside, probably seated next to his father, with *his* senior bodyguard, Ignacio Suarez. His second, Thiago Herrera, sat next to Jorge, scowling. Truthfully, Carlos didn't care for either of Santiago's men. Although they were both dangerous men and ruthless killers, and the kind of men you would want beside you in a fire fight, routine day to day duty didn't suit them well.

Hector Acevido was Amber Machado's head of security, and he was undoubtedly the most dangerous man in the building. As legendary as Eduardo Hernandez was, especially with almost any kind of firearm or knife, Hector was in a league of his own.

It wasn't mere chance that led to Senor Machado assigning Hector as his beloved daughter's protection when she was very young.

Speaking of which, Carlos was surprised she wasn't part of this meeting, unless, of course, it was strictly about illegal operations. Senor Machado had tried to keep Amber out of the family business. When the middle child, Fernando Machado, almost beat a man to death with a tire iron for "disrespecting" his girlfriend, he ended up in Raiford doing five to twelve years. Amber was brought in to learn about the family business.

The legitimate, legal, family business. That consisted of the entertainment division, which included booking agencies, a stable of entertainers, and a growing number of very exclusive, all-inclusive resorts, some of them nude or clothing optional.

Carlos knew from paying attention that she'd cleaned up a lot of messy operations, improved the profitability to the point that Fernando might be hard-pressed to get his old duties back from her. She was very intelligent, focused, worked as hard or harder than anyone in the Machado empire, and had either fixed or got rid of any underperforming businesses. Profits were up significantly, especially considering she'd only taken over her duties five months ago.

Even as he mused, the subject of his thoughts came striding briskly through the conference room.

Amber Machado was wearing black tailored slacks, and a waist-length matching jacket. She had a white silk shirt underneath, with the top two buttons undone, showing a hint of her ample cleavage. The yellow scarf around her neck contrasted nicely with her deep tan. Her thick, silky, black hair flowed down over her shoulders.

She was short, 5'3", had a solid build that was rounded in all the right places, but firm, rather than fleshy, and had dark expressive eyes.

When she laughed or showed her teeth, they were a brilliant white, and looked perfect, which they were.

She rarely did either, and her lips ranged from being full and looking very kissable, to being thin lines across the lower part of her face that warned she wasn't in the mood for nonsense.

"Introduce yourselves," she said brusquely and went right into the conference room.

Carlos winced. She looked pissed. Usually, when she was, he had a pretty good idea why, but today he had no clue. He casually eyed the two women that had followed her into the outer office. They both surveyed the three men without enthusiasm.

They both dismissed Jorge and Thiago after a quick examination. They pivoted their attention to him almost in perfect unison. Carlos showed them his best poker face, even as he took his time looking them over.

They were both about 5'5" or 5'6", but there the similarities ended. One wore a navy business suit, with a matching tie over a pale yellow blouse. It fit her well and she looked attractive and natural, even down to the comfortable-looking shoes with the thick heels. She wore a holster on her right hip, and anyone not looking for it, would never notice.

Of course, it wasn't those people you needed the gun for. *Those* kind of people would spot it right off. As well as the second gun on another belt holster in the middle of her back. He saw it right off when she turned to look at the other two men.

Carlos saw the slight firmness to the right leg of her pants that shouted out "throwaway gun". He didn't have to have read her dossier to know she was an ex-cop.

She was Hispanic, and nice to look at. Her hair didn't quite reach her shoulders. It looked like she'd recently decided to grow it out from the very practical style of her policing days.

The other woman couldn't have been much more different, and yet so similar, all the same.

She wore a matching suit, but where the ex-cop looked natural, she looked uncomfortable. She was heavily muscled, and relatively flat-chested, and Carlos doubted she'd ever worn business suits in any of her previous jobs.

Carlos wondered if she was doing steroids. She looked very tough. She was also growing her hair out, but at this point, it was only perhaps an inch long. He kept his grin hidden as he looked at her face. She was attractive in a very tough, butchy kind of way. Her nose had clearly been broken several times over the years. He would have wondered what tattoos lurked beneath her clothes if he hadn't already read her dossier.

She was also Hispanic. Not that the Machados used anything *but* Hispanic people in their organization.

She wore practical laced shoes, and he was pleased to see she wore her guns in holsters under both arms.

They both looked about thirty years old, and very competent. And at the moment, they both looked at him.

Carlos kept himself from stirring at the attention they gave him, as much because of his attire as because they undoubtedly knew he was one of Amber's original detail.

Jorge and Thiago both wore very nice, tailored suits that concealed their weapons well, Jorge's brown, and Thiago's navy. Their shoes shone and had clearly been polished since the last time they wore them. Their hair was relatively neat, not quite a businessman's cut, and with several unruly locks that would not fall into line.

Thiago had a second day shadow, and the lack of definition of its limits showed it to not be a decision to grow a beard. He simply hadn't shaved this morning.

Jorge was clean shaven. Jose Machado didn't have scruffy-looking bodyguards or attendants. Period. Eduardo Hernandez saw to that.

Carlos had shaved that morning, but had recently decided to grow a stylized beard that was only on the chin, and connected with his mustache by a narrow strand of hair on each side of his mouth. He believed it was commonly referred to as a Van Dyke. His mustache was the same length as the beard, short, as if he hadn't shaved in a week or perhaps two.

He thought it made him look older, and Hector had reluctantly agreed. At least he hadn't told Carlos to get rid of it. Senor Machado saw him for the first time in over a week before this meeting, and his lips had begun to form a smile before he caught himself.

His hair was uniformly three quarters of an inch long and Carlos thought the beard went well with it. It would also give him a slightly different look in Key West, and perhaps provide some cover to his identity. He wondered what Nadi would think of it.

What really made him stand out was his casual sports jacket with a long-sleeved Henley shirt that molded to his body underneath, with all three buttons undone. His worn, but hole-free jeans and old athletic shoes screamed comfort over professional attire. He was glad he hadn't put his Dolphins cap on yet.

"You look comfortable," the ex-cop said, her the tone didn't give away whether she thought that was good or bad.

"I am," Carlos admitted, and stood to shake hands with them. "I'm Carlos Marquiz, part of Senorita Machado's detail. They have me doing other things today, and this is appropriate wear for that."

"I'm Lucia Perez, and this is my junior partner, Rosa Fuentes," she said, and the other woman frowned at her.

"Where were you a cop?" Carlos said quietly, and Perez frowned.

"Who told you I was a cop?" she asked aggressively.

"No one 'told' me anything about you," Carlos said easily, but let a bit of steel enter his voice. "But I've worked with Senor Acevido for more than a decade, and *have* learned a thing or two. So, where were you a cop?"

"Tampa," she admitted.

"Yo, and to set the record straight, she is *not* the senior partner, I am *not* the junior partner," Rosa Fuentes said firmly, and introduced herself. Her handshake was firm, and Carlos could feel the calluses on her hands.

As he released his grip, he looked down at her hand, then up into her eyes.

"MMA?" he asked, and she blinked in surprise.

"Dayam, you're good," she admitted grudgingly, exchanging glances with the other woman.

"Carlos is babysitter for our junior Machado, girls," Thiago said, and Jorge shook his head in disgust, and shifted his chair farther away from him. "Jorge here is in Senor Machado's personal guard, and I work for the oldest kid, Santiago. We're the ones you wanna try and impress."

Carlos rolled his eyes, wondering how this fool had ever risen to his current position. That mouth would get a very swift reaction from either Senor Hernandez or Hector. He idly wondered why Senor Suarez put up with him. He glanced over at Jorge to find the man staring back at him.

"He's tough, and good with a gun, but not very bright, and his mouth will end up getting him killed," Jorge said simply, and Carlos laughed out loud.

Thiago looked at them sourly, but didn't respond. He knew he couldn't bully either of them, and the women seemed impervious to him as well. Carlos didn't envy him having to work for Santiago, but his releases for his frustration and anger would be his undoing.

Carlos turned back to the women, who were now sitting next to each other on his side of the room. He looked at Fuentes curiously. He wondered if she'd had a shaven head or a Mohawk before she began to let it grow out.

"Where did we find you? West coast?" he asked.

"L.A.," she admitted. "So what kind of other things you doing today to get to dress comfortable like?"

"Good question," he said, and leaned back in his chair and closed his eyes. He wondered if the flippant attitude of Tuesday Dumarest was rubbing off on him. When he heard Perez snicker, he decided it probably was.

♦ ♦ ♦ ♦ ♦

Amber closed the door behind her and glanced around the room. Hector was already on his feet, pulling and holding the chair he'd just been sitting in.

Papa was sitting at the head of the conference table, with Santiago on his right, with Senor Suarez to *his* right. Of course, Eduardo sat on Papa's left side, and Hector had been sitting next to him. After she sat, he took the seat to her left.

"You're late," Santiago said immediately, taking the aggressive stance.

Papa made a little sound in his throat, and his son subsided.

"I was not sure if you would be attending this meeting," Papa admitted, looking at her. "Some of what we'll be discussing concerns other divisions of the family business, not under your purview."

"I was here, and I found out that Hector and Carlos would be here," she pointed out, wondering what subjects she was not supposed to be aware of. "They are my senior people, and to lead them properly, I must know what they are dealing with."

"Right now, we are more concerned with what the family as a whole is dealing with," Papa said firmly and looked around the table at them. "Rumors have surfaced, both in regard to Miami and South Beach, as well as the keys. We must identify the threats, and learn more about their intentions, as well as their strengths and weaknesses. This does not really fall into your area of interest."

"Maybe as one of only two of your children currently available, we should be less concerned with the perceived limits to my authority, or protecting me, and more with solving problems." Amber looked at her father's right arm and smiled with no hint of humor whatsoever.

"You were about to comment, Eduardo?" she said, staring across the table at him. He looked at her, clearly amused. He glanced at Papa, and they almost seemed to be talking without saying a word. Shrugging, Eduardo turned back to everyone else.

"Our first and most obvious threat is from Mexico," Eduardo said, any hint of good humor leaving his face as a testimony to the seriousness of the situation. "We know that the event in October at Playa Perdida created a situation, and the balance of trust we had with the cartel is broken. They say they were lied to, and we were not the stated goal, and they may tell the truth. But we can't be certain, and they can't count on our not coming back at them at some point."

"Which we should have, already," Santiago said angrily. "I do not understand why we wait."

"We do not have the numbers to fight a war in Mexico right now, and that is what even a surgical strike would initiate," Papa said heavily. "You and I have discussed this. We believe the local cartel has been infiltrated and taken over by a splinter group of Los Zetas. They have chosen the imaginative name of Los Zetas de la Nueva Escuela. Their numbers and influence is mostly unknown. We need to learn more about them, and what their long-term goals are, as well as their intentions in regards to our presence in their back yard. That is why we are here today."

"Allow me to take a team to Mexico and I will deal with them myself," Santiago said, and Amber rolled her eyes. "Give me that crew that liberated Playa Perdida, and we can accomplish our goals in a couple days."

"They are not on contract for that purpose, and do not do that sort of work," Eduardo said quietly. "We use them for intel, and can call on them in an emergency, but they will not put boots on the ground for a turf war, which is what this would be."

"We pay them well," Amber's brother argued, and she raised her eyebrows at the idea of arguing with Eduardo Hernandez. "They will do as they're told."

"They are a black ops resource of the United States military, and do not answer to us," Papa said, sighing in resignation. "Stop this bickering about sending a crew to Mexico. *If* we decide to do this, it will be *after* we've learned more. Which brings me back to the purpose of this meeting. Los Zetas de la Nueva Escuela is not our only threat. The Russians have a very strong presence in the keys, in Key West in particular. We know they're trying to consolidate their strengths, even as we increase our presence. At some point, our interests will collide, We cannot fight a battle on two fronts. Three, if you count the recent decision by local authorities to increase their forces, as well as federal agencies increasing their surveillance efforts."

"What about our interests in Espana?" Amber asked, praying her father wasn't about to send her into exile far from any danger to protect her. Their new properties in Europe were her initiatives, but all four were at various stages of transition. They merely needed watching to make sure the construction and marketing didn't lag, due to lack of oversight.

"I am sending Ramon Gutierrez to oversee the projects passively, while he gets a feel for whether there is any threat from the Mexicans." Amber watched her father lean back in his chair, observing her closely for her reaction.

"That is good," Amber nodded her approval. "I have many more time sensitive pots to watch here in southern Florida, as well as Branson, Nashville and Los Angeles. I also have a team discreetly researching Las Vegas for more venues for our entertainment division. I would rather not be so far removed from my work."

"You and he will meet before he leaves," Papa said, and Amber nodded her head in approval.

"We are leaving my little brother without protection if you send Ramon to Espana," Santiago pointed out. "Raiford is a dangerous prison, and he is vulnerable to an attack."

"We have several men inside the prison, both prisoners and guards, watching out for him," Eduardo said brusquely. "Pedro Navarro is more than capable of overseeing them. Ramon is wasted resources sitting in Starke, reading their reports. Pedro can handle that, and forward anything he feels needs Ramon's attention. We have many properties and assets, and are currently light on experienced leaders. Your father and I have discussed this at length."

"Santiago, I am counting on you to use your people to try and get answers in Miami and on South Beach," Papa said, and Amber wondered how much of that was true, and how much of it was to soothe the pride of his heir apparent. "We need to stay low key, not use strong arm tactics, simply use favors owed and new friendships to get answers. Is Los Zetas trying to get a foothold in our backyard? That is what I need you to focus on. If you find a cell or even more, report to me, and we will decide together on how you will deal with it."

"I still think a surgical strike at the leaders of the cartel would solve things quicker," Santiago said, but Amber recognized he'd conceded to their father.

"The last thing we want is to be sending our best people to Mexico, only to have them hit Cocoplum," Papa said, staring at him intently. "I need you and Ignacio to work together smoothly, and find out what we need to know."

"What about the Russians?" Santiago asked, and Papa shook his head.

"I have good people checking into that right now, under Hector's supervision. You worry about Miami and South Beach." Papa turned to look at Amber. "Do you have data updates on your projects?"

Amber was taken aback. She hadn't thought that would even be a topic at this meeting, but gamely held up her iPad.

"I have all the data here, Papa," she said, and decided to gamble on a hunch. "As we go through all the projects, I can print out anything you wish to read in further detail."

Santiago made a point of shuddering.

"Unless you're about to tell me you've signed Selena Gomez, or Ariana Grande, I am off for South Beach," he said aggressively, surging to his feet. Ignacio looked at Papa, then Eduardo carefully, and a wisp of a smile passed across his lips. He stood as well, and bowed slightly at Papa.

"Senor Machado, con su permiso?"

Papa nodded and they watched the two men leave, one the son, sure he'd just made a rebellious gesture, and asserted his independence. The other, relieved to see his charge not making a complete fool of himself.

As least, I *think* that is what Ignacio is thinking, Amber mused. She turned back to find all three remaining men looking at her with amusement. She hid her misgivings and smiled at them.

"Well, now that he's gone, what am I *really* here for today?" she asked sweetly, and Hector stifled a chuckle. Both Papa and Eduardo smiled at her.

"How are your new personal aides?" Papa asked, his eyes twinkling. "Do you think they will work out?"

"Right now, they're in fierce competition to prove how much better each of them is, compared to the other," Amber said, smiling back at Papa. "They aren't a team yet, and have no personal ties between them. But they both appear to be very strong, both mentally and physically. I think, as they recognize their place in our family, things will settle down and they will find mutual interests and values. They *do* make me appreciate Hector and Carlos even more than I already do."

"We have added a number of new people to various positions in the business, and have to consider that we may have a plant or two," Eduardo said slowly, watching for her reaction. "Anyone we've added since Playa Perdida should be considered a possible risk. The topics of this meeting are off limits to both of them, as well as a number of other new hires."

Amber didn't look at her father, knowing he was expecting her to.

"I agree," she said, probably shocking all three men. She *did* notice that Hector nodded his head in approval. "So, Hector is going to be making trips to Key West to monitor information gathered by any operatives we have there?" She focused on her father now, watching his face intently. "That seems like a waste of his time. Even with the jet, he will be spending too many hours in transit, and flying back and forth isn't exactly subtle or secretive."

She sat back as she had a sudden revelation.

"I saw Carlos in the outer office, and he wasn't dressed for business as usual. Is he going to spearhead our efforts in Key West?" She let a mischievous expression reach her face. "If so, I think I should pick out a few tropical shirts for him, to help him blend in."

All three men smiled at the idea, and to her relief, Papa nodded his head.

"He has an apartment in Key West, although we haven't sat down with him and discussed details yet. We will do that shortly." Papa pursed his lips thoughtfully. "For now, you can tell your new people, or anyone else that expresses curiosity, that we have Carlos traveling to some of our many properties and interests, doing evaluations, getting answers to questions we don't necessarily ask via unsecured communications." He smiled at her. "Technically, that *is* what he is doing, but in a condensed location."

"Will he be reporting to me, or directly to you or Hector?" Amber asked carefully, and sighed in disappointment as she watched her father's reaction. "Father, you cannot continue to shield me from what we do and who we are. I am not stupid. The average company doesn't have employees that are always heavily armed, sometimes with illegal automatic

Related Matters

weapons. And very few businesses have the armory we do. And that is only the one site I know, here at Cocoplum. I know that the Zetas near Playa Perdida are not our friends, or even business acquaintances we can comfortably work with."

"I know you aren't stupid, Ambita," Papa said, and quickly looked at her closely to see her reaction to his using that term of endearment. She smiled at him to let him know it was okay. "But you are able to honestly, and under oath, swear you have no actual details or knowledge of any illegal activities done either by our people, or by our orders."

"Papa, I am your daughter. I am also your most intelligent child." Amber saw no reason to skirt around the truth. "Santiago does not have the temperament to run your empire. Fernando is in prison, and missing years of opportunity to learn how to lead people in a level-headed way. And his temperament is no better than Santiago's. You may have another son coming soon, but no matter how competent he is, we're talking about twenty-five to thirty years before he can grow into a leadership role."

Amber leaned forward, fingering her iPad nervously, but determined to see this through.

"And you have me." She reached a hand out and her father automatically reached forward and enclosed it in his own. "This is not what I intended as a career choice. But truthfully, I had been floating in life, uncertain of what I wanted to do, until I was pulled into the family business to cover for Fernando until he returns. And I am capable of so much more."

"If I do as you request, your mother will kill me in my sleep some night," her father said heavily, and his hand squeezed hers to show he was kidding. More or less. "Knowing everything we must do to succeed and protect the family will harden and age you. You will not thank me for including you. In fact, there will come a day that you may curse me for being weak and allowing you in."

"I will never curse you, Papa," Amber said fondly, and with a final squeeze, took her hand back. "No one on this earth can call you weak, either. Tell me what I can do to help you. To help the family."

"There can only be four people that know of this conversation," Papa said, and Amber nodded, looking at him, then let her eyes drift to Eduardo Hernandez and Hector Acevido. "I am not agreeing to make you my heir. I am giving you the opportunity to earn that right. And to show me you have the right character to be a good, yet strong, leader. You have not always been the perfect example of being a woman in control of herself. We must also adjust your training. As far as I know, you own no guns, have never even fired one. That will need to change, for your own sake."

"To be fair, Senor Machado, I should have seen to that years ago," Hector said slowly. "Even though she was not to be brought into the business, knowing how to protect herself is critical. I could have done this by making it a recreational activity."

"I already knew how to protect myself, Hector," Amber said, and smiled at him warmly. "All I needed to do was call out. 'Hector, help me.' Or 'Carlos, help me.'"

They all smiled, although Amber was worried to see sadness in her father's eyes.

"I have two new employees that will be introduced to our firing range this afternoon," Amber said slowly, thinking. "I will tell them I think I would be a marksman if I ever tried, and get them to teach me. It will be a good cover."

"You must allow me to teach you, Ambita," Hector said, shaking his head. "This will be our little secret. I do not think you should let anyone know you can use a gun until you need to use it."

"I agree," Papa said firmly, and that was that. He smiled at her sadly and gestured at the door. "For now, take your ladies and introduce them to the staff so no one shoots them by mistake. Carlos leaves this afternoon, so say goodbye to him if you wish."

"Yes, Papa," Amber said, standing. All three men automatically stood as well, and she impulsively stepped around Hector and Eduardo to hug her father. "I will not disappoint you, Papa. I promise."

She gave a quick hug to Eduardo, and a longer one to Hector, and walked out the door.

♦ ♦ ♦ ♦ ♦

Carlos turned as the door opened and Amber appeared. He saw she was in good spirits and was happy to see that. She glanced at the two women sitting beside him and nodded her approval.

"I see you have met Senor Marquiz," she said, and looked at Carlos playfully. "I trust all pissing contests have been resolved?"

"Perhaps," Carlos said, qualifying his answer. He looked down at his clothes. "Senorita, Senor Acevido has given me a task, and told me to dress appropriately for that task…"

"I know of it, Carlos," Amber said, and something in her voice made him look at her. She bit her lip and took him by the arm. "We will be right back, ladies. Please give us a moment."

They left the outer office and walked down the broad hallway. The Machado house wasn't really a house. It was a sprawling mansion, with one wing dedicated to family business. They paused at the door to Amber's office. She looked at Carlos fondly, if a little sadly, as she closed it behind them.

"I have convinced my father that I can handle more duties for the family. He and the others have briefed me on the current situation. I know you leave for Key West immediately. You are going to get an apartment?"

"I have already rented an apartment through our realtor in Key West," Carlos said, and her words suddenly clicked into place. "When you say you're handling more duties for the family, what…"

"It means I will know about *all* of the family business," she said firmly, watching him close for his reaction. "With Fernando in prison, and Santiago so single-minded, I convinced father that an intelligent, less emotional daughter might be an asset at this time."

Carlos stared at her and wondered if he should point out the obvious. It seemed like a suicidal move to him, so he tried to make a joke out of his reaction.

"I did not know you had a sister, Senorita," he said, and waited for her reaction. He didn't expect what he got as a response.

Amber laughed out loud and backhanded him on the arm. She impulsively hugged him and looked up into his face.

"Thank you for not pretending to agree or that you think it is not true," she said frankly. "I know how spoiled I am, and how angry and petulant I can get." She sighed, and a sad expression flew across her face. "Despite how poorly I handled our breakup, I believe the time I spent with Nathan taught me much, and made me a better person."

She shrugged.

"Even if I do not show signs of it very often. At least I have confronted my behavior and try to act more deliberately, thinking before acting, and trying to do better."

Carlos didn't quite know how to respond to that, and made an unintelligible neutral sound, hoping she would continue to speak, so he wouldn't have to.

Amber snorted, and blushed with embarrassment.

"That is a very Nathan thing to do," she pointed out. "I know I have a long way to go to become the person I wish to be. Fortunately, I have a perfect example to observe, to try and model my behavior after."

"Your mama?" Carlos asked, and she nodded. Amber looked at him slyly, and he winced.

"I think you have taken long strides towards becoming the man you will be, and I believe it started at Playa Perdida." She sighed. "Please,

I know you will see Nadi, and almost certainly, Nathan and Tess. And Tuesday," she finished reluctantly, sighing. "Please tell them, all three, that I miss them, and that I've come to accept the reality of the situation."

Her voice sounded strained, and she paused for a moment, then continued.

"I suppose this is evidence that things happen for a purpose." She sighed again. "If I was still involved with Nathan, I would not have told my papa that I was eager and ready to assume my proper place in the family business. *All* the family business."

She stared into his eyes, and her voice strengthened.

"They cannot know I have become my father's daughter," she said flatly. "They will not keep it secret, or ever treat me the same again. I would ask that you not tell Nadezhda, either. I would not ask you to keep a secret from the woman you love, but it does not concern her. I am no danger to her or her employer."

"Of course, Senorita," Carlos said, his heart sinking. He finally caught everything she'd just said, and cleared his throat. "Senorita Machado, we are not in love. Our relationship is primarily…physical."

Amber exhaled and looked at him. "Carlos, I have been Amber to you for years. Please do not stop calling me that, except when around my new bodyguards, or Papa or Eduardo. And deny all you like, I can see the truth. I know you have a…robust physical relationship, but there are feelings there as well. And if they aren't love, they will be. And I firmly believe they already are."

She gave him a little shove.

"Now, go back and tell the ladies I will be staying in the house the rest of the day and will not be needing them. Anna will take them around and introduce them to everyone, show them the range and the gymnasium, and then they can leave. But they should be here tomorrow morning at 8:00 a.m. And I believe Hector wishes to talk to you before you depart. I doubt that meeting will last much longer."

Carlos returned to the outer office to the conference room and told both women what Amber had said.

They looked at each other speculatively.

"Do you think she goes shopping that early?" Perez asked, and Fuentes shrugged.

"What decent shop is open at eight in the morning?"

"Good point."

Anna appeared and they left with her. Less than ten minutes later, Hector came out of the conference room. He glanced at Carlos, gave his face a longer searching look, and gestured to a chair. They sat, and Carlos looked at the closed door curiously.

"Senior Machado and Eduardo are having their meeting to actually decide on a course of action," Hector said dryly. "There are layers and layers of knowledge and authority in this organization. Like the layers of an onion. We all have our places."

"I thought you were of the inner layers, or the heart of the onion, to use your analogy," Carlos said, a bit surprised.

"Oh, they ask my thoughts and advice, and I take part in the logistical side of operations. But when it comes to setting a course of action, I provide information and give advice. They either heed it or don't. All decisions are made by the two of them."

"I would think Senior Machado would have the final word," Carlos said, and Hector shook his head.

"He will give the final decree, but they have always agreed on what course of action to take. Of course, Senor Machado can ignore Eduardo's advice, but in the thirty plus years I've worked for the Machado family, I cannot think of a single instance it has happened."

Carlos nodded his head slowly, not speaking, as he considered Hector's words.

"Here," Hector said, and handed him a portfolio. "Inside is a fake identity kit, with everything you'll need to know to carry it off. You will find another apartment, far enough away to not be seen by anyone staking out your current apartment. You will pretend to live at your current residence, but you will actually live elsewhere, under an alias. This is for your own safety. We are not confident the realtor can be fully trusted."

He smiled at Carlos.

"I know you love driving your car, but I would leave that here if I were you. Go to Juan's Auto and tell them who you are. They will have a car ready for you. It will not be a car you would purchase yourself. This portfolio contains money, a number of credit cards, several passports, a statement for your new checking account, and several burner phones."

"So, I'm snooping around, trying to get a feel for what Russian presence there is, and how much of their businesses are legit, and how many are illegal," Carlos said, trying to think if he was forgetting anything. "I should get names, their places in their organization, and perhaps their addresses."

"You also need to watch for any sign of cartel activity," Hector said heavily, and Carlos looked at him in surprise. His mentor nodded. "We think the cartel we pay off for Playa Perdida has merged or been taken over by a new crew. We believe it is Los Zetas de la Nueva Escuela. You need to keep a watch out for them as well."

"Will I have any backup?" Carlos asked, masking his apprehension.

"We do not want you taking any actions, except to defend yourself, if necessary. Another man with you would make both of you stand out as a team." A flicker of a smile came to his mouth. "Or, in Key West, perhaps a couple. Normally, I would give you one of our female soldiers, but I think the one you already know there might have an opinion on that idea. You would need to sell the idea that the two of you were a couple."

"I can see where that might be a problem," Carlos admitted.

"We have some operatives already embedded, and two of the burners will put you in contact with them, if you need immediate help," Hector said and gave him a stern look. "These operatives are to be activated only if you feel you are in eminent danger. If it's less urgent, call me, and I'll come, with more help if the situation calls for it."

"Understood," Carlos said, knowing Nadi would jump into any situation, whether he wanted her to or not. So technically, he *did* have backup, or support. "I suppose since today is the 20th, I will not be back in time for Navidad. Please pass my compliments and respect to Carmen and the children."

"My boys want you to come over. They say they're ready to beat you at hoops now." Hector's eyes shone with pride for his children, and amusement at their eagerness to salvage their pride after the last time Carlos had joined them in a pickup game. "They have been working hard on their game. You know Ramon has a scholarship at Jacksonville University, for next fall."

"That is wonderful," Carlos said. "I am happy for him. And for you and Carmen. Your children do you honor."

"Did you bring your armory back from Playa Perdida?" Hector asked, and nodded his approval when Carlos told him he'd brought everything. "You might want to take a selection with you. Don't get stopped on U.S.1."

"Good idea," Carlos said wryly, and shook Hector's hand. His mind was already swirling with details he needed to take care of before he could leave. "I will stay with Nadi tonight and find the apartment tomorrow."

"Keep an expense log, get receipts when you can," Hector called after him. "You know how Senora Blanco gets about the accounting."

"Yes, Mama," Carlos said put his left hand out behind him, catching the small square overstuffed pillow Hector had thrown at his head. He laughed and tossed it back to his boss and hurried to his small sleepover room to get his bags and a healthy portion of his personal armory. Or perhaps all of it.

If he didn't waste too much time, he could be in Key West in time for dinner. It was Friday, and he thought Oshba was on duty guarding Lady Yasmin, so Nadi should be free.

His pace quickened, and he took the steps to the third floor two at a time.

◆ ◆ ◆ ◆ ◆

He walked into the saloon, and casually looked around as he approached the bar. He ordered the usual beer, took a healthy swig, and began surveying the room.

At first, he was enthusiastic. This gay bar lived up to its billing. As far as he could see, there wasn't a woman in the room. It was all men, and some of them were clearly alone, and looking for company.

As he surveyed closer, he began to notice the clientele was mostly older men, most of them twice his age. The few younger, sexier men were with partners, all of which were older. He knew what he wanted, and being with an older man that probably had trouble getting it up, and hemorrhoids, didn't appeal to him.

He finished his drink and decided to gamble on staying for one more beer, on the off chance that some younger men would show up. After the third older man approached him, wanting to strike up a conversation, maybe go for a walk, or upstairs to the movie room, he'd had enough.

The last one said the gay porn movies upstairs were very stimulating, and he would love to show him proof. The idea of any form of sexual activity with that old queen turned his stomach, and he finished his beer, shook his head at the old man, and left.

Five minutes later, driving through the drizzling rain, he cursed his lack of success. It shouldn't be this hard to do. To find a good-looking man that wasn't already paired up with someone, to be able to experience anonymous sex with a stranger, it just shouldn't be this difficult.

He unzipped his pants and slid his hand inside. There was nothing to find but flaccid, wrinkled skin, and he swore in frustration as he guided his car one-handed, down the road.

◆ ◆ ◆ ◆ ◆

Chapter Six

Lawrence watched Boston grow smaller and smaller as his jet rose into the sky. The flight was on schedule, and barring unforeseen circumstances, he should be in Key West in time for dinner. It was Saturday, so that meant he would be able to drop by Captain Eddie's and listen to Nathan play the first set with Dr. Leek and the Prime Rib Veggies.

He smiled at the name, and not for the first time, wondered how the band came up with it. He took one last look as Boston fell behind them. They were still over land, but that wouldn't last long. Most of the flight was just off the coast, over the Atlantic seaboard.

He closed his eyes and pictured his host for the last two nights.

Dr. Ronald Underwood had a nice apartment on Marlborough Street, was in his late thirties, and bore a remarkable resemblance to what Nathan might look like in fifteen years. Lawrence had been perusing Successful Singles, with no intention of actually trying to contact anyone, when he came across Ronald.

Ronald wasn't Nathan, couldn't sing like an angel, wasn't the shy man Nathan was when he wasn't performing. But when he smiled, he lit the room up, just like Nathan. And more conveniently, Ronald was gay.

Lawrence knew it had been too long since he'd had a sexual liaison. Ronald had looked intriguing, and was rather handsome. He also turned out to be in very good shape, which made their bed antics all the more enjoyable.

It also gave him the chance to introduce the idea that he had a boyfriend up north to the neighborhood. So, in Atlanta, after changing from Luanne back to a version of himself, he flew up to Logan Airport in Boston. He'd let Ronald pick the meeting site, and it turned out to be the Cathedral Station, a gay pub close to where Ronald lived.

Lawrence hadn't used his own name on the Successful Singles site, so Ronald knew him as Lance Lennon. They agreed to meet at the pub at 4:30. Ronald told him it was comfort food, and a sports bar, and he'd expressed his enthusiasm. When they met, neither of them were disappointed. A couple men Ronald knew passed by their table, and he introduced Lance, and chuckled as he did so. After the third time, he finally let Lance in on the joke.

"You know, every hot romance Superman had, even as Clark Kent, their initials were all LL."

Lawrence laughed, and eyed Ronald seductively.

"Are you saying you're Superman?" he asked coyly.

"Well, maybe more like Clark Kent," he said, and looked boldly into Lawrence's eyes. "But with the right person, I might just feel like, and maybe actually be, Superman."

"As long as you're not faster than a speeding bullet under certain circumstances," Lawrence said, and let Ronald take his hand. "Some things are better if they take longer."

They both ordered light dinners, and talked for a couple hours. As the evening progressed, Lawrence noticed their stools kept getting closer, until they were sitting side by side, their shoulders rubbing.

"Do you have a place for tonight?" Ronald asked, and Lawrence smiled.

"I have a reservation for late arrival at the Doubletree," he admitted.

"I would love for you to stay with me. It's much homier than a hotel, and I have to do rounds tomorrow morning," Ronald admitted.

"It wouldn't be too much bother?" Lawrence asked, and looked hesitant.

"I suspect it would be far more pleasure than bother," Ronald said, and Lawrence smiled.

"I think you're right," he agreed.

Ten minutes later, they left the pub, and twenty minutes after that, Ronald was showing him around his apartment. Ronald led him to his master bedroom, and uncharacteristically looked shy.

"I was hoping we wouldn't need the spare bedroom," he admitted, and Lawrence set his bag on the floor.

"No point in mussing up the covers on two beds, when we can fit quite comfortably on this one together," Lawrence said, and let Ronald take the lead.

They stood in the middle of the room, kissing, for a couple minutes, and then Ronald pulled away enough to look at him.

"I worked the ICU after rounds today, and came to the pub straight from the hospital." He smiled at Lawrence seductively. "I could use a shower."

"I travelled all day, and could use one myself," Lawrence admitted. He glanced towards the bathroom. "Any chance we could both fit at the same time? To save water?" he asked, and laughed with Ronald.

"Excellent plan," his host agreed.

A few minutes later, they were holding each other under the spraying water, kissing and letting their hands roam freely.

"You're so smooth," Ronald exclaimed when they came up for air. "You shave your entire body, every day? Why?"

"I swam in school, and we always shaved everything. I've been doing it so long, if I skip more than a day or two, it feels weird.," Lawrence lied glibly. "Plus, some of the places I'm sent for pickups are not the most luxurious or hygienic sites. It slightly decreases the chances of picking up critters."

"Ew," Ronald said, soaping Lawrence up. Ronald ran the soapy face cloth down his butt crack and worked a soapy finger inside him. The pressure of his insertion pushed Lawrence forward so their bodies were tight against each other, and he could feel both of their physical reactions. "I hope I'm not being too forward." He leaned forward and kissed Lawrence, letting his finger slip in deeper.

Lawrence gasped and their lips separated enough for him to speak.

"Not at all. In fact, I can't wait until you substitute something a little more substantial for that finger."

They kissed again and then both hurried to finish the shower. They dried each other off, and before Lawrence knew it, they were in the bed, him on his back, with his legs wrapped around Ronald's waist. The lights were very low, and in the shadowy room, he could almost picture that it was Nathan, and not Ronald above him.

The next morning, Ronald gave him a key to the apartment, and the code to get him into the building. It was just past six, and Ronald said he'd probably be able to get away from the hospital by mid-afternoon. He would come home, get out of the suit, into something more comfortable, and take Lawrence out to dinner.

"What are you going to do with the day, Lance?" Ronald asked, struggling to maintain eye contact. Lawrence was still naked, and showering together had led to things. Even though they'd both had orgasms, Lawrence's body seemed to remember how infrequent it was to have this kind of action. A certain part of him already looked ready for another round. "Well, there's a sight I'll have running through my head all day."

"I'm going to go for a walk and run, come back and get cleaned up, and maybe check out a museum or two. Or maybe an art gallery," Lawrence said, knowing he couldn't buy anything that would attract attention

Related Matters

to him on this trip. No one in the world knew what "The Fox" looked like, except that she was an attractive woman, and very athletic. He was flying as himself, but attention during boarding, or from other passengers, was out of the question.

Lawrence walked Ronald to the door, they kissed, and Ronald took hold of his penis and gave it a shake.

"We'll deal with this tonight," he said, and Lawrence laughed.

"I'm sure of that. See you this afternoon."

After he left, Lawrence put on some old sweats, with several layers of t-shirt and sweatshirt underneath, conscientiously locked the door behind him, walked three miles, according to his phone, ran three more, then walked about a mile as a cool down.

Showering, he noticed he was a little tender, and laughed ruefully. It really had been a long time, and he was pretty sure Ronald had taken Viagra or Cialis. That part of his body hadn't had that much attention in… well, maybe ever, he mused.

Even so, with Ronald resembling Nathan so closely in the diminished light, he didn't regret a single action. In fact, he hoped tonight turned out as well as last night. And as prolific. If he couldn't sit right for a couple days as a result, so be it.

They'd ended up showering together again, got sidetracked, and finally realized they were both starving around seven or eight that evening. Ronald ended up taking him to a retro restaurant with an upscale American cuisine. It looked like it might have once been a speakeasy, and Lawrence enjoyed the meal and company immensely.

They both got light meals, and sat talking long after they'd finished. Then it was back to the apartment and bed.

Neither of them got much sleep that night.

Lawrence shifted in his seat and winced. He smiled ruefully. It was his own fault. He'd told Ronald he enjoyed being the bottom, and preferred it, which was true. As a result, although he did manage to invade Ronald's body several times over the course of two days, it was mostly the other way around.

When Ronald dropped him at the airport, Lawrence insisted he not come inside. His flight was in less than three hours, and Ronald wouldn't be able to follow him past security anyway. Lawrence promised he would email, message him on Facebook, and try to get back early in the new year.

Ronald thought he was an international courier, and it was easy to tell him that once he left Miami, he would be jumping from London to Paris to Rome and on to Zurich. Lawrence spun a story of how he would depart Zurich for a flurry of stops that included South Africa, the Persian Gulf, India and the Far East.

Lawrence was surprised to realize he really did want to see Ronald again, sooner than later. Normally, in a case like this, Lawrence would have the skeleton of a plan on how he would kill Ronald, all the while erasing any trace of his existence from the doctor's life.

It was impossible to have any sort of relationship that didn't result in the other person trying to snoop into his personal life, or become too persistent. At some point, every man he'd ever slept with had died. And contrary to appearances and assumptions, none of the deaths had been natural.

Dating him was a real killer, Lawrence thought glumly. He liked Ronald, and suspected he would like him even more if they met up again. His resemblance to an older Nathan really was astounding. And they had more than a few traits in common.

He knew he should try and not see Ronald before March, at the very soonest. It would reinforce how hectic and unpredictable his job was. Every time they got together, the risks of something going wrong would increase.

Lawrence smiled as he realized tonight he'd get to see the real thing. Nathan would be on stage, and he would be sitting with his neighbors, listening to every note and word. It would make it easier later tonight for him to replay his nocturnal activities for the last couple days with Nathan's visage firmly replacing Ronald's.

On an impulse, he pulled out his phone, went to the stored photos and found one of Nathan playing solo at Captain Eddie's. It was a good shot of him. His eyes were closed, and he was clearly caught up in the song he was singing. "Simple Man" by Graham Nash, if memory served.

Lawrence sighed, Ronald temporarily forgotten. It would be good to get home.

♦ ♦ ♦ ♦ ♦

Tess and Tuesday stood near Izzy and Diane, and watched Fay, her partner Letitia, and Cindy Drimble walk to the rocky edge of the beach at Fort Zachary Taylor State Park Beach. This stretch of shore was off the main beaten path enough that the mourners had it to themselves.

Fay carried an urn that somehow reminded Tess of a Turkish liquor bottle, which was probably inappropriate, since Fay's brother John Parkhurst had been an alcoholic.

Letitia and Cindy were on either side of her, and they were there in case Fay stumbled. Tess had never liked John. He had played at Captain Eddie's for much of the first year she and Tuesday had lived in Key West, and had constantly rotated flirting with tormenting, being ingratiating and snide in his comments, depending on how drunk he was.

But he was all the family Fay had, except for her long-time girlfriend and partner, Letitia Powell. Her speech about John had been mostly about their youth, and how hard it had been, growing up in the rural south.

They'd moved to Key West almost ten years ago, John to pursue a musical career of sorts, playing guitar and singing in the club circuit of Duval Street. Fay had moved, at least as much because John did, as to get away from the bigotry of the small town in northern Mississippi where they'd been born and raised.

She had lightly touched on John's difficulty with his bad habits, and eventual addictions. She focused more on the strength he gave her, when the other kids teased her for her looks, and the fact that she seemed much more interested in girls than boys in high school.

Tuesday leaned close.

"I hope the wind stays true," she said in an unnaturally, quiet voice. "It would be awful if his ashes got blown all over her."

All three of them wore cargo shorts, and had clipped the legs high, allowing them to wade in up to their knees without getting their clothes wet. They all wore old battered-looking athletic shoes.

"Goodbye, John," Fay said in a clear voice, and took the top off the urn and carefully spread the ashes from waist height towards the open sea. "I release you on a lee shore, and may your voyages be happy."

"Won't they just wash up on the rocks?" Tess whispered, and Tuesday shook her head.

"No, high tide was three hours ago, and the water is going out until low tide at 11:07 a.m."

Tess saw Izzy and Diane both turn and look at Tuesday, and she saw something in their eyes she didn't quite understand. It was pride, indulgent good humor, yet tinged with a sadness. She made a mental note to ask Izzy about that, the next chance she got.

The ceremony went without a hitch, and Cindy and Letitia got Fay back on the rocks safely. She faced the surprisingly big group of mostly women, and looked grateful.

"Thank you, everyone, for coming today and helping me put John to rest. I know he wasn't always someone you wanted to be around, or even liked, but his heart was good. I'm thankful to every one of you."

She began to cry as she and Letitia made their way off the rocks, onto the soft sand. Cindy called out for everyone's attention, even as members of the Amazons began to surround Fay.

"We will be gathering on the roof at the Diane Isis Bar & Girl, immediately after this, and all of you are welcome. The rule regarding no males on the roof is still in effect, however. There will be refreshments available downstairs for any males, until just before the restaurant opens for lunch at noon today."

Tess felt her eyes beginning to water, and she told herself she was being silly. She had never liked John, and he had treated them both badly. But their relationship with Fay had gotten much better, and she actually felt they were friends now. So she cried for her friend, she told herself firmly.

Tuesday sniffed, next to her, and she resisted the urge to look at her girl. Tuesday always projected that she was impervious to pain, sorrow, and any other sign of weakness. But she knew better.

Tess put her arm around the love of her life, and steered them towards Fay.

"C'mon, Tue Bear, let's go console our friend."

"Damn straight," Tuesday muttered, her voice sounding thick.

♦ ♦ ♦ ♦ ♦ ♦

Carlos drove away from Eldamar, the taste of Nadi's lips still lingering. Yasmin had spent the evening with Nathan, and of course, Oshba had stayed with Phoebe, so he and Nadi had the new house to themselves.

Which included the pool, and the hot tub. He and Nadi had an enjoyable evening, first eating an excellent meal at the Hogfish Bar & Grill on Stock Island, and then later, back at the house.

They stripped off their clothes, cooled off in the pool, heated up in the hot tub, and finally overheated on the exercise pad they carried out next to the pool. Carlos barely got a sheet over it before Nadi pulled him down and they were rolling around, at times tender and intimate, then grinding and using their strength to make the love-making bruising and urgent.

Later, they lay in each other's arms, and Nadi ran a finger along the hair on his face, tracing the outline of the beard. She hadn't mentioned it at all when he arrived, and he'd wondered what she thought of it.

"This is a good look for you," she finally said. "One could almost believe you were a Moor from the days we swept through most of Espana, scimitars swinging, pushing the Spaniards almost to Gaul."

"I am glad we aren't in those days," Carlos admitted. "If we met on the field of battle, one of us would surely die."

Related Matters

"Yes, you would," Nadi said, and they both laughed, and another energetic bout of love-making ensued. They finally were both spent, and she sat straddling him, leaning forward so her breasts hung full and tempting, in front of his face.

He watched her face, and wondered what she was thinking. Her gaze was unreadable as she stared at him.

"How long is this visit?" she finally asked.

Carlos smiled.

"It's open-ended," he admitted. "The Machado family has given me tasks that will keep me in Key West for the foreseeable future. I have an apartment, remember?"

"Have you even slept in that apartment?" Nadi asked, looking thoughtful. "Other than that first night, when we 'broke it in'?"

"Like we broke in this pad?" Carlos asked, smiling.

"Not exactly," Nadi admitted with a devilish look on her face. "I'm afraid that like the virgins in paradise, this pad has lost its innocent state."

"Really?" Carlos said, trying to hide his thoughts. He obviously failed, because Nadi started laughing.

"Whoever uses it is responsible for cleaning it afterwards," Nadi assured him.

"And when your princess and Nathan use it?" Carlos asked shrewdly.

"Oshba cleaned it the first time, I did the second," Nadi admitted, her distain easy to see. "But she saw me doing it, and she apparently felt guilty. She told me that henceforth, she would clean up after her and Nathan, do her own bedding laundry as well."

"And how is she doing, keeping that pledge?" Carlos asked, grinning. He knew what the answer was going to be, which made her next words all the more shocking.

"She has been true to her word," Nadi admitted, her tone and facial expression showing her own disbelief. "I gave it a week, as long as they only stayed here twice in that week. But it has been most of a month now, and she has stripped the sheets, as well as any towels and such. Once Oshba showed her how to use the washer and dryer, she has done all her own bedding, towels, and simple clothing."

"Simple clothing?" Carlos asked, grinning.

"Any underwear she bothers to wear, socks, towel wraps," Nadi rattled off. She stared down at him. "She said she needs to learn how to be a good wife and mother, because someday, she plans to be both."

Carlos stared at her, and Nadi nodded heavily.

"I know. I do not know what to think." Nadi's voice was full of wonder. "I've seen some changes in her behavior and empathy to others, but this is totally unexpected."

"Is this simply her growing up as she gets older, or is it all Nathan?" Carlos asked curiously.

Nadi winced.

"I wonder that, myself." Nadi shuddered. "I hope it's her growing up. If it is entirely due to Nathan, what would happen if they broke up?"

"You think she would revert?" Carlos asked carefully, not wanting to offend Nadi when it came to her *princess*."

"I think I could see anything from her shrugging and then having a huge orgy party to find a new toy, to telling me to have Ashley sell the house, we are off to Rome. Or anything in between."

"I would be sad if it was the latter," Carlos said heavily, and realized what he'd just said. He looked at Nadi hurriedly. They'd both accepted that their relationship was a physical one, and one sorely needed by both of them. The stress of their jobs made a need for release critical. But their lives were too volatile to attempt any sort of relationship. No matter how they felt, their lives, where they lived, and who they could consort with, were dictated by their employer's needs.

Nadi glanced at him and smiled cynically.

"Getting soft on me?" she asked, and Carlos tried to shift the focus of the conversation.

"It's a temporary thing," he insisted. "My batteries will recharge very soon."

She laughed out loud, and reached down to cup his cheek with her hand.

"Very nice try, Carlos," she said, and her expression grew serious. "I know what our unspoken agreement and assumption is. But I do not feel I can hold you to it."

Carlos looked up at her questioningly.

"I think our feelings towards each other have expanded beyond purely physical needs and release." She sighed and met his eyes directly. "I would also be sad if something separated us. Even though our schedule is sporadic, I have grown accustomed to our being together whenever we can manage it."

She'd leaned over farther and kissed him, and that led to other things. Eventually, the cooling wind off the water drove them inside, and to another bout of love-making.

Saturday morning, Nadi asked him to drop her off at Eldamar. Yasmin was taking Tess's class after their stretching routine that Nadi tried to describe to him. He'd begged her to stop, because his groin began to ache just picturing trying to stretch that far.

Yasmin told her she wished to walk back to the house, and to please bring a pair of shorts and a top for her to wear. She said they would find a place to have breakfast on the way back. The fact that eating breakfast after walking to stay slim had certain contradictions didn't seem to worry her at all.

Nadi would be with Yasmin all day. After Nathan finished his set with the band, Yasmin would probably either stay with him, or convince him to return to her home, their own private pool, and that pad that Carlos and Nadi had so abused last night.

But, true to her word, Nadi had cleaned it and it was drying in the sun.

Carlos told her he had some things for work he needed to do during the day, and that it might drag into the evening. So they might not see each other Saturday at all.

Nadi frowned at him. "You will be working the entire night?"

Carlos had hesitated, thinking about how much he could tell her. She could see he was deliberating something, and correctly guessed what.

"I am sorry. We do not pry into each other's work related activities. Text or call me when you are free again."

Carlos pulled the car over to the side of the road and turned to her.

"Nadi, this is an odd situation. I wish to tell you everything about what I am doing here." He sighed. "But these are not my secrets to tell. I need to think this through carefully, and perhaps even call Hector and discuss this matter. It is not reasonable to expect I can keep secrets from you, but I must weigh certain factors, see if there are any particular details I must keep private. I trust your discretion completely. I trust you with my life. But I need to think this through very carefully."

"I understand," Nadi said, and hesitated, which was very unlike her. "Is there, *are* there aspects of your duties that would impact my lady, or her family in any way?"

"No," Carlos said in relief. "Amber told me to reassure you. This is not about you or anything to do with Yasmin, Oshba, or the al Nahyan family. Or the Middle East, for that matter. But there *could* be factors you would not want to be in any way associated with. There might also be some elements of danger involved."

Nadi nodded slowly, and knowing her, Carlos suspected she was going down a mental list of dangerous elements he might be dealing with. It wouldn't take her long to think of the Russians, and either the Columbians, the cartels, or both. She might also think they were setting up some sort of illegal operation like drug smuggling, or gun running.

That was Santiago's territory, he thought with amusement. She caught his hint of humor and he shook his head.

"We will discuss everything in the next day or so," he promised, and she gave him a sincere smile that promised...something.

He finished driving to Eldamar, and dropped her off. He was about to drive in search of more coffee, good Cuban coffee this time, and perhaps something to eat, when he felt his phone vibrate.

It was a text from Hector, telling him to go to the cemetery, and gave him instructions on how to find a certain headstone, and to look behind it.

Muttering to himself, he followed the instructions, found a headstone with a flat slab of slate lying on the ground right behind it. He picked up one end of the slab, took the manila envelope from beneath, and walked for a bit, making sure no one was watching him, as he worked his way back to the car.

He drove to Ana's Cuban Café, got coffee and an egg and cheese breakfast sandwich. He sat at the table farthest from the door, out on the porch, and was thankful it was still fairly early, and there weren't very many people around yet.

There was a set of keys that might be house keys, a map of Key West, and a letter with detailed orders, along with the address of his new house, as well as the alarm combination. There was also a burner phone with instructions to call Hector at three in the afternoon, using the contact number for him in the phone.

There were the usual instructions about caution letting anyone know about this house at all. He was to stop by the original house regularly, act as though he was living there, but after dark, he was to leave without letting anyone see him depart.

He was to start hanging out on Duval, or close to it, wherever the action was. He was to act like a tough punk. If he got into a fight or two, that was fine. But he wasn't to give too much away regarding his capabilities, or his identity.

Hector also recommended he not lose any fights, unless he liked hospital food. They would discuss more details at three, when he called. Hector suggested that if he was taking the car to his second home, he park it in the shed in back. It had no windows, was just big enough for his car, and he could padlock it.

He should also do periodic checks under the hood, under the chassis, the front seat, he knew the drill.

Carlos sighed, and wished he had a partner for this assignment. Someone to watch his back. But, the reasoning on why he didn't made sense. But it also made him more vulnerable.

By the time he called Hector at three, he'd found his new house, moved most of his things in, left some clothes in the original one to make it look like he was staying there. His armory was safely hidden in several boxes built into the wall or floor throughout the house.

Anyone searching might be fooled into thinking the first thing they found was his entire armory.

"How is the house?" Hector asked, and Carlos told him it was fine. A bit small, but since there was just him, that was fine. The car fit in the shed, and the yard was mostly gravel, so he wasn't leaving tire tracks coming and going.

"How is Nadi?' Hector asked after they spoke for a few minutes. His question caught Carlos by surprise. As a rule, Hector never brought up anyone he was dating, or just screwing around with.

"She is fine," Carlos said, having second thoughts on what he was going to ask Hector. As usual, his boss beat him to the punch.

"Have you told her about the second house yet?" he asked and Carlos opened his mouth and then closed it without speaking.

"I have not," Carlos told him. "She does not snoop around on my activities, but she is intelligent, so I don't think it will take her long to figure it out."

"What does she think you're doing in Key West?" he asked, and Carlos laughed.

"With my vague, evasive answers and comments, I suspect she thinks I'm here to set up a drug smuggling operation, or perhaps I am running illegal gun shipments."

"I doubt you will fool her for long, and I do not wish you to lose her trust by lying to her," Hector commented. "Tell her what you need to, as you need to."

"Really?" Carlos asked, shocked. "Will Senor Machado approve of such a thing?"

"We have dropped you in the middle of something, and you have very little support or backup," Hector said in a businesslike voice. "We do not wish to discover an operation at the cost of losing you. She is more than competent, probably more so than both of Ambita's new personal protective detail together. If you find yourself in a tight situation, use this phone and call me. If the danger is eminent, call the second number in your directory."

"Protective detail?" Carlos asked, grinning because he knew Hector couldn't see him.

"*Personal* protection detail," Hector said, correcting him. "And quit grinning. You will attract attention."

Carlos quickly scanned his six, and looked around to see if Hector was actually close by.

"No, I am not in Key West," his boss said mildly. "But how many years have we worked together?"

"Good point," Carlos admitted sheepishly.

"Don't get distracted, or become a foolish love-stricken fool, but don't neglect her either, or take her for a fool." Hector paused for a moment. "She is the best thing that has ever happened to you. Do not lose her by lying or causing her to mistrust you."

"We're just…" Carlos started, and stopped, thinking hard. "Truthfully, we are trying to figure out what we 'just' are," he admitted. "But your advice is good, and I thank you for it."

"Watch your six, Carlos," Hector said gruffly. "My boys would be dismayed if you went and got killed so they couldn't get a chance to wipe the floor up with you playing hoops or futbol."

"In their dreams," Carlos said, and wasn't fooled by Hector's sudden bout of gruffness.

"Thank you, Boss."

"Jose Machado is your boss," Hector replied. "I am simply the one that kicks your butt when you screw up."

"Right," Carlos said, smiling now. "I'll try and keep you from having to do that."

"See that you do," Hector said, and the phone went dead.

Carlos smiled and decided to take a walk down Duval.

♦ ♦ ♦ ♦ ♦

Related Matters

Chapter Seven

"Well, there's a break," Houston said, and Felicia looked up in time to see her husband pull their Chevy Traverse into a parallel parking spot.

"Where's the bed and breakfast?" she asked, and he pointed out his side window. She saw a bright white three story building with a long ascending staircase up the left side of the building. The first floor had a front porch behind white bannisters, and there was a matching balcony on the second floor.

It had a sign over the door that said Key West Bed & Breakfast, and the front door was open and inviting-looking. Felicia beamed at her husband.

"Shall we go get our room in paradise?" she asked, and he nodded eagerly. They crossed William Street and went up the steps of the porch.

As they entered, Felicia noticed the wooden stairway on the left side of the foyer. She decided heels were going to be a low priority this trip, and was glad she'd packed plenty of other choices. That was one of the good things about driving to your vacation. You could take a few more liberties in your packing.

Of course, driving seventeen hundred miles each way wasn't one of those positives. But, they were here, the weather was nice, and they had over a week to find out what their son was doing, and what was so alluring about Key West.

They walked into the next room and there was a desk on the left side, with a pretty young woman with long, straight, dark hair sitting at it.

"Hello, our name is Williams, and we have a reservation for the Yellow Room?" Houston said, and Felicia smiled at how he raised the pitch of his last words, making it sound like he was asking a question.

"Ah yes, Mr. and Mrs. Williams, my name is Janice. Welcome." She looked through her stack of papers and pulled out one paper-clipped batch, and looked at it. "Let's get you checked in. I'll show you around and give you the spiel. You're from Michigan? Did you fly or drive?"

"We drove," he answered, and Felicia smiled, watching her husband. He really was like a cute puppy dog in so many ways. "It took us two and a half days."

They filled out the paperwork, got the tour, the spiel, their keys, and were thanking Janice, when another couple came down the stairs and into the room. They were about the same age as Houston and Felicia, and looked happy to be there.

The man was maybe an inch shorter than Houston, fit and tan, clean shaven, with close-cropped hair. He walked up to the desk, opened his mouth to speak, and then looked at them and his mouth snapped shut.

"Go ahead, we're pretty much done, I think," Felicia said, and smiled at him and the woman she assumed was his wife.

She was attractive and only a couple inches shorter than her husband. She smiled back and turned to Janice.

"We were wondering if you were familiar with the local music scene at all?" she asked, and Janice nodded cautiously.

"I don't go out a lot, but we do, sometimes," she said.

"There's a young man that plays piano and sings," she said, and looked at her husband. "I think he's in his early twenties, and does primarily classic rock." Her husband nodded.

"I think he plays in a place called Captain Eddie's Saloon."

Janice smiled and nodded. "His name is Nathan. Nathan..." she looked at Felicia, and then down at the paperwork in her hand. Her mouth twisted with humor. "...Williams. He's quite good. He sings like an angel, except when he sings like Mick Jagger."

They all laughed. Felicia snuck a quick glance at her husband and almost burst into laughter at the proud look on his face.

"Do you know if he's playing tonight?" the woman asked, and Janice nodded.

"Give me a moment and I can tell you," she said. "I can pull up their entertainment calendar. So, it's Saturday. He plays solo happy hour, Tuesdays and Thursday, and in the evening on Sundays." She smiled at them as a group. "That's my favorite time to hear him. He treats the evening as if it were a coffee house, or a concert. His song list is all over the place, and the crowd sits and listens to him, except when they sing along. You have no idea how rare that is in Key West."

"So he doesn't play tonight?" the man asked, looking disappointed.

"I think he does," Janice said. "Whenever Dr. Leek is playing at Eddie's, he sits in on the first set." She looked at the screen. "Yes, Dr. Leek and the Prime Rib Veggies are booked at Eddie's this week. So he'll be onstage from around nine until sometime after ten. Their first set with him is usually extended. And tonight *is* their last night until New Year's Eve."

"Dr. Leek and the, the what?" Houston asked, and Felicia grinned at him.

Janice looked a little puzzled as she looked at him, and Felicia knew what she was thinking.

"Dr. Leek and the Prime Rib Veggies," she repeated. "They're an R&B band, quite good. All four of them are basically studio musicians playing about three weeks a month, around their day schedules."

Houston looked at Felicia, who shrugged. This was news to her as well.

"I'm sorry," Janice said, looking at the paperwork and then at the other couple as she continued. "Their last name is Williams, and I had this thought he was their son."

"He is," Felicia said. "But we live in northern Michigan, and he calls us about once a month if we're lucky. Nathan is playing in a blues band?" She looked at Houston again. "Nathan doesn't play the blues."

The other couple were looking at each other, probably bemused by the karmic coincidence. Felicia knew *she* was.

"He could if he wanted to," Houston said dryly, and she nodded her head doubtfully. Of course he could play it. But they'd had a conversation a year or two ago about the blues, and he found it uninspiring.

"Oh no, when Nathan plays with them, they do rock. And I mean they rock," Janice said enthusiastically. "They're the best cover band I ever heard. When they do Yes, you just *know* it's the lead singer. Or the Who, or Emerson, Lake & Palmer. I even heard them do Thunderstruck by AC/DC last month. It was incredible."

Houston looked at Felicia questioningly. She shrugged. "He has an excellent ear, and you've heard him go from Cat Stevens to Dan Fogelberg. I never thought he was into the harder rock though."

"Excuse me, so Nathan *is* your son?" the woman asked hesitantly. "I think our kids live together."

Felicia stared at the woman, and then the man, and she could see it. She smiled with genuine pleasure.

"Your daughter is Tess, right?"

The woman blinked in surprise, and Felicia hastened to explain.

"Nathan set up a Skype chat with us on Thanksgiving, and both Tess and her girl…" Felicia stopped cold as she realized what she was doing. "…her girl roommate, Tuesday, came on the call and we got introduced. You have a lovely daughter, and I think she's very sweet," she finished lamely.

The couple exchanged looks, and then the woman looked back at her. She extended her hand.

"I'm Kendra Carter, and this is Robert Carter. We're her parents." She nodded in response to a tiny bit of movement by Robert. "And you're very sweet yourself, trying to not out Tess, but we figured that out a couple months ago. Tuesday is her partner, and they seem to be in a very solid relationship."

They all traded handshakes, and hesitated. As one, they all turned and looked at Janice. She blushed and grinned.

"This is better than YouTube. Are y'all going to hear him tonight?"

"Yes," Houston said, and Robert, who'd said to call him Bob, added they were hoping to catch up with their daughter there as well.

"I think you'll find the whole pack there," Janice said. "I have to call my husband. After this conversation, he's taking me out to dinner. *And to Eddie's, for at least a set.* Speaking of YouTube, have you seen the video?"

All four of them exchanged uncertain looks.

"Is it of Nathan, with the band, or playing alone?" Felicia asked hopefully, and Janice shook her head.

"No, it's got a bit of Tess in it, but it will introduce you to the third member of TNT," she said chuckling, as she started a search on Google.

"TNT?" Kendra asked curiously.

"Tess, Nathan, Tuesday, and they are dy-no-mite!" Janice said, laughing. "Here we go." She looked up at Kendra. "This happened a month and a half ago, and Tess came out of it fine. A guy slipped a roofie into her drink at the Smokin' Tuna, while she was standing at the bar."

"Someone gave my daughter a date rape drug?" Bob said, and his voice made Felicia turn and look at him.

"Calm down, Bob," Kendra said. "Janice just said Tess is okay."

He looked like he wanted to ask more questions, and Janice looked like she already regretted bringing it up. But she held a hand up to Bob.

"Watch the video, and I'll answer any questions I can," she said, and he finally nodded.

"You'll have to crowd close to all see," Janice said, and they hung over her shoulders.

They watched Tess standing at the corner of the bar, talking with what looked like a very busy bartender. She was a tiny little thing, Felicia thought, and frowned as she saw the guy slip his hand over Tess's glass for a moment, then step back to wait. The speed of the video sped up for a few seconds, then slowed, and you could see Tess stagger a little, and look dazed.

When the man began to try and maneuver Tess towards the door, Bob made a guttural sound, and Felicia felt Houston's protective nature slip into overdrive as well. But the bartender was right there, blocking the man, getting in his face, clearly calling for backup, and the man fled.

The video changed to a street view, and they all saw a small, solidly built girl go flying through the camera's range. Felicia thought she recognized Tuesday, but it was so quick, and she'd only seen her the one time, she wasn't sure. The next camera angle verified it was Tuesday.

"That is Tuesday running," Felicia said, and Janice nodded.

"She was on the phone with Tess when the drug really hit her, and she heard the guy telling Tess she needed to get some air."

The scene came back to the bar, and Tuesday came flying in, sliding on her knees the last six or eight feet. Felicia was glad she was wearing softball pants and not shorts. When she stood, after checking to see if Tess was okay, she grabbed one of the managers by his shirt. He pointed to the other door and they all laughed nervously. He was twice her size, but clearly intimidated.

The next camera view showed the guy look back and then run out of the camera's range. A moment later, what looked like a cannon ball shot through the picture, and the video switched to another camera that showed Tuesday tackle the guy from behind. When she began pummeling and kicking the guy, Bob turned to his wife.

"I like this girl."

They watched the last bit where the female police officer pulled Tuesday off the guy, and she swung around with a backhand. They started to groan, and Felicia found herself feeling relieved when the officer actually managed to catch her swing. Tuesday's manner changed immediately, and the female officer released her. When she gave the guy one last kick, all four of them cheered, and then looked at each other guiltily.

"I *really* like this girl," Bob exclaimed, and they all laughed. Bob turned to Janice. "Is it happy hour yet?"

"You're in Key West," Janice reminded him.

He turned to Houston and Felicia.

"I think we're ready for a glass of wine. We have a Shiraz, ready to drink, but the Chardonnay probably isn't chilled enough yet."

"Red is fine, and I think we have Chardonnay in the cooler," Felicia said. "We're in the Yellow Room, on the second floor. We need to unload and I want to change clothes and throw some water on my face. Twenty minutes?"

"We're in the Blue Room, next door to you," Kendra said, her hand on Felicia's arm. "There's a front balcony that has a table with four chairs."

Related Matters

"We'll hurry," Felicia said, smiling at her. She turned to Janice. "Thank you so much for helping us connect. We have so much to talk about."

Janice handed her a sheet of paper that turned out to be a map of Key West. "I put an x where there are several places that are excellent for dinner, and close by, in case you decide to eat and come back here before Eddie's. I also marked where that is, as well. And don't forget about the Duval Loop free bus shuttle. It runs until eleven."

"You've been such a dear, Janice," Felicia said. "Maybe we'll see you and your husband tonight at Captain Eddie's."

"You will," she assured them, and grinned. "It's always entertaining when Nathan plays, and I have a feeling tonight might just set a new record."

Felicia turned to Houston, and smiled sweetly. "Is the car unloaded?" He made a face at her, and she laughed. "See you in twenty, no, nineteen minutes, Kendra," she said, and followed her husband out the front door.

"I'm glad we decided to walk," Bob said, as they made their way down Eaton Street. "That meal was delicious, but I ate too much."

"The Eaton Street Seafood Market turned out to be an excellent choice," Kendra agreed. "We'll have to thank Janice."

"I think if we turn right on Duval, and go two blocks, hang a left, it's right there, on the left," Houston said, studying the map.

Felicia tugged his arm so he shifted to the left just in time to not get run over by a bicycler. "Eyes on the road, Huey."

She sighed. It was good that they were taking this walk. She needed to clear her head. The bottle of Shiraz, which was excellent, followed by their bottle of Chardonnay, which she thought was average, had given her a bit of a buzz, and the glass of wine with dinner had kept it going. She switched to water after that for a while, but there was something about a good wine with seafood.

"What time you got, Bob?" Kendra asked, and he grinned at her.

"I got all night, babe," he said, and Felicia grinned at Kendra's expression. They'd been married almost the same amount of time, and she recognized those endearing traits that every now and then made you want to club your mate senseless. Kendra was tolerant of her husband's bad jokes, and occasional earthiness. In fact, she'd exhibited a little of that herself, at dinner.

All in all, a fun couple to hang out with as they rediscovered who their children *really* were.

They turned onto Duval, and she watched Houston looking at the Hard Rock Café. He turned and looked at her.

"Can we?" he asked, batting his eyes, and she laughed.

"Yes, but not tonight."

He nodded his agreement, and watched two young nymphettes walk by.

"Eyes on the road, mister," she said, and Kendra snickered, and slapped her husband on the arm.

"You too, bud," she said, and he looked at her fondly.

They turned onto Greene Street, and walked by several bars with live entertainment. What she could hear of it, didn't impress Felicia much. Of course, she *was* a music teacher, and she'd played in coffee houses herself, in college.

They saw the sign for Captain Eddie's Saloon ahead, and their pace quickened.

Felicia looked at her phone and frowned.

"It's almost a quarter to nine, and Nathan's band starts playing at nine, according to Janice," she said, and the others looked at her inquiringly. She had an idea. "Why don't we try and get a table towards the back a little, and watch them all in action before we make our grand entrance. If we go in there now, there's no way Nathan will be ready to play at nine. It'll distract him. He'll want to be professional and do the gig properly. But he'll also want to show his appreciation that we're here, and it'll throw him off."

"It might be fun to watch Tess for a few minutes and see how she acts in this setting," Kendra mused. She looked at Bob, who shrugged. "Sure, let's play it by ear."

The bar had two entrances, and they could see that the stage was along the back wall, and the band was towards the right side, away from the door. They slipped in and stepped to the side so they wouldn't be silhouetted in the doorway.

Houston pointed at a table about in the middle of the room, but behind two very rowdy, crowded tables of tourists. Felicia nodded and they slipped into chairs and looked around the room.

Bob looked around the room at the tables with people at them. "I don't see Tess or anyone that looks like Tuesday."

Felicia half listened to the duo that had just finished playing, tell the crowd about Dr. Leek and the Prime Rib Veggies, with Nathan Williams sitting in for the first set.

She wondered what songs they would play. She and Huey were huge

Related Matters

classic rock and folk fans. That was why Nathan had heard so much of it as a young child. He'd fallen in love with it as well. When he decided to become a performing musician, he'd applied himself and grew from a very diligent pianist with some potential of getting a musical scholarship in college, to a very proficient piano player. One with a beautiful voice.

Felicia saw him on the stage and nudged Houston. She looked at her husband and realized he'd already found his son, and was watching him talk quietly with the other musicians, handing them each small index cards. She saw the pride in Huey's face, and smiled, turning her eyes to watch Nathan fine-tune his keyboard setup.

She wondered where he'd gotten all of them. That was a lot of hardware, and they weren't cheap. She knew he had a very good keyboard with an amazing capacity, but this setup was far beyond that.

Kendra sat on her left, and leaned over. "Nathan is the boy at the keyboards?" Felicia nodded, and was suddenly near tears. Kendra's arm slipped around her waist. "He's very handsome. He has his father's stature, but I think he resembles you more in his features."

Felicia remembered that Kendra and Bob had come here to see their child, and hoped for their sake that the girls were coming tonight. She looked at the tables close to the dance floor, and thought she saw a familiar face.

"See the girl with the ice bucket in front of her?" she said, and Kendra nodded. "I *think* that's Nathan's girlfriend, Yasmin."

"That is a very beautiful woman," she said, and they both watched as the girl turned to her left and smiled. She turned back and pulled a bottle out of the ice bucket and topped off her glass. Felicia blinked.

"Is that Dom Perignon?" Kendra asked, and Felicia nodded.

"I think so." Felicia shuddered. "I hate to think what they probably charge in a bar. I wonder what the occasion is."

"It's Saturday," a voice said behind them, and a rough-looking woman leaned closer. "We carry it because she buys at least one bottle every time she comes. And she's at every one of Nathan's gigs. Can I get y'all something to drink?"

Kendra looked around the table. "I know we usually drink red, but we had fish tonight." The two men nodded sagely. She turned to Felicia, who nodded her approval. White wine didn't hit her as hard as red did. She needed to go slow for a while. Kendra turned back to the woman.

"Are we going to like your house Chardonnay?" she asked, and the woman looked around the table thoughtfully, and grinned.

"I wouldn't think so," she admitted. Felicia laughed.

"Would you have any Chardonnay that might normally be found a shelf or two higher in a store?" Kendra asked, and the woman grinned.

"I swear Nathan brings them out," she said, as if to herself. "I think I have just the thing. My name is Melanie, if you need me. I'll be right back with a bottle of Chardonnay and four glasses."

Kendra started to thank her, but she was already gone.

The duo that played earlier had packed and left. The tall guitar player with the little goatee on the stage looked at Nathan inquiringly, and Felicia's son nodded.

The drummer, the bassist, and a man on bongos began to play a driving beat, and Felicia recognized it immediately.

"Oh, excellent!" Houston exclaimed. Felicia nodded, her shoulders bobbing with the rhythm.

The guitar player used his instrument for percussion for several measures and then began to play in earnest, and Nathan began adding the offbeat organ chords.

"I know this song," Kendra exclaimed and looked at her husband. Bob nodded with the beat, agreeing with her.

Felicia saw something near the other door and nudged Kendra.

Tess and Tuesday were dancing their way into the bar, taking their time to get to the table Yasmin sat at with several other women. A lot of the crowd were clapping and rooting them on. They dropped their things off and kept right on dancing until they reached the dance floor. Several young ladies following them at a distance, found chairs at the table of women.

Felicia watched in awe as the two girls started doing a fairly complicated progression, and at the right point switched their direction ninety degrees to the right. She looked over at Kendra. Both she and Bob were staring at the two girls, then at the mass of men from the next table, as well as several girls from Yasmin's group who joined them on the dance floor. As Felicia watched, several dozen other people, from all over the room, crowded the floor.

Felicia looked at Houston, who shook his head violently. She nudged Kendra and pointed with her head at the dance floor, raising an eyebrow. Kendra grinned and stood. As they took each other's hand, the song reached that point, and they sang along with the band, and about half the room.

"Hey, big brother, as soon as you arrive."

They hurried to the dance floor and Felicia looked for an opening on the floor. A big black guy, with a wide, infectious smile, saw their dilemma and got several of the couples of men to make room for them.

"Thank you," Felicia shouted, and she and Kendra tried to pick up the steps. She kept watching both Nathan and Tess, waiting for her or Kendra to get spotted, but they were both caught up in what they were doing.

Related Matters

Kendra leaned forward. "Your son is really talented."

Felicia grinned. "It looks like your daughter is, too."

She watched Nathan playing and singing, and he was clearly having a good time. She'd never heard him play this sort of rock music before. As a solo act, there was only so much he could do to sound like a band, without pre-recording numerous tracks. She knew he disliked that almost as much as she did.

His eyes were constantly moving around the room, watching the crowd as the guitar player did a lead part, let his guitar sag with the strap holding it, and picked up a saxophone and did another lead solo.

Nathan came back in on the vocals, and as they finished the song, his eyes finally got to their part of the dance floor. As the song ended, his eyes went wide and he involuntarily said "Mother?"

Most of the people on the dance floor heard him and looked around and then zeroed in on her and Kendra. Felicia heard a shriek that seemed to include the word Mommy behind her, and turned just in time to see Tess rush across the floor and be enveloped by Kendra's embrace. She noticed the little blonde follow her at a slower pace, feigning a nonchalant manner.

She turned back to the stage just in time to lift her arms to hug Nathan as he got to her. They hugged for a long moment.

"What are you doing here? How?" Nathan seemed at a loss for words. He glanced back at the stage. "I have so many questions, but I have to work."

"Go, son. We'll still be here when you finish. Go on, get back to work."

"Yes, Ma'am," he said and hugged her again. Then he hurried back to the stage, where the band seemed to be having a lot of fun at his expense. He took it with a smile, she was happy to see.

Nathan got back on the stage, and glanced at the band. The guitar player nodded and Nathan started playing a very rapid progression with the organ voice on. The guitar player hit a few chords here and there, and then the drummer started up and the band began to play a very complicated sounding progression at what felt like hyper speed.

"Boston. Didn't see that coming," she said, and started as the big black man from earlier lightly touched her arm.

"Ma'am, are you really Nathan's mother?" When she nodded, he beamed at her. "Good job! He is a delightful young man, and loved by everyone in the neighborhood."

"So, you live near where he does?" Felicia asked. He looked at her in disbelief, then with mirth in his face.

"This is going to be so much fun," he exclaimed. "My name is Marvin Lee. And is that Tess's mother?"

"Yes, Kendra Carter," Felicia said. "My name is Felicia. Felicia Williams."

"Everyone is going to want to meet you," he said and looked around in confusion. "Did you and Tess's mother come together?"

"Our husbands are sitting over there," Felicia started to say, and stopped dead as she watched a giant carry a table that might have been theirs over his head with one hand, using the other to make his way through people. He finally set it down bridging the tables of women and the second batch with all the men. He towered over everyone, and was very muscle-bound. Houston and Bob were following him, looking a little chagrinned, and maybe more than a little awed. Melanie had all their drinks and the bottle of wine.

"Steve is one of the owners," Marvin confided. "They like Nathan and the girls a lot, and treat them well."

He saw Houston and Bob approach and smiled. "And these must be the proud fathers."

Felicia realized the big man was approaching her and looked up at him.

"You're Nathan's mother?" His voice was every bit as deep as she would have expected, which actually surprised her. "It's a pleasure to meet you, Mrs. Williams. You have a very talented son. My name is Steve Little. My brother Ted and I own Captain Eddie's Saloon. Please let us know if you need anything."

"Please, call me Felicia," she said, not quite stammering. "Have you met Nathan's father?"

He smiled and nodded. "I'm going to go meet Tess's mother and let you get settled in with the rest of their extended Key West family."

Felicia looked at her husband and grinned at the expression on his face as he watched Nathan play and sing.

"C'mon, Huey, let's go meet our kid's friends."

They walked to the table, and saw that there were now two empty chairs to the right of Yasmin. There were two more across from her and Tess and Tuesday were pointing them out to Kendra and Bob.

Felicia went around the table and approached Yasmin, who'd been watching her approach. She got to her feet, and Felicia realized the Arab girl was nervous. There was a stocky woman sitting on her other side that Felicia thought looked Arabic as well, and she was staring at Yasmin.

Felicia wanted to put her at ease immediately. She reached out and took Yasmin's hand in a shake, and pulled her closer. She rested her other hand on the girl's shoulder.

"Yasmin, I recognize you from the Zoom call on Thanksgiving," she said and smiled at her. "You're even prettier in person. I get the feeling that you and Nathan are in a relationship."

Yasmin smiled faintly at the description.

"We have become very close," she admitted, her eyes flitting towards the stage. "He has told me how nice you are, and I can see that he was not just being loyal to his mother."

"What a sweet thing to say," Felicia said, and gestured at Huey. "His father is far sweeter than I am, but as you can see, he has the attention span of a gnat."

They both turned and watched Huey joking with Bob and the two girls. Tess was looking at her mother, shaking her head, and Kendra was laughing. Tuesday seemed more at ease, and must have felt their eyes on her, because she turned and looked directly at them.

"She must have radar," Felicia muttered, and Yasmin laughed, a little shakily.

"You have no idea," she said, and seemed to gain strength with the words.

"I know my boy well enough to see that you're very important to him, Yasmin," Felicia said, and squeezed her shoulder. "Please feel like we're all family. If you're important to Nathan, you're important to us."

Yasmin stared at her, and her eyes glistened. Felicia realized that the girl was nearly in tears. The older woman on her other side looked at her in alarm, and the woman past her leaned forward and whispered something in the first woman's ear.

"May I hug you?" Yasmin asked in a tiny voice.

"We can do it together," Felicia said firmly, and enveloped the girl in her best motherly embrace. The girl hugged her back, tightly. Finally, she exhaled and loosened her grip enough to pull back and look into Felicia's face.

"Thank you," she said, and sighed. "I am afraid my family is less open to strangers and new faces than you are." She grimaced. "In fact, they are not all that fond of certain familiar faces."

Felicia smiled sympathetically, and wondered what kind of home environment she'd grown up in. Nathan had told her Yasmin was from a very powerful family, and perhaps a warm family environment wasn't included in that.

Yasmin shook herself, both physically and what appeared to be mentally, and shook her head.

"But I forget my manners," she said, and turned to gesture to the women seated on her other side. "May I introduce Nadezhda Ahmadi and

Oshba Salehi. They are my employees and like family to me. Stern, older sisters, disapproving of much that I do, but supportive all the same. They have become very important to me, and I honestly do not know what I would do without them."

Felicia felt a handshake was actually more appropriate with these two. They seemed low key, but looked…ominous, somehow.

She looked past them at the two girls at the end of the table. They were the ones that had followed a safe distance behind Tess and Tuesday. The first one was so pale, she thought the girl had to be an albino, but Felicia realized she wasn't. She had black hair that was wavy to the point of looking like a perm that fell down below her waist. The last girl was gorgeous, and could almost rival Yasmin in beauty.

Yasmin started, and gestured to the two girls.

"I am being rude and forgetful. This is Phoebe Stark, and Aurora Romano. Phoebe is Oshba's partner. They hope to wed next year some time. Aurora is visiting from Italy. Her family is very close with friends of ours. They both work with Tess and Tuesday."

"Pleased to meet you, ladies," Felicia said and shook hands with both of them, which seemed to amuse the Italian girl.

The band picked that moment to start a new song, and Felicia looked at the stage in disbelief.

"Yes?" she asked incredulously.

"Yes!" Yasmin responded and gave her a mischievous smile.

"Honey, do you hear what they're playing?" Huey came around the table, looking excited.

"Yes," Felicia said, and kept her face deadpan.

"Yes," Houston repeated as if she hadn't already said it.

"What band is this," the woman named Nadezhda asked.

"Yes," Yasmin said with a straight face, and the woman stared at her in confusion.

"Yes, what?" she asked, and Yasmin immediately answered.

"No, Yes."

Nadezhda looked around at everyone, and looked irate.

Tess leaned forward and grinned at them before turning to the annoyed woman.

"Nadi, the name of the band is Yes. The song is called "Roundabout.""

Nathan started singing at that point, and both Felicia and Huey turned to stare at him. Then at each other. They sank down on their chairs in unison, watching their son play and sing.

"He's better than I realized," Huey said, and Felicia nodded.

"He's improved so much," she breathed. "And he's expanded his range of what he does. It's…incredible."

"I think he is tremendous," Yasmin said, leaning close to her. She hesitantly reached out, and Felicia took her hand. They watched and listened for a couple minutes until the song repeated the guitar introduction. When Nathan broke into a frenzied organ solo, and began alternating verses with the guitar player, all action at their tables stopped and the group as a whole simply watched, bobbing with the rhythm.

"It was his voice that first attracted me," Yasmin admitted. "I thought he was quite good, but then he sang Cat Stevens. And captured my heart."

Felicia thought that was very romantic sounding, and realized her and Nathan's relationship was far more serious than she and Huey had realized.

When the song finished, they both exhaled heavily, and grinned at each other.

"He has that effect on me," Yasmin admitted, and Felicia saw she was blushing. A glance past her showed Nadezhda, or Nadi, as Tess called her, staring at Yasmin. Beyond her, Oshba was doing the same. Felicia guessed she didn't have a habit of blushing. Nathan had told her Yasmin was twenty-one, but she seemed very mature and sophisticated for a girl that age.

Everyone in the band took a drink. Felicia took a sip of her own, as did Yasmin. She glanced across the table and saw Bob and Kendra bracketing Tess between them, with Tuesday on Kendra's other side. Tess was talking to her father, and Kendra was drawing Tuesday out of reticence.

The band started a song that made Felicia turn back to the stage. She loved this song. It was "Smooth" by Santana with the lead singer from Matchbox 20 doing the lead vocals. It had a great beat to dance to. She looked at Huey and sighed in disappointment. He didn't dance.

A petite, very fit-looking woman in her thirties appeared at Tess's shoulder, and the girl laughed, looked apologetically at her parents, then rushed to the dance floor. Felicia watched them and blinked. They could flat out dance, both of them. And they seemed to be in perfect sync.

"Would you like to dance, Mrs. Williams?"

Felicia started at Yasmin's question. She looked at Tess and the woman and then at Yasmin.

"Can we compete with that?" she asked, and Yasmin shook her head and shrugged expressively.

"Not in technique, but I suspect we can be very graceful and not embarrass ourselves," Yasmin said and stood. She pulled Felicia's hand, and smiled. "And we can enjoy ourselves."

"Good point," Felicia said, and followed her out to the dance floor.

Kendra and Tuesday appeared at their side, and her new friend nudged her.

"I'm glad you two decided to dance." Kendra glanced at her daughter. "Those two are professionals, but we have safety in numbers."

"Kendra, this is Yasmin, Nathan's…girlfriend?" she said, making it a question as she looked at the girl.

Yasmin smiled, and Felicia was struck again by how beautiful she was.

"I am," she admitted, and a wistful smile came to her face. "And possibly more. We are perhaps a little more serious than boy and girl friend."

Felicia noticed Nathan was watching them, even while he played and sang, and she imperiously pointed at his hands and wagged her finger at him.

"Less gawking and more attention to what you're doing," she called out to him, and the tall guitar player next to him started laughing.

The song ended too soon, and Felicia impulsively hugged Yasmin. "That was fun, Yasmin." She turned to Kendra and Tuesday as they left the dance floor.

"It's so good to finally get to meet you in person, Tuesday. Nathan says the nicest things about you."

"I already thanked her for catching that creep that drugged my daughter," Kendra said darkly. She pointed at a table across the room, and her mood lightened. "Did you see that Janice and her husband did show up, just as she said they would."

Felicia looked and saw the young lady that checked them in to the B&B earlier. Nathan started playing something on the keyboard and Felicia stopped dead and turned around just as he began to sing.

"Welcome back my friends, to the show that never ends…"

"First Yes, and now Emerson, Lake & Palmer?" Felicia shook her head. "Nathan has been holding out on me. Karn Evil 9."

When they got back to the table, Felicia pushed Huey's mouth closed with her fingers.

"Quick drooling, dear. It's unbecoming."

"This band is so good, and a lot of it is because of Nathan," Huey said, and she felt she was going to be blinded by the glare of his pride. "I mean, they're all over the place, and every song sounds just like the original. Nathan is great, but the rest of the band is really talented as well."

"They are, and they blend well," Felicia nodded. "So, he just plays one set with them each night?"

"That is correct," Yasmin said, looking thoughtful. "My Nathan told me that he met them the first night he played here, and they spoke about how much fun it would be to play some of the old classic rock and roll for a change. They are a blues band, and I guess they wanted a broader color scheme."

Felicia and Huey exchanged looks. They didn't have to say a word to acknowledge having heard the possessive term of endearment Yasmin used. "My Nathan" was saying a lot more than just identifying him. She got the idea from her casual tone that the girl used that honorific regularly.

She felt eyes on her, and turned to see Yasmin's two employees watching them. Their expressions were masked and impossible to read. But she was pretty sure they were waiting to see if there would be any sort of response or reaction to their employer's honorific of their son.

"So, Nadi, is it?" Felicia decided to go on the offense. "What is it you do, exactly, as employees of Yasmin?"

"We were originally tasked with protecting her. We were simply bodyguards," Nadi said, after a long pause. She was choosing her words carefully, and Felicia noticed that Oshba had a slight smile on her face as she watched her fellow employee respond. "When our lady left the Arabian Gulf, both of us took on additional duties."

"How long are you here for?" Huey asked curiously. "When do you have to go back home?"

"We *are* home," Yasmin said in a distracted voice. "I will never return to the Middle East. No matter how badly my family want me to."

Felicia and Huey exchanged glances. She liked the young girl a lot. But she was going to want to know a lot more about her before she gave any kind of blessing to a long-term relationship.

Not that Nathan was asking her opinion or permission, she thought resignedly.

Felicia saw that Yasmin was intently watching Nathan as the band broke into "Who Are You?" by the Who. She saw the petite dancer friend of Tess's look at the stage, then at the bar area, and say she'd be back, and hurry to the bar.

"This is interesting," Yasmin said, squeezing Felicia's hand. She hadn't even realized they were still holding hands. "Watch the bar area."

Tess nodded her agreement, and started a chant.

"Betsy! Betsy! Betsy!"

Tuesday and all the men at the adjoining tables quickly joined in, and Felicia saw the tall, muscular bartender look over at their tables and visibly sigh, shaking his head. Steve the owner worked his way through the standing room only crowd to stand at the waitress station. Betsy joined him, and Steve gave her a look remarkably similar to the one the bartender had.

"The large bartender is the younger brother of the manager, Steve Little. His name is Ted, and the two of them own Captain Eddie's," Yasmin said, leaning up against her so she could speak over the music and chanting. "They are both avid fans of the Who, and the first song my Nathan played here with the band was a Who song. Betsy is Ted's wife, and was a professional dancer. They have this tradition…"

Felicia saw Ted line up quite a few shot glasses, giving Betsy a fatalistic stare as he did so. He reached up into a cabinet above the bar and pulled down several bottles of what looked like whiskey. Customers were holding up cash or cards, clamoring for a shot. Their waitress quickly made her way around the bar area, taking money or cards, or taking a note to add to a tab. She called out something, and Ted sighed again and pulled three more shot glasses out.

He poured healthy shots into each with a sure hand and a lack of wastage. In no time, the waitress was making sure the right people had their shots. Felicia expected them to start shooting them, but everyone waited, their glass on the bar, watching Ted intently. He said something and heads nodded all around the bar.

Meanwhile, the band was making its way through the song, Nathan sounded just like Roger Daltrey, and Felicia really wanted to watch him play, but she didn't want to miss whatever was about to happen.

The guitar player and Nathan were both playing artsy parts, with the drummer clearly enjoying himself. When Nathan finally sang "I really want to know", everyone shot the drinks as fast as they could on the word 'know', and slammed them down on the bar upside down.

Felicia blinked in surprise. Tess's friend Betsy beat everyone and it wasn't even close. If you went by the speed of the song, she won by about a beat and a half.

"You see that?" Huey said, and Felicia nodded as she watched Betsy give Ted an air kiss before coming back to their table.

"And the girls win again!" Tuesday said enthusiastically. Felicia was glad to see the girl was recovering from her fears about what her probable future in-laws would think of her.

Felicia shook her head at the girl. Tuesday started to look belligerent, and remembered who she was.

"Girls rock and rule, but *Betsy* wins again. She kicks butt!" Felicia sang out.

"Damned straight," Tuesday muttered and grinned at her. "By the way, thank you for having such a cool son. Nate Boy rocks too!"

Related Matters

"Damned straight," Huey said, and looked around the table.

"You think the band will play another Who song tonight?"

Felicia laughed out loud, grinning.

"You're out of your league, Huey."

They all laughed and cheered when Dr. Leek played a Beatles song.

"So I hear that you're who I have to thank for giving birth to such a wonderful young man," a woman's voice said. Felicia looked up to see a weathered looking woman in her sixties or seventies standing next to her. She had a bright sundress on, and Felicia didn't want to look too closely to confirm, but she was pretty sure the old woman was going commando underneath.

Over the course of the set, all the gay men had managed to introduce themselves and declare what a wonder boy Nathan was. Or a wonderful young man, in some cases. About half of them had warned her about an older woman named Marilyn that was a very good friend of Nathan's but was always pushing the merits of a Harold and Maude relationship.

Felicia had looked at Huey the first time one of them had told that story, and his expression was priceless. She smiled up at Marilyn.

"So, you're Marilyn," she began, and the older woman looked around the table of men in disgust.

"I swear you men are worse than gossipy suburban housewives," she declared, and all of them pointed to the fleshy black man named Marvin Lee. She turned back to Felicia. "We meet every Monday, and god knows, I've spelled it out enough times."

Yasmin leaned in close and whispered in her ear.

"She and my Nathan play Scrabble every Monday at the Garden of Eden."

Felicia laughed at the woman's clever pun, then remembered that when researching Key West, she'd seen a bar named Garden of Eden. What was it, again?

"Isn't Garden of Eden a rooftop, clothing optional bar?" Huey asked hesitantly.

"There is no way Nathan would sit in a public place, naked," Felicia said with conviction. "Even if it's only playing Scrabble. He can be so shy sometimes."

"I dunno," Huey began, and stopped as almost everyone at both groups of tables began to laugh. "What?"

That just made people laugh harder. Felicia had a feeling she didn't know her son as well as she thought she did.

She looked across the table, and Kendra and Bob looked as lost as they were. Tess, on the other hand, looked almost distressed. Tuesday couldn't quit laughing.

Felicia noticed that none of the Arab women were laughing, and wondered if this topic was somehow offensive to them. Then she noticed that they all were trying to hide smirks. The two employees were far more successful at it than Yasmin.

The band finished playing a song by Styx that would have blown her away if she hadn't already suffered overkill of amazing songs by what they'd already played.

Nathan began playing a song that stopped the conversation cold. "Maybe I'm Amazed," by Paul McCartney. Everyone turned to watch and listen, and Felicia had to admit it was exceptional. She'd heard a lot of recordings of Paul doing this song that weren't as well played and sung.

When it ended, Felicia sighed and turned back to Yasmin. She was surprised to see tears in the girl's eyes. She was staring at Nathan, and Felicia had an epiphany that she'd just met her future daughter-in-law. If Yasmin had any say in the matter, anyway.

Yasmin's eyes slowly slid away from him and to her. She realized her vulnerability, and blushed again. It made her even prettier, Felicia decided. She handed the girl a packet of travel tissues, and the girl smiled at her.

"You really like Nathan, don't you?" Felicia asked, and Yasmin dabbed at her eyes, and then looked at Felicia frankly.

"I am deeply in love with your son," she admitted. "I know I sound possessive about him when I call him 'my' Nathan, but it is how I feel. He changed me, and my life as a result. And for the better. I hope I do not offend you when I say I love him and cannot imagine a life without him in it."

Felicia was aware that the girl felt she was taking a chance by being so open. Her eyes showed she was relieved she'd said her mind, but now wondered if she'd rushed Felicia and Nathan's father into the situation too quickly.

"I haven't talked with him about you, other than that one Zoom call last month," Felicia said. "But I got the impression the two of you are in a relationship that he expects to be long-term."

Yasmin smiled, and it wasn't a victorious smile, or smug. It was sincere happiness.

"He's told me he wonders what our children would look like," she admitted, and Felicia kept her jaw from falling with an effort. She heard her husband grunt behind her and knew he was listening to every word. Yasmin shook her head. "I've wondered the same."

"You would have had to know me before October to fully realize what an impact he has had on me," Yasmin said slowly. "I was a very selfish young woman that was accustomed to getting my own way, even if it would lead to my being stoned or imprisoned. Even then, I resisted the norms of my family and culture. As a result, when I escaped from home, I think I felt the rules of normal behavior did not apply to me. Nathan opened my eyes, and I am a better person for it."

Felicia was floored. This was a very proud, intelligent, young lady that was used to getting her way. Manipulating people was just a part of her life. But here she was, opening herself up, leaving herself wide open and defenseless, in the hopes Nathan's parents were not the type to abuse that trust.

Something in her eyes must have cued Yasmin into her thoughts, because she smiled hopefully, and her hand tightened on Felicia's.

"You know, Yasmin, I'm not just going to give up on Nathan getting to experience the ultimate cougar," Marilyn said from behind her. Felicia realized she'd been standing there and had probably heard every word they said.

The band started another song, and Felicia looked up in surprise and some annoyance.

"I hope he doesn't sing this one," she said. "It's a great way to screw your throat up."

As if to mock her, Nathan came in on the first line of "Thunderstruck" by AC/DC.

"I was caught, in the middle of a railroad's tracks..."

Felicia shook her head in dismay.

"I'm going to have to talk to that boy," she said, and Yasmin laughed shakily.

Felicia realized they were blocking Huey out of the conversation, and debated about it internally. She looked over at him and saw him stand as the song ended and clap loudly. She bit a lip and turned back to Yasmin. She seemed to know what Felicia was deliberating.

"I think Nathan's papa is caught up in his son right now, and will not miss us. At least until my Nathan finishes singing."

"I think you're right," Felicia said, and sighed as they started another song. "The Guess Who. You don't hear *that* band very often anymore."

"We hear it at least once every time Nathan plays," Yasmin said, looking thoughtful. "I had never heard of them, but now I know at least seven or eight of their songs."

"Nathan said you met at one of his gigs?"

Yasmin uncharacteristically hesitated, and glanced at Nathan as they finished the song "Bus Rider." She nodded slowly, and then seemed to come to a decision.

"We met when he played at a resort in Mexico," she admitted. "I met all three of them there. We were the only young people, so we kind of stuck together, I believe is the phrase."

"Nathan played at a resort in Mexico?" Felicia didn't remember him ever mentioning that. "Which one?"

"Playa Perdida, or Lost Beach, in English," Yasmin said slowly. "My Nathan was involved with Amber Machado at the time, and she was responsible for the company's entertainment division. Technically, he was not *my* Nathan, at that point."

"Really," Felicia said, and kept her voice neutral. That seemed to catch Yasmin's attention, and she looked distressed.

"Please understand, Nathan was a perfect gentleman," she said. She looked at Felicia and took a deep breath. "I tried to seduce him, and failed. Later, he told me he was very attracted to me. But he would not betray Amber. That had never happened before, and it gave me much to think about."

Felicia had no idea what to say. Yasmin was as much as admitting she had tried to have sex with Nathan while he was in another relationship. Whether or not Nathan was weak, it was more a statement about her.

"As I mentioned before, Nathan has made me reconsider many of my routine actions and behavior." Yasmin was watching her closely, and Felicia had a feeling she knew exactly what was going through her head.

"We both walked on the beach in the mornings, and began to walk together. I spent much time with him, as well as Tess and Tuesday, in the club at night. Ms. Machado had to fly to Europe, so he had free time on his hands. But we behaved, and I must admit, it was not my preference. Under the circumstances, it was almost a miracle. And, of course, he helped hide me when the mercenaries took over the resort to kidnap me. In fact, I believe he saved my life, just before forces hired by the Machado family liberated the resort. With a little help from my 'big sisters'," Yasmin said and smiled.

"He also saved Amber's life when the mercenaries tried to execute everyone."

Felicia sat absolutely still, staring at her. She was shocked and frightened for her boy. She wanted to tell Nathan to go home and pack. They were all going back to Michigan, whether he liked it or not. There were obvious flaws with that plan, and what Yasmin was telling her had happened in Mexico.

But still…

The band started playing "Magic Carpet Ride" by Steppenwolf, and it distracted her. She wondered if the fact that Nathan sounded just like John Kay, the lead singer shouldn't be a little disturbing.

Felicia remembered something, and shook her head to clear it.

"So, if Nathan behaved in Mexico, and stayed loyal to this Amber girl, how did you two end up getting together?"

"I tried to forget him, and we visited several other resorts in the Caribbean, but I could not get him out of my mind," Yasmin admitted. "So we came to Key West for Fantasy Fest." Yasmin got a satisfied expression on her face. "As it turned out, Nathan broke up with her that morning. We arrived in the late afternoon. And here we are," she finished glibly.

"Did he know you were coming?" Felicia asked, praying for a particular answer.

"He did not," Yasmin said, a little color appearing in her face. "Later, he told me she was trying to dictate his life, wanted him to move to Miami, sign contracts giving up all control over his bookings. She seemed to think they were almost engaged, but they never talked about a relationship. He thought they were just…"

Yasmin stopped abruptly and blushed. Felicia knew she'd just realized what she was about to blurt out to Nathan's mother.

"He thought their relationship was purely physical?" Felicia said, and had trouble forming the words, when they involved Nathan.

"Maybe," Yasmin said, and looked meek. She went to take a sip and realized her glass was empty. She tried to pour another, but there was barely a shot's worth left in the bottle. "I think I am going to let Nathan tell you any details involving anyone other than myself. I think I might have already dug a tiger pit and fallen in."

She looked at the empty bottle wistfully.

"Would you like some champagne?" she asked hopefully. "I could order another, if there was someone to help me drink it."

"Nice try," Felicia said and laughed at the girl's expression.

The band finished the Steppenwolf song, and the lead guitar player, that Felicia now knew was named Kris, announced that they would be taking a break after the next song. He also thanked Nathan for sitting in with them, and a cheer went up around the room.

Felicia looked across the bar in wonder, and finally turned back to Yasmin.

"He's really popular here," she said, awestruck.

"He is," Yasmin said, looking happy to change the subject.

Nathan picked that moment to start the next song, and Felicia felt her eyes widen as she recognized "Won't Get Fooled Again" by the Who. She looked across the table and saw Kendra looking back at her, even as she stood up. She nodded towards the bar and raised an eyebrow questioningly.

"Honey, can we?" Huey said, and pulled her to her feet. Felicia looked down and saw Yasmin looking wistful. She impulsively grabbed the girl's hand and pulled her to her feet, even as Nadi started to rise, startled by the action.

"Nadi, you are *not* to shoot my Nathan's parents," Yasmin said, using one hand to push her back into her chair. She giggled as she let Felicia lead her around the table. Huey and Bob were already halfway to the bar. Felicia glanced back at the two other Arab women nervously.

Nadi made a point of sighing as she started to rise at a more sedate rate, and looked startled as the other woman put her hand on Nadi's arm. They stared at each other for a moment, and then did rock, paper, scissors. Oshba, Felicia remembered was her name, played paper, and Nadi had scissors.

Nadi sneered at her partner and hurried to follow them to the bar.

Ted looked at them, and a hint of a smile showed briefly on his lips.

"I'm Ted. Welcome to Key West and Captain Eddie's Saloon."

"Shaddap and pour, mister," Betsy called out, grinning at him.

"What she said," Steve said, startling Felicia. He was standing right next to her, and she looked up at him in awe. Both brothers made her feel like a little girl in stature again.

They watched Ted pour the shots, somehow continuously pouring, yet not spilling anything, as far as she could tell. Yasmin leaned in close to her and whispered.

"I have been wanting to do this since the first time I saw it," she admitted. She looked at Nadi. "Nadi, you must win this competition for the honor of our tribe. The al Nahyan tribe of Abu Dhabi is depending on you."

Nadi stared at her employer.

"I am Jordanian."

She said it with such a deadpan expression, Felicia couldn't tell if she was joking or not.

Ted announced when the shots would be drunk, and they all waited as Nathan did a drawn out synthesizer lead part. Then the drummer came back in, and as the guitar and bass joined in, Nathan screamed, and the whiskey flew.

Betsy won again.

♦ ♦ ♦ ♦ ♦

Tess watched her and Nathan's parents do the shot thing, and was glad to see it didn't seem to set them off in a coughing spasm, or chicken out at the last moment. In fact, she was impressed that Yasmin joined them. Of course, it made sense. She had a feeling her friend was desperate to gain the approval of Nathan's parents.

I guess that would finally give her a family that loved her for herself, not some stupid title. And if I'm reading Houston and Felicia correctly, two parents that wouldn't judge her badly for her past actions.

Tess noticed that Nadi had no trouble with the shot. In fact, afterward, she shook it a little, as if to get the last drop. Yasmin, on the other hand, had a slightly queasy expression on her face. Tess heard her tell Nadi that it burned all the way from her throat to stomach.

Tuesday nudged her and looked her in the face.

"I'm glad you're getting to see your parents," she said hesitantly. "Do you think they like me?"

"No, I think they love you, Tue Bear," she said, and kissed her girl on the lips, very softly. They stared into each other's eyes. "It's going to be fine. They like you, and think that you are fun to be around. Do you like them okay?"

"I think they're great," Tuesday admitted. "I wish *my* parents were that cool. If they were here, they'd be telling me to put you out of my mind, and find a guy. A couple of my brothers would be calling our neighbors fags, and you a dyke. Then I'd have to kick their asses."

"Tuesday, I *am* a dyke," Tess said gently. "It's only an insult if I let it become one."

"You're too good for me," Tuesday said morosely. "I expect the insults, and am always defensive about them."

Tess felt eyes on her and looked up to see Phoebe watching them. She got up and walked around the table, Oshba watching her curiously. She sat down on the other side of Tuesday and took her hand.

"No," Tuesday began, and Phoebe shushed her. Tuesday was so startled, she didn't pull her hand free.

Phoebe examined her palm carefully, nodded to herself, ran a finger up the palm almost to the base of Tuesday's forefinger. Then she carefully set the hand down and reached for the other.

"That's enough," Tuesday, began, and stopped cold when Phoebe reached out without looking and placed her forefinger and middle finger pressed together on Tuesday's lips.

"Hush."

Phoebe leaned forward to look closer, and nodded again, looking satisfied. She leaned back in the chair and released Tuesday's hand.

"You have a long lifeline. The base of it was a little muddled, but then it's a clear line. You will have one long-term relationship, and it will be for life. And you will have children."

Tuesday stiffened and hesitantly looked at Tess. Then she looked back at Phoebe.

"How many?"

"Either one or two," Phoebe said and grimaced. "Tess shows the same results, so I don't know if that means you're each going to have two children, or if you will each have one, so that makes two between you."

Phoebe stared at Tuesday.

"It shows a happy lifeline for you. Happy. Somehow, I don't think you would be this happy if your in-laws didn't like you."

"Or love you," Tess said softly.

"That seems more likely," Phoebe admitted. "I tend to interpret conservatively, so the odds of my readings not exaggerating the facts are better."

"I miss anything?" Nathan asked, startling them all. "Is everyone getting along? You all looked like you were having a ball earlier."

"Nathan, you were great, as always," Tess said, and gave him a kiss on the cheek and hugged him. "I really like your parents. Come on, I'll introduce you to mine."

An hour later, the core of them were still there, but they were fading fast.

Aurora had left as soon as Nathan was done, saying she was going to drop in on her roomie at Smokin' Tuna. Tess and Tuesday looked around the group after she left.

"That's Italian for, I'm going to hang out until they close, and then take Mariah home for the night," Tuesday announced, and Tess, Yasmin and Nathan all nodded their agreement. Yasmin had ordered another bottle of Dom, and Tess and Tuesday were doing their best to drink the wine that had been bought for Nathan tonight.

The men of Eldamar had all left, leaving in little groups. Tess noticed every one of them made a point of saying goodbye, and how happy they were to meet the parents of two of their favorite neighbors. Marilyn left with the last of them, asking Nathan if he was ready to go? Both of Nathan's parents had laughed about that for a while.

"So, I don't get this," Tess's mother said slowly, looking like the wine was finally catching up with them. "You live in a community called Eldamar, which is seven houses all owned by the same man, and it's gay only. It *used* to be male gay only, but because your landlord's boyfriend is Tess's old mentor from Florida, he did a favor and let two gay women live there, even though you didn't think you were gay at the time. So

Related Matters

how did Nathan manage to move in? It's pretty clear they all know he isn't gay."

"Uh, that's a long story," Nathan said. "Why don't I tell you tomorrow or the next day, when it's earlier?"

Tess had to laugh at Nathan's feeble attempt to avoid telling he'd pretended to be gay for a dinner party, thinking he was keeping her and Tue Bear out of trouble.

Oshba and Phoebe had left soon after she read Tuesday's palm, much to Kendra and Felicia's disappointment.

"You can always get her to read you at some point this week," Tess assured them. "It's not like we never see her. In fact, I'll see her tomorrow. I work the early part of the day, leading jet ski groups around Key West."

"How long are you here for?" Nathan asked, and Felicia grinned at him.

"What, you trying to get rid of us?' she joked, and Nathan smiled.

"Of course not," Nathan said. "I was just thinking of all the things there are to do, and wondering how much time we have to do them."

"We thought we'd stay through New Year's," Mr. Williams said, and Tess wondered as Nathan frowned.

"That isn't necessary, sir," Nathan said firmly. "I'm fine. I mean, not fine, but I've come to terms with it, and you don't need to babysit me. I'm not going to go throw myself off a cliff or anything."

"Not in Key West, anyway," Tuesday said. "The closest thing we have to a cliff wouldn't do more than give you a scrape on your knees."

"Was it a year ago, this week?" Tess asked, realizing they were talking about one of the main reasons Nathan had just picked up and moved to Key West after he graduated from college.

"Don't worry about it, seriously," Nathan insisted. "Telling the two of you about it was a kind of therapy for me. Actually, with everything that happened that week, it was very cathartic."

"You told Tess and Tuesday about it?" Felicia asked slowly, looking around the table at everyone. Of course, neither of her parents knew about what had happened to Nathan that had made him hate himself for a while. Neither did Yasmin or Nadi, from the looks on their faces, she decided.

"What are we talking about, Nathan?" Yasmin asked, looking worried.

"I'll tell you tonight, when we get home," Nathan said, and Tess felt tears threatening at his sad tone. Clearly his mother heard that same tone. About the same time, Nathan realized what he'd just admitted, and his blush followed quickly. Yasmin saw it and tried to hide a smile, unsuccessfully.

"Are you sure you're dealing with it, and not just avoiding it?" Mrs. Williams asked, and looked at her and Tue Bear curiously. "He told you about it?"

"Yeah, it was the night I got shot in the butt by the Columbians," Tuesday said, and Tess winced. "It's a great scar. Want to see it?"

"Maybe another day," Mrs. Williams responded uncertainly. "You got shot. When?"

"Last June," Tuesday said quickly, before Tess could try and steer the conversation along different lines.

"*And,* when Nathan played a gig at some resort in Mexico, mercenaries actually took it over and tried to kidnap Yasmin?"

Nathan started. "How did you find...oh." He looked at Yasmin, who was biting her lip.

"I'm sorry, I got caught up in my conversation with your mother," Yasmin admitted. "She is very easy to talk to."

"I know *that's* true," Nathan said, at the same time his father spoke. "And *that's* a fact!"

They looked at each other, startled.

Tess watched the four parents look at each other, and realized they were going to gang up on Nathan, on her, even on Tuesday, although they were in for a shock with *that* one.

"Is everyone ready? We have any open tabs?" Tess asked, to sidetrack the conversation.

Her father and Mr. Williams said they were all set. Melanie happened to be passing by and Tess put a ten on her tray.

"Thank you kindly, little lady," she said, and looked at Nadi inquiringly. She nodded and stood and walked with Melanie while she got her wallet out. Tess wasn't snooping, but could tell Nadi gave her six hundred dollar bills for the tab.

"Thank you kindly, miss," Melanie said, and turned to face the table. She looked at the parents. "It was a pleasure meeting all of you. I hope to see you again soon before you leave."

"Tomorrow night," Tess's mother said, and Melanie nodded her approval.

"Good choice."

They all stood and Tess looked at her mother.

"Your B&B is on our way home. We'll walk you there." Tess had a thought. "Um, after all that wine, can everyone still walk?"

"You calling us lightweights, dear?" her mother asked, and Tess smiled and shook her head.

"No, that would be me. I can drink wine, and rum and cokes, fine. But frozen drinks do me in every time."

"I'm tired, but I think it was the drive down from Michigan," Nathan's mother said. "I'll sleep well tonight."

"That reminds me, dear Tess," Yasmin said, and looked at her questioningly.

"Are you teaching your aerobics class tomorrow? And are we doing our stretches?"

"You teach an aerobics class?" her mother asked, surprised. Both she and Nathan's mother exchanged nods and looked at her. "That might be fun."

Tess sighed, and decided Yasmin was definitely nervous tonight, because she didn't have her "A" game.

Nathan nudged Yasmin, all the while trying to keep from smiling, and realization dawned on her face. She looked at Tess.

"Oops."

♦ ♦ ♦ ♦ ♦ ♦

Nathan lay on his back, one arm draped over Yasmin's bare shoulders. She had her face pressed against his chest and her fingers played with the hairs on his chest. Their love-making had been a little more frantic at the start, but eventually settled into a comforting, familiar rhythm.

Their climax was slow in coming, mutual, as far as he could tell, and very intense. He'd rolled off her, breathed for a minute, then started to get out of the bed.

"Please, let me," Yasmin said, pushing him back prone with a hand on his chest. She went in the bathroom, and a minute later, there was the sound of the toilet flushing. She came out with a warm, damp hand cloth and cleaned him up. She took her time about it, and he looked at her face.

She had a troubled look that worried him.

After she finished and straddled him, her body pressed firmly against his, her head resting on his chest they fell into a synchronized breathing pattern that always intrigued him. He waited for her to speak, knowing from her face that she had something to say.

She kissed his nipple and sighed.

"Nathan, I was very foolish this evening. When your mother and I spoke, it was as if I was drunken and babbling. I wanted to please them so much, but I ended up telling them many things I probably should not have."

"You were nervous," Nathan point out. "You wanted to make a good impression, for them to like and approve of you."

"Dear Nathan, I am not in the habit of being nervous." Yasmin sounded almost annoyed. "But when I am in conversation with your mother, it is as if I have become a babbling brook."

She raised her head to look into his eyes.

"Is that the right expression?"

"Yes, not that I'm agreeing with you, though," Nathan said, side-stepping the trap.

She smiled to show her appreciation of his defense of her.

"What all did you tell her?" Nathan asked, wondering if this was a wise question. But he wanted to know what kind of grilling he'd be facing in the morning.

She recounted most of the key points of their conversations, and Nathan winced. Her expressing her love of him told his mother she was hoping for more, and that it was her goal. Which was fine. A young girl, either infatuated or in love, was going to be enthusiastic. He knew his mother well enough to know what her primary concerns were. He was also pretty sure she'd be expressing her thoughts on that to him sometime in the next day or so.

The real concern Nathan had, was Yasmin and Tuesday letting slip the story about the Columbians. And the mercenaries trying to abduct Yasmin at the command of some of her relatives. That was potentially a reoccurring problem that wasn't necessarily solved by winning one battle.

Of course, *that* wasn't the primary concern that *Tess* had, Nathan thought, smiling in spite of himself.

"What?" Yasmin asked, looking down at his expression with suspicion.

Nathan laughed.

"I'm wondering if Tess is quite ready to have her parents taking part in her aerobics classes," he said, and she winced. "And I *know* she doesn't feel ready to share the stretching routine with them."

Yasmin looked concerned.

"I did not think of that at the time," she admitted, shaking her head in embarrassment. "I don't think I've ever been so careless in my conversations before. Your mother has the ability to make me tell her things I do not wish to."

"Like what?" Nathan asked, watching her face, marveling yet another time how lucky he was to have her love.

"That you told me you wondered what our children would look like," Yasmin said tartly, and Nathan laughed nervously. "And that I wondered the same thing."

"Uh, we don't need to hurry to find that out, Yasmin," he said, and cleared his throat nervously.

Yasmin laughed at him.

"In some ways, you are such a typical boy. However, in other ways…"

She cupped his face in her hands, leaned over and kissed him.

When she finally straightened up, her eyes watched him closely. He tried to get his breath back, and was glad it didn't *really* sound like panting. She smiled her satisfaction, then a shadow crossed her face.

"Still, I have worked my entire life to keep my composure strictly under control," she said, sounding troubled. "One minute with your mother, I'm calling you mine, telling her so many things I never intended her to know."

"It's her superpower," Nathan admitted. "Anyway, it's not unusual for a young woman to be nervous and talk too much when she meets her future in-laws."

Yasmin stared at him, shocked. She started to speak, cleared her own throat, tried again, and stopped. Nathan hadn't intended to say that, but didn't regret it, since that *was* what he hoped for, someday. Not today, of course.

She finally swallowed hard and managed to speak. Her eyes were shiny, and she looked very happy. She also looked more than a little frightened.

"Did you just propose to me?" she asked quietly.

Nathan wanted to scream yes, that was it. But even *he* knew it was too soon.

"More like a statement of my intentions," Nathan said, and smiled at her. "I love you, Yasmin. I can't imagine a future that you aren't part of."

"I will say yes when you ask," Yasmin said in a tiny voice. "And I love you, too."

She leaned forward, and all thoughts of his parents, or of much of anything else, fled, leaving him alone with the beautiful woman kissing him.

❖ ❖ ❖ ❖ ❖

Chapter Eight

Felicia came down the stairs, hoping she could beg a cup of coffee from Janice, or whoever was preparing the continental breakfast. She inhaled and gasped at the smell of freshly baked bread. She grinned when she saw the back of Kendra standing in the doorway into the kitchen.

"Whatever you're getting, get two," she called out, and Kendra turned and grinned at her.

"How do you take your coffee?" she asked, and Felicia said a little dairy product of any nature would be fine.

Kendra turned to whoever was in the kitchen and sweetly asked if they had any brie cheese. There was a chuckle from within, and then two hands held out two paper cups with heat guards on them. Kendra thanked her and handed one to Felicia.

They walked out and sat on the chairs on the front porch. Felicia took a closer look at Kendra. She wore short shorts, an Atlanta Falcons lightweight tank top, and old athletic shoes. It didn't look like she'd done any more to primp than she herself had. Brushed the teeth, and splashed enough water on her face to wake up.

As it happened, Felicia had very similar clothes on, except she wore a Beatles t-shirt. She knew Huey would sleep for at least another hour.

"Were you thinking of walking or running?" she asked Kendra, and was intrigued to see her shift her eyes away.

"Maybe," she admitted. "I had to put something on, and I thought I'd keep my options open."

Felicia suddenly got it.

"You're going to sneak over to where Tess lives, and spy on that exercise routine she was trying to keep us from finding out about last night," Felicia exclaimed, keeping her voice down.

Kendra looked at her guiltily, and then with indecision. Her expression changed to playful.

"Want to go with me? It's only about three blocks from here."

Five minutes later, they were looking at the street numbers on the houses.

"This is it," Kendra said confidently. They started to leave the road and walk between their kids' house and the one just beyond it, when a young man walked out of an apartment on the second floor of the building next door.

He had a towel over his shoulder, but was otherwise naked, and Kendra and Felicia turned right around and were back on the road, looking at the house across the street.

"I like the looks of that one," Felicia said in her normal voice, and then added in a whispering tone. "I guess the dress code really *is* very casual here."

Kendra giggled, and Felicia looked at her. She sounded just like Tess when she did that, Felicia decided. Kendra felt her gaze, and instinctively seemed to know what she was thinking.

"No, she sounds just like me," she said primly.

"Ladies?" A man's voice right behind them made them both jump. They both turned around, and saw the man from the stairs standing behind them. Felicia was glad to see he'd wrapped his towel around his waist. He gave them a little smile.

"If you're trying to spy on your kids, this isn't the way you want to go," he began, and Kendra bristled.

"I will be the one that decides where I'm going when it comes to my daughter," she began, and he raised his hand, looking amused.

"That's fine," he said. "But if you try and sneak in here, she'll see you. This goes straight to their patio. If you're trying to spy on them, you need to come in on the far side of the second house over," he finished and smiled at them thinly. "Or, you can simply walk in and wish her a good morning. We're about to do a stretching routine, and Nathan's girlfriend will be taking part, so he'll probably be up soon. In fact, he's started doing the aerobics class after that, so I'm sure he'll be up shortly. Have a good morning."

They watched him walk away, and after he went around the corner of the house, they looked at each other.

"I remember him from last night at Eddie's. Nice tush," Kendra commented, and Felicia nodded, then frowned.

"But he shaves his entire body, and that kind of creeps me out," Felicia said, and made a face.

Without discussing it, they went back to the road and over two houses, then made their way through the unlocked gate, and past some palm trees and several statues that would have made Felicia blush, if she was the blushing sort.

They reached the end of the house, and peeked around the corner. Felicia heard someone swimming in the pool, but ignored that. Kendra pointed at a small cement bench between several bushes, and partially blocked from view by a couple trees. They bent over and scurried to the bench and sat.

They could hear Tess talking, but her words were hard to make out. Kendra gasped and pointed to the right side of the patio. There was a ballet barre fastened to the roof's pillars. Tess, Yasmin, the tiny attractive bartender from the video, and the man they'd talked to were all holding it with one hand, and doing a series of simple stretches. And they were all naked.

Felicia noticed that there were a number of men sitting on pool chairs nearby, some watching, some talking among themselves. Virtually all of them were nude. Some of them had bits of clothing draped on their chair backs.

Their attention came back to Tess and her little circle of followers, as the degree of difficulty went up dramatically. When Tess, Yasmin and the man all raised their legs up to point to the sky, Felicia gasped. Some of the men sitting around groaned at the sight.

"That certainly leaves them in an exposed position," Kendra muttered, and Felicia looked at her. She looked like she couldn't decide whether to be proud of her daughter's skill and flexibility, or to be pissed at her for her lack of concern for propriety.

As they came down from that position, they all reversed their direction so they were working the other half of their bodies, and Felicia couldn't get over how flexible they all were. The bartender couldn't lift her legs as high as the others, but she did well with everything else.

She saw Nathan walk out of the back of the apartment, holding a coffee cup. Thankfully, he wore a pair of those godawful ugly comic book boxers he seemed to love.

They both heard a splashing sound, and turned to see a naked Tuesday coming out of the pool, looking at them.

"Oh, shit," Kendra muttered, and Felicia would have laughed if she wasn't so mortified. They watched as Tuesday mimed zipping her lips shut, fastening a padlock, and throwing the imaginary key over her shoulder. She grinned at them, gave them a thumbs up, and trotted through the throng of men, and past Tess and her class.

They watched her run her fingers over Tess's butt as she passed. She kept going into the apartment. Some of the men waiting called comments after her.

They finished their stretching, and Felicia watched Tess look into the apartment with a smile on her face. She chatted with some of the men as they unrolled two big mats. Several others brought a smaller square one out and put it between them.

Yasmin stepped over to Nathan and gave him a kiss. That is not a chaste kiss, Felicia noted, trying to decide how she felt about this.

"Nathan's girlfriend is so beautiful," Kendra noted, and Felicia nodded her agreement.

"She is," Felicia agreed, watching her mold her naked body against her son. "And she's very dangerous."

They watched the men, and several women begin spacing themselves out on the two mats. Felicia saw one of the Arab women that worked for Yasmin glance at them, and although they were pretty well hidden in the foliage, she had a feeling the woman had seen them. She had no expression on her face, but her eyes centered right on them. Then she turned away.

The pallid girl with the long, thick black hair that had been with the Arab woman last night suddenly stood and looked straight at them. A smile came to her face, and then she too turned away.

Felicia and Kendra looked at each other in confusion.

"There is no way she could have seen us," Kendra said firmly, and Felicia shrugged.

"I don't see any way either of them could have," she said, and felt her phone vibrate in her bag. She saw Nathan pull his shorts down and off and toss them on a chair. "And my son is naked. Time to go," she said, looking at her phone as they made their way back to the street.

Kendra laughed. "C'mon, you've seen your son in the buff," she kidded.

"Not since he reached puberty," Felicia muttered. "Anyway, Houston and Bob are asking where we are." She showed her the text from her husband.

She typed a response.

Kendra and I went for a walk. Five minutes.

"Bob will know we went to snoop," Kendra said philosophically, and Felicia nodded glumly.

"So will Huey."

They briskly strode down Margaret Street.

They heard a motorcycle, and glanced up as it went by. The Arab woman was driving a Harley Davidson, and the pale girl was seated behind her, arms wrapped around the driver.

The girl waved, the woman nodded her head slightly.

"Well, crap," Kendra said. "That's right. Last night, those two were attached at the hips."

Felicia thought for a moment. "Oshba and Phoebe," she finally said. "Yasmin implied they were either engaged, or about to be."

"For all intents and purposes, our kids live in a nude resort," Kendra said, and Felicia sighed.

"Nathan is so shy and reserved, when he's not on stage," Felicia muttered, more to herself. "How on earth did they ever get him to feel comfortable running around naked?"

"I know how you feel," Kendra said, shaking her head. "Tess has always been so self-conscious and shy. And now she's basically showing the southern passage to her tonsils."

"So, which parent did she get *that* trait from?" Felicia teased, and Kendra sighed.

"Yes."

♦ ♦ ♦ ♦ ♦

Tess leaned in close to Sarah, so she could speak privately.

"I'm glad you're still coming to the workouts and stretching exercises, Sarah," she said and the short girl smiled at her as she pulled her panties on. "It's so much more fun with multiple people."

"I wish I was as flexible as any of the three of you," Sarah said. She put her shorts on and slipped into her flats. She looked down at her modest breasts. "Think anyone would notice if I walk home like this?"

"It's only a block, right?" Tess asked, smiling at her. "Sarah, your breasts are beautiful. Trust me, people would notice."

"I suppose," Sarah said, and slipped on her t-shirt.

"You work today?"

"No, I got Sundays and Mondays off."

"I knew that," Tess said, feeling stupid. She looked at the little girl with concern. "Sarah, are you doing okay? I know you've been through a lot the last month. I want you to know, if you need someone to talk to, or a big ole hug, I'm there for you, anytime."

"I'll take one of those hugs now," Sarah said, and Tess immediately embraced her fully, not releasing her. They stood that way for a bit. "Thanks, Tess. I didn't know how bad I needed this." Her voice was muffled against Tess's chest.

Sarah released her and stepped back, looking at her breasts ruefully. "Hugging you like that when you're naked is very disconcerting," she admitted. "But nice."

"Anytime," Tess said. She looked at Sarah closely. "What is it?" She looked over where Nathan and Yasmin were talking with Walter and a couple other residents. "I guess Nathan isn't as available to hang out with, now that Yasmin's back."

"Yeah," Sarah said. "I miss that."

"Anyone on your radar?" Tess asked, wondering if she should pry.

"No, I'm not really looking for a relationship right now," Sarah said. "Nathan and I are great friends, and there's always been the sexual tension, but we both recognized it and dealt with it. There's a guy at work that's interested, but like I said, I don't really want to get into anything with anybody right now."

"I can understand that," Tess said, knowing how hard it could be, working with someone you were seeing. "Who is it?" She flinched. "Wait, I didn't mean to pry…"

"No, that's okay," Sarah said, smiling at her. "His name is Peter, and he's my boss. So there's really a couple reasons why that isn't going anywhere."

"Right," Tess said fervently. "That can create so many issues, and then if it falls apart, you're both still in the same place, every day, and he's in control. Smart to not let that happen."

"Yeah," Sarah said, and looked despondent. "He's a nice enough guy, but I can't be involved with the boss. Everyone at work loses out. And there isn't really any spark between us, as far as I'm concerned."

Tess suddenly giggled, and made a face. Sarah looked at her, curiously. Then she laughed.

"You just pictured yourself in an affair with Wally, didn't you?"

They both chuckled.

Nathan and Yasmin walked by, on their way into the apartment.

"Sarah, you going to be at the bookstore later?" he asked, and Sarah shrugged.

"Probably," she admitted. "I try to stop in to see Suz, and give her some business at least once a week. Gotta support our local bookstore."

"We're going to be there, too." He smiled at her. "Maybe we can get an ice cream together."

"That would be very nice, Sarah," Yasmin said, and they went into the apartment.

Tess looked after them.

"Nathan is sweet, but sometimes he is so clueless," she said, shaking her head.

Sarah smiled, a little sadly. She hugged Tess without meeting her eyes. "See you tonight."

Tess watched her walk around the side of the house, and felt sad. She

120

went inside and got cleaned up, then headed for work. On a whim, she changed her usual route to have her walk by the Key West Bed & Breakfast on William Street. She went inside and saw her and Nathans' parents sitting in a booth towards the back of the common area.

They were having breakfast. Her mother saw her first, and she was surprised to see her blush. She hugged her parents, and then, on a whim, hugged Nathan's as well.

"What do you guys have planned for today?" she asked, when they all got seated.

"The ladies want to shop some," her father said, shuddering. "I think I can hear the credit card screaming already."

"Oh, shut up, Bob," her mother said and grinned at Tess. "Don't listen to him. He knows I'll sniff out all the best deals, at the best prices."

"Yes, but she'll sniff them *all* out," her father said mournfully.

"You said you work today," her mother said, and sighed. "We were hoping to spend a little time with you."

"That could happen," Tess said, smiling. "I lead three jet ski tours around Key West today. The first one is in about forty minutes, but if that's too soon, there're two more. Do you know where our dock is?"

"Freedom Seas," her father read off the map. "I can get us there."

Tess pulled her phone out, and speed-dialed the hut, even as she was speaking. "How would you like to drive jet skis for an hour and a half or so?"

"You go all around the entire island?" Nathan's mother, Felicia asked, looking doubtful.

"It isn't an island, dear, it's a key," his father corrected her, and Tess bit her lip to keep from laughing when she saw Felicia's expression.

"In any case, the answer is yes," Tess said.

"Tess, is that you? How are you doing?"

Tess turned around and looked at Grace and Emily Stark. She smiled widely at them. Phoebe picked that moment to answer the phone.

"Phoebe, this is Tess. How many machines do we have reserved for the first tour?" Tess listened to her, and nodded. "And how many are out on open rental?" Tess smiled at the answer. "Hold on a moment."

"So, want to go jet skiing?" Tess asked. She looked at the two Stark women. "I was just telling Nathan and my parents I'm leading jet ski tours and we have machines available if you'd like to come along. I forgot you were staying here, too."

"You have six machines open?" her father asked, looking serious.

"We have twelve, and I can tell you from experience, we will rent either four or six of those to people before the tour. So I have the machines for all of you, if you'd like to come. You might want to bring your swimsuits." She thought about the pier bathroom and winced. "Better yet, change here. It's a small bathroom."

They all looked at each other and nodded. Nathan's mother looked at Grace and Emily, and Tess realized they hadn't met.

"Look, I have to rush, because I check all the machines before we go out on them, and you have to change." Tess pointed at her parents. "Robert and Kendra Carter, my parents, Houston and Felicia Williams, Nathan's parents, and Emily and Grace Stark, Phoebe's grandmother and mother. Got to go. Phoebe is the very white girl with the great black hair down to her waist. She works with us, as Yasmin mentioned last night."

Tess hurried out and stripped the polo off before she got to the corner of Williams and Eaton. She decided a sedate trot might be in order, and picked up the pace."

"Uh Tess?"

She winced as she realized she never finished her conversation with Phoebe.

"Oh Phoebe, sorry about that. Please reserve six machines for family members, no charge, four to me, two to you. I'm taking our families out on the water today, first tour."

"I kind of figured that," Phoebe said dryly. "I've double-checked everything from last night, the machines are ready to go, I'll get the life jackets out. Where are you?"

"Just going by the Studios," Tess said. "I'll be there in under ten minutes."

"Don't stress yourself out," Phoebe said. "Everything's ready. Oh, and right now, Tuesday's afternoon dolphin cruise looks iffy. But we have a few hours."

"Okay. See you in a couple," Tess said, and slowed to a fast-paced walk. No sense in getting all gross and sweaty, first thing.

She had a thought, and called Nathan.

"Hey, Tess," he said.

"Our parents, and Phoebe's mother and grandmother are going out with me on the first jet ski tour. You and Yasmin want to tag along?" Tess looked at her phone. "You'd have to kind of book it. The tour starts in just about twenty-five minutes."

She turned onto Whitehead, and Nathan said they'd be there in fifteen minutes.

"Where are you?" Tess asked?

"We *were* about to leave and go get breakfast. But we'll have brunch later, instead."

"Don't forget swimsuits," Tess reminded him. "Love you. Gotta go."

She heard him say "Love you" just before she disconnected the phone.

A few minutes later, she was stripped down to her suit, told Phoebe to hold three for Yasmin, Nathan, and either Oshba or Nadezhda, and went to find Tuesday to bring her up to date.

Twenty minutes later, she was leading the pack out of the Freedom Seas wet dock, smiling as she heard her mother whooping it up.

"That was so much fun," Nathan's mother said, for maybe the fifth time. Tess smiled as both Nathan and his dad watched her excitement with happy smiles. "I was afraid I wouldn't be able to drive the machine, but it was easy. And so much fun!"

"So, what are you going to do now?" Tess asked, and all four parents looked at each other, then at Nathan and Yasmin. Tess grinned as she looked at Yasmin's swimsuit. She didn't have a swimsuit at Nathan's, so on that fast walk from Eldamar to the dock, she swung into a shop, tried on a white bikini, bought it, and wore it down Duval to the dock. Needless to say, she looked spectacular in it. She had her regular clothes in her hand, and was about to go change.

"Shop," all three women said, even as both fathers and Nathan said "lunch".

Nathan's mother beamed at her. "It looks like we're going to shop, with a bit of lunch tossed in the middle," she said and winked at Tess. "I wish you could join us. And Tuesday as well. Where is she?"

"She's running back to back Dolphin cruises today, and then the sunset cruise on one of the tall ships," Tess said. "So we won't see much of Tuesday until tonight, when we go hear Nathan play at Eddie's."

"I'm looking forward to that," Felicia said. "The band was incredible, but I've always enjoyed my boy singing his silly love songs the most." She looked at Tess and her mother. "Huey, I'm going to go change, after Yasmin's done. Are you going to wear wet shorts, or change?"

"Well, it really doesn't…" Nathan's dad looked at his wife, and cleared his throat. "Guess I'll get out of these wet things," he finished lamely, and followed her down their pier to the shed.

Tess's mother looked at her, and she knew what her mother was thinking. Her father was looking at Phoebe's products, looking at her and Oshba curiously, thinking he was being discreet.

"So, you and Tuesday seem pretty serious," she said, looking nervous.

"We are, Mother," Tess said firmly, wondering where this sudden strength was coming from. "She will probably ask me to marry her one of these days, and I'll say yes."

"It just seems so sudden," her mother said, and sighed. "We only found out late in October."

"The Thompsons," Tess said, not surprised.

Her mother smiled at her in resignation. "You know how Sean and your father get talking. Neither of them can keep a secret to save their lives. I think Julie was relieved when he screwed up. She was dying to tell me."

"That your daughter is gay?" Tess said quietly, and her mother shook her head.

"No, that didn't matter," she said, and tempered her words. "Well, I mean, it *was* news, but they were eager to tell us that you looked good, seemed very happy, and had wonderful friends. And how awkward it was spending half a week naked most of the time, around the neighborhood kid they'd known practically since you were born."

"There was that," Tess said, laughing lightly. She saw people beginning to show up and wondered if they were for her next tour, or the reef snorkeling cruise on the Free Seas catamaran. She hoped some people would sign up for Tuesday's Dolphin Cruise so she could get some more hours logged on the water. "It wasn't sudden for us. We've known each other over three years, and have been roommates for over two and a half."

"I remember you telling me some things about her back then," Mother admitted. She hesitated for a moment, and then put her hands on Tess's arms. "You know you could have told us you were gay. We would have been okay with it. Surprised, because we'd never seen any sign of that, but it wouldn't have mattered."

"I wasn't hiding anything," Tess told, smiling ruefully. "When Tuesday and I suddenly realized we were in love with each other, we didn't think we were gay then. We just thought we were two girls that loved each other, and the gender was just happenstance. That was a little over two years ago."

"We met her on our way to Orlando for that convention," Mother said, and Tess remembered. She nodded.

"That was about three years ago, and we weren't roommates," Tess remembered. "We ate at the Cracker Barrel."

They looked at each other, and then at Tess's father.

"He loves that place," Mother said in a resigned voice, and Tess giggled. Her mother heard her and smiled. "You seem so happy," she said wistfully. "I would think you would know you being gay wouldn't change anything about the way we feel about you."

"It wasn't really that simple," Tess admitted. "Initially, we kept telling everyone we weren't lesbians, we were just in love with each other. And everyone would smile, like they knew something we didn't, and nod their heads. We only just figured it out back in the beginning of this last summer. Really, our meeting Nathan got us started on the path to acknowledging what we really were."

"Really," Mother said, and looked at her questioningly. Tess laughed.

"Mother, I will be happy to tell you all about it, but it will take a while, and be much easier to tell if there are adult beverages involved," Tess said, and her mother laughed and gave her a big hug. "Oh, and Mother?"

Something in Tess's tone made her look guarded, and Tess kept her face straight.

"Yes dear?" she asked cautiously.

"If you and Mrs. Williams decide to come by tomorrow morning, we'll just be doing the stretching, but please don't hide in the bushes. I had several neighbors say they were about to call the cops, that we had peeping Thomasinas, until they recognized you. Just avert your eyes if you don't want to see anything, and get yourselves some coffee from the kitchen."

"It's Felicia, and we will," Nathan's mother said from behind her, and Tess jumped in surprise, giving a little shriek. "We're sorry we were so weird about it, but you and Nathan are still our little babies, and knowing and seeing some things takes some getting used to."

"I'm going to get changed, honey," Mother said, and hugged her. "You have a fun day. Bob, time to change."

"Into what?" he asked turning away from the hut with a Freedom Seas cloth bag that seemed a little heavy.

"Into something you can wear into a store or restaurant," Mother said, and headed to the shed. "Come on, dear. The day is flying by."

"Seeing what things?" Mr. Williams asked curiously, and Mrs. Williams began walking faster to the hut to look at Phoebe's products. He followed after her.

"Your and my Nathan's parents are so fun to watch and listen to," Yasmin said, startling her. Somehow she'd come back from the shed and had been standing nearby that entire time. "They want to know everything, but are embarrassed about what they might find out. But I think they are very good parents," she said wistfully. She saw Tess's expression, and smiled at her with a little sorrow in her eyes. "My mother tried to protect me, but other than my Grandfather, none of my family approved of, respected, or even liked, much less loved me."

"Well, you are very loved now, Yasmin," Tess said, and impulsively hugged her. "We're all one big extended, dysfunctional family, and you are part of it." She watched Phoebe put a combo pack in a bag, and a couple other bottles as well. "And that includes Oshba and Nadi."

"It does," Yasmin said, pulling away far enough to look Tess in the face. "I love my new, dysfunctional, extended family. You're the first friend I ever had. And you have turned out to be the best friend I will ever have."

"Thank you, Yasmin," Tess said, and hugged her close again.

Yasmin reluctantly pulled away and gave a little sniff that Tess pretended she didn't hear. She looked at Tess, with a little smile. "Your and Nathan's mothers spied on us this morning?"

"Yes," Tess said, grinning at her. "Tommy said they were watching, fascinated, even though they both kept blushing, until Nathan dropped his shorts. They ran like hell at that point."

Tess saw Nathan looking at them curiously, and also that the bulk of the customers milling around were obviously for her next tour and sighed.

"Yasmin, have fun," she said, and winked. "I have to go try and drown a bunch of tourists."

♦ ♦ ♦ ♦ ♦

Nico came awake with a start. He wondered why the alarm on his phone was sounding, and then realized it was the ring tone. He looked at the number and muttered under his breath. He coughed and tried to clear his throat as he turned and sat upright on the side of his bed.

"Sergeant Skourellos," he said gruffly.

"Sergeant, we have a body washed up on Smather's Beach," the dispatcher said in a careful, clear tone. Nico liked her professional, even tone. She was relatively new, and was obviously trying to be clear and accurate. "It was called in by the county maintenance crew raking the beach."

"Where on Smather's?" Nico asked, resisting the urge to sigh.

"Just south of the western end of the salt ponds, approximately one hundred yards east of the western end," she said, and Nico nodded, forgetting she couldn't see him.

"Could you call my partner, Detective-in-training Wilcox?" he asked. "Tell her I'll be there in half an hour. If she beats me there, she can question the county maintenance crew. No one is to move the body until I get there."

"You got it, sir," the dispatcher said, and Nico smiled faintly at her enthusiastic tone.

"Thanks, Julie," he said, as he stood and headed to the bathroom for a quick rinse shower. Then he had a difficult decision to make.

McDonald's or the Doubletree Hotel for coffee? McDonald's was faster service, but he'd have to stay on U.S.1 for about a quarter of a mile, and it was on the left side of the road. Doubletree was on A1A, on the right side of the road, but he'd have to park and go into the hotel.

Nico decided that if he already had a cup of coffee, this would be an easier decision.

♦ ♦ ♦ ♦ ♦

Related Matters

Chapter Nine

Phoebe sat in the hut, holding hands with Oshba, very content. Her mother and Grandma Emily had fun on Tess's jet ski tour, and came back very cheery. She was glad they were enjoying themselves, and didn't need to spend every single moment with her.

Since their arrival, they had juggled their time around dropping in on Phoebe, eating some meals with her and Oshba, doing some shopping, exploring, and spending at least a couple hours every day at their new favorite daytime hangout, the rooftop Garden of Eden. And, of course, her mother was spending more nights than not, meeting Nadine after work, and spending the night with her.

Grandma Emily seemed fine with that. She said Phoebe's mother was too restless in her sleep, so she'd happily take any nights where she got the bed to herself. Unless, of course, she got lucky, at which point Phoebe had sighed in resignation.

They said the jet ski tour was almost as fun as Wednesday night at Diane Isis. Her mother had said she might forget to wear a bra next week. She was quite devastated when she found out that softball season was over, so there wouldn't be any more team get-togethers until after the holidays. Phoebe told her about Ladies' Night, but she was disappointed when told that there was no shirt-removing ritual.

They had adjusted their plans on when to do a simple ritual to recognize and celebrate Winter Solstice so she could join them Saturday afternoon. Tess had covered the hut after her last tour, which also gave her a chance to train Aurora on some of the bookkeeping and maintenance procedures Phoebe usually did.

Mother, Grandma Emily, Oshba and she had gone to Fort Zachary Taylor State Park Beach, found a stretch of the rocky shore that had little foot traffic, and built a small altar from the stones that lined the beach.

Phoebe had been shocked when the famous Running Man appeared, running along the shore. She'd heard of him and the lore, but had never actually seen him before. Tess, Tuesday, and Nathan all admitted they'd seen him before, as did Diane at Diane Isis, but none could explain how he happened to show up when he did at times.

He'd gestured grandly with his baton, as well as his free hand, as he passed. He looked at all four of them carefully, and bowed his head, then focused ahead, and soon disappeared around the curve of the shore.

Phoebe gave a very cursory explanation of him and his sudden appearances, and she could see all three other women were intrigued, if doubtful of any hidden meaning or purpose.

Phoebe wasn't so sure. But she kept her own council, so they could focus on the ceremony of the day.

They had all stripped and gone into the ocean and bathed, thus cleansing themselves with a salt bath. Phoebe observed Grandma Emily looking at the scars crisscrossing Oshba's back, and more than a couple scars that were obviously gunshot wounds. She didn't say anything, but Phoebe knew she was watching Oshba like a hawk.

They lit a candle and talked about the aspects of the previous year they were discarding, and their new intentions for the next year. They did three-card Tarot readings of themselves to strengthen the spells they wove to assist achieving their goals.

Grace and Emily had few changes in mind, except they would maintain closer ties and contacts with the youngest member of their coven, which was Phoebe.

Phoebe said she was going to focus on being a happier person, and that she hoped to become happily married sometime in the year to come. That had gotten serious glances from both older women, and a slight smile from Oshba.

When asked if she wished to declare things to discard from the previous year, and intentions for the new, Oshba nodded, taking the ceremony very seriously. She said she was going to try and kill fewer people in the new year. She would also find the strength and courage to propose to the woman she loved, marry her, and be the best wife she could be.

Grace and Emily had stared at her, and Phoebe knew they had wondered if she was playing with them, or mocking the ceremony, which they believed in completely. She suspected they didn't believe she'd actually killed anyone. She decided she would tell her mother and grandma about the serial killer on the boat at Fantasy Fest. That was a documented death, and she was cleared of any wrong-doing. If they happened to assume that was the entirety of her killing people, all the better.

Phoebe had no way of knowing, of course, but was pretty sure the head count was somewhat higher. Between the attempted kidnapping of Yasmin in Mexico, the man on the boat, and Baltimore, she didn't try and delude herself.

Oshba sighed and looked at her.

"Little bird, I must go home and search the grounds for any more cameras. M'Lady will be *busy* for a few hours at Nathan's."

Phoebe laughed at her euphemism of what Yasmin and Nathan were undoubtedly doing right now, and then shook her head in frustration.

"I guess it doesn't really matter, but I'm glad the feeds were turned off before Thanksgiving, so there aren't any videos of us sitting out naked by the pool at Eldamar floating around the internet."

"I only wish I would have been the one that traced the feeds back to the man that planted all those cameras," Oshba said in a cold voice, and Phoebe shivered. Oshba was usually so dispassionate about when violence was required. Primarily, because it had always been such a major portion of her life. But her voice promised pain and more. "Because of that man, we must worry about whether any film of our lady is circulating, or saved in someone's files. And if those videos could resurface and be found by any of her enemies."

They both stood and hugged and kissed.

"You know, when we decide to get married, if we have the necessary legal license, either my grandma or mother could marry us. They are both ordained Wiccan priestesses and witches."

"Are you, as well?" Oshba asked, smiling at her.

"I am a witch, and part of the Stark Coven, which consists of the three of us," Phoebe admitted. "My skills in witchcraft have been confirmed, although my education is far from complete. Technically, I am not yet a Wiccan priestess, although my powers are stronger than either of theirs."

"Well, my little witch, I will be back, after you've had time to complete most of your work," Oshba kissed her lips gently. "Where *is* the rest of your coven?" she teased.

"Up at the Garden of Eden, prancing around naked, trying to get Grandma Emily laid," Phoebe admitted, and Oshba tried to hide her smile. "They said they'll meet us at Captain Eddie's before nine."

"It would be interesting if they got the chance to meet Marilyn," Oshba said, and gave her one final hug.

"There is always tomorrow, and she and Nathan will be at the Garden, playing Scrabble," Phoebe said. She watched Oshba walk down the dock, start her Harley, and ride away. She smiled, shaking her head. Last week, after walking Phoebe to work, Oshba had disappeared for a couple hours and returned with a four-year old Harley Davidson Softail.

Oshba told her its name was Sahira, which Phoebe figured out from context that it meant 'witch'.

She thought about what Oshba had said yesterday on the rocky beach, and found visualizing them living together was very easy to do.

Phoebe felt something, and stood up to watch a family of five make their way up the dock. Three men, two women. She realized the woman in the middle was probably the mother of at least several of them. In fact, as she looked from face to face, she realized all four of the others were probably her children. They all appeared to be in their twenties, the mother around fifty years old.

Adult children, but the resemblance was easy to see. Also, as she focused on their auras, she could see the commonalities. They were all a little chaotic in nature. In fact, she decided, they reminded her of someone, but it took her a moment to get it.

Even as Phoebe realized who they had to be, one of the men saw her and stepped up to the counter.

"Does a little blond fire plug named Tuesday work here?" he asked.

Phoebe stared at him. She nodded wordlessly, wondering at the odds of four family reunions occurring in such rapid succession. "She's out on the water, captaining the Dolphin Cruise on the Free Breeze. She's due back pretty soon."

"She fishing for dinner?" one of the other men asked, and nudged the third man. "She using dynamite?"

"No, fishing for dolphins is illegal," Phoebe said. "They're sentient beings, smarter than many of our customers, in fact."

The girl laughed and shoved the man who'd spoken. "Ha, you just got burned, Chuckie."

"It's Chuck," he said, and the rest of the family showed one form of amusement or another. He looked at Phoebe, and looked like he was trying to decide whether to be angry or not.

"You're her family?" Phoebe asked, hoping to shift the conversation.

"Did you say my daughter is the captain of a boat?" the older woman asked.

"If Tuesday is your daughter," Phoebe said, wondering how hard it could be to get any one of them to answer a question straight up.

"It's probably a rowboat," Chuck said, and got a backhand on the arm from what looked like the oldest and biggest of the sons.

"I'm Mari Sue Dumarest, Tuesday's ma," the older woman said. "These are her brothers and sister. Bubba is the oldest, then Chuck, and Bobby is the youngest. And this mouthy girl is her older sister, Bobbi Jo."

"Bobby and Bobbi Jo?" Phoebe asked in as neutral a tone as she could manage.

"I was supposed to be a boy named Bobby," the young woman said, and shrugged. "I guess Ma and Pa felt it was a shame to waste a perfectly good name."

Tuesday's mother sighed.

"Pa really wanted a boy named Bobby," she said, and grinned at Phoebe ruefully. "So when the next one popped out and was a boy, he wouldn't take no for an answer."

Phoebe looked at the youngest son.

"Did they name you Bobby or Robert Joseph?" she asked, calling on her years of depression to keep her expression deadpan.

"Ha, that's pretty good," the mother said, laughing and slapping Bobby on the shoulder. "Probably a good thing your pa didn't think o' that."

She turned back to Phoebe. "In answer to your question, yeah, we're Tuesday's family, 'ceptin' her pa, Jackie. He'll be here later."

"Pleased to meet you," Phoebe said carefully. "My name is Phoebe Stark. Tuesday should be returning to port in a few minutes."

"Winter is coming," said Bobby. He looked a couple years older than Tuesday's twenty-four, relatively fit, and clean cut. He was maybe five foot eight or nine. The middle son was about the same size, although his hair was a little longer. The oldest looked to be an inch or so taller, and short-haired, like his youngest brother.

"Looks like she already knows that," Bobbi Jo said, and Phoebe thought she could have been kind of cute, if she took a little better care of herself. She had blonde hair like Tuesday, but not as pretty. In fact, it was so straight, Phoebe wondered if she ironed it. "How can you be so white, living in Key West?"

"She's an albino," Chuck said, earning another swat, this from his mother. Phoebe noticed she put some muscle into that one.

"I'm sorry," she said to Phoebe. "Some of my kids don't think a lot before they shoot their mouths off."

"That's okay," Phoebe said. "I'm really just a whiter shade of pale."

Bobbi Jo laughed, but Phoebe didn't think any of the brothers got it. Mari Sue did, because she grinned.

Phoebe felt something and turned to look west by northwest out over the water. Sure enough, Free Breeze was coming up the port side of the marked channel.

"Here comes Tuesday now," she said, pointing at the powered catamaran. It disappeared behind the cruise ship in the next dock, and a couple minutes later, Tuesday brought it deftly up to the dock, and smoothly brought it to rest in its berth.

Five minutes later, the six passengers were making their way past the hut, stopping to ask about Phoebe's products. Tuesday was securing the Free Breeze, and hadn't noticed her family. Phoebe quickly realized why. All four of her siblings had ducked back where the hut made it hard to see them. Mari Sue hadn't budged, but she wasn't but a couple inches taller than Tuesday, and didn't stand out.

Phoebe finished the sales to the passengers, and stepped out of the hut and a little way down the dock.

"Tuesday, people here to see you," she called out, and the brothers and sister gave up trying to surprise her.

"You're a spoilsport," Bobbi Jo said, frowning at her.

"I'm a loyal friend," Phoebe said, and went back into the hut. She turned around to watch Tuesday's reaction.

Tuesday slowed down as she neared the hut, and stared at her mother.

"Ma?" she said slowly, and then took several steps forward and hugged her mother. "What are you doing here? Is everybody here?" she said as she took in her sister and brothers coming around the corner of the hut. "Did Pa come?"

"Your pa will be here tonight," Mari Sue said, and held Tuesday out at arm's length. "He's driving his rig down, and will be here around dinnertime, he says. My gawd, you been lifting weights? You're as solid as Bubba."

"He's bringing his rig to Key West?" Tuesday looked doubtful. "Where's he going to park it?"

"We're staying at the El Patio Motel," her mother said, and Tuesday shook her head.

"Well, he won't be parking it there," she said, and turned just in time to meet the onslaught of siblings.

"Hey, Fireplug," Bubba said, and enveloped her in a huge bear hug. He basically passed her to Chuck, who hugged her, and then moved her over to Bobby. Phoebe noticed both Tuesday and the youngest brother seemed to actually mean their hugs. Tuesday looked at her older sister, who wagged her head at her and gave her a hug that seemed restrained by Phoebe's new friend's standards.

"Yo, bitch," she said, and looked Tuesday up and down.

"Hey, slut," Tuesday returned, and gave her an inspection as well.

"That ain't no way for sisters to greet each other after two years," their mother said in an aggravated tone.

"Beats 'yo, ho'," Tuesday said, shrugging, and Bobbi Jo nodded. She grinned at Tuesday.

"We saw the video of you on YouTube," she said, and leered at Tuesday, who looked wary.

Phoebe realized she was wondering if it was the famous video of her kicking the rapist's ass, or something off the cameras planted in the neighborhood.

"Yeah, you really kicked that guy's ass," Bobby said, and they were all talking about it. Phoebe heard one of them say it was over nine million hits now, and then Bobbi Jo asked the question Phoebe knew was coming. From the lack of hurt or surprise on Tuesday's face, she did too.

"So, they said the girl that got drugged was the love of your life." Bobbi Jo frowned at her. "Since when did you become a muff eater?"

"I've always been gay," Tuesday said evenly. "I only figured it out last June. But I knew I was in love with Tess for almost two years before that."

"Maybe you just haven't met the right guy yet, Tuesday," her mother said, frowning. "I didn't raise you to be a deviant."

"That's not the way it works, Ma," Tuesday said heavily, and looked at her brothers, as if wondering when they were going to jump in and gang up on her.

"Just because you got infatuated with some pretty girl doesn't make you a queer, Tuesday," Chuck said. "Girls get infatuated all the time in school and stuff. They grow out of it."

"You kids hush for a minute," Mari Sue said, and they all shut up. She turned to Tuesday. "Honey, Chuck does have a point. You meet a girl, you get a crush on her, you're lonely, maybe a little drunk. A lot of women have fallen for that."

"Speak for yourself, Ma," Bobby Jo said, her nose wrinkled up in disgust. "Far as I'm concerned, if there's nuthin' hangin' between the legs, there's no reason to be hangin' around. I've never done nuthin' with no girls."

"That don't mean it don't happen, sometimes," her mother snapped at her. "The point is, most women don't decide that it means they only like girls. Tuesday just needs to get back on the horse, start dating guys again."

She looked at Tuesday.

"What about that boy you met a few years back, in Jacksonville? He ended up following you back to Gainesville. Whatever happened to him?"

"Carl?" Tuesday asked sweetly, and Phoebe knew *that* was a trap. "He's in prison right now. For assaulting me, putting me in the hospital, selling drugs, parole violations, and a few other things, if I remember it right."

There was a long moment of uncomfortable silence. They all turned in relief as the sound of numerous machines grew in volume. Tess led her pack of customers behind the cruise ship. A couple minutes later, she reappeared and led the large group into the wet dock.

"Good afternoon, Phoebe," Aurora said, startling her as she appeared at the hut window. "Would you like me to help Tess get the machines squared away?"

"That would be great, Aurora," Phoebe said, thinking fast. "Would you ask Tess to come here for a moment?"

"Uh," Tuesday began and stopped. She looked at Phoebe, looking indecisive.

Phoebe looked at her, trying to will her the strength to deal with all this. Tuesday seemed to nod to herself and looked as Aurora approached Tess. She nodded and pointed out a couple things to the Italian girl, then hurried up the dock to look at Phoebe questioningly.

Her eyes shifted over to her girl, and she was about to say something when she got a clear look at the family. Her eyes widened, and she looked at Tuesday. Tess didn't appear to be concerned, other than the fact that all she was wearing was a pretty sexy bikini. She just wanted to know how Tuesday was going to play it.

"Man, that looks fun," Bobby said, and looked at Tuesday. "You ever get to play with all the toys around here?"

"Every day," Tuesday said, and for some reason, just saying that seemed to give her strength. She nodded to herself.

"Ma," she said, pointing at her mother, then each sibling as she named them. "Bubba, Chuck, Bobby, and Bobbi Jo, this is my partner, and the love of my life, Tess. Tess, this is my family. Pa will be here later tonight."

"Hello," Tess said, staring at Tuesday in pleased surprise. She turned back to the family and smiled brightly at them. "I'm so happy to finally get to meet all of you. Mrs. Dumarest, what should I call you?"

"Oh, my name is Mari Sue, and her pa's name is Jackie," Tuesday's mother said, staring at her, clearly not knowing quite what to say. "So, you're a, uh…"

"I'm a lesbian, Ma'am," Tess confirmed, and blushed a little. "I never knew I was. But when Tuesday and I realized we were in love, we had to consider the possibility. It wouldn't really matter if we weren't gay. Because we're in love, regardless. Your daughter is the most wonderful person I've ever met. I plan on spending the rest of my life with her."

"Do your parents know?" Mari Sue asked sharply. "What do they think about this?"

"They found out a couple months ago, through some friends that saw us together," Tess admitted. "They're fine with it. They really just met Tuesday yesterday, but already like her. They want us to be happy, and they can tell we do that for each other."

Tess reflexively reached out and put her hand on the woman's arm.

"I'm sorry we've been so slow to tell everyone," she said apologetically. "But we've been working it out ourselves, and we're so isolated down here. It didn't seem like something to tell you over the phone. My parents just surprised me by showing up yesterday." She smiled at the woman. "And here you all are, today. I guess it was fate's way of telling us it was time."

Phoebe saw the older woman was touched by Tess's apparent sincere happiness to meet her.

"What are your plans for the day?" Tess asked. "We've both got to work until around seven thirty, maybe eight o'clock. Then we were going to go to a bar and hear our other roommate, Nathan, play and sing tonight. He starts at about nine, at Captain Eddie's Saloon."

"Well, we're at loose ends until Pa gets here, and then I guess we'll go find dinner somewhere. Jackie said he knew some fancy place he wants to try. A couple of his friends rave about it."

"Ma, I got to take care of my boat," Tuesday said. "Let me go refuel it, do the maintenance and give it a quick rinse. It won't take long."

"I'll help you. It'll go faster," Tess said, and looked at Phoebe. "Do you have the numbers on available berths left for the next couple days?" she asked, and Phoebe nodded.

As she handed the iPad to Tess, she spoke in a very quiet tone. "No one for the dolphin cruise this afternoon yet. Aurora would probably clock in early."

"She better be clocked in now," Tess said, glancing to where Aurora was checking the spark plugs on a jet ski. "She's working, she's getting paid. Not to mention the crap if she got hurt and wasn't on the clock. The insurance company would have a hissy fit. I'll check with her."

Tess followed Tuesday to the Free Breeze, and they talked as they walked. Tess nodded and veered over to the jet ski stations and began talking quickly to Aurora.

"Is she always that bossy?" Mari Sue asked, watching Tess.

"No, she usually goes with the flow. But she's the boss around here, unless Wally, the owner, is on the premises. And he usually takes her advice on just about everything."

"All that and cute too," the woman said, and looked at Phoebe speculatively. "Why aren't you burned? Your hair isn't white, so I don't think you're an albino. But that skin should be blistering, just in the time we've been here."

Related Matters

"I make sunscreen, and I have one I designed specifically for my needs. I call it Level Adamantium," Phoebe said, and Bobby grinned at her.

"So, you wear Captain America's shield," he said, laughing.

"I guess I do," Phoebe said, liking the way that sounded.

"Cool," he said, and looked at her speculatively.

"Don't bother," she said. "My girlfriend will be back in a while."

"Dang, are all cute girls lezzies in this town?" he asked, and blushed. "I'm sorry. I didn't mean to sound hurtful."

"No offense taken," Phoebe said, impressed that he was capable of recognizing his own faults. "In answer, most of the smart ones are."

Bobby laughed and grinned at her. "Good one," he said, and she was surprised to find that she could actually tolerate one of Tuesday's family members.

Tuesday came back to them.

"Ma, do you want to go out on my next Dolphin cruise? It's in a little over an hour." Tuesday blushed. "We've been busy today, but we don't always do this cruise in the afternoon. So far, I don't have any sign-ups. If we don't do that cruise, I'll be crewing on one of the others. All our scuba diving, snorkeling, and kayaking cruises are full. But if you guys want to go out, that would be five people, and Tess said she can get Aurora to take her last Jet ski tour for her. That way, she could come along, and you could get to know her a little better."

"How much is it?" Mari Sue asked dubiously.

"If we have open seats, we can comp family and employees," Tuesday said. "And I can captain the trip. I have a basic captain license with limitations. I've already passed all the tests to get my full captain's license, but I need a lot more hours on the water, either crewing or captaining cruises with no more than six passengers."

"So we'd be helping you out?" her mother asked, and Tuesday nodded. "Well then, that's settled. What do we have to do?"

"Nothing. We'll fill out the paperwork. Have you eaten yet?" Tuesday asked. Her mother shook her head. "Right up at the end of the dock, to the left there, is Gator Joe's Coffee Shop. It's got hot dogs, paninis, and a few other things. It's quick and cheap, and real close."

"You need anything?" her mother asked, and smiled. "You want me to get you a hot dog?"

"I brownbag it, usually, Ma." Tuesday smiled back. "Our other roommate, Nathan, made me a sandwich. I think it's ham and cheese. I'm good. We got stuff to get done before the boat leaves, and we'll take a quick lunch and then deal with that."

"They also cover for me, while I get *my* lunch," Phoebe said pointedly, and Tuesday laughed. "In fact, I'll go first. Tuesday, could you and Tess cover the hut and phone while I eat my lunch?" she asked sweetly, her voice so fake that Mari Sue and Tuesday both laughed.

Phoebe was happy to see Tuesday's mother show genuine affection as she hugged her daughter.

"I'm glad you're happy, honey," she told Tuesday, and shook her head. "I don't know what your pa's going to say, though."

"He'll like Tess," Tuesday said firmly. "Unless he wants to lose a daughter."

♦ ♦ ♦ ♦ ♦

"You okay, Tue Bear?" Tess asked, hugging Tuesday close. "I thought this afternoon went pretty well."

"Yeah, I'm just sick of how ignorant and bigoted my family can be," Tuesday said, sighing. "Now you know why I didn't want to tell them about us."

"I thought they were okay," Tess said, and hoped she wasn't lying. "I mean, Chuck says some thoughtless things, but I think Bubba loves you and will back you up. Bobby loves you and admires your guts. He seems like a really nice young man."

"Bobbi Jo isn't quite so open-minded," Tuesday reminded her, and Tess conceded her that one.

"But it's obvious your mother loves you," Tess said.

"Yeah, but she'll back Pa. And if he starts in, she'll just fade into the woodwork, and anything she says will be standing by her man."

"I'm going to track down my parents, and see what they're doing for dinner," Tess said. "Do you want me to get you a to go, or grab something from somewhere in particular?"

Tuesday shrugged.

"Text me when you know where you're going, and I'll let you know. I'd be fine with a burrito from Amigos."

"We've eaten there a lot lately, and I think your system could use a week or so with no Mexican food," Tess said delicately.

"You saying I'm farting too much?" Tuesday feigned outrage.

Tess embraced her and laughed.

"You *always* fart too much," she said. "But we need to lay off the Mexican for a while, or I need to buy stock in air freshener."

Tess called her parents, and found out they were enjoying happy hour with Nathan's parents at the pool at the bed and breakfast.

Related Matters

"Hey, Honey, we've had a fun day. We went to lunch at Caroline's, and people-watched. We went shopping, went by a bookstore, and saw Sarah, that nice bartender," her mother said. "We told her, she's family forever, and thanked her about fifty times. She's a very sweet girl."

"She is," Tess said. "She's a good friend of mine, and I think, after Yasmin, Tueberry and me, she's Nathan's best friend."

"Between you and me, Felicia and I think she might be a little more than that to him," her mother said, and Tess wasn't surprised her mother picked up on that. Both Nathan and Sarah denied it, but Tess had no doubt that if Yasmin wasn't in the picture, there would be four people living in their apartment. And Tess would be fine with that.

Those thoughts made Tess feel guilty that she wasn't being loyal to Yasmin. They'd grown close. Tess knew Nathan really did love her. But she also could see how he felt about Sarah.

Thankfully, her mother brought her back to the moment.

"Tuesday works until about eight, right?" she asked, and Tess said yes. "Well, what are you going to do for dinner? Do you plan on waiting for her? We were thinking about going to the Prime Steakhouse. You caught us as we were about to call and make reservations. I think Nathan and Yasmin are going to join us."

"Where are they?" Tess asked, and rolled her eyes at her own stupidity. She was sure she could predict exactly where they were, and what they were doing.

"Well, I think they're back at your apartment, and I don't want to say what I think they're doing, because it'll make my new best friend blush," her mother said, and they both laughed. "Oh, she told me she just heard back from Nathan, and they'll join us for dinner."

"That's an expensive place, Mother," Tess said hesitantly.

"Tess, we're CPAs, and very successful ones," her mother reminded her. "We can afford to go out to a fancy dinner every now and then," she said, and giggled. "Although we'll probably be wearing sundresses and the boys will be wearing khaki shorts and polos."

"Let me know when you have a time," Tess said. "I'll meet you there. Or I'll catch up to you before you leave the B&B. But I want to go home, get out of this swimsuit, and wash the salt water off."

"I'll text you, dear," her mother said. "See you in a while."

Tess found Tuesday on the Freedom Wind, and gave her a quick kiss, telling her she'd see her at Eddie's. Then she hurried home. As she went down the hall to their bedroom, Nathan came out, wearing a towel wrap, saw her and blushed. Tess could hear the sound of the shower behind him.

"Got anything left for tonight?" she asked sweetly, and Nathan's blush deepened. She laughed, not slowing down. "Get yourself together, sweet prince. You're having dinner with our parents."

Soon enough, they were walking down Margaret to Caroline.

Tess wore a sundress and had one of Tuesday's in a bag for her to change into. Nathan wore his typical khaki shorts, and a Beatles Let It Be album cover t-shirt. Yasmin wore short shorts, showing a lot of leg, and a cute top that clung to her like a second skin. Her hair was still damp wet from the shower, hanging free down her back. She looked gorgeous, of course.

Oshba wore a crop tee with khaki shorts, and her usual lightweight jacket that denoted she was on duty. Tess doubted any of the parents realized that was because she was packing a sidearm, holstered under her left arm, magazine holder under her right.

They rounded the corner, and saw their parents just entering The Prime Steakhouse. Tess couldn't believe it when they got seated immediately. Everyone was drinking wine, so they ordered a bottle of red and another of white.

"I'm only having one glass," Nathan warned. "I work tonight."

His father looked at him with amusement.

"Nathan, I saw the drinks being bought for you last night," he said and grinned at Nathan's mother. "It didn't seem to affect your performance."

"I really don't drink that much at my gigs," Nathan said, and glanced over at Tess. "Fortunately, Tess and Tuesday pick up the slack on a lot of that, especially Tuesday. She doesn't seem to get drunk, and I've never seen her with a hangover."

"Me either," Tess admitted. "I don't know how she does it. I've built up a tolerance to wine, but frozen drinks seem to do me in." She sighed. "And they're *so* good."

She started as she remembered what she hadn't told any of them yet.

"Tuesday's family is in town," Tess said, lowering her voice. Nathan stared at her.

"Really?" Nathan looked worried. "She didn't seem very eager to introduce us to them."

"Well, it was an experience," Tess said, and quickly gave them a general accounting of the afternoon. Their wine came, and they had to tell the waiter they needed a few more minutes. He nodded, looking around the room.

"What about you two?" Tess's father asked, and Nathan shrugged.

"I didn't have any problem with telling Mother and Dad," he said, and glanced at Yasmin, then his parents. "I wasn't too sure *what* to tell them, until pretty recently," he admitted.

Related Matters

"I wanted to tell you," Tess said looking back and forth between her parents. "But I wanted both Tuesday and I to do it together, and she was as stubborn as I've ever seen her. I wanted it all in the open."

"Really?" her father asked, looking a little skeptical. "You weren't afraid of what our reaction would be?"

"No, I really wasn't," Tess said, smiling at him.

"Hmm," her father said, not looking convinced.

"Now Bob, you stop that," her mother said, staring at him. "You know Tess can't lie to us. If there's one thing she knew would get her a spanking, it was lying."

Tess laughed. "Mother, the closest I've ever come to getting a spanking in my entire life, was when Tuesday..." She stopped abruptly, feeling her face suddenly burning. Nathan snickered.

Nathan's mother was the first one to laugh, and hesitantly, the rest of the "grownups" joined in. Tess watched her parents struggle with not wanting anything that might give them a mental image of their daughter in bed with another consenting adult, and wanting to laugh because she was so clearly mortified.

Again, it was Nathan's mother that recovered first. She looked at her son.

"Nathan? Anything you'd like to add to this discussion?"

"Um," was all he could say, and Tess bit her lip.

Yasmin cleared her throat and all eyes went to her. The parents were curious about what she was about to say. Nathan, and to an extent, for Nathan's sake, Tess, were terrified of what she might say. Oshba sat back in her chair to watch, her face expressionless, but Tess thought she saw a glint of humor flash through her eyes.

Yasmin pulled her phone out.

"I believe I have some video footage here, somewhere," she said, sounding like she was concentrating on her search. "You know they say a picture is worth a thousand words. I suppose an actual video would be worth at least a few thousand..."

"Oh, I don't think that will be necessary," Tess's mother said, and both fathers were stuttering.

Yasmin smiled in satisfaction.

"Here it is," she said. "Want to watch it?" she said and held her phone out in front of both sets of parents.

Nathan was playing and singing "Tiny Dancer" by Elton John, sitting behind his own keyboard.

Yasmin looked around the table with an innocent look on her face, looking puzzled at their relieved expressions.

"What did you *think* the video was of?" she asked, and a small smile came to her lips.

They were all still laughing when the waiter came to take their orders, and they had to ask for another couple minutes to look at the menu.

Tess turned to look as the Maitre d seated a party of six at the large table next to their own. She blinked as she watched Mari Sue Dumarest sit down next to a short man that was clearly Tuesday's father.

It was Bobbi Jo that noticed Tess, and hushed Chuck as he was bitching to his pa about all the faggots and lezzies in this town. They all turned and stared at Tess, then at the rest of her table, and Tess almost burst into laughter as all three of the sons zeroed right in on Yasmin.

Bobbi Jo looked at Tess apologetically, and shrugged.

"Awkward," she said, and Tess had to laugh.

"You have to be kidding me," Nathan said in a low tone meant only for her.

To give him credit, it was actually funny when Chuck leaned forward and stared at Nathan intensely.

"Do I *look* like I'm kidding?"

"Um," Nathan said, and Tess and Yasmin both started laughing.

Nathan's father looked at the other table curiously. He got it and flagged down the waiter.

"We're going to need more wine."

♦ ♦ ♦ ♦ ♦

Carlos decided that the time spent around Nathan, as well as his support group of friends, Nadi, who he knew primarily because of Nathan's prior relationship with Amber, and now with Yasmin, was time well spent. It also had a high entertainment value.

This week, Sunday was Nadi's day off, but she'd told him that she wished to listen to Nathan play for at least a set or two.

"This has been an entertaining week, for more reasons than you can imagine," she said as they sat at the kitchen table in his new house, nude, drinking beer and eating pizza. "I spoke with Oshba a while ago. I have a feeling tonight will be even more entertaining, and stranger than usual. Rather than tell you why, I would enjoy providing commentary."

"Whatever you wish, mi cielito," Carlos said, and watched Nadi glance at her phone. "Shall we get a shower and get ready?"

Nadi snorted.

"If 'we' get a shower together, we will be lucky to make his last set." She stood, unmindful of his eyes running up and down her naked body as she washed down her last bite of pizza with beer. "Behave yourself now, and I *might* reward you tenfold, tonight."

"I'll take those odds," Carlos said, and watched her walk down the hall to the bathroom. He almost stood to follow her, but forced himself to stay seated until she was safely out of sight. Nadi was very aware of his admiration for her naked form, and that it was a very significant tool, or weapon. She never hesitated to flaunt its power over him.

Carlos sighed, knowing resistance was futile. He knew a losing cause when confronted with it.

They walked into Captain Eddie's fifteen minutes before nine, and the bar was already rapidly filling. Lady Yasmin, as Carlos kept catching himself thinking of her as, sat with a couple he didn't recognize on one side of her, and Oshba on the other.

Nadi's partner saw them immediately, and grinned widely for a brief moment. Just as quickly, she reacquired her distant, almost bored demeanor, that gave away none of her thoughts. Her white-skinned lover, sitting next to her, immediately glanced sideways, as if sensing Oshba's visual mood shifts.

Carlos was bemused by the number of unfamiliar faces. There was a couple seated next to Tess, and of course, Tuesday was on her other side. She took one look at him, and nodded her head in approval.

"I'm diggin' your beard, Carlos." Her eyes twinkled. "You kind of look like Spock from classic Star Trek in that alternate universe episode."

Carlos wondered what she was talking about as he pulled out a chair for Nadi, next to Sarah and across from Oshba. She looked at him without speaking, and he realized he'd never held a chair for her before. She sat, and he hurriedly sat next to her.

Although technically, neither of them were working, they were both packing. Nadi had her usual light jacket over a t-shirt to cover the holstered handgun under each arm, and comfortable looking jeans, stressed, but not torn.

Carlos realized they'd unconsciously dressed in matching outfits. He had an older sports jacket to hide his own sidearms, over a dark t-shirt, and the same worn jeans he'd had on Friday.

There were about half a dozen empty chairs to his left, and he wondered who they could be expecting. Most of the usual suspects were already here, plus a few new faces.

Their tables kind of zigzagged, due to the ones that surrounded their staked space. Tuesday and Tess sat at the end of the table on the far side, followed by two couples. The woman next to Tess looked familiar, and he wondered if she might be Tess's mother. The other couple had been talking with Yasmin, and stopped to watch them approach. They obviously recognized Nadi.

Yasmin, Oshba, Phoebe, and two older women finished that side of the tables. Aurora sat at the end, leaning over the corner to one side, holding hands with the blond girl that worked with Sarah at Smokin' Tuna. Her name was…Mariah. The girl next to her had blue hair, and he couldn't decide if it made her interesting or just weird. Then there was Sarah, Nadi and himself.

He looked at the empty chairs again, knowing how valuable they were on a Sunday night at Eddie's. Beyond those, he could see there were at least a dozen or more men from Eldamar filling the last tables, as well as that crazy old woman, Marilyn.

Even as he stared at the chairs, a family started filling them. He opened his mouth, and let it snap shut again as he felt Nadi's hand on his thigh, squeezing it in warning. He sat and watched as four men and two women filled the empty chairs.

Carlos looked at them closely, wondering why they looked familiar. He got his answer quickly as the younger woman looked around the room, at all the business cards stapled to the walls, the stage, and Nathan setting up in his usual place near the west entrance of the bar. Then she looked across the table at Tuesday.

"So this is where you spend most of your free time, Sis?"

He gave her a closer look, and now the family resemblance was obvious. He let his eyes run across the rest of the group, and could now see it included Tuesday's parents, and from the looks of it, three brothers, as well as the sister.

The man next to him was a brother, and looked the oldest. Carlos realized his inspecting them had not gone unnoticed, and wasn't exactly appreciated. The man next to him looked about thirty, and was pretty fit and muscular for his size, which was about half a foot shorter than his own six foot three. The brother looked past him at Nadi, then across the table at Yasmin and Oshba.

"What's your name?" he asked belligerently. "I'm Bubba."

"Carlos," he said, keeping his voice at a normal volume. He thought Tuesday Dumarest was crazy as anyone could be, but he liked her aggressive stance against the world. He didn't wish to offend her by getting into a fight with her oldest brother.

"Carlos?" Bubba asked, incredulously. "What kind of name is that for an Ay-rab?"

"Very unlikely," Carlos admitted, and said no more.

Bubba waited for him to continue, and when he didn't say anything more, one of the other brothers laughed. He immediately got a punch in the arm from the third brother.

"Carlos is a Mexican name," Bubba said, ignoring both the other brothers. "You Mexican?"

"No," Carlos said, stifling a sigh. He didn't want to get into a fight on the third day of this assignment. And he *really* didn't want to have to kick the crap out of Tuesday's oldest brother. And if he did have to, he didn't want to do it in Captain Eddie's. He had a sneaking feeling that getting into a fight was a sure way to get banned.

"No? That's all you got to say?" Bubba turned sideways in his chair, probably thinking it was a good move if they got into it. He was wrong, of course.

"Yes."

This time it was the brother *and* the sister that laughed.

"If you ain't Mexican, where *are* you from?"

Carlos turned his head to look into the man's eyes.

"I'm American."

"Ah, the hell you are, Where's your passport. Let me see it. You even *got* a passport? An American one?"

Carlos stared into Bubba's eyes.

"Yes, I do. Do you?"

"Well, no. But it's obvious I'm American. You're from south of the border somewhere."

"No, I'm from Miami," Carlos said, trying one last time to defuse the situation. "My *grandparents* were from Cuba. They became citizens in the late sixties."

"Let me see your passport."

Carlos became aware he only had one passport on him, and it was for his assumed identity. He began mentally preparing himself for a fight. He was pretty sure at least one of the brothers would jump in, and the father for certain. He hoped Tuesday wouldn't, but it was becoming very clear where her craziness came from, so who could say?

"Bubba, you're pissin' me off, but you're my brother, so I'm gonna let you in on a secret," Tuesday drawled, slouching in her chair. "Carlos is a friend of ours, and he's Nadi's boyfriend. Nadi is one of Yasmin's *two* bodyguards, the other being Oshba, who you met tonight at dinner. Carlos is in the same line of work. And he's *very* good at his job."

"Hey, you folks ready to order drinks?"

Melanie started dropping cocktail napkins in front of each of the Dumarests. "I think I heard this lovely young lady call Tuesday sis, so I guess you're her family. I'm Melanie, and I'll be your stewardess tonight. No wait, that's my day job. I'll be your waitress tonight. I want to personally welcome you to Captain Eddie's Saloon. We all love Tess, Nathan, and Tuesday."

She made a point of looking directly at Bubba.

"Especially the owners. If you look behind you about four tables, you'll see Steve and Ted Little. They're brothers, and when they got back from multiple tours in Afghanistan and Iraq, they took this bar over, and absolutely love their baby. Ted, the younger one, is an Army Ranger, and Steve is a Navy SEAL. I thought they had size limits for those services, but apparently even at six foot six, you can still be a SEAL or a Ranger."

Melanie smiled at each of the Dumarests, her eyes resting last on Bubba.

"So, what are you drinking?"

All four men turned and looked at Ted and Steve, who just *happened* to be standing by a table about four rows over, nodding to them. They both were wearing tight t-shirts that showed off their layers of muscles over muscles. Tuesday's mother made a sound of disgust, and the sister couldn't quit laughing.

"I'll take a Bud lite, long neck," the mother said. "Hold the testosterone."

The sister nodded her head in agreement, grinning at her mother's words. One by one, all four of the men agreed that sounded good, and Melanie smiled brilliantly at them.

"Excellent choice," she said, and looked thoughtful. "Tell you what, if you get a bucket of five, you save some money, and I'll have them toss a sixth one in for free. It's a pleasure meeting y'all."

She left, and Tuesday covered her face, shaking her head.

"Tess Mess, I can't take them *anywhere*."

Tess immediately stood up.

"We have so many new faces, I want to introduce everyone by name, at least." Tess smiled around the table, and Carlos was impressed to see the tension visibly lessen. He already knew what a sweet girl Tess was, but he got the feeling she was tougher than anyone gave her credit for. "I want to personally welcome my Tue Bear's family, her sister, Bobbi Jo, her youngest brother Bobby, her mother, Mari Sue, Jackie, her dad, and Chuckie and Bubba, her other two brothers."

She smiled at them and Carlos relaxed as well, knowing she'd finished easing the tension, at least for the moment.

"Then we have Carlos, who is *very* close to Nadi, Sarah, Robbi, Mariah, that's Aurora down at the end, Phoebe's grandmother, Emily, her mother, Grace, Phoebe, Oshba, Yasmin, Nathan's mother and father, Felicia and Houston, me, and Tuesday you know."

Tess actually blushed as she said that, and there was some laughter. Her blush deepened and she hurriedly kept going.

"This is my mother and father...oh. Uh, Kendra and Bob," Tess said, and laughed self-consciously. "I don't know if I've ever introduced them by their names before. Then there are the men of Eldamar, the owner, Philip LeBlanc, Paul, Marilyn, Marvin, Simon, Richard, Leon, Mohsen, Gerald, Lawrence, Daniel, James, Tommy and Walter."

She started to sit down, and popped right back up.

"Oh, Marilyn isn't one of the men of Eldamar. She just hangs out with them, and us, a lot." Tess got an impish look in her eyes. "And when I say 'hangs out', I mean just that."

"What?" Marilyn asked, playing dumb. There were some chuckles around the table. Carlos knew her breasts seemed to fall out of those sundresses she wore with alarming regularity.

There was applause and cheers for Tess getting through everyone. She gave a little curtsey and giggled as she sat back down. Tuesday gave her a hug, and Carlos watched the father, Jackie, scowl.

That was not going to be an easy sell, Carlos decided.

"My name is Nathan Williams. Who's ready for some music?" Nathan called out, his P.A. system carrying his voice to every corner of the room and out onto Greene Street.

He got an energetic response and nodded his approval as he started to play a song Carlos recognized by Maroon 5.

"Sunday morning, rain is falling..."

Carlos had to struggle to not smile as Nathan's mother turned to his papa, exclaiming how much she loved this song.

Nathan got to the first chorus, and Carlos flinched as the room erupted into a vast choir of people singing as loud as they could. As leadoff songs went, this one was a home run. He watched as Tuesday dragged Tess without much resistance to the dance floor, and they merged into one as they danced on the empty floor.

That didn't last for long as couples appeared from all parts of the room. Carlos realized Nadi's hand was still on his thigh and reached to cover it with his own. He felt Nadi lean against him a little and they sat listening to the rest of the song, enjoying the moment of normalcy.

For normal people, anyway, Carlos thought stoically.

Nathan finished "Sunday Morning", took a sip of his wine, which immediately caused a flurry of people calling out for Melanie to get the piano man another drink. Carlos estimated seven people bought him drinks before he even started the next song. She symbolically brought him a fresh glass of Chardonnay, setting it next to the one he was drinking.

Nathan nodded his thanks to the room in general, then hit a full chord hinting resolution. Carlos realized what he was about to play and leaned towards Nadi, only to discover she was already leaning so close to him, their heads were almost touching.

"I recognize this next song. It's a good one."

Nadi smiled at him and nodded her agreement, and he realized she knew the song as well as he did.

Nathan started a dynamic piano introduction, and the dance floor immediately filled again.

Carlos held his bottle towards Nadi, and she clinked it with her own, even as Nathan began to sing.

"Hey kids, shake it loose together, the spotlight's hitting something that's been known to change the weather…"

♦ ♦ ♦ ♦ ♦

Lori Lynn watched Melanie defuse the situation and shook her head.

"As a waitress, that woman is worth her weight in gold," she said, and looked at Steve with amusement. "Did Tuesday's brother not realize how much bigger Carlos is than him?"

"You ever see Tuesday back away from anyone, no matter how big they are?" Ted asked quietly.

"Good point," she admitted. She smiled and leaned closer to Nico as Nathan began to play. "Jeez, I like this song."

"*Everyone* likes this song," Ted said morosely.

She looked at him curiously, and then got it as Nathan reached the chorus. At least a hundred voices began singing along with him, with a wide variety of quality.

"That may be all I need. In darkness she is all I see…"

Lori Lynn realized that she was one of those voices, shrugged, and sang even louder. About half the table joined her. She nudged Nico, who shook his head, and called out over the voices.

"You'll thank me for not singing, later."

Too soon the song came to the ending.

"Driving slow on Sunday morning, and I never want to leave."

Nathan played "Bennie and the Jets," by Elton John, and then went into a Cat Stevens song, "Morning has Broken." Lori Lynn sighed and reached under the table to take Nico's hand. She felt the eyes of her friends on her, and realized they weren't fooling anyone, but she didn't pull her hand free.

A song or two later, she turned to Nico, who reluctantly released her hand.

"So, tell me about your body," she said, and saw him fight a grin. She realized how vague her question was, and narrowed her eyes at him. She lifted her jacket enough for him to see the butt of her service weapon. He laughed, and so did his partner, Annette Wilcox, sitting with her husband Justin, across the table from them.

"Don't make me ask again," she warned, keeping her expression menacing. He shook his head and looked at Steve's wife, sitting on the other side of Annette. She was a Key West City uniform officer, and was always no-nonsense. She was also one of the toughest cops in Monroe County, of any police force, including the state troopers.

"Officer Little, would you please show Lieutenant Buffington what a menacing stare looks like?"

Marisela stared at him, and although he knew she was having fun with him, he suddenly looked nervous. He shrugged.

"Okay, I was kind of hoping you'd use it on her, not me, but you made my point," Nico said, his tone even and strong. He turned back to Lori Lynn and she cleared her throat.

"The body?"

"White male, six foot three, about two hundred and fifteen pounds, his throat slashed, only wearing underwear." Nico cleared his own voice. "Tighty whities. We're trying to I.D. him by fingerprints, facial recognition, and by his tattoos. We sent in a DNA sample, but that could take weeks. Based on the tattoos, I think he's probably Russian."

"You didn't call me?" Lori Lynn asked, disappointed she'd missed out on being there at the start of the case.

"There wasn't much to do," Nico pointed out. "I had my partner, and it gave her some good experience. And why should your Sunday get messed up? Even with the fact his washing up eliminated any chance of evidence where the body was found. There was literally nothing on him, except his tats and tighties. And we were *still* out there until almost four o'clock."

"I guess," Lori Lynn agreed reluctantly.

"You said you had personal matters to deal with until tonight," Nico reminded her.

"Yeah," Lori Lynn admitted.

"If you're good, and don't hold a grudge, I'll show you what we got tomorrow morning. If you're *really* good, I'll get you a Dilly Bar from DQ."

"Well, with *that* at stake, I guess I can wait," Lori Lynn said, letting the smile out. Nathan started another song and she shushed him. "Another Cat Stevens song. I want to listen to this."

They sat back in their chairs, and she snuck her hand back into his.

"Subtle," Marisela Little said, and Lori Lynn scratched next to her left eye with her middle finger.

"Shaddap."

♦ ♦ ♦ ♦ ♦

He had a beer in Sloppy Joe's, and then another in Rick's Bar. He looked around the Bull, made his way up to the Whistle Bar, then to the roof, and the Garden of Eden. There were some people milling around, some undressed, many not, a few were getting body painted, but it was mostly older people, primarily couples, and he went back downstairs and continued his way on Duval.

He looked into Margaritaville, and then Willie T's, but the action wasn't what he was looking for, and he kept going. Cowboy Bill's looked like fun another night, or maybe at happy hour, but he wasn't going to waste his time there tonight.

He looked in the Aqua Bar, but it was a drag queen show, and he wasn't interested. The Bourbon Street Pub might have been interesting, but to get inside, you had to walk by these people at the bar that seemed to be sitting there for the sole purpose of drinking and staring at anyone that approached the entrance.

The 801 Bourbon Bar looked intriguing, and he got another beer there, watched the crowd for a few minutes, saw some men go in a door in the back left corner of the room. He thought it might be where the bathrooms were, but when he went through the door, he found himself in another bar entirely. It had a dance floor, but no live entertainment. It was clearly a gay bar, and the numerous televisions hanging from the ceiling around the room had gay porn playing.

The first television showed one man giving a blow job to another, and after watching for a minute, he went in search of the bathroom. He walked towards the back part of the bar, and found a room with a wall partitioning it from the rest of the bar, but the wall was only about six feet tall, leaving at least a couple feet of open space to the hanging tile ceiling.

The small room behind the partition had six or seven men standing around, looking at each other, not really talking or anything. He saw the bathroom door and went in to piss. He'd thought he'd go into a stall for privacy, but all the stall walls had been removed. Anyone needing to use the toilet was either standing or sitting, totally exposed. There were two urinals, and they didn't look gross, so he chose one.

Related Matters

While he was using it, a man stood at the second, a few feet away, looking him over while he was peeing. He didn't say a word, but the man looked interested. He finished his business and left the bathroom.

He stood looking at the group of men standing around, and walked over so he wasn't quite part of any group, but he could see what was happening.

One older man looked at a guy's face, and the guy gave a tiny nod. The older man knelt, unzipped the other man's pants, reached in and leaned forward. His head began bobbing, and he stepped a few feet over to the side to get a better look.

He could feel someone next to him and looked to see it was the man from the bathroom. He looked at him, and the man made a slight gesture towards his crotch. He nodded his head, as slightly as he could, and the man knelt in front of him, and opened his fly.

The moist warmth of the man's mouth made him breathe in sharply. He stood, trying to think about other things, but his eyes kept looking down to watch, and the sensation began to build.

Suddenly it was too late for him to think about anything except the knee-shaking release he was experiencing. When he was spent, the man closed his fly, stood, and left. After a minute or two, so did he.

He walked for a block or two, and a chicken wandered in front of his path. He violently kicked at it, but the chicken avoided his foot, and went squalling across the sidewalk.

He continued down the street.

♦ ♦ ♦ ♦ ♦

Chapter Ten

Felicia carefully made her way down the stairs, and wandered back to the kitchen. She knew it was too early, but thought maybe Kendra would be there to work her magic with whoever was preparing the continental breakfast. Get her to slip them cups of coffee.

Kendra wasn't there. She stuck her head around the frame of the door and peeked into the kitchen. A woman a few years older than she was busy cutting fruit. She looked up and stared at Felicia, and raised the outside corner of her right eye, and nodded.

As she moved to the coffee maker, Felicia saw her glance past her, as if to see if there were more people. She prepared two cups of coffee and handed them to her. She saw there was a capital F on the side of one, and a K on the other.

Felicia opened her mouth to mention she was alone, when a hand reached around her and took the cup with the K.

"I believe this is mine," Kendra whispered, and sniffed it, sighing.

The woman handed Felicia a small plate covered with a paper towel.

"Bring the plate back later, after we're open. Now, disappear," she said sternly, with what might be a British accent, and went back to cutting fruit.

Felicia turned and looked at Kendra, holding up the plate. They both sniffed, and their eyes widened. Giggling, they hurried out to the front porch. They sat on the love seat, uncovered the plate, looked at the two slices of bread and the little plastic cup of butter. There was a plastic knife, and Kendra picked it up and put a liberal coat on one of the slices.

She took a bite, and her eyes softened and nearly closed.

"Ish ish sho good," she mumbled, covering her mouth in embarrassment, but it didn't stop her from taking a second bite.

Felicia tried a bite before she added butter, and sighed.

"That's cranberry, and those are walnuts," she sighed, and thought about the flavor. "There's something tart in the bread. Key lime? Lemon?"

"Orange zest, I believe," Kendra said, and Felicia nodded.

"That's it."

They took their time eating their slices, sipping coffee in between bites. Felicia grinned at Kendra. "Are you going to spy on your daughter this morning?"

Kendra blushed and shook her head.

"I'm giving my girl some space," she said. "She's going to have enough on her hands with the in-laws."

"Oh, so it's in-laws now, is it?" Felicia asked, grinning.

"You saw the two of them last night. They're a couple," Kendra said, and smiled as she stared into space, probably picturing her daughter. "They are so right for each other. I can't believe I'm saying this, but it's true."

Kendra turned to look at her.

"How about you? Ready to invite a daughter into the family?"

"I think Nathan and Yasmin are a little behind the girls on that," Felicia said, and shook her head. "Have we really been here less than forty-eight hours? So much has happened. Our kids have so many friends, and know so many people. It's almost too much to take in."

"I know," Kendra sighed. "I feel so bad for Tuesday. Her family doesn't approve, and they don't hesitate to make that clear. I hope she realizes we're on her and Tess's side, and that we welcome her with open arms."

"Tuesday's family was pretty brutal about her at dinner, and then it seemed like there was always at least one of them digging at her all night at Captain Eddie's." Felicia grinned. "Did you see the look on Bubba's face when both he and Carlos happened to stand up at the same time?"

"His 'pa' and at least one of the other two brothers were going to jump in. I could see it in their faces," Kendra said, frowning. "Even so, I'm not so sure he couldn't handle any two of them himself. I accidentally bumped into him, and he's all muscle. But he moves like a cat."

"If all three went after him, they would have found out how tough his girlfriend is," Felicia said. "I'm not so sure she couldn't take any two of them herself. Even so, why these guys feel the need to fight is beyond me."

"I so wanted to get in their faces about the things they kept saying to Tuesday," Kendra admitted. "I mean, she's their sister, for cripes' sake."

"I can't imagine being that mean-spirited to someone in my own family. If they aren't careful, they'll lose her completely. That's a very tough little girl. There's a limit to how much she'll take before she says screw it."

"Well, my job is making sure she knows she's welcome with us," Kendra said, and looked at Felicia. "Seriously, Nathan and Yasmin look as serious as any couple I've ever seen. I wonder if anything ever rattles her. She was nervous the first night, but after that, she's cool as a cucumber. She has this constant calm state that makes me wonder if she's on Quaaludes."

Felicia nodded, grinning. It was true. She was always watching, evaluating, but any reactions she had were deeply buried. After that first night, she'd recovered her poise, and seemed unflappable.

"Her two employees," Felicia mentioned. "Are they just bodyguards? Or, like, companions, nurses, maids? Spies reporting back to her family? You're right about Nadi. She looks tough."

"They're *her* bodyguards," Houston said, and pulled a chair from the table around so he could sit facing them. He had a bottled water, and eyed their coffee cups and the empty plate suspiciously. He glanced at his wristwatch and sighed. He reluctantly refocused on what they were talking about. "I know the bigger one, Nadetama, or Naztemida, whatever, was packing last night. When she and Carlos danced or hugged, I could see they both had guns."

"Her name is Nadezhda," Kendra said, saying each syllable slowly and enunciating carefully. "Everyone seems to call her Nadi. Why would a young girl like Yasmin need armed guards?"

"We met her the same day we met Tess and Tuesday, on the Skype call," Felicia said, thoughtfully. "Nathan said she was from a powerful family in Abu Dhabi. Maybe they worry about kidnapping. Remember they talked about mercenaries that were sent to that resort in Mexico to kidnap her."

"Mercenaries? What young girl has mercenaries after her?" Kendra said, sounding bewildered. She stared at Felicia.

"Hired by someone in her own country," Felicia said slowly, already regretting her slip.

"There was a murder in the neighborhood, back in June," Kendra said slowly. "That's how Tuesday got shot in the butt. We need to quiz all three of them and get more details on these things, and find out if there's anything else that's happened around them."

"I checked into that resort, and it's a very exclusive, totally inclusive nude resort," Felicia said. "Nathan played poolside and dinners for a week. The girls all hung out naked at the pool all day, and they all partied in the club at night."

"I can't see either of those women stripping down to guard her poolside," Kendra said thoughtfully. "Plus, the guns would have stood out.

Related Matters

They might have had a room with a view, and sat above, watching."

"Well, they clearly aren't there to protect her chastity," Houston said, and leaned back out of Felicia's backhand reach.

"Don't be crass," Felicia said, although she knew her husband was right. "So, what are we going to do today? Kendra?"

"They have a couple ways to get around Key West and see the sights," she said, and shrugged. "It's a touristy thing to do, but they have a Conch Tour Train of the old town area, and a Town Trolley that takes you around the entire island."

"Phoebe says Yasmin is a princess in Abu Dhabi," Emily said, startling all of them as she suddenly popped through the door. "Part of the royal family. There's more to the story, but I don't feel comfortable telling you what I heard second hand."

They all looked at her in confusion. She smiled at them.

"I was sitting upstairs on the balcony," she said, holding up a to go coffee cup from the Old Town Bakery. It was her turn to look hesitant. "Did you say you're going on the Conch Train?"

"Either that or the Old Town Trolley," Felicia admitted, and realized what she was hesitating about. "Would you and Grace like to join us?"

"We'd love to," Emily said, and smiled. "Well, really, *I'd* love to. Grace and I can only spend so much time with just the two of us before she starts to drive me crazy."

"I heard that," a voice came down from the balcony above, and Felicia and Kendra looked at each other, trying to keep from laughing.

"Before *we* start to drive each other crazy," Emily conceded, with a smile.

Felicia looked at Houston. "Honey, if you get right on it, you have time to shower and get ready before the kitchen opens."

He sighed and stood, looking at the rest of them with resignation.

"In our house, that's called a subtle hint," he said with a deadpan voice, and headed for the stairs.

"So, Emily, you and Grace have been here a couple days longer than us, so you're experts," Kendra said, and all three of them grinned. "Anything we should know about in particular, today?"

Emily shrugged, and looked like she was taking the question seriously.

"I guess you know about your kids' neighborhood being kind of like a gay nude resort. They're hosting a Christmas dinner Wednesday. So there will be a very broad spectrum of new experiences for you to deal with." She scratched her head. "Oh, and tonight is ladies' night at the Diane Isis Bar & Girl. The girls will probably try and get the two of you to go there for dinner."

"Is that the lesbian bar?" Kendra asked hesitantly. "Both Tess and Tuesday did mention it, last night. We're not gay. And can our husbands come?"

"Grace and I have only been there once, last Wednesday, and it was a hoot," Emily admitted. "The main floor is a restaurant with a very specific subject matter represented by a plethora of art. One of the owners is a sculptor and painter, and she is astounding. And the food is excellent. They have a lounge up on the roof, and it's for women only, no exceptions. Phoebe tells me they had a fire up there three years ago, and no male firemen were allowed to go to the roof. Depending on who you talk to, they almost lost the entire building, or, it wasn't that big a deal. Small fire, put right out."

"The boys can fend for themselves," Kendra said, looking at Felicia. "My girl spends a couple nights a week in that place, so I want to scope it out."

"You got a wingman," Felicia said, and then grinned. "I mean, wing person."

They heard voices down the hall and Felicia glanced at her phone.

"It's eight thirty," she said, and they turned as one towards the kitchen.

Kendra sighed as they walked through the house. "I guess I'll call Mari Sue, and see if she and Jackie want to join us this morning on the Conch Train."

"Working on the Conch Train, baby," Felicia sang as they got into the short line of guests into the kitchen.

Mari Sue and Jackie did end up joining them for the tour. They all ended up eating lunch at Margaritaville afterwards, so they could say they did. Felicia thought it was okay, if not exceptional. They told Mari Sue their plans for the evening and she glanced at Jackie. She looked doubtful, but said she'd see what the kids and Jackie were going to do before she said for sure.

Kendra said she wanted to go because she wanted to understand their kids better, and seeing their other gay friends might help.

"Tuesday ain't gay," Jackie said shortly, and Mari Sue looked resigned.

"Where are your kids today?" Felicia asked, to deflect Jackie from going on a rant, like he did the night before.

"They went jet skiing," Mari Sue said, sounding envious. "When they found out that Italian girl was leading the tour, the boys definitely wanted to check it out. I guess Bobbi Jo went with the flow."

"We did it yesterday morning," Kendra confessed. "It was a lot of fun. Those machines feel like they're flying."

Related Matters

She turned to Felicia.

"What's Nathan doing today?"

"He meets a friend every Monday afternoon for a rousing game of Scrabble, and then he has band practice in the early evening," Felicia said. "I guess they have a big gig New Year's Eve, and the booking includes the rest of the week, so they're learning some new songs."

"Jackie, I think Bob and I are going to eat dinner downstairs at the place the girls are going tonight, if you want to join us," Kendra said, and looked at Felicia. "Houston and Felicia are, too."

"I'll probably do something with the boys tonight," he said. "Thanks for asking, though. I doubt I'd fit in very well." He looked troubled, and turned to his wife. "Honey pie, maybe you *should* go with them, or meet them there. See what we're up against."

Mari Sue looked surprised, and even more so when he continued. "Let's have Bobbi Jo go with you. Me an' the boys will find someplace on Duval. I think I saw a sports bar or two when you were shopping yesterday. I'm pretty sure there's a bowl game or two on tonight."

He looked at the rest of them.

"Your daughter is a very sweet girl, and I don't want you to think we don't like her." He looked uncomfortable. "But we need to nip this in the bud, before it gets out of control. I'm hoping we can talk Tuesday into moving back to Jacksonville, find herself a good man, move past all this nonsense."

Felicia felt her husband stiffen, and knew how he felt. She looked at Bob and Kendra and saw they were controlling their faces, but they were fuming.

Grace suddenly pulled a deck of cards out of her bag, and Felicia saw they were Tarot cards. She shuffled them deliberately, and everyone's eyes fixated on her hands and the deck. She finished shuffling and set it on the table top.

She then proceeded to pull another deck out, with different art, and shuffled it as well. When she was satisfied, she set it a little away from the first. She moved the first in front of Jackie.

"Jackie, would you mind cutting this deck?"

"Why?" he asked suspiciously.

"Why not?" she answered whimsically.

He looked nervous, but went ahead and cut the deck. Grace smoothly put the bottom half on top of the cut cards, and then set the other deck in front of Mari Sue.

"Would you?" she asked, and Mari Sue looked nervous. She stared at Grace, then at Emily, and sat back and finally nodded her head. She cut it about two thirds of the way down the deck. Grace put the bottom portion on top and thanked them both.

"Now what?" Jackie asked, frowning.

"Do you believe in people telling fortunes by reading Tarot cards, or palms, or seeing auras?" she asked mildly.

"I don't know what auras is, but hell no, I don't," he said firmly.

"What about you, Mari Sue?" Grace asked, and looked at her curiously. Her eyes narrowed as she did so, and she looked a little surprised.

"I don't reckon I do," she said slowly. "But I don't reckon I disbelieve in it, either."

"Keeping an open mind to the idea," Grace said, nodding her approval. "Sound thinking."

She packed the cards into their boxes, careful to not disturb their order, and put them into her bag. She turned to Emily.

"We should probably grocery shop today for Christmas Dinner," she said, and her mother nodded. Grace looked at Kendra and Felicia. "Phoebe said we're all invited to Tess, Nathan, and Tuesday's home Christmas Day, and we're going to bring an old family recipe. Do any of you *not* like spicy food?" She looked at Mari Sue as well.

"Thai food is a bit tough on us, but other than that, no, a little spicy is nice," Kendra said, smiling. "What are you bringing?"

"Corn Glop," Emily said with a broad smile. Everyone kind of chuckled at the name. "It's kind of a cornbread casserole, with more corn, a few other ingredients, and a good dollop of hot sauce tossed in to fight the overall blandness of holiday dinners in general."

"Sounds good," Houston said, and Felicia smiled at him. She looked at Kendra. "I guess we better think about that as well. Nathan said he's grilling a turkey and a ham, so the oven should be available."

"Or some obscure family recipe for Cheese Danish that resembles something you might find at the Publix Bakery," Kendra said, innocently staring up at the ceiling. She turned to Mari Sue. "You're all coming, right?"

"We haven't really talked about it yet," Jackie started to say, and Mari Sue cut him off.

"Yes, we are," she said firmly. "I don't know if I'll take something to prepare there, or get something take out, if anything's open Christmas Day. I guess I better check on that."

Jackie looked at her in surprise, and his forehead furled. Then he shrugged to himself. "We could probably find someplace that has platters of wings, or cheese, or sumthin' like that."

"Like the Publix Deli?" Kendra asked with a straight face, and Mari Sue laughed.

"A lot like that," she admitted.

Felicia talked with Nathan a little later, while Houston looked at hats in the Banana Republic clothing store. When she asked where he was, he got vague, and of course, that just peaked her curiosity even more. She'd met Marilyn, the woman he played Scrabble with, last night, and she was a hoot. She remembered hearing that they played at the Garden of Eden, and were both nude. She didn't know whether to believe that her son wasn't too self-conscious to sit naked in a clothing optional bar where anyone might show up. She decided she didn't need to know today.

He told her he'd be going to practice in a while, grab a bite for dinner, and probably be over at Diane Isis sometime around ten or so to wait for Yasmin. But there was no hurry. He'd have a book to read.

"Your father and Tess's father will probably be downstairs waiting for us as well," Felicia said, and Nathan started laughing.

"Maybe I'll get there a little earlier than that, then. It's a pretty cool restaurant. They have excellent grouper, and their fries are the best I've ever had. They call them chips."

"Ah, like in Great Britain," she said.

"Or Australia," Nathan said, and she wondered how the heck he knew that.

They went back to the B&B, and hung out at the pool for a while. The Dumarest family was still finding things to do on Duval Street.

"You know, if we were at the kids, we wouldn't have to bother with swimsuits," Kendra said, musing. She looked at Felicia. "Oh, and I found out that Liz, the lady in the kitchen, is from South Africa. She's the owner."

"Hmm," Felicia said, trying to remember if she'd ever met anyone from there before.

"Oh, suits are no bother," Houston said nervously, and Felicia struggled to keep her face straight.

She turned to her new best friend.

"Houston is a hopeless prude," Felicia confided in a quiet voice that could be heard by anyone within ten feet. She looked at Kendra. "I have the feeling that nude settings aren't new to you and Bob."

"No, we've been to a few beaches and resorts," Kendra admitted, her voice lower. "It's a comfort thing, but it's kind of exhilarating, too. You've never gone to any nude resorts or skinny dipped?"

"I don't even know if Michigan *has* any nude resorts," Felicia confessed. "We've skinny dipped before, lots of times before we had Nathan, and when he was very young. When we were in college, the dunes of Lake Michigan were only an hour's drive away, and even up around the Traverse Bay area, there are a lot of secluded beaches and dune areas where you can frolic in a natural state."

"I think our kids are all experts, compared to us," Bob said with a smile. "You know they all met Yasmin at some ritzy nude resort in Mexico that Nathan was playing at."

"Getting stories out of Nathan is like pulling teeth," Houston said. "You'd think he'd be a little more open with his dad than his mother, but he's always been such a private person. I guess he started changing a little in college, and we just didn't pick up on it."

Felicia and Kendra exchanged knowing looks, but kept quiet about their already knowing about the resort. Felicia wanted to find out more about what happened there before she started freaking Huey out.

"What are you going to wear tonight?" Kendra asked suddenly, and Felicia thought about it.

"Maybe some leggings, and a button shirt with tails?" Felicia said. "It's been a little cool at night, and we'll be on a roof."

"Good point," Kendra said, and frowned. "I was gonna wear a sundress, but it's got bare shoulders, and I'll probably feel it." She suddenly grinned. "I got leggings. And a husband with a couple button shirts. And he's only a couple inches taller than I am."

"Alright, let's start a rumor," Felicia said, laughing, and they grinned at each other. She turned to Houston and Bob. "Huey, you know where the Diane Isis is? The Duval Loop has a stop half a block away, Tess told us."

"We'll find you ladies just fine," her husband said, and took a drink of his wine. "Have fun, and don't get pregnant."

An hour later, Felicia and Kendra got off the bus, and could see the sign for Diane Isis Bar & Girl a half a block down the side street, on the left. They looked at each other and made minor adjustments to each other's new fedoras.

They both laughed.

"I want pictures of this, but I don't know if I want pictures of this," Felicia admitted, and Kendra nodded her head.

"I know what you mean," she said. "I don't know if we look gay, affected, or butch dyke, but this is kind of a rush."

"I know," Felicia said, and offered her arm. Kendra looked at her, and smirked.

"Let's go impress some ladies," she said, and took her arm.

They admired the sign out front, and the nude archers on the storefront. Kendra made a point of holding the door for Felicia, and she nodded.

"Thank you very much, m'lady," she said, and they both giggled.

They walked in and stopped cold, thunderstruck by all the artwork. Felicia didn't think there was this much artwork of nude women in the state of Michigan, much less, one location. They made their way slowly towards the bar, where a young black girl was working. She looked them over approvingly and smiled.

"Have you been here before?" she asked, and they both shook their heads. The girl looked at them, and actually licked her lips. "I'm Shanda. If you'd like to order your drinks, I'll bring them upstairs to you. Do you know where to go?"

They both ordered Shiraz, and she led them to the back door. "If you're eating finger foods and such, we can bring it up to you, but if you're having a regular meal, we recommend you eat down here. There isn't regular seating on the roof. There are menus up there, and I'll be back and forth a lot. Just catch me and tell me what you need. Or, come down and order while you're seated." She smiled at them and pointed out the back door at the stairs.

As they started up to the roof, Kendra leaned in close to Felicia. "Why did I get her unspoken words were 'on or off the menu'?"

Felicia laughed and nodded. "I think I heard the same thing."

They reached the top step and looked around in wonder. The row of archer statues, numerous other pieces of art, and about two dozen women filled the roof. They took a couple steps to clear the stairs, and stopped, not quite sure of what to do next.

"Kendra, Felicia, you made it!"

Felicia was relieved to see two familiar faces, Emily and Grace.

They both wore tie-dyed dresses, that fit loosely, and were anything but modest. Whereas Grace's dress had a low-cut neckline, and revealed much if she happened to lean forward, Emily's dress, at first glance, had a bit more modest neckline, but was sleeveless, and the gaps for her arms were much larger than one would expect. You had the feeling her breasts were going to peek out at any point.

Shanda swept between them, gave Felicia and Kendra their drinks, and smiled invitingly.

Both Stark women hugged them and held them at arm's length, looking them over with approval.

"This is a very good look on both of you," Emily said in approval. "I would happily shag either of you."

"Um, well," Kendra said hesitantly, and both Stark women laughed.

Their greetings to Kendra and Felicia caught the attention of a very attractive woman that looked to be about forty. She had classic Italian features, and Felicia suspected she'd been gorgeous when she was young. She looked pretty darned good at forty, Felicia decided enviously.

"So, who do we have here?" the Italian woman said, giving them both casual glances that Felicia could tell missed nothing. "I'm Izzy Martelli. Welcome to Diane Isis Bar & Girl."

"She and her wife, Diane Sparks, own this place," Grace told them, and they nodded.

"I'm Felicia Williams, and this is Kendra Carter," she said, shaking hands with the woman.

"My daughter comes here often," Kendra confessed, and Izzy looked at her closely. Her expression changed to shock, and she stared at her, then at Felicia. She looked back at Kendra.

"You're Tess's mother," she said, and swept Kendra into an all-enveloping embrace. "We don't shake hands with family here, we hug. And Tess is definitely family."

She looked at Felicia curiously, and seemed puzzled. It occurred to her that Izzy thought she might be Tuesday's mother, and was having a hard time seeing it.

"I'm Nathan's mother," she said quietly. "I guess he's never been up here, being a boy, so I don't know if you've met him or not."

"Oh yes, I certainly have met Nathan," Izzy said, and Felicia got her own enthusiastic hug. "He has a beautiful, versatile voice, and is very sweet." She grinned at Felicia. "For a boy. But he is part of TNT, and we love him."

"Everyone seems to know our kids as TNT," Kendra said curiously. "I know it's their initials, but it seems like *everyone* knows them by that."

"Well, with all the things that happen to them, all the situations they find themselves in," Izzy said, and stopped cold. "Uh, do they keep you up to date on their lives down here?" she asked cautiously.

"Obviously not enough," Felicia mused, and Kendra nodded.

"What *kind* of situations?" she asked, and Izzy looked uncomfortable.

"I think you should probably quiz them a bit," she admitted, and her voice was firm. "But you won't hear it from me." She immediately lightened her mood. "But please, let me introduce you to the love of *my* life, my wife. I'll get her."

"Mrs. Williams, Mrs. Carter, I am happy to see you came this evening."

They both turned to see Yasmin, standing alone, looking at them. Felicia saw she looked uncertain. She'd bounced from feeling very insecure two nights ago, to being comfortable and confident last night. It appeared she'd regressed a little over the last twenty-four hours.

Related Matters

She looked beautiful, of course. She wore jean leggings and a form-fitting white tank top that told Felicia she wore no bra. A Spanish bolero jacket that didn't reach her waist gave her some cover for her shoulders.

Felicia set her drink down on a convenient small table, and stepped forward to hug her.

"You look beautiful tonight, Yasmin," she said, and held her close. She felt Yasmin's arms close around her as well. "I think you should call me Felicia."

They stood like that for a few moments, and she could feel the tension ease out of the Arab girl's body. They reluctantly released and Felicia was startled to see she actually looked shy.

"Thank you, Felicia," she said quietly. "Thank you for making me feel welcome to your family. I know some of the thoughts that must have flown through your head about me."

Kendra and she hugged then, and when they parted, Yasmin was smiling. It wasn't her self-assured smile, but it was a happy one.

Izzy introduced them to her wife, Diane. Felicia was intrigued. They owned a restaurant, and Diane was clearly a very talented artist, but they reminded her of nothing so much as a lawyer and a cop. Izzy had already shown she had verbal skills, and Diane looked very alert, like a cop. She also looked like she could fight like a cop. And she had more tattoos than any two people Felicia had ever seen.

They talked to the couple for a few minutes, and people kept coming up to introduce themselves. Kendra was a huge hit with most of them, and Felicia had a feeling Tess was much-loved in this community.

Something made her look at the stairs. Mari Sue and Bobbi Jo were standing at the top, looking at the variety of ladies with misgivings on their faces. Felicia immediately went over and greeted them.

"Ladies, c'mon, let me introduce you to the restaurant owners."

Mari Sue took her daughter's hand and firmly pulled her along. They both looked at Felicia, and then over at Kendra, then back at her.

"Y'all drink the Kool-Aid?" Bobbi Jo asked, and Felicia laughed.

"No, no, we're kind of just playing dress-up, or celebrating Halloween a little late," Felicia assured her. "We're both going home to our men tonight."

Bobbi Jo looked at two girls that were clearly twins walk past them. "Lesbians come in twins?" she mused, her voice carrying a little more than she intended.

"Oh, hell no," one of them said. The other shook her head and did a fake shudder.

"We're ringers," she said, and saw the looks on their faces and sighed.

"We're straight. We *like* the Y chromosome."

Shanda slowed as she passed between them "That one's Carrie, and she's Carla," she said and kept going, carrying four buckets, each with five long-neck Bud Lights packed in ice. Bobby Jo looked at her thin arms and whistled under her breath. "That's a lot of weight she's carrying."

The twin Shanda identified first leaned in closer. "I'm Carla, and she's Carrie," she confided. "No one around here can get it right, except one girl named Tuesday. She isn't here yet."

"I'm her sister," Bobbi Jo admitted, and the twins stared at her, and slapped her on the back, and shook hands with her.

"Our softball team, the Amazons, went from being pretty damned good to being champions the last two seasons, because of that crazy girl," Carla said, and the other twin agreed.

"That girl can flat out run," Carrie said, and turned to a clump of women. "Hey, ladies, and I use that term very loosely. This is Tuesday's sister!" She turned and looked at Bobbi Jo questioningly.

"I'm Bobbi Jo, and this is our Ma, Mari Sue," she said, suddenly sounding shy.

"Whoa, and her ma as well," Carla yelled out. "Ma Mari Sue and Sis Bobbi Jo, to Ms. Perkiness herself."

"Perky!" at least a dozen voices shouted out.

Mari Sue nodded her head. "At least I get that one," she said, and watched her daughter be surrounded by ladies, and a beer suddenly appeared in her hands. More women came over to Mari Sue, and Felicia looked at Kendra with a bewildered look on her face.

"Your future daughter-in-law is pretty darned popular around here," she said, and Kendra nodded her head, out of her element, every bit as much as she was. Felicia felt her stomach grumble. "You hungry? My stomach just registered seven on the Richter Scale."

"I think I heard it," Kendra said, a serious expression on her face. She started laughing as Felicia felt her face warm a bit. She turned to Tuesday's mother. "Mari Sue, we're going downstairs to grab a bite to eat. You want to join us?"

"Oh, hell yes," she said, feeling her stomach. "I didn't eat that much for lunch."

"Ladies, would you mind if I joined you for dinner?" Yasmin asked, looking from mother to mother, a little nervously, as they walked down the stairs. "I know Nathan will have dinner tonight at Smokin' Tuna, so he can chat with Sarah, so I am on my own for dinner."

Nadezhda, who apparently had been standing nearby all along, and had followed them down the stairs, cleared her throat. Yasmin laughed and turned to her.

"Nadezhda, you are off for the evening. Oshba will be here in an hour or so, and will stay near until I am in Nathan's competent hands." She looked at her employee slyly. "Your boyfriend is still in Key West, so I'm sure you have much to…talk…about."

The woman rolled her eyes.

"Carlos will wait as long as needed," she said. "He is well aware of my duties. And he has moved here."

Yasmin stared at her, and a thoughtful expression flashed across her face. Felicia wondered what that was about.

"Hey, Yasmin girl, how's my bestie?"

They all turned to see two women, both in cutoff jean shorts that bordered on being mini-skirts, they were so short, and cute tops that showed both their cleavages prominently. Both were tall, one blonde, one with some shade of auburn that Felicia was sure was a dye job. Although both had breasts that Felicia occasionally dreamed of having, the auburn-haired one had clearly paid money for hers. She was the one that had spoken.

"Ashley, how are you? And Lieutenant," Yasmin said, and she got a gleeful look on her face. "May I introduce you to Nathan's mother, Felicia, Tess's mother, Kendra, and Tuesday's mother and sister, Mari Sue and Bobbi Jo?"

The blond woman Yasmin called Lieutenant smiled at them.

"I saw you last night at Captain Eddie's," she admitted. "I wasn't quite sure who was who, at first. You had quite a crowd at your tables." She looked at the auburn-haired woman.

"I forgot to tell you, Ashley."

Ashley pulled both Kendra and Mari Sue close to her, hugging them close. In Mari Sue's case, her head was right at chest level, and she was blushing furiously.

The blonde woman embraced Felicia, and held her by the shoulders at arm's length.

"My name is Lori Lynn, and I want you to know your son is the sweetest young man, with the most beautiful voice, I have ever known. If I was ten years younger, and not already…" She stopped abruptly and blushed, apparently able to tell that Ashley had turned to stare at her.

"I may be seeing someone," she said shortly, and glared at Ashley, tapping on her hip expressively. Ashley just laughed. They traded places and Felicia found herself trapped between two surprisingly strong arms and two moderate-sized mountains attached to Ashley's chest.

The introductions over, Ashley pointed at a table for six over near a statue.

"Grab that table while it's empty, ladies," she said, and took Lori Lynn's hand. "It's the best seat down here. Diane did that statue. You might see us back down here for dinner in a bit. But right now, we have to go drive some lezzies crazy."

She grinned at them.

"No, we aren't gay, and aren't hookers, either." She dragged Lori Lynn behind her as she called back over her shoulder. "We just love driving them crazy."

They got seated and Yasmin looked at Nadezhda.

"Are you still here? I have Lieutenant Buffington for protection, as well as Diane and Cindy. And Oshba will be here before you know it. Go. You and Carlos can have the house for the night. I will stay with Nathan." She froze, and turned to look at Felicia, who couldn't help but laugh.

"That boat sailed, Yasmin," Felicia said. "As much as we want our children to be angels, his voice is as close as Nathan will ever get. Plus, he can't keep a secret from me to save his life."

"It does not appear that I can, either," Yasmin said, looking a little bewildered.

They all looked up as there was a roar from the roof.

"I believe Ashley and Lori Lynn have caught everyone's attention," Yasmin said, and continued.

"My Nathan is very stubborn about not telling secrets, or being pushed into anything he does not wish to say or do," Yasmin said, and shook her head in self-incrimination at her choice of words.

"*Your* Nathan is still *my* son, and he has been slipping up when he talks with me since he *could* talk," Felicia said sweetly. "The three minutes after you left the Skype call, and before Tess and Tuesday paraded through, he slipped and told me how he feels about you, and about how you don't spend *every* night at his place."

"No, some nights we go to my…" She stopped, and reluctantly, a smile of concession came to her face. "You are indeed very good," she admitted, looking at Felicia ruefully.

"Moms one, kids none," Mari Sue said triumphantly, and there was some high-fiving by the mothers. Yasmin and Bobbi Jo glanced at each other and shrugged at almost the same time.

"I believe I will follow your directive, M'lady," Nadezhda said, and nodded at Yasmin. She went to the bar, and spoke briefly with Shanda. The slender black woman nodded and texted something.

Related Matters

A few moments later, Diane came in the back door, nodded to Nadezhda, and went behind the bar, disappearing into the back room. In no time, she emerged, holding two holstered handguns. Nadezhda had already taken her jacket off, and Felicia stared at her biceps in awe. The woman efficiently strapped her holsters in place, reloaded both weapons, and put her jacket back on.

She nodded to them as she passed, pulling a phone out of her pocket as she left.

Kendra looked at Yasmin.

"Not a maid, then."

Yasmin laughed out loud. "Please, ask her that tomorrow, when I can watch."

Felicia knew just enough about guns to know those were high caliber handguns. She thought about her boy in such a turbulent environment and resisted the urge to sigh. But it worried her.

"Ladies, here are the menus, there are no bad choices, but the chips are really fries, and they're the best in Key West, or anywhere else outside of Australia," Shanda said, passing out laminated sheets to them.

"I'll be the judge of that," Mari Sue said, sniffing as she looked at the menu.

"Those are the best fries I ever had," Mari Sue admitted as she polished her plate with the last one.

"They were," Kendra agreed, and looked around the table. Bobbi Jo had made short work of her dinner and gone back upstairs. Yasmin had eaten most of what was on her plate. She'd had rice instead of fries, but her meal had looked very good. Felicia watched them all and sighed. She wished she hadn't finished the fries, or chips, as they said.

"We need to dance or something, work this food off," she said, and slowly rose to her feet. She looked at Shanda, who was helping someone at the next table. The girl turned away from it, and she called to her. "Shanda, do you want us to take care of the tabs now, or all at once?"

"We'll settle up at the end," Shanda said, and smiled.

They went upstairs, and the action hadn't slowed down, including the pace of the drinking. There were close to thirty women on the roof, and the mood was festive.

Felicia watched Mari Sue look at her daughter talking with the blonde twins. Both mother and daughter seemed much more comfortable with the setting, and being surrounded by women that liked women.

She stood next to Mari Sue and put her arm around the woman.

"I hear Nathan and Tuesday are best friends, and they're very supportive of each other," Felicia said, and gave her shoulders a quick squeeze before releasing her. "I hope we become good friends. I know Kendra wants that. We all need to stay in touch after this trip."

"Jackie isn't going to let this go on," Mari Sue said, looking around the crowd. "He isn't going to see any of this. He's going to make Tuesday move back home, and they'll have one hell of a fight, because I think she'll try to say no."

"From what I've seen of Tuesday, if she tries to say no, she'll probably succeed," Felicia said gently. "Everyone tells me, when she makes up her mind, no one, with the possible exception of Tess, can make her change it."

"Her pa can and has, and he'll do it again," she said, and sighed. "She does seem to have a lot of friends that like her, and care about her though. It's a shame they can't just find men and be friends."

"I'm afraid it doesn't work that way," Felicia said, and Mari Sue nodded unhappily.

"Mama Perky, we need you for pictures," one of the girls said. Felicia thought her name might be Stacey. Mari Sue acted hesitant, but Felicia could tell she liked the nickname they'd given her. She was clearly enjoying all the attention.

They got group shots of the team players present, and then of those with softball widows, as they called them. The partners that didn't play, like Izzy, and some of the others.

Diane wanted pictures of the straight women present. She wanted to show how it was a fun place for women, whether they liked women or not.

Izzy insisted on getting shots of the Mothers of TNT, in order of initial, and a couple of Kendra and Felicia, with their fedoras cocked jauntily, arms around each other's waists.

They both jumped when the roof erupted in a loudly shouted "Perky!"

Tuesday grinned, and Tess smiled, blushing, at the ribbing. Behind them, Oshba led Phoebe to a couple chairs, and then found Yasmin, and briefly checked in with her. Aurora and Mariah brought up the rear, and the party went on.

Felicia looked at the glass mugs in Tess and Tuesday's hands. She saw that both Oshba and Phoebe were drinking the same thing. They were white, thick, and frozen, and Tuesday held her head for a moment.

"Brain freeze," she cried, and some of the women Felicia thought were on the team cried out "Barbies!"

"Frozen lime daiquiris," Emily said, standing next to her. Felicia looked at Kendra, who looked doubtful.

Related Matters

Tuesday went over to the woman that had lost her brother recently and spoke to her quietly, and gave her a hug. The woman sighed sadly at Tuesday, but she sat a little straighter, and a glimmer of a smile came to her lips.

Hours later, Felicia saw Kendra staring at her phone. She looked over her friend's shoulder. The only thing showing was the time. Felicia blinked. It was almost midnight.

"Oh my god, where are the boys?" she said, feeling a little panicked, and Kendra shook her head. "Downstairs, apparently."

"We should go, shouldn't we?" Felicia asked, sighing. They'd had so much fun tonight. She felt like Kendra was a friend for life, and she guessed she probably was.

The crowd had shrunk, but there were still a lot of cheerful people She looked around and saw Tess and Tuesday making the rounds, wishing everyone Merry Christmas, Yasmin was doing the same, while Oshba stayed nearby. Behind her, Phoebe was talking with her mother and grandma. She watched Lori Lynn and Ashley say their goodbyes to Izzy and Diane, and come over to them.

"Felicia, Kendra, it was a pleasure meeting you. We might see you in a couple days at the Christmas dinner, if duty permits," she said, and they hugged. Ashley hugged them while Lori Lynn found Mari Sue trying to talk Bobbi Jo into leaving. She was having a good time, but Felicia doubted she had the slightest idea of how to find her motel at this point.

Izzy came over to her, and they hugged.

"We're here until sometime next week, so you'll probably see us next Monday," Felicia said, and hugged her again. "We had such a great time. Now I know why our kids like it here so much."

"You know you don't have to wait until Ladies' Night to drop by," Izzy said. "The food's good on boring days, too."

They laughed and headed downstairs. As they all trooped in the back door, Felicia smiled as she saw Huey, Bob, Nathan and some tall skinny guy shooting pool. Fay, the woman who'd lost her brother, caught her eye as she scurried away from the Wonder Woman juke box. She smiled at how appropriate the motif was for this venue.

A song started playing and Tess and Tuesday stopped cold in their tracks. Felicia realized belatedly that a lot of the women from the roof had trooped down behind them, and they all started chanting.

"Barbie! Barbie! Barbie!"

Tess and Tuesday looked at each other, and Felicia thought Tuesday looked a little spooked, but Tess's good humor was infectious.

As the singing started, Tess lip-synced it, dancing all the while, using classic ballet moves. Felicia snuck a peek at Kendra and burst out laughing. She was staring and they both laughed when Tuesday faked singing the perv guy in the song's part.

"C'mon Barbie, let's go party," Tuesday sang and did some strange Mutant Ninja Turtles kind of martial arts dance routine, acting as a counter to Tess.

Tess did a graceful kick high in the air and Felicia felt her eyes widen. That was a serious ballet move with a hint of Kung Fu. She heard the women behind her all singing along to the song. When it ended, everyone in the house was cheering and clapping.

Nathan walked over to them and put his hands on his hips.

"So *that's* what that song was about," he said, and both girls burst into laughter and hugged him. He shook his head. "All those nights I hear…" He stopped abruptly and looked at Felicia with resignation, and sighed. He didn't look at Kendra or Mari Sue. "Nuthin'," he said, and went over to Yasmin.

Kendra nudged her.

"You really *do* get him to blurt things out he normally wouldn't. Is that, like, a super power?"

Felicia laughed and told Houston to get their bill. She watched Yasmin pull Nathan out the door, Oshba and Phoebe casually walking behind them. She wondered where Oshba could possibly be concealing a firearm.

Houston came back and said it was all set. Felicia frowned at him.

"You didn't have to take care of it," she said. "I'm paying for Yasmin and the girls' dinners and I wanted to make the tip a good one."

"I didn't pay it," Huey corrected her. "Shanda said the bill's already paid."

"By whom?" Felicia said, and looked out the door in sudden comprehension. She *thought* Yasmin had been hurrying Nathan along.

"Did you pay our bill?" Kendra said, frowning. "You didn't need to do that."

"I didn't," Felicia said. "I think Yasmin did. I think she bought all of us dinner."

"I want you to let me give you some money for that bill," Mari Sue said, suddenly appearing beside them. "I thank you, but we can afford to pay our way."

"We didn't pay it, we think Yasmin did," Kendra said, and the woman frowned.

"She's just a kid, she can't afford to rack up these kind of bills on her credit cards," Mari Sue said, and Felicia's thoughts about Tuesday's mother climbed much higher.

"Ladies, Shanda told me that Yasmin paid your bills," Izzy told them, hearing what they were saying. "Don't worry about her being able to afford it. Her family rules the Arab Emirates, and she has her own software writing company. She just bought a three-million dollar house and paid cash for it. Trust me, she's not on a budget."

"Still…" Kendra said, and Felicia found herself nodding in agreement.

"I remember when Yasmin first showed up here in Key West," Izzy said, and smiled at the memory. "She was confident and bold on the outside, but absolutely terrified of being alone and not having anyone care if she lived or died. I think that's what it was like in her home."

Izzy looked sad for a moment.

"Bisexual girls don't do well in some countries. She's lucky she got out with exile, and not being married off, hung, or stoned to death. Nathan and the girls were the first people in her life that took her on face value and treated her like a person with feelings."

"She seems so sure of herself," Kendra said thoughtfully.

"She does, but inside there's this frightened little girl that wanted someone to like her, or maybe even love her, just for herself. Not for her family, her money, her beauty. Nathan fell for her in a big way in Mexico, but wouldn't let himself show his feelings because he had a commitment. Tess and Tuesday befriended her the first day, and they all helped her hide when the mercenaries came to kidnap her."

"We really need to talk to all three of these kids," Kendra said slowly. "I want to know more about these mercenaries."

"I was going to find out more details from Nathan. But the last two days have been so hectic, it slipped my mind," Felicia admitted.

"Mercenaries slipped your mind?" Kendra asked incredulously, and Felicia winced.

They both turned to stare at Izzy.

She shook her head, clearly annoyed with herself. "I'm cutting back," she muttered to herself, and Felicia laughed, despite the seriousness of the subject.

Izzy shook her head. "Anyway, the thing is, Yasmin feels she has a place in this world, and friends around her. I think she's actually enjoying life for the first time ever. She loves and respects your kids. And me? I think she was thanking all of you for doing such a good job raising them. And for accepting her without misgivings."

"Kids do the darnedest things," Mari Sue said, and led Bobbi Jo out the door.

They all stared after her, and then at each other.

"C'mon, or we'll never catch up to them," Kendra said, and Felicia nodded. Everyone else had already left, including their husbands, and they hurried after them. As they went out the door, Felicia turned and looked at Kendra.

"Yasmin is bisexual?"

Kendra grinned.

"And she's royalty. A real princess."

♦ ♦ ♦ ♦ ♦

Nathan sighed and rested his forehead on Yasmin's flat stomach. He looked up at her.

"They had a relapse," he said, and she laughed, and started singing along with the song playing in Tess and Tuesday's bedroom.

"I am a Barbie Girl…"

Nathan groaned and did the only thing he could think of to distract her. Yasmin gasped and her singing trailed off, although she did try for a line or two.

♦ ♦ ♦ ♦ ♦

He walked down Duval, knowing where he was headed. He did stop and try to look in the Bourbon Street Pub, but it was too busy. If he went in there, he'd have to talk to people. It looked to be part of the New Orleans House, and it was hopping.

He crossed the intersection and went into the 801 Bourbon Bar. He made his way into the back bar, bought a beer, and went into the open room next to the bathroom. There were a few more people than the night before, and he wondered how to show what he wanted.

It looked like that wasn't hard to figure out, because within a couple minutes a guy in his mid-twenties faced him and looked down. He gave a slight nod, and the man sank to his knees. He closed his eyes and concentrated on delaying his climax as long as he could.

Afterwards, the man zipped him up, and looked like he might be about to ask for the same in return.

He left without a word.

Tonight, he could settle himself down enough to recognize that he liked it, and would do it again. Maybe nothing more, but the combination of excitement and self-loathing wouldn't leave his thoughts as he walked down Duval.

Related Matters

Chapter Eleven

Tess woke, realized she didn't hear the alarm, and exhaled heavily in frustration. She looked at her clock, and saw it was still six minutes until the alarm would go off. She gave in, turned it off, and rolled out of bed. At some point in the night she vaguely remembered waking up cold, and putting a flannel pajama top on.

After using the bathroom, she checked on Nathan and Yasmin. For a change, Yasmin had her arm around Nathan, and his face was pressed against her breast. His arm was around her waist, his other kind of pinned between them.

They were out like a light, and Tess was careful as she closed the door, so not to disturb them. She poured herself a cup of coffee and walked out onto the patio. It wasn't cold, but it was definitely cooler than she was used to. She drank about half of the cup, and decided that swimming would warm her as fast as anything, tossed her pajama top on a chair and got to it.

She was well over half done with her laps when Tuesday came running into view. She was wearing her usual, short shorts and a sports bra, which she pulled off as she ran alongside the pool.

She gave a wolf whistle to Tess and kept right on going into the patio area, and then into the apartment. Sarah walked around the corner of the house right about as Tuesday came busting back out the door, naked.

Tuesday high-fived Sarah, rinsed just long enough to say she did it, and was wading to an empty lane as fast as she could.

"It was brisk this morning," Tuesday said to Tess, and started swimming her laps with a passion. Tess finished a couple minutes later and came out of the pool, grabbing the towel Sarah tossed to her. She hurriedly dried off and put the top back on.

Tess eyed her coffee with distain. If only…

Answering her unspoken prayer, Yasmin walked out of the apartment with a tray containing a china coffee pot and four matching cups. She poured a cup, handed it to Tess, nodding her head forward as she did, poured a second for Sarah, repeated the action, and then poured herself a cup.

Tess didn't bother checking to see if she'd put cream in hers. Yasmin knew how they all took their coffee, and took great pride in preparing and serving it to them.

"We missed you at Diane Isis last night, Sarah," Tess said, looking at her curiously. "I thought you had Mondays off?"

"I usually do," Sarah admitted, taking a sip. She looked at the cup appreciatively. "This is really good coffee, Yasmin."

"Thank you, Sarah," Yasmin said, nodding to her.

"Mariah wanted to go to Diane Isis with Aurora, so we switched days," Sarah said, and Tess was curious about the suddenly solemn expression on her face.

"That is good, Sarah," Yasmin said. "Since you were working, Nathan could come see you, so you could chat. I know you both value the opportunity to spend time together."

Sarah looked at Yasmin with a quizzical expression on her face.

"He's my best friend," she said simply, "Thanks for being so understanding about that."

"I have only recently come to fully understand how important good friendships are," Yasmin admitted. "I am glad you share this bond."

Tess stared at them. She and Yasmin both knew how close Sarah and Nathan were, and Tess had seen the sexual tension between them while Yasmin was visiting friends in Finland the first two weeks of December. It happened to be when Sarah's fiancé dumped her, and Nathan had been a life-saver to her. In fact, she'd stayed with them, and shared Nathan's bed for about a week while she found a new place to live.

Somehow, they'd kept their feelings under control, and there had been no weak moments. At least, none that resulted in sex. Tess decided to shift the conversation to a safer topic.

"Sarah, do you think Aurora and Mariah would like to come over for Christmas Day dinner? You know how much food we'll have, and they're part of the gang."

"Aurora will be at her aunties, Christmas Day," Sarah said, and there was a sadness in her voice. "And I'm afraid Mariah didn't make the cut. I heard them talking this morning when I got up."

"Oh, is she okay?" Tess asked, feeling sad for the girl.

Mariah would be the first to say she wasn't a lesbian or even bisexual, but she'd felt something towards Aurora, and had turned out to be an easy conquest for the Italian girl. She'd looked very uncomfortable around anyone other than Aurora the first week, but Jess had watched her relax, as she realized she enjoyed her relationship with *this* woman, bisexual or not.

Unfortunately, Aurora had a track record of breaking hearts. None of her first conquests since arriving from Italy had lasted even a week, and everyone had been surprised to see her and Mariah still acting as a couple, after two weeks had passed. But that, apparently, was now history.

"If you get a chance, can you tell Mariah she's invited to spend Christmas with us? You know the details. And tell her Robbi is invited, too."

"For the day, or do you want them to arrive later on, like Nico and Lori Lynn do?" Sarah asked.

"Their choice. You know what to tell them. They're invited for the day, and it's up to them, as far as what they want to do."

"I'll tell them," Sarah said. She looked around. "We stretching today?"

"Yes we are," Tess said, suddenly feeling exhilarated. "Let's get this show on the road."

"What about the aerobics class?" Sarah asked. "You're out of school until after New Year's, right?"

"You're right," Tess admitted. She looked at Yasmin. "You up for both, Yasmin?"

"Certainly," she said. "I have no pressing engagements."

"Let's get at it, then," Tess said, and they took their final sips of coffee and stood.

♦ ♦ ♦ ♦ ♦

Nico absentmindedly sipped his coffee from McDonald's. He resisted the urge to make a face. He wondered when he got so damned picky about coffee. For most of his life, he'd drunk black coffee, and could care less where it came from, what brand, whether it was piping hot, cold, or lukewarm.

Of course, he knew exactly when he started getting picky. It had been when he and Lori Lynn started partnering up, because his old partner Latrelle Harper was trying to track down and map a system of cameras around the city to try and catch a serial killer. Lori Lynn started going with Nico when he was pursuing a lead, or just hanging around Old Town, hoping to be in the right place when something happened that would lead them to the killer.

He and Lori Lynn began getting coffee and donuts almost every day. She was *very* picky, and the more he was exposed to good coffee, the more he started caring about the details.

Away, witch, he thought, smiling to himself. You have made these things matter.

He looked at his notes, and the stack of photos of the sites Geoffrey Neilson had installed hidden cameras. He dug through the stack and pulled out several of the woman that killed him for his troubles.

He stared at them for a minute, pulled a magnifying glass from a drawer of his desk, and carefully looked at every inch of her, on both photos. Then he turned to his computer, pulled the short clips of the woman walking from the Neilson file, and watched the one of her walking towards Neilson's house. A home security camera caught her walking by the house. He reran it four or five times, trying to decide if the gait of the woman was at all familiar.

Then he watched the other five second clip of her returning to her vehicle, same camera. Again, other than the fact that it looked like it *might* be the international assassin known as "The Fox," he couldn't be sure if he recognized the way she walked because he knew her, or because he'd seen the video clip several hundred times, at this point.

He turned at the sound of the door opening, and Lori Lynn came bustling in. She carried a coffee holder with two large cups, and something in a paper bag.

"I'm expanding your horizons," she said crisply, and set one of the coffees in front of him. She pulled the extra chair at the end of his desk over from her desk and sat, setting the bag down between them. "This is from El Mocho, over on Maloney Avenue. Café con Leche, y Croquetas de Jamon."

"Isn't that place a dive?" Nico asked, sniffing the coffee with trepidation. He didn't usually drink coffee with cream or milk, but it was clearly still steaming hot, and smelled pretty good.

"It's…unpretentious," Lori Lynn said primly. "Merry Christmas Eve Morning."

"Thank you," Nico said, looking in the bag. He tried to decide what the little rolls were, and took a whiff. Whatever it was smelled pretty good, even if it wasn't a donut or some other kind of sweet pastry. "What are Croquetas de Jamon? And who *is* Jamon?"

"Jamon is ham," Lori Lynn said, staring at him as if to decide if he was pulling her leg. She set a couple paper towels down on his desk, and he removed one of the croquetas. He looked at the paper towel and then at her, and raised an eyebrow as he bit into the fried ball.

"They're very, very fresh, and might be a little…" Lori Lynn began, and tried not to laugh as he started inhaling hard, trying to cool his mouth. He lifted his coffee and saw the steam still rising from it, grabbed his original coffee, which had cooled down, and took a gulp and let it swish around his mouth for a minute before swallowing.

"...hot," she finished, and smiled at him sweetly. "So, you look like you've been here a while. What are you obsessing about that made you get up early?"

Nico swallowed finally, and just breathed for a moment. He looked at the other half of the croqueta on his paper towel cautiously. "That might have tasted good," he admitted.

Lori Lynn blew on hers, and nibbled on one side. She closed her eyes and smiled.

"Yummy for the tummy," she said, and Nico snorted. As he slowly ate the other half, she looked at what he had spread on his desk as she spoke. "So, have we got an I.D. for the John Doe yet?"

She frowned as she recognized the pictures.

"You back to this again?" she asked. "You have an active case, so working on cold cases isn't necessarily the best use of your time."

Nico winced, recognizing a bit of Lori Lynn the cranky department head emerging.

"We've established from the tats that he's Russian, but his fingers aren't in any of our databases, and facial recognition didn't give us anything. That might be because the nibbling fishies didn't leave us a good photo op, or he might just not be in there."

"Did you...?" Lori Lynn began, and Nico continued with his update, staring at her.

"I sent his prints off to the FBI, along with pictures of his tats and face, but I haven't heard back from them yet."

"Drink some more coffee and have a Snickers bar," Lori Lynn said crisply, then relented. "Sorry I interrupted you. It's a bad habit I'm trying to break."

"Don't be sorry," Nico said, feeling guilty that her attempt to cut in actually *had* annoyed him. He knew she had little patience with dawdling, and that one of her favorite sayings was "Cut to the chase."

"When did you send them everything?" Lori Lynn asked, and he noted she was being careful to not sound aggressive.

"Early yesterday morning, when our computer told us to go fish," Nico admitted. "I called back a few minutes ago, and they said we might not get a response before Thursday, what with tomorrow being Christmas and all."

"Curse these family holidays and HR, keeping us from overworking everyone to death," Lori Lynn said in a deadpan voice, and then they both grinned. She put her hand on his arm. "I didn't mean to get impatient. You don't need motivation, or shoving. So, any ideas?"

Annette walked in, closely followed by Latrelle, Gary, and Chris.

"Hey, Partner," Nico said, and Annette nodded back at him. She had a big, flat Tupperware container, and after stashing her other things, opened it to show rows of cookies, four different kinds.

"Ooh, I love the holidays," Nico said, and looked at them. He started to reach in for a peanut butter blossom, and she snapped the lid back on, just missing catching his fingers. "Whoa, what the…?"

"These are for the Christmas lunch today," Annette said primly, and set the container down out of his reach. Behind her, Chris Anderson, Lori Lynn's partner, reached out stealthily, and his hand snatched back quickly as she pulled a police baton out of somewhere, and tapped it on the table top, very close to his fingers. "Doan be raiding my cookie jar, dude," she said casually.

She reached into her backpack and pulled another container out, a good-sized round metal tin. She pried the lid off and set it down on the desk.

"These are for us."

"Are those Snickerdoodles?" Lori Lynn asked, and picked up two at Annette's nod. "I was told to eat a Snickers."

Annette leaned forward to watch Nico take a Snickerdoodle and a peanut butter blossom.

"Aren't we getting bold?" she said, and sat down at her desk, which was backed up to his.

Nico frowned at Lori Lynn, who was looking up at the ceiling, smiling.

"*I* was the one told to have a Snickers," he said, and shrugged. "Whatever."

Latrelle Harper, his old partner, took a peanut butter blossom and a chocolate chip cookie, followed by his partner, Gary Yurke, who took two oatmeal cookies. Everyone stared at him. He flinched under the flood of attention, but stood his ground.

"I like oatmeal," he muttered.

"He's just a regular kinda guy," Latrelle muttered, and everyone except Gary smiled.

Chris eyed Annette cautiously as he reached into the tin. He flinched as she pulled a taser out of one of her drawers, but carefully selected two chocolate chip cookies.

"I like simple," he said, feeling everyone's eyes on him. Nico liked him, and thought he showed great promise, once he got some experience. He'd been a Sheriff's deputy for Monroe County before applying for de-

180

tective. Detective work was quite a bit different from being a uniformed deputy. It took a different mindset.

As the others went to their desks to log in, and get up to speed on the day, Nico reached into the bag from El Mocho and, after carefully checking to make sure it had cooled some, popped another croqueta into his mouth. Sure enough, it was ham, along with some other things, and quite tasty.

Lori Lynn watched him as she nibbled on a snickerdoodle. She set it down and got one of the fried balls from the bag and bit into it.

"I forgot about these," she admitted. "Sugar always did have an unnatural hold on me. Where were we, regarding the dead Russian?"

"His throat was slashed, from ear to ear, as the pirates say," Nico said, picturing the corpse. "His face was a little mutilated, as if the murderer slashed and stuck him several times in the face, before giving him his second smile."

"*That* is gross," Lori Lynn said, wrinkling her nose. "You thinking the Columbians?"

"It would make sense," Nico admitted. "The Columbians are bringing all these drugs to the states. Hell, over half of what they bring in goes right on to Europe. The local Russian mob has a pipeline from Europe to here, and back, as well. They're probably trying to horn in on the second leg of the trip, and the Columbians don't want to play with them."

Nico paused, thinking. He absentmindedly ate another croqueta and took a large sip of his coffee. He frowned.

"What is it?" Lori Lynn asked. She watched him closely, and Nico hesitated. He saw that Annette was listening to every word, even as she casually leaned forward to peek into the bag. Lori Lynn nodded for her to try one. Then she turned back to Nico. "I know that look. What's the problem with our hypothesis?"

"Hypothesis?" Nico asked, smiling.

"Bite me," Lori Lynn said, and Annette began choking on her coffee. "What's running through that twisted mind of yours?"

"All kinds of things," Nico admitted. "But something feels too easy about this. Okay, we have a dead Ruskie, and everything about the method screams Columbians at work. If I'm the Columbians, I don't know that I want to sign this job. It catches our attention, we automatically assume Columbians, we start snooping around their action, digging into things. Heck, they have from here to South America to ditch that body. Why put it in the water where the tides and normal weather conditions almost guarantee it's going to wash up on our beach?"

"Maybe as a warning to the Russians," Annette said slowly. "Maybe they don't care if we know about it. With budget cutbacks, on us, city, the state, hell, even the feds are cutting back on their operations, the coast guard is stretched thin. Why should they worry what we think?"

Nico and Lori Lynn looked at each other, and she shrugged. "She has a point."

"I don't like it," Nico said. "That screw-up by those idiots that were running the money-laundering last spring cost them a pretty bundle. Right now, they don't want hassles, extra expenses, like upping the bribes, covering losses, bringing in more gunslingers. This seems sloppy and foolish, and the Columbians are neither. I think they would have left something with the Russians identifying the dead dude, and the body would be somewhere south of the Cayman Islands by now."

"What's your plan?" Lori Lynn asked, and Nico shrugged.

"I thought I'd send Annette alone to confront them, accuse them of a lot of different things. To calm them down, she could take some of her oatmeal cookies to placate them. We're keeping the good stuff for ourselves."

Annette's head shot up and she stared at Nico a moment, and then grinned sheepishly.

"Touche," she said, taking a bite out of her own oatmeal cookie. "By the way, even if you don't like oatmeal cookies, you try one of mine, you'll change your mind."

"I figure we wait for the autopsy, see if there are any surprises, and then start bugging the FBI for the results of their search." Nico watched Lori Lynn for her reaction. "I don't want to talk with the Russians before I know who the dead guy is."

Lori Lynn nodded her approval. She gave him a speculative look.

"Okay, so that's on the backburner for a few hours, or a day or so. Tell me more about your thoughts about the Fox."

"Ooh, I wouldn't mind hearing about that," Annette said, and leaned back in her chair with her coffee. She felt Lori Lynn's eyes on her and slowly brought the chair upright again, took a sip of coffee, set the cup down, and pulled a notepad from a drawer and wrote something at the top of the first page.

"There's not that much to tell," Nico stated slowly, letting what he knew run through his head. "I know Oshba Salehi has an ironclad alibi. There is no way she could have killed Geoffrey Neilson. But it feels like her work,"

"How so?" Lori Lynn asked.

"First, if you look at the still pictures, or the five second clips, the Fox is about her size. She has stiletto heels on, so you can't get a firm estimate. But she's about Oshba's size and build. She's athletic and a martial artist. We know the perp took Neilson down with one very sophisticated kick to the side of his head. We know Oshba can do that in her sleep, according to Mari."

"You asked Mari about this?" Annette looked shocked, and Nico saw Lori Lynn grin at her reaction.

"Sure," Nico said. "Since Lori…uh, since I've been going to Captain Eddie's, I've gotten to know most of the people at the Sunday night Little table pretty well. And I already knew all the Littles from years ago. She's sparred with Oshba. She said that reverse flying roundhouse kick would be simple for her."

Nico opened a drawer and took out a file. He didn't open it at first.

"I've been researching the Fox for quite a while, and have studied all the different ways she's killed people, or all the ailments people have died from around her, and tried to figure out how she would have done it. Most of that information is very hard to come by."

Nico took a gulp of his coffee, which was now cool.

"I've also tried to research Oshba's background, and it wasn't any easier." Nico looked at Lori Lynn, then at Annette. He had their complete attention, although Lori Lynn looked a little distressed. "Look, I don't want it to be Oshba. I would almost rather never solve it than have it turn out to be her. She saved our lives when we caught the Fantasy Fest serial killer couple. The husband had us dead to rights, and she took him out with a thrown knife. From about twenty yards. With her left hand."

"That's a good throw," Annette said, and Nico nodded.

"From what I've been able to put together, Oshba was four or five when her tribe got mostly wiped out by the Houthi in Yemen. They raised her to be a terrorist from the start. When she was eight, she was put into a youth brigade, and her life was nothing but learning ways to kill people. She also got training in unarmed combat, and learned quite a little list of styles."

"Mari has sparred with her a couple times," Lori Lynn admitted. "She says she could take Oshba, but it would be the toughest fight she ever had. Since Oshba doesn't stick with one style or school, she's totally unpredictable." Lori Lynn smiled. "She also said that if it was a real fight, Oshba would probably cheat and use knives. In a fight to the death, Mari actually said she wasn't convinced she'd win."

"Mari said someone was a better fighter than she is?" Annette stared.

"No, she said she thought Oshba would cheat and use knives, because she was trained to survive, to do the maximum damage she could, and any moral issues wouldn't even occur to her."

"And yet she's so in love with that girl, Phoebe," Annette said wonderingly. "Around her, she's the doting girlfriend, and treats Phoebe like she's a princess."

"Maybe to her, Phoebe *is* a princess," Nico said, and shrugged. "Maybe with Phoebe, she is redeeming herself for all the things she's had to do to survive. Or because she was ordered to by a superior officer."

"How did she ever get out of that life?" Annette asked, looking sad.

"That I know," Nico said heavily. "After a successful strike against a Saudi Army unit, her superior officer took her back to his quarters and wanted to have sex with her. When she refused, he slapped her and tried to rape her."

"I know where *this* is going," Annette said quietly.

"You got it," Nico agreed. "She killed him, cut some, uh, *parts* off him, and fled the camp. Part of her own unit pursued her from Yemen into Oman, back into Yemen, across a good-sized hunk of Saudi Arabia, where she finally ditched them, and she eventually ended up in Bahrain. She joined a security company providing many services to corporations, eventually got partnered with Nadezhda Ahmadi."

"Nadi," Annette said, nodding.

"Nadi," Nico agreed. "She kind of took Oshba under her wing, they developed into a topnotch security team, and eventually got their contract bought by the al Nahyan tribe. Because they were women, they were tasked with guarding some of the children of the royal family. When Yasmin went to Europe for school, they were assigned to her. They've been with her ever since."

"Nico, I see what you mean about how similar she is to the Fox, but I want to show you something." Lori Lynn had been going through the file Nico had compiled for the Fox, as well as video compilations of the assassin going through airports, walking down streets, anywhere she'd been caught on camera that she'd been recognized. "Picture Oshba walking through the Diane Isis with Phoebe last night, or coming and going at Eddie's."

"Okay," Nico said, and began to run those occasions through his head.

"Now, watch the Fox here on the screen," Lori Lynn said, pointing to his computer monitor. She'd shifted her chair around while Nico was talking and he hadn't even noticed.

All three of them watched the woman on the screen stroll down a side street in Florence, Italy, then going in and out of a bank in Switzerland. The file had her passing through about two dozen camera views, all over Europe, and even in Japan and Hong Kong.

"Okay, they both move very smoothly," Nico said, and tried to see what she was picking up on. "They both walk very confidently, and with grace. They both look like athletes. Hmm. The Fox usually has spiked heels on, and Oshba hardly ever wears them. In fact…"

Nico paused, knowing he was missing something right there, but he couldn't come up with it. Then he got it, smiled, and looked at Lori Lynn, who nodded in satisfaction.

"You and I are the only ones who would know this," she said and Nico conceded she was right.

"The Fox looks like she was born in heels, could go up steps in them. In fact, there is one eight second clip where she *does* go up steps, in Rome. After you and I got shot, and Oshba killed Randy Sheldon, she used the *same* kick on Vicky Sheldon as the Fox used on Neilson. That was one of the details that kept sticking in my mind. The vision was so strong, I forgot about a few other details.

"Oshba was naked and barefoot at the time. When she put her thong and her shoes on, you asked if her heels were comfortable," Lori Lynn said, putting her hand on his arm.

"And she shook her head no," Nico said exultantly. "I remember noticing she could walk fine, but that she didn't look very natural in them. She clearly hadn't grown up wearing heels to social events, and certainly not to do reverse crescent kicks with."

"It's not conclusive," Lori Lynn admitted, and Nico shook his head.

"It might as well be," he said. "Oh, I'm not abandoning her as a suspect, but between her ironclad alibi, her different moving style, her lack of experience with heels, she's barely registering on my charts now. And I'm glad."

"I am too," Lori Lynn said and sighed. "I would feel just awful for Phoebe if we ended up having to arrest her girlfriend. It's the only relationship she's ever been in."

"That either of them have probably ever been in," Nico added, and both women nodded solemnly.

All three of them stared at the video playing of the Fox caught on camera.

"Oshba moves with more of a power stride," Annette said, and both the others nodded.

"I think she's probably more muscular than the Fox, the more I think about it," Nico admitted. "She has those amazing six pack abs, and even though she doesn't look like she carries a lot of muscle weight, she's got a lot of muscles."

"Yes, she's an athlete, whereas the Fox looks more like a dancer," Lori Lynn said, her eyes on the video. "There's one place where the Fox turns around, and it is so graceful. It's the kind of turn a dancer would make."

Nico and Lori Lynn looked at each other.

"Oshba's an athlete, the Fox is a dancer." Nico stated it as fact, not as a question.

"Right," Lori Lynn agreed, excitement in her voice. "So, we have an assassin that started off doing girlie things, ballet, perhaps cheerleader or majorette, and then at some point begins to apply herself to becoming an athlete, as well as a martial artist."

"And a specialist in poisons, explosives, traps, a marksman, probably with most weapons," Nico added. "One of her confirmed kills was a single shot from over three thousand meters."

"That's almost two miles," Annette said in awe.

"One point eight six miles, to be precise," he said, and Lori Lynn slapped his arm.

"Quit showing off," she said, and Nico snorted. He thought about what they'd just discussed.

"So why did she start off as a dancer, and then suddenly become an assassin?" Nico asked. "And she didn't just switch. She would have, at some point, had to change her lifestyle from dance and the arts, to athletics, including martial arts, and eventually a plethora of other skills for killing people."

"Maybe when she hit puberty, she realized she was gay," Annette said. "At that point, she puts away her Barbies, and starts playing sports."

"And then she finds she likes Barbies after all, but not Kens," Nico continued, and Lori Lynn slapped his arm again, harder this time.

"Please don't get yourself sent to detention and have to watch those HR videos. I need you working, not watching TV."

"Yeah, yeah," Nico said, and Annette laughed.

"*I* thought it was funny," she said, and Nico snorted.

"Suck up."

♦ ♦ ♦ ♦ ♦

"We need a waitress," Huey said, and Bob nodded his agreement. Felicia looked at Kendra and winked.

"What a sexist thing to say," she said, and stared at her husband. "Huey, especially in this town, it could just as easily be a waiter. Or are you trying to delegate all women to the service industry?"

The four of them were sitting by the pool at the bed and breakfast next door to their own. The Key West Bed & Breakfast didn't have a pool of its own, but had an agreement with their neighbors to allow access to theirs.

"C'mon, you know I'm not," Huey protested. "But waitresses are a lot easier on the eyes, and..." His voice trailed off as he recognized the trap he was in. He sighed. "What would you like?"

"Sitting out here in the sun, I think a nice white wine is the best choice," Felicia said brightly. "I bought some this morning, and there are two in the refrigerator in the kitchen downstairs. Don't forget to either open them or bring a corkscrew."

"I know you bought the wine," Houston said shortly. "Don't you remember who carried it back? I do tend to remember things like carrying a case of wine across town."

"You might want to put a couple more bottles to chill while you're getting those," Felicia pointed out. "Oh, and do we have any more of those jars of mixed nuts we bought in Georgia, on the way down here?"

"Just Bob and I," Huey said with resignation. He sighed and stood up, slipping his feet in his sandals.

"I'll give you a hand," Bob said.

"Don't forget to bring four of those plastic cups," Kendra called out and nudged Felicia. "Well played."

"I could just ask him to do it, but what's the fun in that," Felicia said, smiling, and Kendra laughed, then looked pensive.

"I'm glad Nathan moved here and got to know the girls." She sat back in her lounger. "This is a lot more fun with you and Huey. If it was just us and the Dumarests, it would be kind of grim."

"Tell me about it." Felicia looked at her new friend with sympathy. "The youngest boy is nice, Bobbi Jo has mellowed out, and Mari Sue is alright when Jackie isn't around. But he and his two oldest boys are a pain in the ass. We're glad we're here, and we got your back."

Felicia bit her lip. "I'm just glad Nathan seems to be doing so well. He was a mess at the beginning of the year, and we were hoping he'd stay in Kalamazoo after he graduated, or maybe move to East Lansing or Ann Arbor."

"University towns," Kendra noted, and Felicia nodded.

"He fits in well in a more enlightened environment. Key West caught us by surprise. It's a tourist trap, and so far away. And it's so chaotic. He was very fragile when he moved here. We didn't hear from him for almost two weeks, and were about to call the local authorities." Felicia's voice caught with emotion, and she didn't speak for a minute.

Kendra reached over and took her hand.

"He seems to be doing well," she pointed out. "The three of them are as tight as I've ever seen any roommates be. And he *is* dating what might well be the most beautiful girl in Florida." She hesitated. "You and Houston have made several references to last year, and something happening that had a huge influence on him. Were you afraid he might hurt himself? He seems very level-headed."

"He is," Felicia said heavily. "But he's always been kind of reticent. Oh, when he's on stage, he's the ultimate showman. But watch after he finishes and as time passes, he kind of retreats back into his shell. Except when he's around Tess and Tuesday. The three of them are…"

"Dy-no-mite!" Kendra finished for her, mimicking Tuesday's way of exaggerating her speech. She looked at Felicia. "What happened last year? Both the girls know, but wouldn't tell me."

Felicia looked at her friend, and opened her mouth. Huey and Bob picked that moment to show back up, carrying an insulated cooler, and a plastic bag. In no time, everyone had their wine, and were passing the mixed nuts around.

"I was just about to tell Kendra about why we were worried about Nathan moving down here," Felicia said, and Huey didn't look particularly surprised.

"Tess and Tuesday already know," he pointed out. "If Kendra has half your superpowers, she'll get Tess to blurt it out before she leaves anyway."

"Good point," Felicia admitted. She looked at Kendra, then at Bob. "Nathan had a gig last year on December 28th. It was a Friday, and at a neighborhood pub. He got there early, had dinner, and after his gig, loaded his car up, and headed home."

Huey exhaled heavily, his eyes distant, as Felicia spoke.

"It had been unseasonably warm that day, and after dark, it began to get quite a bit colder." Felicia felt Kendra's hand creep back into hers and she gripped it tight. "What Nathan didn't know was, while he was inside, there was a light, but steady rain, just before dark. So when it got cold, the rain turned to ice."

"And then it started snowing," Huey said, and Felicia nodded.

"We got about four inches, which is no big deal, normally," she said. "Nathan has snow tires, he's driven in bad weather, which this wasn't, really, and he's a very good driver. Confident, but not careless."

"He had an accident," Bob said, and flinched as Kendra swatted him on the arm. "Uh, sorry."

"He barely got out of the parking lot, was making a turn, and his tires lost traction. The car began to slide across the road." Felicia's voice cracked a little, and she cleared her throat and took a sip of wine. "He tried tapping on the brakes, then applying gas, but the road was like an ice rink under the layer of snow. The car slid across the road, and Nathan told us he could see he was going to hit the cars parallel parked across the street. He wasn't even moving all that fast. But he couldn't get any control of the car."

She stopped talking and took another sip. Kendra and Bob were listening with concern, but Huey had his eyes closed, and Felicia could see his lower lip tremble.

"A woman stepped out between two cars, and didn't see Nathan's car sliding towards her," Felicia said with a strained voice. "She was really still just a girl, Nathan's age. In fact, he told us he dated her when they were freshmen, but it never developed into anything serious."

She stopped talking, and Kendra gently squeezed her hand.

"Nathan's car hit her?" she asked gently.

Felicia closed her eyes and nodded. "It hit her, pinning her and her baby against her own truck. She was talking on the phone, carrying the baby in the other arm, and the car pinned her against the truck, bounced off it, and she and the baby fell on the icy road."

"Oh my god," Kendra breathed.

"Nathan's car kind of fishtailed a little as it bounced off, and the left rear tire ran over them both again, before it stopped with them pinned against her own truck." Felicia closed her eyes. She went to take another sip, but set the glass down instead.

"How bad were they hurt?" Bob asked hesitantly, and Huey shook his head despondently.

"The mother fell on the baby, and the doctors think it caused the baby's head to hit the road hard. The baby died immediately. The mother had internal injuries, and her baby dying seemed to take the life out of her. According to Nathan," she finished somberly. "She just seemed to slip away, and died two days later."

"Poor Nathan," Kendra said sadly. "Even in the few days we've known him, it's clear he's a very sensitive person, and having any part in their deaths had to be devastating."

Bob cleared his throat uneasily. Felicia took one look at him and knew the question he wanted to ask. For an instant, her temper flared, but she sat quietly, until she got her breathing back under control. Nathan had been a college student, leaving a bar. It was a reasonable question, and of course, the police would have asked it immediately.

"He had one glass of wine, through the course of the evening," she said evenly, not looking at Bob. "What with his having dinner, playing the gig for four hours, and the pub confirming he only had the one, not to mention he blew a very low number, and was nowhere near the legal limit, the police, and then the district attorney said alcohol wasn't a factor."

Related Matters

"I'm glad for his sake," Kendra said quietly, and Bob nodded his agreement, relief showing on his face. "He's a good boy, with a good heart. I suppose he blamed himself anyway."

"He argued with the police, and then the D.A.," Huey said heavily. "He said he was tired from finals, a long semester, playing gigs, and it probably made the drink affect him more than they suspected. He insisted he was guilty, of manslaughter, at the very least."

There was a long silence as Felicia watched Kendra and Bob look stunned, stare at each other, and then at them.

"That is...extraordinary," Bob finally said. "What did the authorities say?"

"The pub is a very popular one, and there was a good number of people in the parking lot, or driving towards it, and everyone questioned said he was driving very slowly and carefully. He did all the correct things to try and regain control of the car. It was just a freak of conditions and circumstances. Nathan was totally exonerated."

"Thank god for that," Kendra said in heartfelt relief. She looked at Felicia with concern on her face. "Did he get some help?"

"The judge finally told him to see a psychologist from a court approved list. He told me later that Nathan was so adamant that he needed to be punished, it seemed like a good way to appease him *and* get him the help he needed." Felicia sniffed and pulled a tissue out of her beach bag. She dabbed her eyes and smiled wanly at Kendra, and then Bob. "Nathan went to her for three months, he quit drinking at any gig he had to drive home from, and lost about fifteen pounds."

"He's not a husky kid," Bob said. "I wouldn't think he had fifteen pounds to lose."

"Towards the end of the semester, he started eating a little better, and got some of that weight back," Felicia said, and frowned. "He's still thinner than he needs to be, but Key West seems to agree with his health. He looks good."

"Judging from the expressions on some of the females in his audiences, he looks better than good to some of them," Bob said dryly, and they all smiled.

"He always could attract girls with his voice," Felicia admitted. "I remember telling him a couple years ago that he had an advantage, and with great power comes great responsibility. If he treated any girls around him poorly, it would get back to me."

"And there would be hell to pay," Houston said dryly. "Like me, Nathan totally believed every word."

They all laughed at that, but then they sat for a while, mostly silent and introspective.

"He's surrounded himself with very good people," Bob pointed out, and everyone nodded their agreement. "Time is really the only cure for such a tragedy."

"Are you worried that his attraction to Yasmin is in reaction to the accident?" Kendra asked, and Felicia thought about it.

"Not exactly," she said. "But I can't help but notice he's moved to a community where he almost never needs to drive anywhere. He has a decent SUV, better than that piece of crap Volvo he used to own, but I haven't seen any sign that he ever even drives it. Maybe to the grocery store."

"Tess pointed out Fausto's as where they do most of their shopping," Kendra said. "They walk right by it every day, going to work, and coming home."

"I hope Yasmin didn't buy it for him," Felicia said. "According to Izzy, she could afford to, but I know my son well enough to know he'd feel obligated by that."

"I don't know how he could afford to buy another SUV, with how expensive it is to live here," Huey said, and grinned. "But I have a sneaking suspicion that if she'd bought it for him, it would be a Lexus, not a Buick."

"Good point," Felicia noted.

"On an unrelated note," Kendra began, and they all looked at her as she paused for a moment. "It's Christmas Eve, and we have three families to try and fit into one restaurant."

"And all three kids insist on working their shifts until eight or nine, because they're too danged loyal and dependable to tell their bosses they need Christmas Eve off on one day's notice," Bob said dryly.

"Who taught these kids such good work ethics, anyway?" Huey demanded to know.

"Hoisted by our own petard," Felicia said idly. She grinned at them. "I always wanted to say that."

"That's fifteen people, once the kids join us," Kendra pointed out. "Sixteen or seventeen with Yasmin and one of her ladies. Where can we hope to seat seventeen people together on this short notice?"

"I was thinking about that," Huey said slowly, not looking at his wife. "I noticed two places on Duval, not all that far from Captain Eddie's, or the docks."

"I hope it's not Sloppy Joe's," Felicia said. "It'll be too chaotic, and I'd like to be where we can sit and have a drink or two, waiting for our kids, and then have a good meal, without feeling rushed to get in, get out."

"What about the Hard Rock Café?" Huey asked hopefully, and Felicia couldn't hide her grin. He'd made it clear the first night he wanted to go there. "And if they're too busy, there is a place right across the street, almost, called Caroline's Café. Lots of outdoor seating."

"I don't know about lots, but certainly enough," Kendra agreed.

"I'll call the Hard Rock and see if we can reserve something," Bob said, picking up his phone. He winked at Huey. "Good choice. I've been eyeing that place too."

Felicia sighed and leaned back to relax, and let the boys work it out. She felt worn out by telling them about Nathan's accident, but she was glad she'd done it. Kendra and Bob felt like lifelong friends already, and it had only been three days. She felt her hand get squeezed and realized she and Kendra were still holding hands. She looked at her questioningly.

"Thank you for sharing," Kendra said, sympathy in her eyes. "It helps us understand Nathan so much more, and his sharing that story with Tess and Tuesday is a clear sign that their friendship is strong and will endure."

"I'm glad we met," Felicia admitted, and returned the hand squeeze.

"BFFs for life," Kendra said, leaning back in her own chair.

"BFFs for life," Felicia agreed. They both took a sip of their wine in a toast to each other.

Neither of them showed any inclination to release the other's hand.

◆ ◆ ◆ ◆ ◆ ◆

He walked into the 801 Bourbon Bar and was a little surprised to see it was fairly busy. He thought most people would be home, or somewhere else on Christmas Eve. But there were maybe thirty people in the back bar area. He looked in the room by the bathroom, but it was empty.

Frustrated, he went to the bar and ordered a beer. It *was* Christmas Eve. Maybe people had more willpower on such a major holiday. Maybe the guilt bothered them enough to avoid the room.

He felt someone sit on the stool next to him. He looked over and thought the man looked familiar. He was handsome, in a faggy sort of way. The man looked at him and smiled. He nodded, as if confirming something.

"I saw you at work a few days ago," he said. "You're cute."

"Thanks," he said, not knowing what else to say.

"Ah, the strong, silent type," the man said, and put his hand on his leg. He gasped at the sudden rush. "I saw you look in the foyer when you came in." He smiled and leaned closer so their faces were very close. "Were you looking for something in particular?"

"Maybe," he somehow managed to say. The words were hard to form, and his voice sounded hoarse to him.

"Maybe, we should go and see if anyone else is there," the man said, and he nodded without speaking. He was breathing heavily, and could feel the blood rushing through him. A lot of it was gathering in one place in particular.

The man took his hand and led him back to what he'd called the foyer. He didn't know why he let this man hold his hand, except he was gorgeous. He was very fit, his hair immaculate, and as they turned to face each other, he saw the man's lips were full, and moist.

The man leaned towards him and he wanted to back away. He didn't kiss men, but he let it happen. And then they were holding each other as they kissed. He felt the man's hands run around his body, hinting at approaching his crotch, only to move away. He realized the man was now cupping his ass cheeks in both hands as they kissed, but didn't stop him.

Finally, the man brought his hands up to gently push him back a step. Then the man reached down and unzipped his own pants, pulling his dick out. He felt his eyes widen as he realized what the man wanted.

The man wanted *him* to go to his knees and take it into his mouth. But he didn't do that. He was here to *get* a blowjob, not to *give* one. As that thought dominated his mind, he felt himself sink to his knees and stare at how huge it was. And it didn't even look hard yet.

He decided to leave, but touched it with one hand, rubbing it and taking it in his hand. He was going to climb to his feet, he swore, as he leaned forward and kissed it, then took it into his mouth.

The man held his head in his hands and guided him in a motion that made it easier to please the man.

His mind felt as if it was on disconnect as the penis hardened, and he continued to let the man's hands guide him, following the man's directions on how to keep his teeth from nicking him. Despite the obvious signs, he was still shocked when it erupted in his mouth, and wanted to pull away, even as he kept his mouth in place, somehow not choking until it was over.

The man zipped his own fly up, and leaned over and kissed him on the head. There still wasn't anyone else in the foyer with them.

"I think I was your first," he said. "You did good. Maybe I'll see you here again soon."

And the man was gone.

He walked out of the back bar, carrying his warm beer. He drained it to get the taste out of his mouth. In the outer bar, he bought another, and drank it as he walked numbly down Duval.

♦ ♦ ♦ ♦ ♦

Chapter Twelve

Tess rolled over and looked at the clock.

Seven minutes before the alarm was set to go off! Muttering, she climbed out of the bed and went into the bathroom.

Five minutes later, feeling a little more alert, with a mouth tasting like peppermint, she walked down the hallway, pausing to peek into Nathan's room. Nathan and Yasmin were all tangled up, their limbs wrapped around each other.

Yasmin opened an eye, saw her and smiled sleepily, patting the bed behind her. Tess smothered a giggle and silently closed the door. You had to admire her consistency, Tess conceded. She saw the coffee was ready and poured herself a cup, adding some creamer.

She walked out onto the patio and saw Sarah sitting at the table, wearing old sweats. They smiled at each other and Tess set her cup down and gave her a quick hug.

"Hey, girlfriend," she said. "You're early today."

"I am," Sarah admitted. "In fact, if you don't mind, when you start your laps, I'd like to swim a few. I can't do as many as you, but I could probably do fifteen or twenty."

"Of course," Tess said, sitting down and taking another sip of coffee. She looked at it, and sighed. "Yasmin has ruined me for coffee. I was fine with this until Yasmin started making me a cup every morning, even if I already had coffee made. That darned machine of hers."

Tess sniffed. "I guess I need to learn how to use it."

Sarah laughed. "I'll show you sometime. What's the plan today?"

"We'll have the meal around five," Tess said. "As far as we're concerned, people can come over all day, hang out at the pool, get drafted to help prep things for the meal. We'll probably have some munchies for lunch, like wings or something."

She leaned forward, resting her elbows on the table.

Related Matters

"I've been reminding everyone, especially the family units, that there will be nude men out by the pool all day, and we can't control that. If anyone wants to be here early, enjoy the ambiance, that is fine. Until around one." She sighed. "We think anyone here for the dinner might want to get cleaned up and put something on then, and I told everyone the apartment would be non-nudist, from two on."

"That seems fair," Sarah said, smiling. "Oh, Mariah said she and Robbi will be here today. They didn't say what time. I have nothing planned today. I could be here and help you, maybe work on my tan line, or getting rid of it, for a while, in the process."

"I was counting on you," Tess said, and put her hand over Sarah's. "As far as we're concerned, it's a family holiday, and *you* are family."

She stared at Sarah in consternation.

"Oh my god, I forgot!" She beamed at Sarah. "Merry Christmas, Sarah!"

"Merry Christmas, Tess," she said, and they both stood and hugged each other. "You have no idea what it means to me to have you guys make me feel so at home."

"You ready to swim?" Tess asked, and Sarah nodded and stripped.

Tess thought Sarah did well. She pulled about a lap ahead of the tiny girl over the course of her swim. When Sarah stopped, Tess thought she had done about twenty-two laps, which wasn't bad for the first time.

Tuesday showed up right about then, whistled at her, and kept right on going into the apartment. Two minutes later, she came bursting back out, naked, rinsed off and started her laps. Tess finished soon after.

Yasmin was sitting drinking coffee with Sarah, both of them naked. Tess inhaled and knew they were both drinking freshly brewed, with Yasmin's machine. Yasmin smiled at her, and gave her a hug.

"I thought you would climb in with us, Tess," she said, wiggling her eyebrows suggestively. "I haven't been double-spooned in, well, a couple weeks now."

She walked into the kitchen, and Tess wondered what exactly that meant. Nathan hadn't shared his and Yasmin's discussion about fidelity with either Tess or Tuesday. She sat down and looked over at Sarah, who had a bemused look on her face.

"You checked up on them this morning?" she asked quietly, smiling faintly.

"Of course," Tess admitted. She felt a little frustrated. "Even Tuesday couldn't get Nathan to tell what they said, or decided." She looked at Sarah and blinked. "You know!" she whispered, accusingly.

"I do," she admitted, looking guilty. Sarah glanced at the kitchen, and before Tess had a chance to grill her, Yasmin came out, carrying a china pot, and cups. Tess watched as the girl poured her a fresh cup of coffee.

Tess thanked Yasmin, sipped it, and sighed in satisfaction.

"This is so much better than Mr. Coffee," Tess admitted, feeling guilty.

"Then you should lose your fear of the machine and learn how to use it," Yasmin said dryly, and they all laughed.

Lawrence came down the steps, towel over his shoulder, and there was a wolf whistle from the road. Tess looked at Yasmin speculatively.

"Do you think that's a different person each time, or has Lawrence acquired an audience?" she asked, and Yasmin smiled.

"Ask him," she said sweetly. "I am sure he knows. He is quite observant. And, of course, if you really want to know what happened in Finland, ask me. Nathan will certainly never tell you. You know how he is."

"Uh, I'll um, keep that in mind," Tess stuttered. Sarah started laughing, as did Lawrence. Apparently, his hearing was as good as his observational skills.

Nathan wandered out of the kitchen, naked except for the Batman cup in his hand, and Tess could smell the old coffee from where she sat. Yasmin sighed, and poured him a fresh cup from the pot. He saw her doing so, and shook his head, going to take a sip. His head reared back, and he blushed as he nodded, put the Batman cup down on the table and accepted a fresh cup from Yasmin.

Tess looked at Lawrence.

"Are you joining us for Christmas dinner, Lawrence?" she asked, and he nodded.

"If you're sure it won't be too much trouble," he said. "You planning on the same timeframe as Thanksgiving?"

"We are," she said, and pushed herself to her feet. "But it'll never happen if we don't get started. Let's go, ladies and gentleman."

Part way through the stretches, Tess saw Nathan and Tuesday sitting together, drinking coffee, both relaxing and casually watching them. Tuesday, of course, was looking at her, but her eyes wandered over Yasmin and Sarah casually as well. Nathan had eyes only for Yasmin.

A minute later, she was surprised to see Bobbi Jo walk around the corner of the house, and sit down with her sister and Nathan. Tess almost started laughing as Nathan started, looked down at himself, and sighed.

The guys from the neighborhood that did the aerobics routine began showing up, some with their significant others. Tess discreetly watched Bobbi Jo look at the men with interest, and then look sheepish as she realized none of them were looking at her.

Tuesday said something to her. She shrugged and proceeded to undress. She glanced around after a minute or two, and seemed shocked that didn't change anyone's interest, or lack of it.

Tess almost toppled over when she saw Phoebe and Oshba walk in, with the pale girl's mother and grandma in tow. But that wasn't what almost threw her off balance. It was her and Nathan's mothers walking behind *them*.

Nathan happened to look up as they came into the patio area, and blanched. He pulled the towel he was sitting on around so part of it covered his crotch. Tess wished she could do the same.

Both women teased him, smiled at Tuesday, who clearly wasn't bothered, and then waved at her. The routine ended, and Tess looked around for something to put on. Her mother appeared at her side.

"Don't bother, Tess," she said, and smirked. "We told you we're occasional nudists. Now, Felicia, on the other hand…"

Tess glanced over where Felicia was standing near the patio table, talking to Nathan, trying to act nonchalant. She looked nervously at all the strangers and new acquaintances around her, none of them really paying her any mind as they got the mats out.

She sighed, got a towel and went into the house.

"First one on the right," Tuesday called after her. "The one with the Captain Marvel poster."

"I'll see you in a minute, honey," her mother said, and got a towel herself and followed Felicia. A couple minutes later, they both walked out, towels wrapped around them, her mother talking reassuringly to Nathan's mother. When they dropped their towels, Tess was a little shocked at how good they both still looked. For older people, of course. Nothing was sagging, which surprised her. She pulled her mind back to the task at hand.

"Alright everyone," Tess called out. "Let's find a spot on the mats. We can all fit. It might be a little closer today than usual, but, it's Christmas."

By the time everyone had a spot with enough space to do the exercises, all the participants were naked, facing her, and ready to go.

"Okay, this first one is to loosen us up," Tess called out. "We don't have any alcohol, so we'll have to do stretches instead." There was some laughter, but everyone paid attention to her.

"First, keep your shoulders square, lean your head to the left, and up, and again, and again, and again. Now to the right, and…"

Fifty minutes later, she dismissed the class, and everyone clapped. Tess was surprised to see Bobbi Jo get through all the repetitions, and her mother and Felicia had come close. Much to her amazement, Phoebe's mother and grandma did all the reps, as did she.

Oshba, of course, had no difficulty doing the entire routine, but managed to not look bored. Phoebe looked proud of herself for making it through, even though she *did* look a little winded.

Tess's mother came up to her, breathing heavily.

"That was so much fun, honey." She hugged her impulsively. "Your class was very good. I take classes like this at the gym from time to time, and yours is better." Nathan's mother approached them.

"Tess, that was a very good class," she said. "The songs fit the routines perfectly." She looked down at herself and blushed a little. "I have to admit, in this setting, the dress code makes sense. And feels very liberating."

She looked at Tess's mother.

"What do you think, Kendra? Should we go get the boys, try and convince them getting some sun in a natural setting won't scar them for life?"

"You wouldn't have to convince Bob of that," her mother laughed. "He got comfortable with this a long time ago. I don't know about Houston, though."

"Huey is very shy," Felicia admitted. She sighed. "I don't know if I could convince him to sit out here wearing only a smile. Heck, a week ago, you couldn't have convinced *me* to do it."

Tess's mother hugged her again and kissed her on her temple.

"We're going to try and motivate the men, sweetie," she said. "Hopefully, we'll see you in an hour or so."

"Okay," Tess said, not all that sure how eager she was to have the dads 'hanging out' at the pool.

The crowd from the class quickly cleared away, but Tess could see that a number of them would be back soon to hit the pool for a few hours.

She, Tuesday, and Nathan had a quick powwow to talk the plan over. Walter told Nathan that Tommy would be available to carve the meat again, and both of them were happy to help on any of the grilling duties. Yasmin told them she would be happy to help as well.

All three of them looked at Yasmin, and Tuesday was the one who asked the obvious question.

"So, Yasmin, have you ever cooked, or prepared a meal?" she asked, smiling at her.

Yasmin looked regretful.

"I have never actually done anything in a kitchen, other than make coffee, or dishing myself a bowl of ice cream," she admitted, and looked embarrassed.

Tess stepped close and put her arm around the girl's waist.

"Not to worry, girlfriend, I'll give you a lesson on working in the kitchen," she said, and grinned. "We'll make a housewife out of you yet."

"Probably not," Yasmin demurred. "But there are things I should learn."

"I dunno, girl," Tuesday said. "I think you'd look dy-no-mite, wearing just an apron and a smile."

"Perhaps I should get a French maid's uniform," Yasmin mused, looking at Nathan questioningly.

"Oh no," he said, backing away from them. "You're not dragging me into this conversation. It's the no-win scenario. The Kobayashi Maru, all over again."

Sarah showed back up, with homemade macaroni and cheese, in a casserole dish, ready to bake. She said the witches of the Key West Cemetery were close behind, along with the Assassin of Abu Dhabi. Mariah and Robbi were with her, with what Mariah said were ham rolls. Whereas Mariah was trying not to look gloomy, Robbi was looking around, intrigued, at the growing crowd of nude sunbathers. Tess noticed her bright blue hair, completely shaven on the left side, was getting a lot of intrigued looks from their guests, as well as the neighbors. Robbi thanked Tess for inviting them.

The three women decided to take the opportunity to get some sun, and put their towels down, asking Tess where they could go to change. She sent them to her and Tuesday's room.

"Where's Nathan?" Tess asked Yasmin curiously.

"He decided it would be prudent of him to do a 'load', as he put it, of towels," she said, shaking her head. "He was concerned we would run out with so many people. He said he will join us shortly."

"Nathan is becoming Mr. Mom," Tuesday said, and Tess started to chide her, but shut her mouth. Her girl had a point. He did a *lot* of the general housecleaning and daily maintenance, not to mention shopping and cooking. He always had, since he moved in with them.

They both happened to look at Yasmin at the same time. She laughed and shook her head.

"No, my Nathan does no housework in *my* house." She looked thoughtful. "I told Nadi she should find a housecleaning service, as well as someone to maintain the pool and yard. One we can trust, with the right credentials. But she is quite picky, and has not selected one yet."

"That will probably be at least two different services," Sarah said. "You won't find a company that does both yard maintenance and housecleaning. Not in Key West."

Nathan walked out with a towel and insulated plastic glass of ice water. He was barely settled next to Yasmin when Walter and Tommy took the next two chairs. They were the most recent residents of Eldamar, and Tess was glad to see them. They were developing into good friends, and were already good neighbors.

"Where's that stud muffin of mine?" a raspy woman's voice rang out, and Tuesday was quick to respond.

"Hey, Nate boy, there's a cougar here to see you," she quipped, and people laughed, Marilyn included. Tess was surprised to see a man about her age, or maybe a few years older, with her. They all stared as Marilyn led him around to where they could face everyone comfortably camped out on recliners.

"Hey, everybody, let me introduce you to a lust interest of mine." Marilyn leered at them, and almost everyone tittered at her expression. The man looked fit, for someone in his mid-seventies at least, with minimal gut or love handles. He was tan, and his face looked weatherworn, but he was still handsome. Tess thought he had nice looking eyes. "This is Michael Stein, but he goes by Mitch. So technically, this is a visit from Mitch and the bitch."

"You're anything but, Marilyn," Tess said firmly. "You are family. That weird aunt that everyone loves, even if she does set a bad example."

"Thank you Tess," Marilyn said, and looked at Tuesday pointedly. "You always were the *good* niece."

"Hey!" Tuesday said, grinning, but didn't argue.

Marilyn turned to Mitch. "Darling, this is Sarah, that dear boy is Nathan, his main squeeze, Yasmin, sweet Tess, crazy Tuesday, neighbors Walter and Tommy."

"And Lawrence," Lawrence said, walking by, naked except for his ball cap, carrying a travel mug and towel. He took the chair next to Tommy.

"And Lawrence, another of the men of Eldamar, and a pretty hot one at that," she said, and winked at him. Lawrence took it in stride, and smiled as he sat down.

"I'm surprised Timothy isn't up yet," Tess said, and most of them looked at Lawrence.

"No," he said, without even looking at anyone. "It's not for want of his trying, but I've made it very clear. He may have picked up a shift today at the restaurant he works at."

"Well, my goodness, I'm glad I talked Simon into an hour or so poolside, before we go to our dinner date," Marvin said, surprising them all. He wore a very short silk robe, as did Simon, standing next to him. They looked at Lawrence. "My dear Lawrence, may we sit next to you for a while?"

"Of course," Lawrence said, and the couple settled into the chairs at the end of the group.

Tess noticed there was actually a pretty good crowd already sitting around the pool area, mostly on the other side, or on the end nearest the hot tub.

Within a few minutes, they were joined by Phoebe and company. Oshba got the three Stark women settled in the second row of chairs, right behind Tess and Tuesday. She checked in with Yasmin, briefly, then claimed the chair on the open side of Phoebe with a towel, and went into the apartment.

Bobbi Jo showed up in a cute sundress, which she immediately ditched in the patio, grabbed a towel, and took a chair next to Emily. Tuesday went over and wished her a Merry Christmas. They both hugged. Bobbi Jo looked startled and then laughed.

"I ain't never hugged a naked chick before," she admitted, and there was a lot of laughter. "It's even weirder when it's your sister." She looked at her sister. "Bobby said he was going to get away from the rest of them and come join us."

"He going to be okay with this?" Tuesday asked, gesturing at the group of people.

"If he ain't, he can go sit with the naked men, or alone in the apartment," Bobbi Jo said crisply.

When Bobby showed up, he got a towel and put it on the chair next to his sister. She looked at him with amusement.

"Why don't you make some new friends," she said pointedly, and he stammered something Tess couldn't quite make out. Bobbi Jo saw something and laughed.

"Calm down, little brother. You ain't getting lucky today."

"I'm married," he protested, his face going beet red. "I don't screw around on Darla."

"You married, Bobby?" Emily asked, and he nodded, looking eager to move the conversation away from any sort of physical reaction he'd had to all the bare skin.

"Yes, Ma'am, three years in February." He seemed to be relieved to talk with someone that he clearly wouldn't be perceived trying to pick up.

"He's the only one of us kids that ain't been divorced, and the only Dumarest that don't sleep around from time to time," Bobbi Jo said cynically, and Tuesday looked back at her. "Exceptin' our kid sister, I guess," she admitted.

Bobby glanced over at Phoebe.

"You still wearin' Captain America's shield?" he asked, and Phoebe nodded, looking pleased.

Tess noticed Nathan look up at that, a puzzled look on his face. His expression became guarded, but she watched his face as he battled between curiosity and caution.

"Is that some sort of euphemism for something I'll regret asking about?" he asked Phoebe slowly.

"Not like you think," Phoebe said crisply. "I told Mari Sue that I didn't burn because I use a sunscreen I designed myself that I call Adamantium. Bobby said that meant I was protected by the equivalent of Captain America's shield."

Phoebe smiled, which still tended to spook Tess. She watched Nathan's forehead wrinkle as he frowned.

"Adamantium is what Wolverine's claws and skeleton are laced with," Nathan said slowly, and looked at Phoebe apologetically. "Captain America's shield is made of Vibranium, from Wakanda."

"Oh," Phoebe said, and Tess saw her disappointment briefly, before she tucked it away out of sight.

"Still, Wolverine's claws are pretty cool," Bobby said, clearly recognizing her disappointment, and trying to cheer her up.

"*I* wouldn't mind having Wolverine's claws," Oshba admitted, and Tess resisted the urge to laugh at the mixed reaction that comment got.

Tess glanced over towards their patio, and gulped when she saw her and Nathan's parents walking between their house and Lawrence's. "Uh, Nathan?"

"Oh crap," Nathan said.

"Please, don't anyone get up," Tess's mother said firmly. "We brought wings, and a cheese platter, and a veggie platter. We'll put the cooler in the kitchen and get um, changed, and be right out. Please, stay in your seats."

"Please," Nathan's dad said in a very nervous voice, and Nathan looked at Tess and Tuesday in panic. Then he looked at Marvin.

Marvin saw his expression and laughed. "No, dear Nathan, you may *not* hide in our apartment. But we'll move to the second row so your parents can sit right next to you."

There was a lot of laughter, at Nathan and Tess's expense, and all five men ended up moving a row back, leaving plenty of chairs to the right of Tuesday available. When Tess and Nathan's parents came out, wearing towels and an anxious look, in the case of Nathan's dad, they paused when they saw where the open chairs were.

"Here you go, folks," Tuesday said cheerfully.

They settled in, and after a while, began to loosen up. Tess's parents were comfortable with being nude, if not used to being around their adult daughter in that state. Even Houston and Felicia began to act more natural as time passed.

It was warm enough that people started going into the pool to cool off, with people sitting on the shallow steps, or standing in the deeper areas.

Time passed, Marvin and Simon had to go to their other event. They put their robes on, gathered their things, and headed back to their apartment. When they were inside, and well out of hearing, Tess's mother turned to Felicia and said in a quiet voice.

"In the beginning, God did not hand out assets in an evenhanded manner."

"No she didn't," Emily said, and there was a lot of laughter.

Soon after, some of them went inside to prepare the platters of finger foods and such for a light lunch. Afterwards, some went back out to the pool, and others began prepping for the main meal.

At some point, Tess looked at the clock and went out to where Nathan was prepping the coals in the two charcoal grills. He had two casual helpers in the form of her and Nathan's fathers. She noticed that Oshba was standing with them, asking Nathan questions from time to time.

Yasmin came out of the kitchen and put her arm around Tess's waist.

"I think Oshba is trying to learn the secret art of grilling meat from my Nathan," she said merrily, and Tess nodded. She saw that the Stark women were still poolside, talking to Tuesday's siblings, as well as Marilyn, Mitch and the men. Yasmin looked down at the hot pot gloves she wore. "I guess I'm trying to learn some things from you, as well."

"I appreciate your help," Tess said. "And this way, we get to spend time together." She called out to Nathan. "Nathan, it's almost one. We'll probably be seeing some new faces soon."

He nodded at her, and said something to the two dads. They nodded and came into the apartment. Her father wrapped the towel around his middle as he walked, and Houston hurriedly did the same.

"Honey, your mother and I are going to use your room to get cleaned up a bit, and Houston and Felicia will use Nathan's."

"That's fine, Dad. When you guys are showered, or whatever, Tuesday and I will get ready. We still have time."

In short order, most of them had put some clothes on, with the exception of their neighbors, Bobbi Jo and Bobby, as well as Marilyn and Mitch. Tess looked at her girl.

"Tue Bear, should we warn your sister and brother what time it is?"

Tuesday looked pensive, and finally sighed.

"As fun as it would be, they've both been pretty nice, and sorta supportive," Tuesday admitted. "I guess we should warn them, although I'm sure Pa would tell them when he gets here."

"Do you really want to start things off on that note, today?" Tess asked gently, holding her girl by the shoulders.

"You're right," Tuesday admitted, and walked outside and talked with them. Bobby stood up immediately, and began heading back to the apartment, but Bobbi Jo seemed reluctant to give up the sun. She finally nodded and followed Tuesday back inside. She saw Tess and nodded reluctantly.

"I got to admit, I could get used to hanging around here," she said. "You guys have some cool friends. And everyone is nice. Nobody's pickin' on anyone."

She walked naked back to Tess and Tuesday's room, towel in one hand.

"Tess, you have more guests arriving," Sarah called to her.

Nico and Lori Lynn stood in the kitchen, cakebox from the Dirty Pig in Nico's hands. Lori Lynn saw where Tess was looking and grinned.

"It seemed to go over well, last month, so we thought, stick with the winner," she said as they hugged.

"Kimmy's cakes are always a good choice. What'd you get?" Tess asked curiously.

"Kimmy's Carrot Cake," Lori Lynn said, and Tess laughed.

"Tuesday doesn't like carrot cake, but I got her to try a bite of mine, when the Dirty Pig opened, and she stole the piece from me. It's incredible." Tess grinned. "She likes carrot cake now, at least from one place."

"Nico," Tess said, and gave him a hug. He seemed a little surprised, but pleased at her personal gesture.

"Hey, girlfriend," Ashley said, as she directed Wally to put a large bowl on the kitchen counter. "Antipasto salad," she said, as they hugged. She frowned, faking anger. "We missed the nude sun-bathing portion of the program, didn't we?"

"I'm afraid you did," Tess admitted, and looked at the four of them with a grin. "But we still have a few friends out by the pool. Make yourself comfortable, we got plenty of towels."

Ashley looked at Wally affectionately. "Getting Wally naked anywhere except the bedroom or our hot tub is pretty darned tough."

Sarah suddenly popped up next to Tess. "Just thought I'd warn you, Tuesday's family just got here."

"The important part of it already is," Bobbi Jo said snippily as she walked by, wearing her sundress, her hair still wet from the shower.

Bobby followed after her as they went out to greet their parents.

Tess saw Mari Sue and Jackie talking with her and Nathan's parents, and sighed in relief. She saw that Nadezhda and Carlos had arrived at some point, and were holding hands, which usually wasn't the case. She looked a little closer and sighed. Of course, they both appeared to be armed. Neither of them ever went anywhere without a weapon. They had another cake from the Dirty Pig. When Carlos said it was called a Chocolate Bourbon Cake with salted caramel filling, both Nico and Lori Lynn looked interested.

She saw Tuesday's oldest brother, Bubba, bristle when he saw Carlos, but not say anything. She also saw him notice their weapons as they turned to talk with someone. Bobby said something as he walked by, and Bubba gave him the finger, even as he shrugged. A rueful smile came to his lips, and Tess exhaled in relief.

The afternoon seemed to fly by. With the exception of a couple of crude remarks by Jackie and Chuck, it was a cheerful group. When the gay neighbors got dressed and came and joined them, they got a couple of stares from the Dumarest clan, but no one said anything, as far as Tess could see. She didn't think they even noticed Lawrence.

Tess thought Nathan impressed his dad with his grilling. The turkey and the ham came off the grill at the same time. Tommy and Walter took them, shooed Nathan away, and went into the kitchen.

"Tess girl, you all did a hell of a job putting this together," Marilyn surprised her by saying. "The food is great, plenty of drinks, and the company is as eclectic as you could ask for. This is a real treat."

"It truly is," Mitch said, and smiled at Tess. "Marilyn has been bragging you kids up, and I thought she was exaggerating. But she was just telling it like it is."

"I'm glad you could join us, Mitch. It really was a team effort. The three of us had a lot of Santa's helpers," Tess said. She glanced at Marilyn, who winked at her and leered, staring at Mitch's crotch. She smothered a laugh, and let her eyes wander around the group, enjoying the moment, the company, and everything else. She decided the three of them truly were blessed.

◆ ◆ ◆ ◆ ◆

Lori Lynn sipped her whiskey sour, watching the group interact, kind of envious about the friends from all circles that these three kids had. She was also wondering if she was going to waddle when she tried to walk.

"I *really* liked that ham," Nico said out of the blue, and Lori Lynn nodded. She watched him look around the pool area, pointedly zipping by the naked couples scattered across the deck. She grinned and reached over and put her hand on his. He automatically turned his, opening it so their fingers intertwined. A little smile came to his lips, and he sighed.

"I really want to risk getting shot and try and kiss you," he said quietly, and she nodded in agreement.

"I might miss," she said pensively, and he snorted.

"We shoot together, remember? You don't miss," he said.

"I ate so much, I might," Lori Lynn said softly, and then laughed. "But I'm so full, I'd probably shoot you just so I wouldn't have to make the effort."

"The effort to kiss me back?" he asked, and grinned.

"No," she said in a tone so low, Nico looked like he was struggling to make out her words. "The efforts we'd probably both be making after you kissed me."

"Oh," Nico said, and said no more. They sat in comfortable silence for a while, and he finally laughed. "Our luck, kissing in a place with this many people, we'd probably end up on YouTube before the night was over."

"That would be unfortunate," Lori Lynn admitted, thinking it might almost be worth it to get past that point. She noticed he was looking around the grounds, looking at the buildings, the trees, the foliage. "What?" she asked.

"Well, in related matters, this beautiful common area, to catch all the scenes he did, how many cameras do you think Neilson used to cover Eldamar?"

Lori Lynn blinked, and looked around herself. A lowlife named Geoffrey Neilson had set up networks of cameras on private areas around Key West. He sold access to the camera feeds in the form of a website membership.

Neilson would probably still be profiting from people like Tess, with her nude aerobics and stretching classes, people's private pools in their back yards, Yasmin's pool and deck area in her new home. In fact, Eldamar, for a while, had a large number of cameras around the pool and hot tub area, as well as some of the resident's patios.

They only found out about Neilson's voyeur business when someone hired an renowned hitman to take him out. Except, the hitman was really a hit woman, known in certain circles as "The Fox." She'd called 9-1-1, just before she left his home, leaving his tortured body tied to a kitchen chair. Before she did so, she blanked all the records and files for the website, leaving only one picture per location frozen on the monitor screens

Related Matters

in his spare bedroom he referred to as his control room, in his notes.

Nico led the investigation. There were still scenes of every location except for two, which were blank. With much perseverance, Latrelle and Gary were able to reconstruct several deleted scenes which allowed them to identify the sites. One had been the old WWII submarine pens on the north side of Boca Chica Key, the last key on U.S.1 before you reached Stock Island and Key West.

The other was Eldamar, the collection of seven houses with traditional Key West architecture, that had been broken into apartments. It was an all male gay community, with the exception of Tess, Nathan, and Tuesday.

TNT.

Eldamar was the only site where all the cameras had been removed, and Nico and Lori Lynn, as well as their partners, were still trying to find out why. They were only able to identify Eldamar and the sub pens by tracking down a website member, and finding still screen-saves of both sites.

TNT's patio area had been blanketed with camera coverage. She remembered there was more than one angle filmed of Tess and her nude classes, and there had been at least one, yes, there it was!

"Remember the first image Latrelle found, of a building? It was that one, right there."

Nico looked at it a moment, and nodded. "Yeah. So?"

"So, there's no hot tub there, no aerobics mats with classes every weekend, why have a camera dedicated to that building?"

"Good question," he admitted, and stirred. "Another question. We found all but two of the sites. Every one of them, including the other scrubbed site, the submarine berths, still had cameras in place." He gestured with his arm.

"This place is big, and there had to be dozens of cameras. Why did they all get taken out? Did Neilson take them out himself, just before he was killed? If so, why? If he didn't do it, who did? The security firm LeBlanc hired didn't find a single one."

Nico swung around to face her.

"Lori Lynn, it had to be the killer. So, why did she take just these cameras out?" Nico looked straight through her, as if he wasn't even seeing her. "And when? We know she killed him, and called 9-1-1, using Neilson's own phone, which she left stuffed in his mouth, from his own house. She almost would have had to come straight here and remove every camera, in the middle of the night, so she wouldn't get caught. And how could she have been sure she'd have time to find them all?"

"She either lived here, or knew someone that did," Lori Lynn said, feeling excited. But then she was confused. "But the only females living here are Tess and Tuesday, and I don't see any way it could have been either of them. The Arab women have already established an alibi. Who does that leave?"

"I'm missing something," Nico muttered, looking very frustrated. He looked back at the house that had been in the image. "I want to know who lives there."

Lori Lynn looked over where Tess and her parents were sitting with Tuesday and hers. She didn't envy the girls at the moment. Tuesday's parents were *not* okay with the situation, and she had a feeling the father was just waiting for his moment to explode.

"Tomorrow, hon," she said. "It's Christmas, and they have thirty guests."

"Yeah," Nico said, and she looked at him. The mood in his voice had changed. What could have caused that? She replayed the last minute in her mind, and resisted the urge to grin. Nico really was an old-fashioned romantic if he got that sappy look, just because she called him 'hon'.

♦ ♦ ♦ ♦ ♦

Tess watched Tuesday's father get more and more worked up. He'd been quiet, but it was clear he was unhappy about something. And she was pretty sure she knew what.

"Tuesday, we need to put the brakes on this before you do something stupid," Jackie said, and Tess winced. "We know this group that does interventions, and can show you that what you're doing is unnatural, and against God's wishes. Their success rate is high."

"Are you talking about gay conversion therapy?" Tuesday asked quietly, and Tess shifted forward in her seat, knowing that tone.

"Our pastor says they've helped a number of misguided kids to learn the error of their ways," he insisted, looking grim. "You need advice and guidance, and yes, even prayers, to bring you back to a normal lifestyle."

"Pastor Baker says they do very good work," Mari Sue said hesitantly.

"It's a form of torture, Ma," Tuesday said in a biting tone. "I ain't doin' it. Anyway, the church is in Jacksonville, and I'm not going back there."

"Yes, you are," her pa said, and Tuesday sat on the front edge of her chair and stared at her pa. "I'm your pa, and you'll do as you're told."

"I am not going to Jacksonville. I am *not* going to let anyone torture me. I *am* in love with Tess, and I *am* going to marry her!"

Tuesday's voice had gradually gotten a little louder with each word, and although she didn't shout, a lot of their friends heard her words. No one said anything, but as Tess looked around the faces, she saw nothing but support. In fact, even Tuesday's family didn't appear to be entirely on the same page.

Bobby looked disturbed, and like he wanted to say something, but Tess suspected none of the kids ever argued with their pa. Except for Tuesday, of course. Bobbi Jo didn't look happy, but didn't seem inclined to jump into things.

Tuesday's mother looked upset, and she said something in a low tone that Tess couldn't make out. Whatever it was, it didn't seem to mollify Jackie at all.

Tuesday stood, and put her hands on her hips, looking at her pa.

"Pa, I know you don't approve, and I'm sorry about that. But I don't really expect your approval, and I don't need it," Tuesday said firmly, although her face was pale, and she actually looked scared, which didn't fit her at all.

"Don't you get mouthy with me. You'll do as you're told!"

Jackie stood with his hands on his hips, and his voice was carrying to all corners of the pool area, and probably beyond.

Tuesday stood mere inches away from him. She stared up into his face and showed no sign of backing down.

"You don't approve of what I am, and who I love. I guess you'll approve of this even less."

Tuesday turned and faced Tess, and with one step, was in front of her. She knelt in front of Tess, and her hand quickly went in and out of her pocket. She held a small box in the shape of a cube, and her hand was shaking so much, it distracted Tess from realizing what it had to hold.

Tess gasped as she realized what her Tue Bear was about to do. Her hands flew to cover her mouth, and she felt tears start pouring down her cheeks.

"Now you hold on. Don't say another word." Jackie began, and both Mari Sue and Bobbi Jo actually hissed at him. He was so startled, his mouth snapped shut and he stared at them. Looking around, he realized it was a hostile crowd and he kept silent.

Tuesday ignored him. She seemed to have difficulty speaking for a moment, and cleared her throat noisily. She started to speak, and nothing came out. Tess wanted to help her by just saying yes, yes, yes. But she knew her girl wanted to do this right, and she wouldn't steal her thunder.

"Tess Carter," she finally managed to get out, and it seemed to settle her down a bit.

"Tess Carter, love of my life, you're the most important thing in the world to me," Tuesday said, and tears were rolling down her face as well. "Would you, could you, do me the honor of marrying me?"

She held the box out and opened it, showing a thin band of gold with a modest diamond mounted on it. Tess held her hand out, but it was shaking so hard Tuesday had to hold her wrist with one hand, slide the ring on with the other.

Tess looked at her girl tenderly. "Oh yes, Tuesday Dumarest. I will marry you. Then they were in each other's arms, kissing. Tess looked around the room, at all her friends, no, *their* friends. And family. Then they were surrounded by everyone hugging them, congratulating, wiping tears of their own away.

Nathan wrapped his arms around them, and Tess could see tears in his eyes. "I'm so happy for both of you," he said, and choked up. "I love you both so much."

Then Tess's mother was there, hugging them both, and much to Tess's surprise, so was Mari Sue. They hugged each other.

"Pa's in shock, but he'll probably have the brains to hold off reacting until tomorrow," Mari Sue told Tuesday. "But I think you can count on a pretty strong reaction then."

"I ain't goin' back to Jax, and I *am* marrying Tess," Tuesday said firmly. "You remind him that we plan on having kids, and if he wants to be a grandpa to them, he's going to be a father to both of us. And approve."

"I don't know that *I* think this is such a good idea," Mari Sue said shortly, and then relented. "But I know love when I see it. I'll do what I can, but you know Pa."

The rest of their friends began to press close, wanting to see the ring, wanting to know when the wedding was going to be, and where. Marilyn asked if it would be clothing optional, were they going to take the same last name, and if so, which? Or would it be one of those hyphenated ones, Carter-Dumarest, or Dumarest-Carter?"

"It might be one of those combined names," Tuesday said, grinning. "You know, like Carmarest, or Dumarter."

"It won't be either of those," Tess said firmly. "And sorry, Marilyn. We probably won't have it clothing optional. Not if we want to get some of our friends to come. Can anyone here picture Ted and Steve stripping down?"

"Oh, I can, just before they climb into my bed, both of them," Marilyn said dreamily. She grinned at Mitch. "Sorry dear, you'll just have to watch."

"You get them both into your bed, and I'll do just that," he said, and everyone laughed.

"Watch out, Marilyn," Lori Lynn called out. "Steve's wife is Mari Little."

Tuesday's family didn't stay much longer, except for Bobbi Jo, who told them she'd be along later. Jackie glared at her, but she didn't make eye contact with any of them.

The fun continued for some time, and the alcohol flowed much faster. Bobby showed back up, and finally got a chance to hug his sister.

"It took me a while to ditch everyone," Bobby admitted, wincing. "Pa is somewhere between furious and erupting like a volcano. But I'm on your side, sparkplug," he said, grinning at her. "Let me know when the wedding is, and Darla and I will be here."

The crowd finally began to thin.

Ashley whispered to her that Wally and she were thinking about setting a date in June.

"I was thinking the same," Tess admitted.

"We need to coordinate, so we don't have a time conflict," Ashley said, and hugged Tess for the sixth or seventh time. "We need to be able to attend each other's weddings. And the receptions," she said, smirking.

"I agree," Tess said, and hugged her right back. Tuesday frowned.

"Why don't we just get married now?" she asked. "We got the families here, and it won't be a hundred degrees in the sun."

"Weddings don't just happen," Tess said primly. "And anyway, even if we went and got our license and everything tomorrow, we'd still have to wait three days. Florida law."

"Hey," Tuesday said, and grinned at both of them. "Wanna do a reenactment Monday night at Diane Isis?"

Tess laughed, but shook her head. "I couldn't reconstruct that reaction to save my life," she admitted. "No, let's just be giddy and show my ring off, and laugh and cry, and get hugged by everyone."

"Even Fay," Tuesday said, grinning, and Tess smiled sadly.

"Even Fay," she agreed.

"They did what?" They heard Marvin shriek in astonishment and excitement out on the pool deck, and Tess and Tuesday looked at each other. Her girl snapped her fingers. Tess looked at her questioningly.

"We're gonna need a box of tissues, stat," she said, and they laughed. Even so, Tuesday dashed into the house to get one from the kitchen.

♦ ♦ ♦ ♦ ♦

He sat at the bar, wondering if he was a fool. He'd been here an hour, and the sexy man hadn't shown up yet. He'd checked in the foyer, but he wasn't there. He went back and checked again twenty minutes later, and one of the men indicated he wanted to service him, so he let him.

Then he went back to the bar, nursing a beer, wanting to be able to perform if the man showed up. Tonight, their roles would be reversed. *He* would stand and hold the man's head as that pretty mouth worked its magic.

Time passed, he had a second beer, and decided the man wasn't going to show. He was about to get up, when the man he'd been fantasizing about for the last twenty-four hours settled on the stool next to him.

"You weren't giving up on me so soon, were you, lover?" he asked, and placed his hand on his leg. The sudden rush was every bit as electric as the night before. "Trust me, I'm worth the wait."

The man stood and offered his hand, and he took it and let himself be led to the foyer, which had several couples making out. They glanced at him enviously, and went back to what they were doing.

He was about to take the initiative and unzip his fly when the man took him into his arms, and they kissed. He felt the man's hands sliding over his body, and just like last night, eventually came to grip his buttocks firmly with both hands. The man's fingers played with his butt crack through the fabric of his pants, and he gasped, grinding his pelvic area against the man's.

They made out for a while, and he gasped as the man's fingers tried to probe his ass through the material. Then the man pulled back and deftly undid his own fly. Despite all his intentions to receive rather than give, he found himself sinking to his knees and kiss, lick, and eventually take the swollen end into his mouth.

He did as the man's hands directed, and eventually got the same result as last night. Swallowing, he was dismayed to find he enjoyed the act, and regretted when the man was spent. He kept it in his mouth, even as it began to shrink. After a minute or two, the man pulled his head away, and fondled it with one hand, even as he arranged himself, and zipped up with the other.

The man pulled him upright and hugged him.

"You did even better tonight. I have to work tomorrow night until close, but I'll be here around one thirty. I know a place we can go and I can complete your education, and give you the experience of your life." The man kissed him on the cheek, and let one hand slide down beneath the beltline of his pants in the back. His fingers slid down his butt crack, and one finger actually penetrated a little. His back arched from the shock of the action, but he didn't pull away. The man smiled and pushed in a little deeper with the finger.

"Tomorrow, we'll pop *this* door wide open."

With that, the man pulled away, and walked out of the bar. He stared after him, too shocked to move. Did the man really think he wanted that? He stumbled back to the bar proper and ordered another beer, remembering the feel of the finger inside him.

He pictured the man's enormous penis, and imagined it where the finger had been, and chugged his beer down. He started at the empty bottle, and looked at the bartender.

"Another," he said.

♦ ♦ ♦ ♦ ♦

Chapter Thirteen

Felicia made her way down the hall, trying to think thin thoughts. She idly wondered how many pounds she and Huey had picked up on this trip so far.

I guess I *could* have put the bathroom scales in the car, she mused to herself.

At least she wasn't sounding very heavy as she went down the old wooden stairs of the B&B. As she turned to the left at the bottom, she met Kendra creeping towards her. She'd clearly been to the kitchen already, because she had two paper cups with coffee, and a small plate with a napkin draped over it

Felicia had been determined to skip the wonderful breakfast bread, no matter what kind it was, and what it had in it, and have a banana instead. That thought disappeared the moment she saw her friend.

They scurried out to the front porch and claimed the love seat. Kendra handed her one of the cups, set hers down, and quickly buttered one slice of the fruity bread on the plate. She spread the butter pretty thick, and then spread butter on the second piece. Leaving about twenty percent unbuttered. She took the first piece and handed the plate with the second piece, as well as the little cup of butter. There was still plenty in the little cup, in case Felicia decided to coat the entire surface.

"You know me so well, and we've only known each other for five days," Felicia said, and took a delicate bite of the unbuttered end. "Mmm, zucchini bread, with brown sugar, cinnamon, and apple?" She looked closer at the bread, and then nodded. "Ah, I bet it's applesauce, in place of some of the oil, pecans, and I'd swear I taste dates."

Kendra looked at her with respect.

"You do," she admitted, and held up a piece of paper. "I asked Liz yesterday if she'd give us a copy of the recipe every day. Thank god she's not one of those people that hoards their recipes and never share."

Felicia buttered the rest of the piece, and nibbled at it, eyes closed.

"I *knew* you two were getting special treatment," Grace Stark said, from right next to her.

Both Felicia and Kendra gave a little shriek.

"You about gave me a heart attack," Kendra said, looking at what remained of her slice of bread guiltily. Felicia knew how she felt.

Grace grinned at them.

"Don't worry," she reassured them. "We can wait until the breakfast officially opens."

"We?" Kendra said, making a show of looking around. "I don't see your mother with you, or are you talking about your invisible friend?"

"No, you had it the first time," Grace said, and stared above them at the deck on the second floor. "You coming down, Mother? Your coffee is hot, but I'm hanging out down here with the cool kids for a while. I know you could sense me coming, and probably saw me as well. I can certainly sense you up there now."

"Be right down, dear." Emily's voice wafted down to them, and they heard a bit of creaking on the wooden deck above.

"You can't really sense her, can you?" Felicia asked skeptically. "I know both of you and your daughter, Phoebe, say you're witches, and can sense things, but you're pulling our legs, right?"

"No, we are all witches, as well as from the same coven, so we can't help but feel when each other is near." Grace shook her head. "As good as Mother and I are, Phoebe's skills are so much stronger, if unrefined. You cannot sneak up on that girl. I've known her to wake up from a sound sleep and stare at the front door, just before someone comes up on the porch and knocks."

"Hmm," Kendra said, clearly not convinced.

"Don't believe me," Grace said, clearly not insulted by her doubts. "Try sneaking up on her at the hut. Ask your daughter if she can sneak up on our Phoebe."

"Tess probably has never tried," Kendra said.

"Have your nearly daughter-in-law try," Felicia suggested. "I get the feeling she lives for playing with people's heads. She would take this as a challenge."

Felicia watched Kendra react to her mention of Tuesday, and finally shake her head in amazement.

"That sounds so weird when you say it, but you're right." Kendra stared ahead as she took a sip of her coffee. "I'm about to have a new daughter in the family, and she's going to be Tess's...wife" She stared at the three women. "My little girl is getting married. To another girl."

"Still trying to wrap your head around that one?" Emily asked knowingly. "She's still your little girl, and as far as I can tell, very sweet. When we first got here, I had three or four people all say that Tess was the sweetest, kindest person they knew. And they all kind of consider Tess their best friend."

"So who is *her* best friend, then?" Kendra asked thoughtfully.

"Not to brag, but I think it's Nathan," Felicia said quietly. They looked at each other and smiled. "That must be why you and I hit it off immediately."

"What about you?" Kendra asked her. "Are you ready to have an Arabian princess for *your* daughter-in-law?"

"You think they're really considering marriage?" Felicia said, and then nodded. "I guess, since they're talking about what their kids would look like, I would like to think marriage was tucked into their plans somewhere."

"That's not a huge deal," Emily said gently. "I don't even know who Grace's dad was, although over the years, I think I have narrowed it down to about five possibilities."

Felicia and Kendra both stared at her, and Emily grinned.

"Hey, I was at Woodstock, summer of love, summer of lust," she said, and glanced at Grace ruefully. "Anyone that started off with condoms, ran out pretty darned fast, that weekend."

"I wish I could narrow it to five," Grace said solemnly. "I *did* eliminate the two black guys as possibilities. With her complexion, I don't see Phoebe's father being black. But, I'm pretty sure Phoebe was conceived the week I was at Hedonism II, in Jamaica. And the resort was packed, and pretty much everyone were swingers. I thought we practiced safe sex pretty consistently, but I have to admit, I may have had a couple memory lapses. There was a lot of booze and drugs being consumed that week."

"Phoebe turned out pretty good," Emily said, shrugging. "And I do think she's going to end up more powerful than either of us."

"It also looks like she's going to end up married, too," Grace said thoughtfully. "I must admit, a year ago, I wouldn't have given any chance of her falling in love with someone that loved her as much as Oshba clearly does, and that they would both decide on marriage. I think they'll beat Nathan and Yasmin to the altar."

"They're all so young," Felicia said, glad she could talk about this with someone besides Huey. "Nathan will be twenty-three in a few months, Yasmin is still twenty-one."

"Hard to believe *my* girls are the old maids of the group," Kendra said, ruminating. "Tess is twenty-five, and Tuesday is twenty-four."

"Technically, that's not true," Grace argued. "Sure, Phoebe is twenty-one, turning twenty-two next month, but Oshba is thirty, or about to be. Eight years difference, at this point in Phoebe's life, is a big gap between them."

"They *are* in love, though," Felicia said, and all four of them nodded.

"I *do* worry about Oshba," Emily admitted. "Her aura is so chaotic. Phoebe has told us she had a very difficult youth, and has had to do certain things to survive, most of her life. I think she would do anything for Phoebe, but at the same time, I think expediency is more important to her than moral issues. We know she killed a serial killer two months ago, but Phoebe has hinted there might have been others."

"Where was she, to run across a serial killer?" Felicia asked, feeling a chill.

"Here in Key West," Grace said shortly. "And before that, when they were in Mexico at that resort, she killed the ringleader of the kidnapping attempt, and maybe one or two others, besides."

"And then there's her days as a Houthi terrorist," Emily reminded her, and Felicia and Kendra stared at both of them as they nodded solemnly. "But, she loves Phoebe dearly, and would do anything for her."

Felicia didn't know how to respond to their comments. She knew the kids had found themselves in dangerous situations several times, since Nathan had moved down here. If nothing else, Nathan's back and right buttock were a testimony to that. He had quite a few small scars spread across his back, and the backs of his legs. And he had one thick gnarly scar on his butt that had to hurt like hell when he got it.

But when she'd tried to ask about the scars, that one in particular, Tess, Tuesday, and Nathan had all made light of it, and their stories were vague and didn't quite match up.

Felicia happened to glance over at Kendra, and saw a reflection of what her own reaction to all this was on her friend's face.

"I've tried to pin Nathan down and make him tell me everything that has happened to them since he moved here, but he's been uncharacteristically illusive," Felicia admitted.

"I had the same results with Tess," Kendra admitted, and looked at her with some amusement in her eyes. "I will tell you, don't bother to try and quiz Tuesday about it."

"Oh?" Felicia asked curiously.

"That girl thinks fast, has the craziest imagination I've ever known, and a perfect poker face," Kendra said glumly. "It's going to be tough prying secrets out of her."

"I guarantee it'll be a funny experience, though," Emily said thoughtfully. "If maybe a little frustrating."

"Yeah," Kendra said dolefully, and Felicia laughed at the expression on her face.

♦ ♦ ♦ ♦ ♦

Tess checked the last couple of jet skis, and conceded everything was in good shape. She considered Phoebe her protégé of sorts, and was proud of the way she'd taken ownership of the hut, the condition and upkeep of the jet skis, and the docks in general.

That also included pushing whoever needed a kick to keep events on schedule. She had never shown any leadership traits in the relatively short time before Tess hired her, but she kept Aurora focused, dealt with customer service issues, made decisions and justified them to either Tess or Wally afterwards.

Tess had even seen her remind several of their captains that they needed to be leaving dock and starting their excursions.

"How is Tuesday dealing with her parents?" Phoebe asked her, and Tess sighed.

"You know my Tue Bear. She's impervious to pain, insults, hurtful behavior, or at least, that's what she would have us believe," Tess admitted. "But deep down, it's hurt her. She so wants their approval. She loves her father so much, and just wants to hear him say he's happy for her."

"Judging from last night, I don't see that happening," Phoebe said with genuine regret in her voice. "At least *your* parents seem to have accepted the fact that you're gay, you have a gay girlfriend, fiancé now," she amended. "And you're going to marry her. They seem very open to welcoming her into the family."

"They've been wonderful," Tess admitted, and forced herself to not get choked up. "They've made it clear that Tuesday is family now, and they're happy with that. But she needs her own blood relatives to accept the circumstances, as well."

"Bobby seems genuinely happy for her," Phoebe pointed out, and Tess nodded.

"Tue Bear has always said that he was the open-minded one, which made him weak in the eyes of his brothers, his parents, and I guess his other sister too." Tess said, shaking her head.

"I think Bobbi Jo might come around, and her mother seemed more philosophical about it," Tess said hesitantly. "But I don't think Mari Sue will do anything that will piss Jackie off."

"Tuesday is coming," Phoebe warned, and Tess looked down their dock for her babe, but didn't see her.

"I don't see her, but it doesn't matter," Tess said. "She knows we're worried about her parents coming around."

Tuesday came out onto the deck of the Freedom Schooner, looked over at them, and waved. Then she was walking briskly down the dock to them.

"Hey, babe," Tuesday said, and gave her a hug. "You going to work today?"

"I'm just going to check the numbers and schedule for the month to date, prep payroll, do a few other things like that," Tess said. "I think I'm going to meet Mother and Father for lunch, and then hang out with them for a while. I'll be here when you get off. I thought we might have dinner at Diane Isis. I don't know if they're going to go listen to Nathan first or not. I'll find out."

"Whatever, I'm good with it," Tuesday said diffidently. "I'm always up for eating at Diane Isis, you know that."

"What about your parents?" Tess asked hesitantly, not wanting to make Tuesday either sad or mad. "Have they called yet?"

"No, and I'm not sure how eager I am to see them," Tuesday said forcefully. "If Pa is going to keep that crap up from last night, I'm not going to put up with it."

"They've had a night to think about it, and talk," Tess said hopefully. "Maybe they've recognized how we feel about each other, and will let things happen as they happen."

"Yeah, right," Tuesday said dismissively. She looked up, and ducked her head. Both Tess and Phoebe instinctively glanced upward, but there was nothing there.

"What, you didn't see that pig flying by?" Tuesday said grinning, but Tess could see it was a strained grin, and her heart wasn't into it. "You're lucky it didn't think it was a bird, and drop a load on us."

"That *would* be unfortunate," Phoebe said in a monotone.

Tess sighed, and slapped her girl on her butt. "You startled me," she accused, but smiled to show she was joking.

"Well, pigs flying, my parents understanding. The odds are about the same," Tuesday said, and gave her a quick kiss before going to her catamaran to prep for the next Dolphin Cruise.

♦ ♦ ♦ ♦ ♦

He knew where the man worked. He couldn't wait until after he was off. In this setting, he would be strong, able to say the things he needed to. If he waited until late tonight, if the man touched him, he would surrender. He knew it.

He walked around to the back door of the restaurant. There was a dumpster, and he knew some employees came out here for a smoke, or to make phone calls. He'd walked by several times today, as well as yesterday. He'd seen the man talking on his phone on a break once yesterday, and had to fight the urge to approach him.

But today, that was precisely what he needed to do. Walk up to him, tell him what *he* wanted, what *he* expected, and to tell him what wouldn't, couldn't, happen.

The little courtyard, more a driveway really, was empty. No employees or homeless, or anyone else hanging around. He looked at his watch and decided he could wait a minute or two. He'd come by several times a few hours ago, but hadn't seen the man.

Even as he thought about giving up on the trip, the back door opened quietly, and the man slipped out, looking at his phone, carrying a trash bag with his other hand. The man opened the heavy polyethylene lid, flipping it backwards, and swung the lightly filled trash bag inside.

He hung back as the man spoke with someone. When the call was over, he stepped forward, and the man looked up in surprise. That expression was quickly replaced with a pleased one.

"Well, hello there, hunk," the man said, and winked at him. "I'm at work, so I can't oblige you now. You will get your chance tonight, as I told you."

"What about my chance to have you go down on me?" he said, his voice sounding hoarse to him. He looked around, but couldn't see anyone. "I went down on you the last two nights. Tonight, it's your turn to go down on me."

The man laughed, and it wasn't a pleasant sound. He felt his resolve weakening under the man's incredulous stare.

"No, no, I don't go down on anyone," the man said, his lips twisting into a smile stained by a sneer. "I don't bend over, or bare my beautiful bottom to anyone. If I think you have promise, I let you go down on me. And you know you loved doing it. After you'd drained me of every drop, you still kept trying to milk it for more. And you swallowed every drop."

"I did it so you would…" he began, and the man gestured swiftly with a hand, cutting him off.

"You did it to please me, which you did. That doesn't mean it's my turn to please you." The man stepped closer and cupped his cheek with an open hand. "My mouth and ass aren't open to anyone. Like I said, if you interest me, I let you go down. If you satisfy me, and I like you, I reward you by riding you like a pony."

The man stepped close to him, tucking his phone into a pocket, and running his fingertips down his chest.

"You're a virgin, or you were, anyway. And you worked hard to please me, and you did," the man said, and his lips were dangerously close to his. "And tonight, I know a place we can go, and I will deal with that last bit of virgin territory of yours. You know you want to, you know we're going to do it, but you need to understand, it isn't reciprocal. It never will be."

The man reached around him and grabbed his ass, his middle finger digging into his butt crack.

"Tonight, I'll be buried right here, up to my balls inside you." The man made a kissing gesture with his lips. "And you will be sad when I'm spent, and slowly pulling out."

"No!" he cried out, hearing the shame and pain in his voice, because he knew everything the man said was true. He shoved the man with both hands, hard. He had to get him out of arm's reach.

The man's expression flashed changes from lust to surprise, to anger, to fear as his slick, polished shoes slipped on the oily concrete, and he staggered backward, out of control.

The back of the man's head slammed against the corner of the dumpster, and he saw the light go out of the man's eyes. For a terrifying moment, the man was suspended against the corner of the dumpster, and then seemed to collapse and fold in on himself to the ground.

Even from where he stood, he could tell the man's skull was no long in the exact same shape it had been. When he looked at the dumpster, he could see the dark, wet stain covering the closest top corner.

He backed away, then turned and walked as fast as he could until he was out of the drive, and down the sidewalk to Caroline Street. He looked both ways, then made his way across the street at a firm but not hurried pace. But his mind couldn't slow to match his gait.

The vision of the man, crumpled like an under-stuffed toy, with the back of his head caved in, would not leave him.

◆ ◆ ◆ ◆ ◆

"That was good," Nico admitted as they got into his car. "I haven't been to Santiago's Bodega in years. Thanks for thinking of it."

"I forgot how much I like eating there," Lori Lynn admitted. He felt her eyes on him as she clicked her seatbelt. He had very good peripheral vision and hid his grin at her sighing as the pressure of the belt dug into her midriff.

She seemed to make a slight adjustment to where it crossed her midsection, and stifled a sigh of relief. Her belt was still attached, so he was pretty sure he knew what she'd just done.

"You don't have to stop on my account," he said cheerfully, and she swatted his arm.

"I shouldn't have tried your lamb and chicken skewers," she muttered, and then shrugged and unzipped her pants an inch or so. "How the hell did you see me unbutton my pants?"

"Eyes in the side of my head," Nico said, smirking. "I've been an adult male for almost twenty years, and a teenager for seven more. My DNA is fine-tuned to the sound and motion of a beautiful woman's pants being unfastened."

"Shaddap," she said, and rubbed his arm where she'd swatted him. He grinned.

"Thanks, Tess."

"She's a bad influence on me," Lori Lynn admitted. "I see her swat Tuesday, and then rub the spot. I swear it's a form of foreplay to them."

"Hmm," Nico said, and Lori Lynn laughed.

"Well, *that* didn't come out the way I intended," she admitted.

Nico decided changing the subject would do wonders for her self-consciousness.

"You wrapped up your case today in hours," he said, glancing over at her. "Was it that slam dunk?"

"It was," Lori Lynn said, and he could hear the sadness in her voice. "It was an old couple, Arnold and Pamela Miller, and she'd been having flashes of dementia for a couple years now, and it's been getting worse. Plus, she was diabetic, and her liver and kidneys were on their last leg. She took almost a full bottle of sleeping pills. The city cop was pretty sure the husband assisted in her suicide, but he was devastated. I talked to him, listened to his voice and watched his face."

Lori Lynn sighed.

"He was the picture of heartbroken. They'd been married sixty years. She'd been living in her own little world more often than not this month. She missed his birthday two weeks ago, their anniversary last Sunday, and late last night, the doctor thinks she became lucid. Her husband was sleeping in the chair next to her, and his iPad was on. She looked at the date, and realized that she'd been out of it almost all month, and had also missed Christmas."

"I'm sorry," Nico said, hearing the pain in her voice. A drawback of being homicide detectives, was that almost everyone they met was either dead, somehow related to the deceased, or the murderer. It was hard, and no matter how calloused you thought you were, how tough, how many times you'd seen the same tragedy, sometimes it really hit you hard. He could tell Lori Lynn was feeling down, and wished there was something he could say or do to make her feel better. But his day hadn't been much better.

"He woke up this morning to find his wife dead, and a note from her, telling him she didn't want him to have to take care of her any more. She was setting him free." Lori Lynn dabbed at her eyes with a tissue from her purse. "He was devastated. There's no other word for it. I copped out and left Chris to write the report and make sure the city cops didn't try and charge him or anything. He canvased their neighborhood to find out if there were any children, or grandchildren, or any other family or close friends we could call. It's not fair to him, to stick him with such a downer case the day after Christmas."

"It's how they learn, how they develop the strength to work through the painful cases and moments," Nico said softly, and rubbed her cheek lightly with his right hand. She pressed her head against his hand and held it close with her left hand.

"What was your case?" she asked, giving his hand a squeeze and sitting upright again.

"Two guys overdosed," Nico said. "Annette is following up on the lab results, but I've seen reactions like that before. The dope was either made by incompetents, or it was deliberately mixed with rat poison or something like that. She texted me a while ago that she was going home for dinner, and didn't think the test results would be done until sometime tomorrow. Two young men, or boys, really. Maybe a couple, or maybe just close friends. They shared a room and bed." He shook his head in annoyance. "And now, they're dead."

He pulled into her driveway, and she looked at her house in surprise.

"Did you speed?" she asked suspiciously, and he shook his head.

"Must have been the clever repartee of our conversation," he said, and got out of the car with her.

"You need to let me be designated driver more often," Lori Lynn said, looking at him contritely. She suddenly seemed to realize he was walking her to her door, and looked at him suspiciously. "What are you doing? You *know* I'm not drunk."

"No, you're not," Nico agreed with her amiably, continuing to walk with her.

"Seriously, let me drive next time," she said. "You only drink a beer or two if you're driving. I feel like I'm depriving you of your whiskey."

Nico smiled at the thought, but shook his head.

"Plenty of that at home if I need some," he said. "Anyway, we Uber on Sundays, so I drink whiskey then."

Nico watched Lori Lynn unlock her door. She turned to him, shaking her head in bemusement.

"You know I *am* not just a Lieutenant and a detective, but also a trained police officer, and carry one of these," she said, raising the side of her jacket enough to show him the butt of her handgun.

"I like walking you to your door," Nico said easily, knowing the real reason was he didn't really want the evening to end. "You sure you don't want to watch a movie or play some cards or something? It's not that late, even for a weeknight."

Lori Lynn smiled sadly at him, her eyes giving away her fatigue.

"Watch a movie, eh?" she asked, feigning disbelief. Then she quit teasing. "No, I need to do some laundry and chores around the house if you and I are going out on the boat this weekend."

"I'm very good at folding dainties," Nico said with a straight face, and she grinned at him.

"Nobody says dainties," she said, and shook her head in derision. "And why would I need to fold them? Stuff them in the drawer, close it, chore done."

"You don't fold your socks and undies?" Nico asked, teasing her. "How do you find both in the pair, and see what your choices are?"

"I choose the ones on top," she retorted. "I own very few panties or bras that are that specific, or much in the way of clothes that it matters what color my undies are, or if they match."

Nico wanted to hug her, but knew he couldn't. He saw her expression and realized she'd just read his mind.

"Get out of here, Nico," she said gently. "I want you to stay as much as you do."

Nico nodded, and as he turned away, he felt his phone vibrate. He waved goodbye as he walked back towards his car. It was the dispatcher, telling him of a body found off Margaret and Caroline, behind the Prime Steakhouse.

"Okay, contact Detective in Training Wilcox, tell her to meet me there," Nico said, and sighed. He had casual slacks, a Key West casual shirt with a light-weight jacket, and comfortable shoes on. It would have to do. He and Annette were on call tonight. He hoped she had a chance to have dinner and spend a little time with her husband since she got home. Usually the day after Christmas was not a big day for finding dead bodies, but 2019 had been that kind of year. He was now glad he'd only had the one beer.

"Hey Nico, you get a call on a body?" Lori Lynn called to him.

"Yeah, Annette and I have this one," Nico said, waving at her. "You go do your laundry."

"You sure?" She sounded uncertain. He wasn't sure if it was because she felt a sense of duty, or whether she didn't want the evening to end any more than he did. But they needed to be sensible about things. She's had several whiskey sours, and shouldn't drive. And if they showed up together, it would just make more mouths flap.

"Yeah, I got this," Nico said, reluctantly. "You've had a couple tonight, and we don't need even more chatter."

"Yeah," she agreed reluctantly. "Give me a call if it's anything interesting."

"Okay, Lute," he said, and didn't dare look back at her as he quickly got in his car and pulled away.

Fifteen minutes later, he pulled up next to a Key West City police cruiser and parked illegally, putting his own blue light on his dash. He walked down the alley and was glad to see he was the first detective on the scene. So, jurisdiction was settled. He watched the city cop take pictures of the body, as well as the stained concrete and asphalt around it.

He stepped over to the side, and crouched to get a closer look at the body. There was a very impressive dent in the back of the head, and he instinctively looked around for a possible weapon or cause. His eyes caught the dark stains on the corner of the trash dumpster.

"Hello, Sergeant," Annette said from behind him. He was glad he hadn't jumped at the sudden voice. It would have been embarrassing and he might have disturbed some evidence. He frowned at the dumpster and sighed.

"If the lid on this dumpster hadn't been open, he might have got off with just a concussion," Nico mused, and pointed out the blood on the front right corner. He looked at the body and tried to gauge the height of the dead man, but in that position, it was impossible. "Detective, I already called and asked the county crime scene photographer to come here. I think we're going to need a couple more uniforms to help us canvas the area and interview people. Can you call that in?"

"Sure, boss," she said and stepped off to the side, pulling out her phone.

Nico straightened and stepped well around the body and looked at the dirty concrete. He looked down the driveway, but the photographer hadn't arrived yet. He pulled out his phone and began taking pictures. He covered the ground thoroughly, then tried to shoot the body from all angles. He finished with several of the dumpster.

He walked down the drive slowly, and took several more pictures. He got to the entrance, and looked both directions. He walked towards Caroline Street and took more pictures. He glanced both ways, and quickly crossed the street. He looked the sidewalk over carefully, but found nothing.

He looked at the Off the Hook Bar & Grill thoughtfully. He turned and headed back to the crime scene. Annette looked at him curiously, from where she was either questioning or comforting a waiter from the Prime Steakhouse.

She clearly wanted him to join them. The waiter was sobbing, and Nico really didn't want to comfort a hysterical gay guy, but maybe he would hold together. As he walked over, he began to get the sense the waiter looked familiar.

Annette looked at him curiously, but introduced Timothy Riley, a waiter at the restaurant, that knew the deceased. The dead man's name was Maurice Renault, and he was a bartender. He thought Renault had come out here to either make or return a call. He often did that, according to Riley.

Nico suddenly knew where he knew the waiter from. He was one of the four gay men that had come to the Thanksgiving Dinner at Eldamar. He was the one that *didn't* make it yesterday, because he'd picked up an extra shift.

About the same time, Riley recognized him.

"Nico, this is horrible," he cried, and Nico had the sudden fear he would burst into tears and collapse into his arms.

"It's Sergeant, sir," Annette said, and patted him on the shoulder. "I think I have everything I need from you right now. You should go inside and sit down for a few minutes, and recover from the shock."

"Thank you, Detective," he said in a broken voice. He made his way inside, and Annette exhaled in relief.

"Dennison is here, and taking pictures," she said. "I think Mr. Riley was in a casual romance with the deceased. From what he told me, it sounded like it was all physical in nature."

"Yeah, he's one of the Eldamar men that come hear Nathan play," Nico said, and sighed. "Make sure Dennison takes pictures of the concrete drive and down the sidewalk to Caroline."

He looked at Annette, and didn't try and hide his annoyance.

"This has become a homicide investigation." He wasn't surprised at the shocked look on her face. "We're going to need the city to send us copies of all interviews and pictures. We're going to need to talk to the other employees, and any open businesses adjacent to the scene of the crime. Later, either you or I need to question Tim in more detail about Renault's personal routine away from work, where he hangs out, what he does with his free time. I have a feeling we should check out across the street at Off the Hook, and talk with the hostess and staff, as well."

"The city cops think it's a cut and dried accident," she said carefully.

Related Matters

"I don't think they're going to like your theory much."

"I don't imagine they will," Nico said, and sighed. "We're going to need to get into his phone, so get that process started, and get his home address. We'll probably find his keys on him. We'll go to his place after we're done here."

He looked at her sympathetically. "Were you doing anything fun when you got the call? Sorry to mess up your night."

"That's okay, sir," she said, and grinned at him. "I got into this division so I'd have the opportunity for things like this. At least we got a chance to have dinner out first."

"Oh, where did you go?" he asked, not really that interested. But he needed to develop a rapport with her. They were going to be working together a lot, and needed to be able to know what to expect from each other.

"Santiago's Bodega, same as you and Lori Lynn," she said, grinning at him. "You noticed that sneaker track in the grease, and tracked it clear out to Caroline, but you didn't see your partner and her husband, sitting three tables over?"

"Oh, you saw that, too?" Nico said, stalling in embarrassment.

"Hell no, but I saw what you were doing, so I went back and looked closer. Still took me ten minutes to figure it out. Good catch, partner."

"Yeah," Nico said and sighed. "I'm sure it'll get me on next year's Christmas card list with everyone working this case."

Annette laughed as she turned away, pulling out her phone.

Nico sat sipping coffee from Burger King, frowning. His frown was based on a number of factors. There was so much data to look at, to decipher and grade as to importance, there was the matter of writing his report of yesterday, and trying to come close to having it be comprehensive.

There was a surprisingly long column of emails from various city police sources, as well as news agencies covering all local media outlets. And all these e-mails appeared to be duplicated in the form of phone messages and texts.

The communication attempts from the city cops were all very argumentative about this being an unfortunate accident, not a homicide investigation.

The journalists all wanted one thing. They wanted to know his reasoning for calling it a homicide. They were fine with it being one, unlike the city, but they wanted to know why he thought it was, when everyone else seemed convinced otherwise. And was it a hate crime?

Nico just wanted two things.

One, he wanted Burger King to learn to make good coffee. An unfortunate side-effect of living conveniently close to headquarters, was the lack of places on the way to buy good coffee in the morning.

And just as importantly, he needed sugar. He would have even accepted Krispy Kreme, which he called sweetly tinged air pockets.

Nico had gotten to the station very early, and he should have taken the time to drive to Dunkin' Donuts. No one else was here yet. He could have had decent coffee *and* sugar snacks to fuel his ridiculous metabolism.

Lori Lynn walked in with a large plastic bag from Dunkin' Donuts, as well as a cup holder with six large coffees. He jumped up to help her and froze at her icy eye contact. He started wondering what he'd done wrong when he realized she was just telling him she could handle it.

He settled back into his chair as she came forward and set the coffees down. Then she pulled out a half dozen box and set it on his desk. He opened it and saw three lemon-filled glazed buns and three apple fritters, with a fourth fritter on top of them.

He looked up at her as she set one of the coffees near his right hand, and set a small stack of napkins next to it. He tried to stifle a smile but clearly didn't, because she looked at him suspiciously.

Nico touched the right corner of his mouth with his forefinger, and raised an eyebrow. She used her tongue to check her own mouth, and the bit of lemon filling disappeared.

"A baker's half dozen, *plus* one," Nico said and grinned, taking the top apple fritter and taking a bite. He closed his eyes to savor the moment. And the fritter. "And plus *another* one. Ooh, Lori Lynn Buffington, I love you."

His eyes popped open, startled by his own words. Clearly, so was Lori Lynn. She stood staring at him, and he felt his face flush.

"I was talking about the fritters and coffee," he said, not quite stuttering. Lori Lynn nodded, her face expressionless. He threw caution to the wind. "But I meant it the way it sounds, too." He flinched, waiting for the reaction.

He looked up to see her putting Latrelle and Gary's coffees on their desks, then one for Chris, and finally Annette's. She looked at it and shuddered. "Pumpkin coffee," she muttered. "They hung witches at Salem for less than that."

She pulled a dozen donut box out of the large bag and set it on the corner of Latrelle's desk.

Lori Lynn set her own cup on the end of Nico's desk, and pulled a chair over. She sat and took the lid off, not looking at him as she spoke.

"For the record, Nico, I love you too." She liberated another lemon-filled from the box, and set it on a napkin next to her coffee. She looked at it for a moment, but Nico was pretty sure she wasn't even really seeing it. She finally picked it up and, holding it, looked him in the eyes.

"So, tell me why the Key West City Police Department has placed a contract on you, and hired a hitman out of Jersey to take you down?"

Nico smiled, despite the seriousness of both topics they were discussing and skirting around.

"Okay," he said, marshaling his thoughts. "Their theory, and at first glance, I don't blame them, is that Renault came out with a bag of trash to mask his making a phone call. He slid on the slippery concrete, fell backwards into the corner of the dumpster, hitting his skull and crushing it, killing him instantly. But the math doesn't work. And neither does the corroborative evidence."

"Math," Lori Lynn enunciated carefully. "Go on."

They both started as Annette and Chris came in the door, with Latrelle and Gary close behind. Annette was animated in her speech.

"So, he pulls this tiny little steel tape measure out his pocket, and measured the distance between where the victim slipped and the corner of the dumpster." She laughed. "I asked how he knew to bring that, and he said he always carries it, and has, every day for the last fourteen years."

Lori Lynn gave him a questioning look, and he pulled the well-worn two by two-inch little steel tape measure out of his pants pocket and set it next to his fritter.

They all saw Nico and Lori Lynn at the same time, and their mouths snapped shut. Annette saw the tall cup on her desk, and made a little dance as she approached it.

"Who's got the best partner in the world? I do, I do," she said and breathed in the aroma. Her head snapped back in shock, and she looked at Nico in awe. "Pumpkin Spice? How did you know?"

"I didn't," Nico said dryly. "Apparently, Chris has the best partner in the world. Thank the Lieutenant for the caffeine and sugar rushes we will all soon be experiencing."

He turned back to Lori Lynn, with a smile. "So, when I got there, I noticed the slippery pavement, and his ridiculous hard leather shoes. My first thought? He slipped and bashed his head in. Just like everyone else. There was a clear mark where he slipped and lost control of his movement. What bothered me was how far he had to stumble back, and still lose his balance to hit his head that way, and that hard. The math didn't work."

"Details?" Lori Lynn asked, encouragingly. "You know either you or I are going to have to defend this stance when the city is so adamantly on a different path."

"Right," Nico agreed. "So, was he just standing there, took a step, or was klutzy, and fall backward? He wouldn't have been anywhere near close enough to hit his head dead on the center of the back. And if he was turning, thus giving him momentum, the slipping marks would have been different, and a different part of his head would have made contact with the corner."

He stopped to take a quick bite of his fritter, and washed it down with a quick sip of coffee. He saw her eyes and hurried to continue.

"I thought the dumpster might be a roll-off, and was actually closer, and the contact caused it to move. But it's an FEL container." He saw her expression and quickly clarified. "Front End Loader," he said, and added for her benefit. "This style doesn't have wheels."

Lori Lynn smiled faintly and nodded for him to continue.

"So, he didn't just slip and fall, he didn't turn, slip, and stagger into it, which really only leaves one choice. And the marks on the grease confirm it." Nico said in satisfaction. He realized what he'd left out and finished lamely. "He was pushed. Hard."

"Somebody pushed him that hard?" Lori Lynn asked skeptically. "We're talking Marvel superhero strength push to send him that far."

"No, we're talking about someone high on adrenaline shoving him, starting him stumbling backwards, trying to keep from falling on the filthy concrete, and not quite being able to right themselves. And when they finally reach the point of no save, the back of their skull collides with the closest corner of the dumpster." Nico shook his head. "Sad thing is, he probably opened it to toss the bag in, and if he'd closed it, he would have hit the hardened Polyethylene lid instead of cast iron, or steel. He would have maybe been knocked unconscious, but it's highly unlikely it would have been a fatal blow."

"Pushed." Lori Lynn said, picking up the stack of photos on Nico's desk and beginning to look through them.

"He was talking with someone wearing athletic shoes, or maybe light-weight treaded boots. But you can see the smudged track when he pushed Renault, taking a step forward doing it. And you can see faintly where he stood, feet squared, either while they were talking, or in shock as he saw the results of his shove." Nico sighed again. "He probably didn't mean to do anything more than shove Renault away."

"Who?" Lori Lynn asked. Nico noticed the rest of the crew had pulled chairs over and were listening as well.

"We don't know," Nico admitted. "I went back and spoke with the waiter that found the body. You know, Timothy Riley, from Eldamar? He's the one that keeps hitting on Nathan and Lawrence. He's at Eddie's every Sunday night."

"Oh, right," Lori Lynn said and gave him a bemused look. Nico belatedly remembered the rest of the crew, and resisted the urge to look at them. He hurried to continue.

"So, we asked him if he could give us any insights on how Renault spent his free time, and if he hung out anywhere in particular." Nico winced. "Unfortunately, he knew exactly where Renault spent most of his free time, and what he was usually doing. This led to Detective in Training Wilcox and myself going to these locations. The restaurant had closed, so Riley volunteered to go with us, because he knew people."

Nico looked at Lori Lynn. "801 Bourbon Bar was very reticent about allowing Detective in Training Wilcox to enter the back bar area. It is a male only club, and they were quite insistent. As unlikely as it seems, Riley was quite helpful in getting us in. Her being armed might have been a contributing factor, as well as the fact they couldn't really be certain she wasn't a cross dresser or transgender."

Lori Lynn stared at Nico. "You told them that?"

"Not in so many words." He shook his head, and Annette chuckled.

Lori Lynn covered her face. "Continue."

"We spoke with the bartender, as well as just about every other man in the building," Nico said wearily. "They all seemed to know him well, and considering the size of the crowd, the percentage of how many of them might well have had a biblical relationship with him was, frankly, disturbing."

"Apparently he has, uh, supersized personal equipment," Annette said, and bit her lip. "I'm sorry. He's dead, and it's not funny. But last night…"

"I get it, I get it," Lori Lynn interrupted her. "Please do *not* go into detail on this."

"Long and short of it," Nico began, and Chris snickered. "Alright, already, enough. Let me finish telling this, so I can get back to work."

Chris nodded, looking abashed.

"We found out," Nico began, choosing his words carefully. "Renault has been gifted with a, uh, manhood, I mean, oh hell…"

"His 'equipment' is of industrial size," Annette said for him, and he looked at her with a mix of irritation and gratitude.

"His attentions are highly coveted. But he only allows others to, uh, experience his industrial equipment," he said, nodding to Annette. "Well, apparently, there's been a number of new faces in the bar this week, and one of them has come every night." Nico stopped as Gary laughed, looking around at them.

"I got that one."

"Well, good," Nico said shortly, and glanced at Latrelle with a raised eyebrow. But his old partner had his eyes closed, shaking his head.

"Well, the suspect has been the recipient of oral attention by one regular or another the first few nights, but Christmas Eve Mr. Renault noticed him, and actually convinced him to uh, kneel, instead. And again, Christmas Night, even though the stranger had already received some *attention* from someone. We found four people in addition to the bartender that were willing to give detailed descriptions, and they all agreed to come here today and sit with the sketch artist. Their descriptions didn't seem all that close to each other, so I don't know how the final product will turn out. Or if it will even prove useful."

"So you think this guy went and confronted Renault at his place of work, out of the blue?" Lori Lynn asked skeptically.

"I don't know," Nico admitted. "But they all said the man was young, maybe late twenties, athletic looking, and pretty quiet, sullen even. One of the men that serviced him hinted he'd like the favor returned, and the man walked out on him without saying a word. It's worth a shot since we don't have any other leads. At least not on *this* case."

Lori Lynn looked at him, and Nico panned the other detectives around him and sighed.

"Okay, so sometimes Renault takes some men to a place that appears to be someone's back yard. This is for when he's going to *reward* some man with his uh, supersized equipment, but not in the mouth." Nico wished he was somewhere else. "Tim has been there with him a number of times, apparently. He showed us last night. We're checking, but we think the owner is a snowbird that doesn't come south until after the holidays."

He turned quickly and stared at Gary. "Don't even think of saying it." Officer Yurke nodded his head meekly.

Nico fanned the photos Lori Lynn was looking through, and pulled the second from the bottom out. He set it where they could all see it."

Lori Lynn looked at the photo and stiffened.

"That's one of the two," she began, and Latrelle excitedly finished her words.

"That's one of the two locations we haven't identified that Neilson had under surveillance," he said, and ducked his head as he saw her head turn towards him. "Sorry."

"So, is Renault somehow connected to the Neilson case?" she asked, looking bewildered.

Related Matters

"He may just have been a victim, like everyone else, so far," Nico pointed out. "That reminds me, we need to talk to someone at Eldamar, find out who lives in that house."

"Right," Lori Lynn said, and looked thoughtful. "Maybe we could…" She got a look of consternation on her face, and pulled out her phone. As she typed, she asked Nico if there were any other tidbits regarding the dumpster case for him to tell them, and he shook his head.

"Whatcha doin'?" he asked. She showed him the text she'd just sent to Nathan. It had the picture recovered of the Eldamar site.

Nathan, can you tell me who lives in this house? Thanx, LL.

That reminded Nico of something.

"You know, the killer tortured Neilson, and it might have been to find out how many cameras there were, and their locations," he said. "Remember, she stuck him several times with knitting needles. Or, she might have already found all the locations, based on the views in the feeds," he pointed out.

"Eldamar is all male with the exception of Tess and Tuesday, and their female friends," Lori Lynn said, frowning. "How could a woman do that comprehensive a search and remove the cameras, without anyone noticing?"

"Maybe we're looking for more than one perp," Nico said mildly. "If someone in the neighborhood hired her, maybe they went around and found all the cameras, and maybe they had help." He stared into space. "It feels like I'm missing something. Something important."

Anything further they were going to say was interrupted by Lori Lynn getting a text.

She looked at it, and blinked in surprise. She sighed and showed it to him.

Lori Lynn, we lived in the ground floor apt before where we are now. Simon Coker and Marvin Lee live upstairs. New tenants are in their late 60s, retired. Chris Cole and Mark Wilde.

"Doesn't look like it leads us anywhere," Nico said morosely, and started as his phone vibrated. He saw Lori Lynn was also getting a text. No one else seemed to be. "Well, that can't be good."

Lori Lynn stared at hers, and held it up for him to see. He sighed, stuffed the rest of the fritter he was eating in his mouth and took a healthy drink of his coffee to wash it down. "We'll be back in a bit," he told Annette. "Keep an eye out for the witnesses. I'm eager to get an idea of who we're looking for." She nodded and glanced at his phone curiously. He showed her the text.

My office, now.

Annette winced and did some sort of salute with her right hand, slapping it against her chest as she spoke.

"To those about to die, we salute you."

Nico winced and followed Lori Lynn out of the room and to Sheriff Raines' office.

♦ ♦ ♦ ♦ ♦

Related Matters

Chapter Fourteen

Phoebe heard Oshba turn the shower on, and reluctantly sat upright. She pulled on a short, black, silk bathrobe with an embroidered Pegasus on the back. It had a unicorn's horn, and was rearing up on its hind legs.

She decided that the water would take a minute to heat up, so she walked down the hallway to the kitchen. She felt something, and frowned. Whatever she'd sensed was familiar, but not part of this house. She heard a step on the stairs to the second floor creak, and turned, expecting to see either Sarah or Aurora.

Grandma Emily, wearing the sundress she'd had on last night and carrying her shoes, froze for a moment, shrugged, and came the rest of the way down. Phoebe stared, and realized her mouth was hanging open.

She didn't know why she was surprised. Both her mother and grandma made no bones about sex for the sake of having sex was a fine way to spend an evening. But this, this was so inappropriate, or somehow wrong, or maybe just disgusting. She was at a loss for words.

"Really? Really?" Phoebe put her hands on her hips.

"Grandma Emily, you just slept with a girl that is *my* age. Your granddaughter's age." Phoebe turned and went into the kitchen to start the coffee. But she couldn't let it go yet, and whirled around. "And she's your granddaughter's roommate. *My* roommate!"

Phoebe saw Aurora appear behind her grandma, looking at Phoebe curiously, but, as far as she could see, with no hint of shame.

"Aurora, she's *over* three times your age! She's my grandmother! You don't think that's maybe just a little bit gross!"

"She has used those years well. She is a wonderful, and very accomplished partner in bed." Aurora shrugged. "Last night was the best sex I've had since I left Italia. She knows exactly how to turn me on, and she did. A number of times," she said, smiling dreamily.

"Fine, fine," Phoebe said, checking the pot to see that the levels of both the water and coffee in the filter were right. She switched the machine on and turned to go back to her room.

"Maxwell House it is, this morning, then," Phoebe muttered to herself as she left the room, knowing Aurora thought this pot made terrible coffee.

"Have a good day, dear," Grandma Emily called after her. "And it wasn't gross for either of us."

Phoebe immediately felt a spike of shame at her own words. She loved her grandma, and she was still a very sexy woman, even at sixty-eight. Saying it was gross was hurtful on her part. She knew they had a limited social life in Cassadega, and she knew they overcompensated for that when they travelled.

Sighing, she turned back.

"Grandma Emily, I am sorry I said it was gross," she said, and forced herself to meet her grandma's eyes. "It was hurtful, and not true. I know you're still very attractive. I was taken by surprise, and not prepared for this. I apologize."

"I told someone just yesterday, that it was impossible to surprise you," her grandma said thoughtfully. "And you prove me wrong, less than twenty-four hours later."

"Whatever," Phoebe said in a low tone. "I'm going to go drown myself in the shower."

Tess gaped at her. Phoebe wondered if she perhaps should not have told her friend. She knew Tess was a bit of a prude in many ways, and very easy to embarrass.

"Your grandma spent the night with Aurora?" she asked, and her shock was quickly tempered by humor. "Way to go, Emily. She's still a very hot lady. She's getting older and a whole lot bolder." She winced. "I'm starting to sound like Tuesday."

"Both my grandma and my mother are always trolling for a good time," Phoebe admitted. "They were wild when they were my age, and never really changed. But their circumstances did. Cassadega isn't that big. If you're on the make, eventually it will be common knowledge. At some point, they both decided that trying to hook up at home was not a good idea. But because of their little shop, and their mail order business, they don't travel near as much as they used to."

"Are you *sure* you weren't adopted?" Tess said, and her smile told Phoebe she was kidding.

"When I was young, we didn't travel a lot, but I did notice that often one or the other of them wouldn't return to wherever we were staying, and the other would watch over me." Phoebe made a face. "Then when I got a little older and figured out what was going on, they sat me down to have the talk."

"The birds and the bees talk?" Tess asked knowingly.

"They had their own spin on it," Phoebe admitted. "First, that it was okay to have these physical urges and needs, and to act upon them. Mother has hated men as long as I can remember, and was sure I was gay from early on. Grandma Emily wanted me to keep an open mind, and if I decided to have sex with a boy, to make sure that I was protected. But that either boys or girls were fine. Or both. Whatever I felt most comfortable with, or attracted to."

"That was your birds and bees talk?" Tess asked, looking thunderstruck.

"Oh, they told me the physical and medical sides to it as well, but they supplemented that with giving me way too much detail on the actual physical actions. What felt good, what boys usually didn't know, and didn't satisfy, how to please another girl." Phoebe sighed and her face got a little pink.

A group of people approached the hut right about then, and they worked together to convince them to sign up for either jet skiing or one of the cruises later in the day. They sold out Tuesday's first cruise, and most of the jet skis for Aurora's first tour, as well as a good portion of the second.

Eventually, they got a break, and Phoebe continued as if they'd never been interrupted.

"Of course, they were telling me all this, and showing me way too many visual aids about sex, and I wasn't sure I would ever even *have* sex with anyone." Phoebe sighed. "I got so much teasing and bullying about my being an albino, or a vampire, or the visual representation of Death, like the girl in that DC comic book."

"But now you have Oshba," Tess pointed out, and Phoebe smiled at her, feeling a warmness in her belly.

"And now I have Oshba," Phoebe agreed. She thought about last night. "I guess I should have seen this coming. Aurora sat by Grandma Emily poolside Christmas Day, and they spent a lot of time talking. And then when we got off work, and swung by Eddie's for a few minutes, Oshba asked if I would be okay with eating barbeque, so we went to the Dirty Pig."

"We just went home," Tess admitted. "We have leftovers like you wouldn't believe. I brought a couple extra sandwiches if you want."

"What kind of mustard?" Phoebe asked, and Tess looked at her with amusement.

"Yellow on the ham, and spicy brown on the turkey," she said. "Provolone and mayo on both."

"Hmm, I'll let you know," Phoebe said, thinking they both sounded good. She returned to their conversation. "So, when Mother said she was going to see Nadine, that was no big surprise. I think she's spent one night at the B&B since they met. Maybe two. And, of course, Grandma Emily going with her makes sense, since her wandering alone on Duval is probably getting old."

"Aurora is always looking for new adventures, so since she'd never even heard of the Garden of Eden, and it being clothing optional and kind of weird, and on a roof, her wanting to check it out made perfect sense," Tess pointed out. Phoebe nodded her head sagely.

"Truthfully, I thought she might be trolling for another conquest," Phoebe admitted. "It never occurred to me she'd found her next victim already, and was just cinching the deal."

"After having met Emily, I'm not so sure who the victim, or the temptress, is," Tess said thoughtfully.

"Good point," Phoebe conceded. She paused, and let her eyes almost close as she concentrated. "Speak of the devil."

Tess automatically looked down the dock and sure enough, Aurora was just coming up Front Street, nearing the Island Bike Rental. She frowned, as if trying to remember something. She nudged Phoebe.

"Could you sense someone that far away when you started working here?" Tess's face flushed with embarrassment. "I can't believe I'm saying this, but I think your range is getting longer. You used to be able to tell when they were right at the dock's edge."

"I thought you didn't believe in my abilities," Phoebe said quietly.

"Hard to argue with proof," Tess said, and followed Phoebe's sudden shift in attention. Sure enough, a moment later, Tuesday walked out of the shed.

"Now you're just showing off," Tess said, and they both laughed. As one, they turned back to the dock and watched Aurora approach. She could see them laughing and her expression was full of misgivings.

The young Italian girl sighed and came in and clocked in on the computer. She looked from one of them to the other.

"I believe the saying is that my ears are burning," she muttered, and Tess put her hand on the girl's arm.

"No, Phoebe was just giving me a demonstration of her radar abilities," Tess said dryly, and Aurora's suspicion lessened appreciably.

"I thought she might have been telling you why she is angry with me,"

Aurora said to her, not looking at Phoebe.

"I'm not angry with you, Aurora," Phoebe said, and a new wave of pinkness began to cover her face. "I am sorry about what I said this morning. I was caught by surprise, but I still had no right to over-react. I flashed back to trips we would take to the beach, or Disney World, and I was too insecure to meet people easily. Yet both Mother and Grandma Emily would not only meet people, but they'd score with college age girls, and in Grandma's case, sometimes boys, and it would seem so weird to me. It seemed like they were flaunting how easy it was for them, and I would never, ever find anyone interested in me."

Aurora looked crestfallen.

"Dear Phoebe, it never occurred to me that you weren't okay with their willingness to meet new people, and spend time sharing their intimacies so freely."

"That was then, this is now, Aurora," Phoebe said, smiling. "I have no problem with your enjoying their intimate company, as you say. I am not the insecure little girl I was then. And I am not alone, and never feel that way, anymore."

"What am I missing?" Tuesday asked, leaning over the counter, looking at the three of them. "Phoebe, you giving Aurora the heads-up that Emily is hot for her bod?" She glanced at Aurora. "Watch out for that one, A-Girl. She's a hottie, and a beautiful young Italian would be a fine conquest for her. Don't let her age fool you."

Tuesday looked in confusion at the three of them laughing. "What?!?"

♦ ♦ ♦ ♦ ♦

Nico stuck his head in Lori Lynn's office door. Idly, he wondered if she was going to keep it, since she had a work station in the cubicle room.

"I just got the word about the I.D. of the Russian dead guy," He said, and stepped inside, started to close the door, and looked at her questioningly.

She nodded and motioned at a chair. "Sit!"

Nico grinned as he sat.

"Ruff, ruff," he said, and then got serious.

"His name is Borya Koslov, and he's, well, he *was* considered one of their heavy hitters." Nico referred to his notes. "When they had a meeting with dangerous folks, he'd always be standing just behind and to the side of whoever was running the Russian side of the meet. Rarely spoke, just glared and looked dangerous."

"*Was* he dangerous?" Lori Lynn asked curiously.

"Sure *looked* that way," Nico said noncommittally. "Raines wants us to go right to the Russians and tell them what we have, and can they send someone to the morgue to confirm his identity. And then try to question them about what he might have been up to."

"I could see that meeting going very poorly," she said, and he nodded his agreement.

"I want to have a body or two with me at that meeting," he said, and grinned at her. "You think the Little brothers are doing anything this weekend?"

Lori Lynn laughed out loud, and then sobered up.

"I'm going with you, and we should take at least one more guy," she said thoughtfully. "Someone that is built like Latrelle, but isn't Latrelle."

"Right," Nico agreed regretfully. "They have a baby, and I'm keeping him off the streets until that kid is at least in college, or high school, maybe," he conceded.

"It's moments like this that make me really wish Mari was county, not city." Lori Lynn said glumly.

"No, we don't take anyone with a trace of Latino in them," Nico said firmly. "The Russians are going to be sure it's the Columbians. Columbians, Mexicans, Cubans, it's all the same to them."

"I told the sheriff I wanted to wait until tomorrow to call for a meeting," Nico said. "I'll have the sketches of the Renault perp by late afternoon, and I'd like to follow up on that right away. I got a plan."

"Ooh, a plan," she said, smiling at him to show she wasn't mocking him.

"Let me check and see what progress they've made on the sketches. I'll get back with you around four."

"Okay," Lori Lynn said, making a face at her computer terminal. "I have to finish up this Miller report. Chris did a good job of writing it up, and I don't have that much to add, but I don't want to deal with it Monday morning. I want it done and behind me." She got a long face. "It's cowardly of me, I know, but there it is."

"There is absolutely nothing cowardly about you, Lori Lynn," Nico said, and stood. "I'll see you in a bit."

"Scoot," she said, and stared at the door long after he closed it behind him.

A little before five, Lori Lynn heard a knock on the door, and looked up as Nico stuck his head inside.

"Annette has an in-law event tonight. Justin's mother's birthday, I think she said. I told her to go on." He shrugged. "I have the sketches from the artist, and I think I'm going to check at 801, as well as Off the

Hook. See if they're as close as I think they are."

Lori Lynn nodded.

"After that, I thought I'd swing by Eldamar and check with the residents of that house. Nathan thinks they'll be home tonight, although if I wait too late, I might have to talk with Coker and Lee while they're soaking in the hot tub."

Lori Lynn grinned at him.

"You want to catch Lee before he's in the buff," she said lightly, letting her amusement show. "Tim Riley made a point of telling me that Lee is the only man on Key West with bigger…equipment than Renault. It might drive you to therapy."

"Whatever," he said dismissively. He blushed a little. "What did you want to do tonight? Ride with me and we grab something after? Or have me get some takeout to bring over later?"

Lori Lynn watched him try to be casual about the fact that they both assumed that whatever either of them were doing tonight, they were doing it together. She could tell he was trying to not sound like it was something to be taken for granted, and she loved that about him.

"Let's ditch my car, and I'll go with you," she said. "I want to look at those sketches."

"I sent you the files," Nico pointed out, and Lori Lynn smiled at him.

"I saw, but I want to look at the copies you made." She got her holstered handgun out of the drawer and strapped it into place, then stood as she pulled her jacket on. She got her purse and decided anything else could wait until the morning. Even though it was Friday night, she was pretty sure she was going to be in tomorrow at some point. "Sometimes bigger is better," she said teasingly.

Nico sighed and shook his head in resignation.

Ten minutes later, they came out of her house, both of them dressed more comfortably. Lori Lynn carried the prints of the sketches. They got in his car and headed across town.

"Unbelievable," she muttered. "I know that face. I'm sure of it."

"That's what I said," Nico agreed. "What's funny is, the witnesses all had very different verbal descriptions, but they kept correcting themselves, and saying, rounder chin, deeper-set to the eyes, eyes aren't that deep-set, more angular jaw, bigger ears, flatter ears."

He gestured at the prints in her hand.

"And yet, this is what we end up with."

Lori Lynn looked at five different versions of the same guy, and a sixth the artist had made that more or less combined the minimal differences, and said he thought it might actually hit the subject better than any of the individual pieces.

Nico pulled into the parking lot next to Off the Hook, and parked close to the fence between them.

"You know this isn't legal parking, right?" she asked, and shook her head when he pulled out his blue light and put it on the dash. "You don't think every Key West cop on duty tonight wouldn't love to give you a ticket right now?"

"Then we should be prompt," Nico said virtuously.

Inside, they found the hostess, a waiter, and a waitress that all agreed they'd seen the man in the sketches before. They also thought the composite version was the closest.

"I remember him," the waiter said. 'They were all rednecks, but he was the most abusive in the party of six with his talk about all the gays in Key West."

"He didn't use the word gay either, did he?" Lori Lynn asked, and he shook his head.

"It was last night," he said, and the other two agreed with him. "Two older people that I think were the parents, and then four adult children, three men and one woman."

"They were definitely a family, and they all had hick names," the waitress said.

"Like Bubba, Bobbi Joe, Lori Lynn? That sort of thing?" Lori Lynn asked softly, and she more felt than saw Nico cringe.

"Yeah," the waiter agreed. "The one, this guy in the picture, he excused himself and we thought he went to the bathroom, but he was gone a long time. He may have gone to the outside bar and had a drink. The parents were riding him about his drinking."

"Was he drunk?" Nico asked, and the waiter shook his head.

"No, he only had two beers while he was here," he said, and then nodded. "Maybe he *did* sneak out to the bar for another."

The bartender behind the patio bar had worked last night as well, but he said he didn't notice that guy at all, and was sure he didn't sell him a beer at the bar.

Nico made sure he had everyone's personal information, and said he might be in touch in a few days about this matter, and they all shrugged.

"We're not going anywhere," the waitress said gloomily. "We're all working New Year's."

While Nico was getting their information, Lori Lynn went outside and called in to request driver's license information on all three brothers. It came through pretty fast and she went in and showed the pictures to all three of them. She covered the names with her thumb, and they all agreed which brother it was.

Nico and Lori Lynn walked outside and she sighed. "Damn, want to guess the name?"

"Chuck Dumarest," Nico said, and she nodded sadly.

"Poor Tuesday," she said, and was glad to see him agree with her.

They got in the car and Nico looked at her questioningly.

"We need to come up with a plan to get a confession out of him," she said, and shrugged. "Otherwise, it's circumstantial, unless we find some physical evidence, forensic, a security cam, or a witness."

"The body didn't give us anything," Nico said. "Although the shoes may come through, if the tread matches, and there's some sort or residue unique to that driveway."

Lori Lynn looked at him.

"What do you want to do?"

"If we're sure he's not going to flee, I'd rather wait until the morning to bring him in," Nico admitted. "Annette would come if I told her to, but she needs to improve her relationship with Justin's mother. Apparently, that woman doesn't appreciate her like we do, or her son does."

"Go figure," Lori Lynn said dryly. "No, don't call her until later, to tell her when you want her in. Let's go to Eldamar and see if anyone is home at that house. Then, once we get done there, I want to go someplace relatively quiet and eat. And I am more than ready for a drink."

Eldamar was just down Margaret Street, and they got there fast.

They stood on the edge of the road, looking at the houses.

"Which one do you think it is?" Lori Lynn asked, and Nico shook his head.

"No idea," he admitted. "We've only seen the pool side of the building."

"I don't know that I feel comfortable just walking back there," Lori Lynn admitted. "We don't have permission, and we're working. I guess I could call Nathan and ask him."

"Ask him what?" Tuesday asked, standing right next to Lori Lynn.

It was everything she could do to not automatically draw her piece. Nico wasn't any better. She heard Tess giggling and turned to see them both standing there, grinning like fools. They must have just come from work, because they both wore Freedom Seas polos.

"I'm sorry if we startled you, Lieutenant," Tess said. "You look like you're here in an official capacity, or I'd call you Lori Lynn."

"We wanted to try and meet the couple that moved into your old place," Nico said. "And if Mr. Coker and Mr. Lee are home, them as well. Which house is it?"

"It's the second one around the corner," Tess admitted, and Tuesday looked back and forth between them.

"Is this about the surveillance thing that happened?" she asked, and Nico nodded reluctantly, which surprised Lori Lynn. "I think everyone is home in both apartments. You want to knock on the front door or sneak in the back patio?"

"I think we'll knock on the front door this time," Lori Lynn said, and Tuesday nodded.

"Are either of you hungry?" Tess asked. "We have a lot of leftovers, and were just going to make ourselves a sandwich. We still have ham and turkey, and some of most of the rest of the side dishes, as well as the desserts. We also have the whiskey you left Christmas Day."

"You have..." Nico began, and Lori Lynn could swear he was about to start salivating.

"We do," Tess said. "When you're done, just come to the patio. We'll be sitting out there, and we'll have something on."

"A hat, maybe some socks," Tuesday mused. "Ow!"

They met Chris Cole and Mark Wilde, both in their late sixties, and quickly realized that nothing they were doing would have warranted any attention. They were both retired librarians and, although they weren't prudes, were still getting used to the very free dress code of the pool area. Mark Wilde was in a wheel chair. They weren't really getting out to the pool much yet, they told Nico.

He got their personal information and thanked them for their assistance, and then rang the doorbell to the upstairs apartment.

"I *told* you they would want to talk to us as well," Marvin's voice carried down the steps, and Lori Lynn looked down and smiled.

They explained why they were there, and although Marvin looked aghast, and wrung his hands, Simon actually looked angry, Lori Lynn thought.

"He always was a surly employee," he said through gritted teeth. "He may have been trying to catch Marvin and me in an indelicate moment, but we obey the rules of the pool area religiously."

"Although we really aren't very religious," Marvin confided to them. "Please don't hold that against us."

"Not a factor with either of us, I can assure you, Marvin," Lori Lynn told him, and he looked relieved. She looked at Simon again. "Do you think he might have been targeting your bedroom window, in the hopes of catching you with your blinds not totally closed?"

"We *are* on the second floor, and he *might* have thought that would make us careless," Simon admitted.

"But we aren't," Marvin whispered to them. "Neither of us want pictures of us in ecstatic bliss showing up at our places of work."

"I can understand that," Nico said in a deadpan voice.

"One of the burdens I've always had to deal with," Marvin admitted to them confidentially in a whisper. "It has made us very conscientious regarding drapes or blinds."

"Well, there you go, then," Nico said, standing up. "He probably assumed otherwise and hadn't yet realized it. Thank you both very much for your assistance, gentlemen. We'll probably see you Sunday at Captain Eddie's."

It took ten minutes, but they finally got away and outside. Lori Lynn heard her stomach growl and looked at Nico. He started laughing, and gestured to the gate between the houses. It was dark and he put his arm around her shoulders as they walked around a large palm tree, and between two bushes. Her arm slipped around his waist, and they walked to the corner of the building and, as if by plan, both stopped. She rested her head against his shoulder for a moment and they stood in silence, holding each other.

As if timed, they started forward, and their arms slipped away.

"That was nice," Lori Lynn said quietly, and sensed Nico nod.

"It was," he agreed.

They came out into the open area and walked over to the girls' patio. Lori Lynn saw they'd set out a spread of containers, and a couple extra plates. She noticed they both had men's dress shirts on, and probably nothing else. Nathan's, almost certainly.

"Occifers, please eat a lot," Tuesday said, and Lori Lynn resisted the urge to laugh. Five minutes later they were sitting with Tess and Tuesday, with full plates of a variety of dishes, as well as oversized sandwiches on rye.

"So where is Nathan tonight?" Nico said, and Lori Lynn looked at him in disbelief. "Ah, over at Ms. Al Nahyan's?"

"That's some pretty good detecting there, Sarge," Tuesday said, and Lori Lynn tried to muffle her laugh.

"Tuesday, don't tease the detectives," Tess scolded her. "They've had a long week, a long year, for that matter."

"You both seem a little somber tonight," Tess said with sympathy. "Poor Tim is distraught. He kept thinking he would get somewhere with that bartender that died, Maurice Renault."

"Oh, he was getting somewhere," Tuesday quipped. "He was on his back, on his knees, and his hands and knees…"

"Don't be crass, Tue Bear," Tess said, and looked at Lori Lynn apolo-

Related Matters

getically. "Tim did say he helped you out, Nico. I'm not sure he actually did, but he *thinks* he did. He says he thinks it's been declared a homicide."

Lori Lynn was very aware that both girls were staring at them to see their reactions.

"Lori Lynn, Nico," Tess began, and blushed. "I think you're working tonight, but I figure while you're breaking for dinner, here at our place, you're Lori Lynn and Nico, and not Lieutenant and Sergeant. Please correct us if we're wrong."

"No, that's fine," Lori Lynn said, and Nico nodded his agreement.

"Well, you both seem kind of down, or at least very quiet, for some reason," Tess said hesitantly. "If you need someone to talk to, or to vent to, we understand what you're going through. When we first got together as a couple, we didn't really understand, and tried to keep a lid on things. So we know what it's like to feel a certain way, but feel you have to keep your relationship secret."

Lori Lynn stared at her, and then at Tuesday. She shook her head. "I appreciate your concern, girls, but you have to understand, our relationship isn't secret, because we can't have one."

"That doesn't have anything to do with the way you feel though," Tess said gently. "We see you both often enough, and we see more than just a working relationship or friendship. I know working together makes that an issue."

"So, you're working two cases tonight?" Tuesday said suddenly. "Where are your junior partners?"

"Annette has something in the family going on," Nico said, and Lori Lynn nodded.

"Chris is off, because this isn't our case. I'm just keeping Nico company and riding shotgun, so he doesn't have to call Annette away from her event."

"And if you were both off, you'd be having dinner together anyway," Tuesday said, and Lori Lynn became aware she was looking at Nico closely. He was staring at just about anything so he didn't have to look at Tuesday, and she realized the girl was sharp enough to know it.

"So, Nico, could you tell me something?" Tuesday asked, and both of them looked at her a little apprehensively. With her, you never knew which direction she was coming from. He nodded cautiously. She smiled her thanks, but Lori Lynn saw it was a pained smile.

"Did Chuck kill Renault?"

All three of them stared at her.

❖ ❖ ❖ ❖ ❖

Chapter Fifteen

Tess sat in a state of shock. Tuesday told Nico that he usually watched her like a hawk, because he never knew what she might say or do. But after the initial greeting, he hadn't looked either of them in the face directly, even once.

There was more, but to Tess, it became a buzzing sound, and threatened to distract her thoughts. She thought about what was about to happen.

"Tuesday, we intend to bring your brother in for questioning, and I would rather do it in the morning," Nico was telling her girl. "He's been drinking by now, and if we bring him in, he's going to sit in jail all night. We would rather start fresh in the morning, unless we think there's a chance you'll warn him. Then we would have to bring him in immediately, and it might get sloppy."

Tuesday had nodded, and said that by now, he probably had drunk at least a six-pack. He'd acted out of character all day, at least when Tuesday had seen him. She'd wondered what was eating him. Now she knew.

"I'll be right back," Tess said, and stood up. She felt Lori Lynn's eyes on her as she walked into the apartment and back to their room. She grabbed her phone and went into the bathroom. She used the toilet, flushed, and then checked her contacts list and made a call, putting the lid down and sitting on it.

Izzy answered, and Tess could hear the sounds of Diane Isis in the background.

"Izzy, this is Tess," she said hesitantly, and Izzy sounded worried as she asked if everything was okay. "Well, I need to see you, as soon as possible. I know it's short notice, and you're always busy, but this is very important."

"Are you calling me as a friend with a personal issue or problem, for either you or Tuesday?" Izzy asked shrewdly. "Or in a professional capacity?"

Tess hesitated. It was a valid question, but the answer was confusing.

"I'm calling as a friend, and as the fiancé of a girl who may have a friend or family member in legal trouble, and needing help," Tess said slowly. "I know it's short notice, but is there any way I could see you yet tonight?"

"Tonight would be problematic," Izzy said delicately. "We have people in town from up north, and Italy. And everyone has been drinking, so I would not feel comfortable offering any sort of advice or aid. What about first thing in the morning?"

"Well, I lead a stretching routine, and then an aerobics class here at Eldamar, but I can always cancel out of that," Tess said. "This is very important, and I think someone will be picked up in the morning and brought in for questioning."

"Don't cancel your classes," Izzy said. "To be honest, I'd like to come over and watch what you do. I've heard very good things about it, and have been meaning to get over there. We can talk either before the class or after, or both, if need be."

"Um, I would love to have you come, either to watch or to take part," Tess said, and continued delicately. "Just remember, both programs are done in the nude, both by myself and the students. And most of them are residents here, and male."

"So you're saying it looks gross?" Izzy asked, and Tess smiled faintly.

"Something like that," Tess admitted. "But I think I'm going to have to head out to work fairly soon after the class. We're going to be short-handed if Tuesday is at the county jail."

"Tess, is this regarding the death of Maurice Renault last night?" Izzy asked quietly. "Initial reports from the city said accidental death, but the Monroe County Sheriff's offices upgraded that to homicide late last night."

"Yes," Tess admitted softly.

"Tess, I will listen with an open mind tomorrow, and please do not give me any particulars right now, or you may be leaving yourself open to being charged with obstruction," she said. "Having said that, his head was crushed in, and based on what little you *have* told me, I can narrow the possibilities down, or could if I were so inclined."

"Okay," Tess said, not knowing what else to say.

"Tess, I love you like a daughter, and Tuesday as well, but some of her family members have made a very negative impression on a lot of people, considering they've only been in town for five or six days. If we are going to be talking about one of the family members that has been very outspoken in his, shall we say, disapproval, for certain life styles, if he was charged, it would almost certainly be upgraded to a hate crime. And I will not defend someone that has earned being charged with that."

"I understand," Tess said in a low voice. "But I have a thought. And I don't know that it's quite that simple. I think Tuesday knows better than me, but we haven't had a chance to discuss this yet."

"How did you find out?" Izzy asked curiously, and Tess blushed.

"Two detectives were working a different case with ties to Eldamar, and we invited them to have leftovers from Wednesday with us," Tess admitted.

"Ah, Lori Lynn and Nico, poor kids," she said, and sounded sympathetic. "Dear Tess, I have to go, but I will see you early in the morning. Oh, and congratulations on your engagement. I can't believe Tuesday didn't wait to propose here at Diane Isis, so we could all see it."

"I think she was going to, but her family was pressuring her to move back to Jacksonville and work on stopping this silly gay thing. I think she wanted to shut them up," Tess admitted.

"I understand," Izzy said. They spoke a few more moments, and then Izzy hung up.

Tess sat on the toilet for a moment, fighting the urge to have a good cry. Then she sighed, and opened the door to go rejoin them on the patio.

Lori Lynn was sitting on the corner of the bed, looking at her with no expression on her face.

"Oh, hi, Lori Lynn," Tess said, trying to hide her shock. "You need to use the bathroom?" Lori Lynn just stared at her. "Um, is it Lieutenant, now?" she asked timidly.

Half an hour later, Tess and Tuesday watched the two detectives walk out of sight between their building and Walter and Tom's. Tuesday turned and looked at her thoughtfully.

"I bet that if that had been me, and not you that made that call, they'd be putting me in the back seat of Nico's car right now," she said pointedly.

"Then I'm glad it was me," Tess said crisply, trying to hide how shaken up she was. "And don't pretend you weren't going to call her."

"I would have waited until the fuzz was gone," Tuesday pointed out, and Tess nodded her head, conceding that point.

"Now, you and I have to talk, and make sure we're on the exact same page on this," Tess said. "You're going to take Nathan's car in the morning, to be at the jail when they bring him in. I will talk Izzy into following you there, and getting involved. I think I know what you're seeing, and I agree. We have to figure out how to use it to change perceptions."

"It won't be easy," Tuesday warned, and Tess nodded glumly.

"If it was, it wouldn't be our style," Tess admitted. "I think we should try and track Tim down, too." Tuesday nodded, and listened closely as Tess explained her plan.

Twenty minutes later, Tuesday looked at Tess in awe.

"You really *did* know what I was thinking."

Tess opened her eyes and looked at the alarm clock. It wasn't set to go off for another twenty-seven minutes. She glanced over, but of course, Tuesday was already up and gone. Muttering, she rolled out of bed and started her usual weekend routine.

She looked in Nathan's room, and belatedly remembered he'd stayed at Yasmin's last night. She poured a cup of coffee and walked out the back door to sit on the patio. She saw Izzy and Diane already seated, with travel cups and a plate of small cinnamon buns. They were facing the back door and both grinned as Tess froze, and glanced down at her own very naked body.

"We've seen hot naked ladies before," Izzy said, and Diane nodded.

Tess muttered to herself as she got a couple towels off the stack. She put one on the chair to sit on, and wrapped the other around herself. Diane gestured at the buns, and she stared at them for a long minute before reluctantly shaking her head.

"I'll have one after my workout," she said, digging deep for resolve. Tess looked at Izzy and winced. "It turns out Lori Lynn was listening to our phone conversation."

"Ouch," Izzy said, smiling with sympathy. "And you're able to sit down, less than a day later?"

"I know," Tess said, remembering Lori Lynn's biting comments last night. "I convinced her I wasn't warning Chu…" Belatedly she remembered who she was talking to, and what she did on weekdays. "That I wasn't warning anyone, that she didn't have to worry about you giving him advance notice, or assisting his avoiding being brought in. I told her you probably wouldn't even consider taking the case."

"Last night, you seemed to think there were factors that would sway my conviction." Izzy selected a bun, looked at it, and meticulously took a bite. Her eyes met Tess's and her features hardened. "Okay, I'm here. Talk to me. Tell me what extenuating circumstances would make me give the slightest damn what happens to that hateful shit."

Tess took a deep breath and told her what she and Tuesday had discussed last night after the detectives left. It took almost half an hour, and

Sarah showed up before she was done. She said hello to them, and asked Izzy and Diane if they were going to do the stretches and aerobics this morning?

Izzy said maybe, and Sarah got the hint.

"You ladies go on with your talk. I'm going to go make a cup of real coffee with Yasmin's machine." She disappeared into the apartment. Almost immediately, music began to play in the kitchen. Izzy nodded her approval. "My respect for that girl grows every time I see her," she said, and Diane nodded her agreement.

"Isn't she great?" Tess asked, and gulped as Izzy transferred her attention back to her.

"Weren't you trying to make a point just now?" she asked pointedly. Tess nodded and hurriedly continued her spiel.

Eventually Tess ended her monologue, and Izzy began to hit her with questions. She answered as best she could, and eventually Izzy sat back, staring into space.

Sarah came out of the apartment carrying two cups of coffee. She set one down in front of Tess, and moved her first cup out of her reach, shuddering. She walked to a table near the pool showers and proceeded to strip, and neatly pile her clothes next to her coffee. She took one last sip, and rinsed off. Then she waded in and began doing laps.

Diane picked up Tess's original cup of coffee, sniffed it and shrugged. Izzy laughed at her, and turned her attention back to Tess. "Diane and I share quite different opinions about what is acceptable coffee."

"Nathan and Tuesday will drink anything," Tess said. "I need to learn how to use Yasmin's coffee machine. This is very good." She held it out and Izzy leaned forward and sniffed it, and her expression showed grudging approval.

"Is that everything?" Izzy asked Tess, and she nodded, feeling depressed.

"Everything we know, or suspect," she said. "Tuesday is going to try something this morning when Nico questions him, if he'll let her."

"She'll probably end up getting arrested," Izzy said dryly. She nodded, more to herself than anyone else. "I guess I should be there, if nothing else, to keep her out of jail."

"You'll help?" Tess asked, and Izzy shook her head.

"I'll listen," she corrected Tess. "Tess, I have a reputation and responsibility to represent and help Key West's gay community survive and protect themselves legally. If I represent someone charged with hate crimes, I risk losing all credibility. My ability to make a difference will be zero." Diane reached over and put her hand on Izzy's, and both hands instinctively wrapped together. "If your theory is true, and it is evident, I might be able to affect things."

Izzy looked at Sarah swimming, and turned back to Tess.

"Don't you usually swim every morning?" she asked.

"I do, but this was more important." Tess shrugged. "Missing one day won't kill me."

"Tess, you're an emotional mess right now," Izzy said. "Swimming will help clear your head. I wanted to take your class today, but I want your A game. Maybe I'll come back tomorrow morning, if that's okay. Go swim. If you don't have time to do a full session, use the remaining time you usually allot for this. Try and stick to your routine today. It'll help take your mind off what's going on."

"Good idea," Tess admitted. Izzy and Diane climbed to their feet. Tess impulsively hugged them both. "Thank you for giving me the chance to talk with you. We'll understand, no matter what you decide."

"Bring the plate back Monday night," Izzy said, pointing at the cinnamon buns. "I'll let you know how this morning goes."

Tess watched them leave.

A minute later, Tuesday ran around the corner of the house.

"Running down Margaret Street, I thought I saw Izzy and Diane ride off on a Harley Davidson," she said, looking at Tess questioningly.

"Izzy says she'll be there this morning, and she'll listen, but she said she's making no promises." Tess wrapped her arms around her girl. "It's all on you, Tue Bear."

"No pressure," Tuesday muttered, and her embrace tightened.

"Ooh, cinnamon rolls!" Tuesday exclaimed, and Tess sighed in resignation. At least it wasn't a squirrel or butterfly.

"Leave some for Sarah and me. And Yasmin. She'll probably be here soon."

♦ ♦ ♦ ♦ ♦

Chapter Sixteen

Lori Lynn walked into the County Sheriff's Offices, and rued that it was Saturday morning, and she was here. She saw Tuesday sitting in the lobby. She was uncharacteristically dressed in a nice collared shirt and dark slacks. She sighed and walked over to her. The girl's eyes were closed, but they popped open as Lori Lynn neared her.

Tuesday stood up, and glanced behind her.

Lori Lynn shook her head.

"Nico and Annette are bringing him in for questioning. They came in a different entrance. He clearly wasn't expecting us," she said, nodding her thanks. "Your family was universally pissed off, according to Nico."

"I bet," Tuesday said, and looked thoughtful as she fell into step with Lori Lynn. "So, are you guys moving, being evicted, or migrating? These buildings look like portable classrooms."

"I don't want to talk about it," Lori Lynn muttered, wishing Sheriff Raines had heard Tuesday's question. "C'mon, I'll explain the ground rules while we walk. Nico and Annette are bringing him to one of the, um, conference rooms."

"Is that anything like an interrogation room?" Tuesday asked, and Lori Lynn winced.

"As much as anything in a portable classroom *can* be," she responded crisply.

Tuesday nodded, and followed her into a darkened room. There was a large window into the next room, and Lori Lynn could see Annette get Chuck Dumarest settled into a chair at the only table in the room. Since at the moment, he'd only been brought in for questioning, he wasn't restrained.

Nico sat down across from him, and Annette looked like she was about to sit in the second chair on that side of the table. The door to the room opened and Tuesday walked in. Lori Lynn stiffened and looked around the room in surprise, but she was alone. But only for a moment. The door from the hallway opened and Sheriff Raines walked in with Izzy Martelli.

"Got a visitor for you that says this may concern her," he said, giving her a stern look.

The sheriff looked through the window and blinked.

"What is *she* doing in there?" he asked, frowning.

"She was in here with me just a moment ago," Lori Lynn said, frustrated. She noticed Izzy hide a grin. The ludicrousness of the situation didn't escape her. She turned on the sound from the other room. There were cameras on all four walls, as well as a number of strategically placed microphones.

"You can't be in here, Ms. Dumarest," Nico said formally, and started to turn to Annette.

"Sergeant, I would like to talk with my brother, in your presence." Tuesday said politely. "I assume you told him his rights, and he waived a lawyer, at this time?"

"Uh, yes," Nico said guardedly. Lori Lynn felt for him. Tuesday was acting so unlike herself, he had no idea how to deal with her.

"I think if you let me talk with Chuck, you will get the answers you're looking for," she said carefully. Tuesday looked at Annette. "Detective in Training Wilcox, I think my brother will be more open with just myself and a male detective in the room. I'm sorry, but could you go join Gibbs and Ziva?"

Lori Lynn saw Annette stop herself from looking at the mirror, which is what it seemed from the other side. Her mouth was clamped shut and she looked at Nico. He looked bemused as he panned the suspect, the sister, and his partner. He finally nodded, and gestured with his head subtly at the door.

Annette looked at Tuesday.

"I hope you know what you're doing, girl," she said, and knocked on the door. A uniformed deputy immediately opened it and nodded to Annette as she passed him. He saw Tuesday and stared in surprise. His expression turned to guilt as he looked at Nico, who thanked him and told him to close the door.

Annette walked into the room and looked at Lori Lynn.

"Hi Ziva, heard you was dead!"

Lori Lynn resisted the urge to smile at the reference to NCIS, as well as the movie "Escape from New York."

"How did she sneak by him?" the sheriff asked, and Annette shrugged.

"Sir, I wouldn't even hazard a guess," she admitted. "Tuesday is *always* surprising people."

As one they turned to watch through the window.

"Chuck, we need to talk," Tuesday said. "They've got all kinds of witnesses and evidence to put you in 801 Bourbon Bar, and tell what you were doing there. As well as two nights ago, when you snuck out of the restaurant across the street from where Maurice Renault was killed."

"I don't know nuthin' about that, and I don't know who the hell 'Maurice Renault' is," Chuck retorted.

"Technically, he's a figment of his own imagination," Tuesday admitted. "His real name is Morris Reinhold, and he's from South Bend, Indiana, not New Orleans, like he told everyone. You would know him by his big, oversized dick."

"I don't know anything about anyone's dick," Chuck retorted. "What kind of sick joke is that to make? I ain't no faggot!"

Tuesday sat in the second chair, next to Nico, who was staring at her in shock.

"Chuck, something has changed you over the last five or six years," she said, leaning forward. "I know you're not a hateful person, I know you don't like bullies, or people picking on them that's smaller than themselves. Remember Oliver Wilson?"

"Oliver? From Sandalwood High?" Chuck asked guardedly.

"Yeah, but you knew him from six grade on," Tuesday said in a casual tone. "Remember how he'd always get picked on, and some of the bullies would beat him up, or mess with his stuff?"

"Yeah, he was a good kid," Chuck admitted, looked at her suspiciously. "He helped me with math and grammar. You couldn't have remembered him from that time. You were in first grade, or kindergarten."

"Right, but when you and he were upperclassmen, I was in sixth and seventh grade, and I remember him from then pretty well. You always stood up for him. I remember you kicking Art Sloan's ass one time, when he was trying to mess with Oliver. You two were friends."

"So what?"

Lori Lynn could see that Chuck didn't have a clue where she was going with this, and neither did Lori Lynn. But she had him talking.

"So Oliver was gay, Chuck," Tuesday said. "He wasn't out, but pretty much everybody knew."

"He never told me that," Chuck said nervously, and glanced sideways at the mirror. He had to know there were more people behind it, listening. "We never did nuthin'."

"No, you were chasing chicks around," Tuesday admitted. "Twelfth grade, you were already chasing Becky O'Malley. Probably caught her, too. Hell, you married her two years later."

"So what's with all this about Oliver, then?" Chuck demanded.

"The thing is, you were into girls, but you were still his friend, you still stuck up for him, you were a good person, doing the right things," Tuesday said forcefully. "Four years later, you were divorced, but so what. Lots of people get divorces. I always liked her. She treated me nice. Not like that skank, Tori Winslow, your second wife. She was a bitch. But I always thought the world of Becky. In retrospect, I probably had a crush on her, and didn't recognize it for what it was."

"You weren't gay then," Chuck scoffed, and Tuesday shook her head.

"Chuck, it doesn't work that way. I've always been gay. I just didn't *know it* back then." Tuesday propped her chin on her fists as she leaned forward. "I kept trying to make it work with boys, and didn't know why no matter how hard I tried to really like a dude, I just didn't. I faked it a lot, but, there was nothing there."

She sighed and stared into Chuck's eyes.

"Chuckaduck, Becky and I talked. She was really sad you two didn't make it. She blamed herself, said that you two were hotter than chili peppers when you started off, but after you got married, things seemed to cool down. She thought it was her, maybe she was getting fat, or you thought she was stupid. She was sad, but she said that whatever the two of you had when you met, it was gone. Both of you were just going through the motions."

"People fall out of love all the time," Chuck said tonelessly. "I always liked her, but it got to be we just didn't cause any sparks anymore."

"Could it be that when you were a little older, and your body wasn't running just on hormones, she didn't interest you or turn you on, because she was a woman?"

"That's crazy," Chuck protested. "I dated around a while, and then Tori and I hooked up, and we were married within six months."

"And divorced in less than two years," Tuesday pointed out. "I went to confront her. I was pissed because I heard she'd been sleeping around on you." Tuesday reached over and took his hand. Nico stirred and then sat back. "She said you either weren't interested in sex, or when the two of you got together, you had trouble."

"Everybody goes through spells," Chuck said, and pulled his hand away. "You got no right to come in here and start talking about that kinda stuff. I dated plenty of women after the divorce."

"That's not what I heard," Tuesday said, and leaned back in her chair. "It must be tough to realize you're not really attracted to women like you always thought. And living your whole life in Jax, it's not like you could go hit the gay bars without someone seeing you."

"I never went to any gay bars in Jacksonville," he snarled.

"No, you probably didn't," Tuesday agreed. She stared at him. "You probably drove to Savannah, or Gainesville, or both, thinking a different town would be full of strangers, and you could figure this thing out. You were becoming obsessed by the urge, and frustrated by not being able to find release. Both those towns have gay bars, but they're set up different, more like neighborhood bars full of gays, or cross dressers. You couldn't just go into a room and find other people wanting to experiment, and see if your urges were real, if your suspicions and fears were confirmed."

"This is crazy!" he shouted, but neither Tuesday nor Nico even flinched. "You can't hold me here and make me listen to all this."

"Ma let it slip a few days ago that it was your idea that the family come down and see what I was up to, and if the gay rumor was true." Tuesday laughed to herself, a little bitterly. "You knew that Key West was full of faggots and dykes, and there was probably an easy way for strangers to hook up without all the usual social steps."

"What you're saying is sick!" he shouted, but it was a weaker shout this time. "I would never..."

"You would never want to," Tuesday finished the sentence for him. "You're scared to death at the idea that you might like having sex with a man. But the pressure, the need to know, drove you to check Duval out until you found the 801 Bourbon Bar. And it had that room in the back, by the bathrooms. Men would be standing there, and if you just walked in, stood there for a couple minutes, some faggot would come up to you and want to kneel and open your pants."

"No," Chuck said weakly, and wouldn't look directly at Tuesday.

"You forget where I live," Tuesday said gently. "I live in a community where every man except one is gay. They know the ins and outs of Duval. Some of them much better than others. I talked with a guy who knew the man who went down on you the second night. And *he* knew the guy that went down on you the first night. And the fourth. He also knew that when he hinted you returning the favor would be nice, you walked out."

Tuesday reached for his hand again, but he snatched it away.

"They *all* know that when a guy is trying to see if his urges are real, he's scared, he's nervous, he's sure it isn't true. And he's going to be stubborn about actively performing a gay act. Receiving a blow job is just a pleasant experience. A mouth is a mouth. But if you kneel, it's *your* mouth, which means it's all true. You might be gay, you might be bisexual, but you crave sex with a man."

"No, no, that's not the way it was," Chuck said, shaking his head vigorously. "I didn't know, and there was no way I was going to put another man's..." He couldn't finish the sentence.

Related Matters

"That *was* the way it was," Tuesday corrected him. "Several men saw Renault come in the bar that first time, and he's a hot commodity for the single gay men that hang out there. He treats them all like shit, and acts like he's bestowing an honor on you by letting you go down on him. But they all say his dick is magnificent. Beautiful, huge, always ready to perform its duty. He taunts the men in there. He saw you at the bar, figured out you were a virgin to men, and as the bartender said, he could charm the skin right off a snake. By comparison, you were easy. Because you wanted, no, you *needed* to know. So you let him lead you back to the room. And you did as he said."

"No," he whispered. "I didn't. I…"

"Chuck, you know you could never lie to me, and you know I'll never lie to you," Tuesday said. "He basically set you up in what seemed to be an empty room, and let your curiosity and fears drive you to an act you didn't want to do. But you really did. Because you *had* to know. And then you were disgusted with yourself, because not only did you do it, you liked it."

He didn't say anything. He sat and stared at the surface of the table, tears streaming down his cheeks.

"He found you again the next night," Tuesday continued, although Lori Lynn could see she was struggling to remain impassive. Her face screamed compassion for her brother. "Even though you'd already gotten serviced by one man, when he led you back to the room, you went willingly. And you enjoyed what you did."

"I didn't." Chuck's protest carried little strength, and Lori Lynn watched in fascination as he seemed to shrink into the chair.

Nico stirred, and looked at Tuesday, obviously expecting her to continue, but she was struggling for control. He leaned forward.

"Mr. Dumarest, he talked about you with a couple of the men at the bar, later, when he came back in. He asked if you were still around, because he said you were primed like a pump, and he was ready to pop that cherry." Nico clearly wasn't enjoying this type of questioning, and Raines leaned closer to Lori Lynn.

"Is he blushing?"

"He's quite modest, and doesn't really do the locker room raunchy thing," Lori Lynn muttered. "Of course it could just be he's sunburned."

She heard Izzy make a sound, which was good. She'd forgotten the lawyer was still with them. Her attention came back to Tuesday's brother.

"Did he say anything about that to you, Chuck?" Tuesday said in a low tone and put her hand out between them on the table.

"When we were done, Christmas night, and he hugged me, he slid his hand down the back of my pants. I didn't have a belt on and he stuck his finger right inside of me," Chuck said, raising his face to look directly at Tuesday. "He was telling me he knew I liked that, and tomorrow night, he was going to stick something much bigger in the same hole, and all the way in. And I was going to love it." He looked like he was hyperventilating.

"All the while, he's wiggling that finger around inside of me, and I knew, if I let him touch me tomorrow night, it would happen just like he said, because, because, I *did* like it," he finished. His shoulders shook with the sobs, and he slowly reached out to take her hand.

"Tuesday, I don't want to be gay, I don't want to like men, to have sex with them." He took a moment to get control. "But, God help me, I liked it. I liked everything I did. If I'd still been there that night, I would have gone with him."

His mouth worked desperately, and Tuesday handed him a bottled water. Nico looked at it incredulously, and then at the door with a grim stare. Lori Lynn grimaced and glanced over at the sheriff. He felt her inspection and shook his head.

"Hell, for all we know, she just teleported the damned thing in," he said, and she gave a little snort.

Chuck took a drink from the bottle, carefully screwed the cap back on and set the bottle on the table.

"Thank you, Sis," he said, and looked like he meant it. He stared at her, then at Nico, then back at her.

"I didn't know we were going to that restaurant for dinner that night," he said, and shrugged. "I remembered where we first saw each other. It was the first night in town when we ate at the Prime Steakhouse, and I'd walked by a couple times during the day on Christmas Day, and at least once on Thursday."

"At dinner, I slipped away, figuring I'd have enough time to go check the back door to the kitchen. That's where the employees seem to slip out to when they want a smoke, or need to make a call. I decided I could walk across the street, watch the door for maybe five minutes, then go back if he didn't come out."

"What were you going to do?" Nico asked in a calm, measured voice. "That's a pretty public area for what you're talking about."

"No, no," Chuck protested. "I didn't go looking for him because I wanted to do anything. I wanted to tell him that I wasn't going to do anything that night. I felt I needed to tell him somewhere he couldn't get close to me and change my mind. I figured with the kitchen door right there, I could stand clear of him, and be firm. But if I waited until that night, and then tried to tell him I wouldn't do what he said, he would get close, and touch me. And then he'd be holding my hand, leading me out of the bar." Tears started running down his cheeks again, and his shoulders shook.

Tuesday started to say something, and Nico nudged her. She looked at him in surprise, but stayed silent. Chuck kept speaking.

"I got back there, and sure 'nuff, he walked out the back door, talking on the phone, holding a bag of trash. He threw it in the dumpster, saw me as he finished the call, and gave me that smile that made me forget what I was there for, at first."

He opened the bottle and took another sip.

"He told me he couldn't do anything right now, because he was at work, but he walked right up to me as he said that, and planted a big kiss on my lips, and I let him," Chuck said, sounding a little breathless. "He had his arms around me, told me that tonight he was going to put his big, well, he said he was going to stick it all the way inside me," Chuck said, his face going flame red.

"Meanwhile, he's trying to get his hand down the back of my pants again, but I had a belt on. He just reached down and grabbed my ass with one hand and acted like he was trying to force his middle finger right through the material."

Chuck was almost hyperventilating again, but this time Lori Lynn didn't think it was from fear. She kept any reaction from appearing on her face. She knew the sheriff was watching her as much as he was watching the suspect.

"I told him, I'd gone down on him twice, and tonight it was his turn. He laughed at me. He laughed at me!" Chuck stared at Tuesday. "He said he didn't take it, he gave it. He said my *penis* was never going to enter his body. All the while, that finger is digging into my pants and ass, and I thought he was going to tear a hole right through. He said that night he'd be by when he got off work, and I was going to lose the last of my virginity." Chuck looked back and forth between the two of them wildly. "And I knew he was right. If I let him get that close to me, it would happen just that way."

Chuck's hands were shaking.

"I knew if I stayed another second, he would have me. I knew I had to get away, so I yelled no at him and shoved him to make him let go my ass."

"Were you trying to kill him?" Nico asked quietly. "Did you push him back and keep pushing?"

"No, that's not the way it was at all," Chuck said, his eyes seeing the memory, or maybe nothing, as he stared at the space between Tuesday and Nico. "I gave him one hard shove, to break his grip on me, but as he stepped back, one of those shiny black shoes slid, and he stumbled backwards, trying to catch hisself."

"What did you do at that point?" Nico asked, and Tuesday slid back in her chair a little.

"Nothing," Chuck said, and Lori Lynn could see the agony in his face. "I was so surprised. I mean, I just shoved him. That should have backed him up a couple steps, but I wasn't trying to knock him down or nuthin'." He closed his eyes for a moment. "I'm not even sure I really wanted to push him away. But he slipped, and kept stumbling backward, and just when it looked like he was going to get his balance, he hit another greasy spot on the pavement. His foot shot up, and he fell back."

His shoulders started shaking again, and he was struggling to speak. Finally, he was able to say something.

"But then, he just stopped dead, as he hit the dumpster. His head hit that corner, and it was like I could see the light go out of his eyes." Chuck looked almost hysterical. "But he just hung there, like he was impaled by the dumpster. Then his body just kind of folded up and he fell forward, and I could see the back of his head."

"What did you see?" Nico asked.

"It was a different shape. He had such fancy hair, used that jelly stuff I guess. But it was all caved in. And his body didn't move."

"Chuck, please think carefully about this, and answer as truthfully as you can," Nico said. "Did you go there with any intent to hurt him?"

"No," Chuck said in a low voice.

"When you shoved him, were you trying to hurt him, to punish him in any way, for the way he treated you?"

"No, I just wanted to get away. To run." Chuck looked at his sister, and his voice sounded desperate. "I was afraid, Sis. I just wanted to run away."

Tuesday looked at Nico questioningly, and he nodded, eyeing her carefully. She turned back to her brother.

"Chuck, Tess and I have gotten you a lawyer. You can trust her." Tuesday looked at him closer. "Chuck, I need to know you can hear me."

"I can hear you," he said listlessly.

"She's a good person, and she will help you," Tuesday said carefully. "You're going to be charged, and she will give you good advice. Please, for your own sake, and for all of us that love you, do as she says. She's a lesbian, just like me, and she's one of the best lawyers in the keys. She will help you, if you let her. You're probably going to have to serve some time, and get help and counseling. But you need it."

Related Matters

"Okay, Sis," he said in the same lifeless voice. "I've been so mean to you. Why are you helping me, after I've said so many nasty things to hide my own weakness?"

"Being gay isn't a weakness, Chuck." Tuesday told him earnestly, and sniffed. "You're my brother. We're family, and related." She leaned forward to stare at him intensely. "Related matters, Chuck, and I love you."

"I love you, too, Tuesday." He finally looked her straight in the face and she came around the table and hugged him. He began to cry into her chest and she held him, soothing her older brother as if he was her own child.

Lori Lynn resisted the urge to reach for a tissue, even as she realized she didn't have any with her. She heard Izzy stir behind her.

"Sheriff Raines, if you don't mind, I would like to speak with my client," she said.

Lori Lynn turned to face her, and took her offered handshake. Izzy Martelli followed the sheriff out the door, and Lori Lynn looked down at the little travel pack of tissues Izzy had palmed to her, and smiled.

◆ ◆ ◆ ◆ ◆

"Sergeant Skourellos, would you mind giving my client and me a few minutes alone? We need to confer." Isabella Martelli glanced at the large mirror. "Is there a place without surveillance cameras and microphones we could move to?"

"Sure, it's in the next cla…, uh, building," Nico said, and turned to Annette. Detective-in-Training Wilcox, would you please escort them to #3?"

Annette nodded and took Chuck Dumarest by the arm. The officer at the door fell in step behind them. As Izzy passed him, she leaned over and whispered. "It reminds me of my sixth grade classroom building, too."

Sheriff Raines followed her, and nodded to him.

"Good job, Nico, if somewhat unorthodox," he said, and shook his head in amusement. "You think she's looking for a job?"

"Izzy Martelli?" Nico asked, confused.

Raines laughed and shook his head.

"Hell no, we can't afford her. I'm talking about Tuesday Dumarest."

"You'd fire or kill her, within a week, Walt," Lori Lynn said, and the sheriff laughed again. He glanced around, curiously.

"Where did she go?"

Nico and Lori Lynn both looked back into the conference room, but she wasn't there.

"I didn't see her leave," Nico admitted, and Lori Lynn shook her head.

"She has a very unnerving skillset," she said. "I have to wrap up a couple things in my office. Can you try and figure out if she's still somewhere in the buildings?"

"Yeah," Nico said, watching the door at the end of the hallway close behind the sheriff. "Annette is going to get his statement on paper and signed. And we have the recordings of everything, and will have more when she goes over his story with him. I'll check her work later, but this afternoon, I plan on playing Russian Roulette."

"Damn, I actually forgot about that for a couple minutes," Lori Lynn admitted. She squeezed his arm, and they went back to their building. "I have your back. More importantly, I have two very large non-Hispanic plainclothes from Vice to back us up when we go to see them."

Nico left her at the door to her office and walked down the hall to the cubicle offices reserved for the Detective Division.

Latrelle and Gary were deep into some discussion on cameras, and Nico blocked them out. Chris was off today, as Lori Lynn would be if she didn't have things that needed her personal attention.

He sat down at his computer and pulled up the security camera array for the entire sheriff's office. He sighed as he saw five people streaming into the front lobby. He pulled out his phone, took a picture of his monitor screen, and texted Lori Lynn.

Guess who just arrived.

He stood and walked out to the lobby. He could hear Jackie Dumarest's voice before he even got to the security doors. He walked out, and pushed them shut behind him, even as Bubba, the oldest son, began to move towards it.

Jackie saw him, recognized him, and quit yelling at the officer at the check-in window. He turned and marched right up to almost chest butt him. Chuck's father was only about five foot eight, but he seemed to think he towered over Nico, even as he raised his head to stare up into Nico's face.

Jackie had probably been in pretty good shape when he was the same age his sons were now, but the years had been tough on him. His face sagged in places it shouldn't need to, and his muscles had begun to soften, as had his gut.

Bubba stood slightly behind him, and to one side. He was bigger than his pa, and in much better shape. Nico had a feeling he lifted a lot of weights.

"They're trying to tell me I can't get Chuck out," Jackie said in a loud voice. "That ain't goin' to cut it. We're here to bail him out. They tell me

I can't even talk to my son, when he's been arrested. He has rights, you know."

"And he's exercising one of them right now," Nico said evenly. "He is meeting with his lawyer."

"He ain't got a lawyer," Jackie said derisively. "We've only been here six days. He don't know any lawyers from around here."

"Fortunately for Chuck, his sister knows one of the best lawyers this side of Miami," Nico said. "They're meeting right now."

"Oh, that's a relief," Chuck's mother said, and Nico turned his head towards her without letting his eyes leave Jackie or his oldest son. "Jackie, that's a good thing. Tuesday is looking out for her brother."

Mari Sue Dumarest was standing as far back as she could be, and still be indoors, along with her daughter and Bobby, her youngest son. She looked very upset, but Nico wasn't so sure it was at him, as much as at her husband.

"What's his name?" Jackie demanded.

"*Her* name is Isabella Martelli," Nico corrected him. "Tuesday and Tess hired her to defend Chuck."

"A woman lawyer?" Jackie made a face and shook his head violently. "What kind of lawyer is she? Wills and real estate? We need a *real* lawyer. Take us to them. We need to get him bailed out of this place."

"He won't be leaving today," Nico said shortly, growing tired of this man. "He's going before Judge Ramsey in the morning, and will almost certainly be charged with manslaughter or worse."

"My son didn't kill anyone," Jackie snarled, and Nico prepared himself for the man to throw himself at him.

"Chuckie's a nice boy," Mari Sue said, sounding very distressed. "I'm sure there's been some kind of mistake."

"No mistake, Ma'am," Nico said, looking at her. "I interviewed him this morning, and he admitted to shoving Mr. Renault, causing him to slip and crush his skull on the corner of a dumpster."

"That's a lie," Jackie shouted, and Nico felt more than saw the officer behind the counter lift their phone and make a call.

"No, Pa, it's the truth," Tuesday said from just inside the door. She walked over to her mother and hugged her, then turned back to her father. "Chuck has some problems to deal with, and his causing Renault's death is only one of them. Izzy is going to help him with his court case, and get him the help he needs, but he's going to be in jail or prison for a while."

"My son didn't kill anyone. And who is this Renault man, anyway?" Jackie was so furious he was almost spitting.

"Pa, I was there when he confessed. It's on video, and recorded."

"How the hell could you have been there?" Jackie asked contemptuously. "They don't let people into the room when they're being questioned. And how did you even know to be here?"

"Because I knew they were going to bring him in this morning," Tuesday said evenly.

"You knew Chuckie was going to be arrested and didn't warn him?" Bubba asked incredulously, and his face reddened with fury. "He's your *brother*! You don't leave brothers *or* sisters hanging out to dry. You have their back. Just like we have yours."

"I do have Chuck's back," Tuesday said evenly, standing firm, with her hands on her hips. "He's my brother and I love him. I have his back a hell of a lot more than most of you had mine this week. How many comments did you make about my being a pervert, living against god's will, being a deviant?"

"You shut your mouth, little girl, before I shut it for you," Jackie said, and took a step forward. "I don't know what you did, but you had a hand in this somehow. Right now, getting Chuck out of this hellhole is first on my list. And then you're coming home to Jacksonville, and we're going to get this gross idea of you having a wife right out of your head. And if you give me any more mouth, you'll ride back home in the trunk of the car. Hell, I'll throw you in there myself."

"That's not going to happen," Tuesday said shortly. "The days of you scaring me into submission are over. And the days of *anyone* bullying me are long gone."

"Mr. Dumarest, perhaps you lost track of where you are right now, and I'm going to give you the benefit of a doubt, and assume you were being rhetorical," Nico said evenly, and stepped over to stand beside Tuesday.

"Tuesday Dumarest is a well-respected citizen, and she is a resident of Key West and Monroe County." Nico pulled out a pair of handcuffs. "We have a number of empty cells, and I have no problem with arresting every Dumarest in this room that isn't named Tuesday. And then *you* can see the Judge in the morning. Unless his schedule is getting full. Then it would be Monday morning. It'd be a hell of a way to end your vacation in Key West."

"You think you can arrest all of us?" Jackie sneered at him.

"All of you that need it," Nico said, staring him in the eyes. "I know I can."

At that point, the front door opened and two large uniformed deputies walked in and stood near the door, watching Jackie and Bubba, their faces expressionless.

Lori Lynn walked through the security doors into the guts of the Sheriff's Office, two more deputies in plainclothes behind her.

"Hey boys, we playing nice out here? The criminals are complaining about the noise," she said with a saccharin smile that was totally insincere. "Charles Dumarest is going to be busy for a couple hours, but then, we could allow some guests, one at a time. It'll be over there in the county jail. There's a visitor's entrance you can go check in at, later this afternoon, if you like. But I suggest you cool down first. Maybe go find some lunch somewhere."

"Jackie, c'mon, let's go." Mari Sue looked at Lori Lynn and then Nico, and nodded her head, looking miserable. Jackie turned to her and looked like he wanted to argue. Bobby Jo and Bobby were already out the door, and Bubba was moving fast behind them. "Jackie, I said let's go. Now."

Jackie reared his head up and stared at his wife, his face a battle of conflicting emotions. Then he nodded shortly, and followed her out the door.

Nico, Lori Lynn, and Tuesday watched her family go out and get into a Ford Expedition. Bubba got behind the wheel, and when they were out of the parking lot, Lori Lynn turned and nodded to the four deputies.

"Thank you, gentlemen," she said. "Carry on with deciding where you're eating lunch." She looked at the two plainclothes deputies. "We'll see you in a couple hours."

The men nodded and went through the security doors.

"Thank you for the support, but I had this," Tuesday said in a low voice. "Thanks for letting me talk to Chuck this morning."

"You may have saved his life," Nico said. "In the long run, you've probably started him on the path to learning to live with himself."

"Yeah, if he plays his cards right, his family will hate him as much as they hate me."

She turned around and walked out the door. Nico and Lori Lynn watched her cross the side road to the small triangular break area, not walking in her usual fast pace. In fact, to Nico, every step looked like a giant effort on her part.

She went to one of the park benches and slowly sank down to sit on it, her head up, but her mannerisms listless.

Lori Lynn squeezed his arm.

"You did great with her and her brother this morning," she said softly. "I know Walt was impressed with how you handled the situation and her. We may get a still print made of when she pulled that bottle of water out of thin air and gave it to her brother. Your expression was priceless."

"Great," Nico said dourly. She smiled, and nudged him as she passed.

"I'm going to go talk with Tuesday," Lori Lynn said and sighed. "She's one of the toughest people I've ever met, but today I think she reached her limits."

Nico watched Lori Lynn walk over, stand next to the bench and say something to Tuesday. Then she sat next to her, and said something. Tuesday responded, and Lori Lynn put her arm around the girl.

They talked for a minute, and then Tuesday buried her face in Lori Lynn's shoulder. Nico could see her shoulders shaking with her sobs from where he stood. Lori Lynn cradled the girl's head with her other arm and held her.

Nico watched them for a minute and their positions didn't change.

"Those are two exceptional women," Sheriff Raines said, and Nico jumped. He hadn't heard the sheriff come through the doors, and didn't sense the man standing next to him. "Getting a bit jumpy, are we?"

"Well, we *are* going to talk with the Russians today," Nico pointed out, and Raines winced.

"Take whatever you need in the way of support," he said, and Nico nodded.

"Lori Lynn put a call in for the 109th Airborne Division," he said, and both men snickered.

♦ ♦ ♦ ♦ ♦ ♦

Lori Lynn followed Tuesday to the bench and stopped at one end.

"Mind if I join you for a minute or two?" she asked, and Tuesday shrugged.

"It's y'all's break area," she pointed out.

"So it is," Lori Lynn said and sat next to her on the bench. She thought for a moment.

"You know, that was one of the finest interrogations I've ever witnessed, this morning," Lori Lynn told her. "You impressed a bunch of cops and at least one lawyer, I can tell you that."

"Yeah, and when my family hears the story, they'll call me Judas, and Bobby will be all the family I have left." Tuesday sniffed, and pulled a couple tissues out of a pocket. "They'll say I betrayed my brother."

"Well, I think you're cutting your ma and sister a little short, and I'm pretty sure that at some point, Chuck will recognize that you probably saved his life, and gave him a path to finally being himself." Lori Lynn smiled at her. "And if memory serves, you're getting married soon, and you'll have a wife, another set of parents, and you already have that huge family of friends I saw at Christmas. And that doesn't even include your extended Diane Isis family. You are loved, Tuesday."

"Even though I turned my own brother in?" Tuesday asked fearfully, and looked at her. "I got my brother to confess to killing someone."

Related Matters

"Even so, Tuesday, you are loved." Lori Lynn put her arm around the small girl's shoulders for support, and she leaned against Lori Lynn, not speaking.

She felt the girl's shoulders begin to shake, and Tuesday put her face into Lori Lynn's shoulder and began to sob. Lori Lynn turned and reached around with her other hand, cradling Tuesday's head, petting her head as she would a child's.

Lori Lynn spoke quietly, and later she wouldn't really remember anything she said. She only knew someone she called friend needed her love and support, and she gave it.

♦ ♦ ♦ ♦ ♦

Chapter Seventeen

Nico pulled into the lot of the Parking Come & Go on Simonton and Greene, and looked at Lori Lynn. She nodded her approval, and pulled up one foot enough for him to see she was wearing sneakers.

"It's only two blocks to Duval, and word is, we'll either find them in Rick's or in the construction site just north of Greene."

"They got the lease on that building?" Nico asked, and frowned. "There have been some premium establishments over the years that did well there for a couple years or so, and then faded. Tough to compete with so many bars and restaurants so close."

"Word on the street is they bought it," she said soberly, and Nico sighed again.

She knew how he felt. She'd spent so much of her life in this community, from the day she was born until her mid-teens, when her parents moved to Birmingham, Alabama. After she got her college degree, passed the police academy, she spent two years as a deputy in the Jefferson County Sheriff's Department. She applied for, and got into, the detective division, in one of the poorest state capitals in the country.

After one year, she applied for an opening in the detective division of the Monroe County Sheriff's Department. She remembered interviewing with Detective Sergeant Richard Carlson, and then Sheriff Raines, after going through the usual HR steps. Both of them wanted to know why she was looking for a new job after only one year in her current position as Detective.

Her answer to both of them was the same.

"I'm a natural born Conch. I'm ready to move back home. And have you ever been to Birmingham, Alabama?"

Both men had laughed, and it was only a year or two later that she found out her asking that had gotten her the job. That and the fact that Richard actually remembered her from her years as a teenager in Key

West. She suspected Walt Raines remembered her as well, although he hadn't been sheriff when her family moved to Alabama. They both remembered her parents.

Key West kept changing, and not always for the better. But that was life in a nutshell.

"Where do you want to start?" she asked Nico. This was his case, so she was going to follow his lead.

"Let's start with Rick's." Nico glanced behind him, and when his head came back around, she saw he was grinning. "If he's there, we're set. If he's somewhere else, there's a chance someone will tell him we're looking for him, and he'll come to find out why. If he's somewhere else, and doesn't want us to find him, we aren't going to. At least not this easily."

"What are you grinning at?" she asked him and he gestured with his head behind them.

"How on earth do we have two big deputies that are almost identical in size, weight, demeanor, everything, except that minor detail of one of them being white, and the other black?" He grinned at her. "And both named Smith."

"I wanted two that both had the first name, John, but you can't have everything."

"Heh," Nico said.

"Annette okay with our not bringing her along on this?" Lori Lynn asked casually, although she was very curious.

"She wanted to come, but one of us needed to stay at the office and coordinate the confession, and incarceration of Charles Dumarest," Nico said mildly.

They turned left on Duval, turned right into Rick's and went up to the second floor. They approached the bar, and looked at the bartender. She looked like she might be Russian.

She asked what they'd like, and Lori Lynn thought she detected a slight accent that *might* be Russian or east European. Nico ordered them both whiskey sours, and when she asked what kind of whiskey, he said Jameson. When she brought them, he leaned forward and asked to speak with Viktor.

"Who?" the girl asked, her face carefully blank.

Nico smiled, but it was a smile Lori Lynn had never seen before, and it actually creeped her out a bit. He leaned forward again.

"Viktor. Viktor Medvedev," he said carefully. "He is missing something, and I think I can help him locate it."

"I don't know any..." she began, and stopped as Nico raised his hand.

"Please, young lady," he said graciously, his mouth in the shape of a smile that didn't reach his eyes. "Tell your manager I have found something that I believe he will wish to know about. He is missing an employee."

The girl's eyes grew wide.

"You know where Borya is?" she asked anxiously, and looked at him closer, then at Lori Lynn. "You are police."

"We are police," Nico agreed. "And we aren't looking for anything, except the opportunity to speak with Viktor for a tiny portion of his very busy day. We have information he will want to have."

"Where is Borya?" she asked, her eyes pleading for an answer. "Is he okay?"

Nico didn't say anything. He just waited. Even as the girl looked like she was going to press him for details, a man made his way to stand next to her.

"Anika, there are customers at the other end of the bar that require your attention," he said, and she hurried away without giving Nico or Lori Lynn a second glance.

The man looked at Nico, barely bothering to glance at Lori Lynn.

"Where is Borya?" he asked, and Nico shook his head.

"I would prefer to speak with Viktor," he said delicately, and then put some steel into his tone. "I feel telling anyone else would be disrespectful."

"But you *will* tell me, now," the man said firmly. He lifted a hand, and a man appeared on either side of Nico and Lori Lynn. The man smiled. "I insist."

"Insist all you like, but don't try and convince me you are going to threaten me in broad daylight," Nico said, not unkindly. "You and I both know people with power know exactly where I am. And we also both know we didn't come here alone. Please, Mikhail, tell Viktor I would like to give him some information. It won't cost him anything more than a few minutes of his time."

Lori Lynn watched Mikhail begin to turn red with irritation. He stopped himself from speaking, and stood motionless, as if thinking something through. Then he muttered under his breath, and deliberately turned his back on Nico and Lori Lynn.

He got a snifter and poured some brandy into it. He stepped off to Nico's left and set the snifter down. A moment later, a man in his forties walked out of a back room and picked up the stemmed glass. He rolled it to move the liquor, and inhaled over the mouth of it, then took a sip, barely wetting his lips.

He had a cruel face, and his eyes were always moving, seeing everything, evaluating quickly. He was an inch or two taller than Nico's own six feet, and outweighed him by at least thirty pounds. None of it looked soft, either.

The man stared at Nico, and then at Lori Lynn. Finally, he turned and looked at the two burly men, one black and one white, carrying Coronas with slices of lime stuffed in the top.

"Who are you?" he asked, his eyes on the bulge under Nico's left shoulder.

"My name is Sergeant Skourellos, from the Monroe County Sheriff's Office," Nico said, and reached slowly and carefully into his right jacket pocket. He pulled out his badge, along with his I.D. "Viktor Medvedev?"

"Yes," the man said, and examined Nico's detective license closely. "What is so important you needed to speak to me in person?" He handed the license and badge back.

Nico looked around and sighed, then shrugged. He stared at Viktor, meeting his eyes.

"You have an employee, Borya Kozlov. May I ask the last time you saw him?"

"Has something happened to Borya?" Viktor asked, and looked in irritation at the girl Mikhail Belyaev had called Anika. She was trying hard to keep from sobbing, down at the end of the bar. She was having very little success with that.

"We aren't sure. The last time you saw him?" Nico pressed him, and Viktor looked at him in amusement. He turned to Mikhail and raised an eyebrow.

"Thursday night, nine days ago, when he got off work, he went to the Smallest Bar in Key West," Mikhail told him, and Viktor turned to Nico.

"Borya enjoys going there, taking up space, getting tourists to buy him drinks, pretending he's lived here all his life, was a pirate, and is Hemingway's illegitimate son," Viktor said, smiling for a moment, then grew dead serious. "I ask again, has something happened to our dear Borya?"

"We found a body washed up on Smather's Beach last Sunday. Based on forensic evidence, we think it is Kozlov," Nico said. "We need someone to come to the morgue and identify him."

"Surely you do not need me for this?" Viktor asked sarcastically.

"No, anyone that can positively I.D. him will do," Nico said, looking at Anika. "I simply wanted to meet you, to have a face to go with the name, so if I see you having lunch at Sloppy Joe's, I will know to say hello."

"Right," Viktor said shortly. He looked at Mikhail. "Take Anika with you. See if it is our good friend Borya Kozlov. Make arrangements to have the body transferred to a funeral home and cremated. Anika might wish to keep him around. If not, perhaps we will bury him at sea the next time we go fishing." He gave Lori Lynn a good look for the first time. "Borya was very fond of fishing. It is what he would want."

"I believe we've finished with the body, so he can be released to you," Nico said to Mikhail, who shrugged.

"And who are you, pretty lady?" Viktor asked, looking at Lori Lynn. "Another detective?"

"I am," Lori Lynn said politely, and both she and Nico turned to go.

"Wait," Viktor said imperiously, and he was looking much closer at Lori Lynn now. "First, I will see your identification and badge, since you have admitted you are police. Second, do you know what poor Borya died of?"

Lori Lynn sighed and showed her badge and I.D. She handed it to him and waited until he reluctantly handed it back.

"Someone carved a smile on his throat," Lori Lynn said quietly, too low for Anika to hear. "Any idea who might want to do that?"

"Borya was a dark, dangerous man, and women found that attractive," Viktor said dismissively. "Perhaps it was a jealous boyfriend."

"I hope this doesn't get blown out of proportion," Lori Lynn said slowly. "It may well be a personal matter. I hope you don't try and use this as an excuse to misbehave."

"Really," Viktor said, and gave her a vicious smile. "Will you spank anyone that does, *Lieutenant* Buffington? A spanking by you might be the most enjoyable thing that happens to me the rest of this year."

"We're into the busy season, and the town is full of snowbirds," Nico said shortly. "No one needs a war. It's bad for business."

"But it *does* keep the boredom away, *Sergeant*," Viktor said, and nodded his dismissal. He turned and walked into the back offices.

Lori Lynn looked at Nico, and he had a troubled look on his face. She wasn't sure their finding a way to finally get a look at the Russian boss had turned out to be a good idea after all. From his expression, Nico was having the same thoughts. They went down the stairs, and when they were back on the sidewalk again, he shook himself and looked at Lori Lynn.

"What do you think about the Sunset Pier for dinner?"

◆ ◆ ◆ ◆ ◆

Tess stood upright, and sighed in relief. All the jet skis were back, the tours were over, the machines were serviced, fueled, clean, and locked up for the night. Technically, she could leave any time. Tuesday was first mate on the Freedom Wind that had just left, and wouldn't be off until around eight.

She shivered, and was glad she'd brought practical clothes to change into. She loved this new lavender bikini, but it was December Twenty-eighth, and late in the day, and it was getting brisk.

"Aren't you cold?" Phoebe asked as she carried some things down to the shed.

"Yes I am," Tess said, and remembered she wore the sweats she had with her over her swimsuit to save time, which meant she had no underwear with her. Oh well, it wasn't like she hadn't gone commando before.

She walked up to the hut and pulled her sweats out of her bag. They were Florida Gator sweats, primarily blue with orange trim, with a big Albert on the chest. More importantly, they were long-sleeved and had a hood.

"Did you remember to bring undies?" Phoebe asked as she walked by her.

"No, Mom, I didn't," Tess said, and wondered if her parents were back from their fishing excursion yet. They'd chartered a fishing boat for the day, along with Nathan, his parents, and Yasmin. She hoped they had fun. She felt guilty she hadn't spent more time with them, but she did see them every day, at least for a while. Both mothers had come for the aerobics class this morning.

Tess was glad that her parents and Nathan's had hit it off so well. They were already talking about maybe traveling together the next time they came down, which would probably be for Tess and Tuesday's wedding. The very thought made her feel warm and fuzzy.

They had synchronized their lunch breaks so Tuesday could tell her how this morning went. Apparently, she'd pulled it off. Chuck had confessed to shoving Renault, causing his tragic accidental death. Lori Lynn had told Tuesday that her getting the story and confession out of him changed everything. There was very little chance he'd be charged with a hate crime, which would have moved it into federal court. The state sentencing guidelines were much more flexible. Both Lori Lynn and Izzy had already spoken with the prosecuting attorney, and it looked like a deal would be worked out if Chuck pled guilty. According to Tuesday, that was the current plan.

When Chuck appeared before the judge, tomorrow morning, he would plead not guilty, but that was to put certain conditions into play, so they could bargain and work out a deal. Then his plea would change.

Phoebe was doing a quick inventory of her products, checking to see what had been sold, as well as see what samples she should restock.

"How is it looking?" Tess asked, and not for the first time, marveled when Phoebe gave her a bright smile.

"Sales have been very good," Phoebe said, rubbing her hands. "Wally is going to be writing me a nice check at the end of the month."

"He's never going to write that check," Tess said with a straight face.

"Why not?" Phoebe asked, looking thunderstruck.

"He'll make it as an electronic deposit," Tess said. "Since we already have your banking info, for your paychecks, we'll simply deposit it into your account."

"Oh," Phoebe said, and laughed. She saw Tess's expression and laughed harder. "I don't blame you for being freaked out by my good moods. My grandma and mother both think I'm bipolar, I'm so cheerful."

"You were never cheerful and happy as a kid?" Tess asked, feeling kind of sad for her.

"Once I got old enough to understand how people saw me? Never," Phoebe admitted. "I was pessimistic, dour, paranoid, and more than a little bitter at the way humanity saw and dealt with me."

"That's so sad," Tess said, and felt silly as her eyes welled up.

"But then I met Oshba," Phoebe said, produced a tissue and wiped the tear from the corner of Tess's eye. "And then I fell in love."

"And now you're happy," Tess said, smiling in honest pleasure at the girl.

"And now, I am ecstatic," Phoebe corrected her, and impulsively hugged Tess. "I have met my soulmate, we will be married in the eyes of Gaia next time my mother and grandmother visit, and in the eyes of the law sometime next year."

"I look forward to attending both," Tess said, and Phoebe laughed, but didn't say anything. She stood and looked down the dock. Tess stood with her, and saw some of the Dumarest family headed their way.

"Should I call Oshba?" Phoebe asked quietly, and Tess had to smile.

"No, I'll be fine," Tess said, although she was a little intimidated by the fact there were three of them, and only one of her.

Mari Sue nodded to her.

"Hello, Tess, is Tuesday out on the schooner?" she asked, and Tess felt her eyebrows raise. She didn't know Tuesday's mother knew that much about Tuesday's schedule.

"She is," Tess admitted. "They just left a bit ago, and she probably won't be back until around eight. Or that's when she'll get off, anyway."

"I reckon Tuesday told you about what happened to Chuck," she said, watching Tess as she asked.

Related Matters

Tess really wanted to plead ignorance, but knew she couldn't lie to the woman. Really, she couldn't lie to anyone. She was terrible at it.

"She did," Tess admitted. "She told me at lunch."

Mari Sue sighed, looking ten years older than the last time Tess had seen her. Maybe more. "I guess the police already knew, and Tuesday didn't really squeal on her brother, but everyone was pretty angry for a while today. Her pa and I had some words about it, and he took off for Jacksonville in his rig about an hour ago. Bubba went with him to try and calm him down so he don't wreck his rig."

"He was pretty mad?" Tess asked, and both Bobbi Jo and Bobby snorted.

"You could say that," Bobby said, and Bobbi Jo shook her head.

"You could say the ocean is wet too," she retorted, and looked at Tess. "He swears you two will never marry, and he's going to hire some high and fancy lawyer in Jacksonville to get Chuck off."

"I don't think that will work," Tess said carefully. "And Tuesday and I *will* be getting married, probably in June, in case any of you are coming."

"I would like to," Bobby said, and Mari Sue frowned at him. Bobby's jaw set, and he looked determined. "She's my kid sister, and I'm going to her wedding, no matter who she marries, and whatever sex, race, or religion. My wife and I will both be here."

"I plan on coming," Bobbi Jo said flatly. "Hell, I might be moved down here by then. I can bartend anywhere, and I'm sick to death of all the drama in Jacksonville. And I'm tired of my boss trying to get into my pants." She looked at her mother. "Ma, you decide to give up on Pa, you can come too. It's pretty cool down here, even with all the lezzies and stuff."

Mari Sue shook her head. "No way in hell am I living with you, girl," she said. "You're the biggest slob in the family."

Bobbi Jo shook her head firmly. "Bubba is worse than I am."

Mari Sue opened her mouth to respond, and looked thoughtful. "Yeah, okay, that might be true," she conceded. Mari Sue looked at Tess. "You know, all this talk, and all these plans and stuff, it would all go better with a beer or two. You working 'til Tuesday gets off, or could you go grab some dinner with us, have a drink or two, get to know each other better? If you're going to be a member of this family, you need to know what you're getting into."

"I can leave anytime now," Tess said impulsively. "I can text Tuesday on where we are if we're still someplace at eight."

"Well, we'll be someplace alright," Bobbi Jo said, and looked at them. "And the sooner we leave here, the sooner we'll be there."

Mari Sue looked at Tess. "Aren't you cold, just wearing that bikini? Not that you don't look great in it."

"I brought sweats," Tess said, holding them up.

"Anyplace close that's worth eatin' and drinkin' at, that ain't too hoity toity?"

"The Sunset Pier is a couple blocks away and outdoors, you can watch the sunset, and there's live music," Tess said. "Or there's the Conch Republic. It isn't too much farther from here."

"It's our last night," Mari Sue said. "I guess we could fit in one more sunset. They got food?"

"It's mostly sandwiches, burgers, shrimp," Tess said. "It's pretty decent. And they have a lot of those specialty drinks, you know, umbrella drinks. I'll go change."

"Did you bring undies?" Mari Sue asked, and Tess sighed as she heard Phoebe laugh. She hurried to the shed without answering, and was back in three minutes.

"They got beer at this sunset place?" Bobbi Jo asked, and Tess nodded. She and Bobby high fived. "Well then, what are we hangin' 'round here for?"

"Shall we go, Mama Dumarest?" Tess asked, and impulsively offered her arm. Mari Sue took it and stared at her.

"Let's go, with the understanding that, if you call me Mama Dumarest again, I'm going to spank your bare ass until it bleeds," she said bluntly.

"Okay, Mari Sue," Tess said, and was rewarded with a tired smile.

"I guess, as daughter-in-laws go, I coulda done worse," she said, and they all walked up the dock. She glanced at Tess, and there was a hint of humor in her expression. "Come to think of it, what with Bubba and Chuckie's brilliant choices, I *have* done worse."

♦ ♦ ♦ ♦ ♦

Lori Lynn sighed and took a sip of her drink. She glanced at Nico, and he was actually relaxed as he lifted his Corona to his lips. They were sitting at one of the umbrella tables out on the pier, holding hands, and the mood couldn't be more different from what they'd had to deal with all weekend, so far.

Nico stiffened slightly, and stared down the pier. She followed his eyes and watched Tess walk up to the umbrella table next to them, along with Tuesday's mother, daughter, and youngest son. It wasn't until they got seated that both Tess and the daughter happened to glance over and see them.

A look of shock, and then pleasure, flashed across Tess's face, and Lori Lynn realized she was looking at their held hands.

"Not as secluded as we thought," she muttered, and Nico snickered involuntarily.

Tess and the daughter turned and looked at each other. Tess smiled, but the girl, Bobbi Jo, was her name, Lori Lynn remembered, grinned widely.

They both spoke in unison.

"Awkward!"

♦ ♦ ♦ ♦ ♦

Chapter Eighteen

Tess felt the wind go through her sweats like they weren't there, and resisted the urge to shiver. She knew it wouldn't have made a difference, but she really wished she'd remembered to bring undies with the sweats.

"That wind is getting worse," muttered Bobby Jo. "My nipples are hard as rocks, and I ain't even turned on."

"I don't think we need that much info, girl," Mari Sue said primly. "Let's not be giving the wrong impression to your future sister-in-law. Both you and Miss Commando there, could stand to be wearin' bras. At least your nips would be warmer."

"Would you like to go to another place?" Tess asked, embarrassed to be the subject of the conversation.

"What was that Conch place you were talking about?" Bobby asked, looking at his ma and sis. "Can you sit inside, there?"

"Yes, most of it is weather protected," Tess said, praying they would decide to go there. "It's only a few blocks from here."

She saw Bobby Jo and Bobby both look at each other, then at their longneck Buds.

"They have beer," she hastened to add, and Mari Sue waved at the waitress and made a checking motion with her hand.

"Well, let's get there, then," Tuesday's mother said briskly. "I'm thinking my youngest problem child would have a fit if you got pneumonia while pretending you weren't cold to impress us."

Tess laughed, although she knew she did a lousy job of hiding her relief.

"It's not that bad," she said, and saw the waitress set the bill next to Mari Sue. "Let me help with that, give you some money."

"We got this, girl," the woman said crisply. "We had kind of a rocky start, but I want you to know you're welcome in this family." She grinned widely. "And this is Jackie's card, so he's welcoming you into the family too, whether he knows it or not. Now let's get you inside."

Tess texted Tuesday to tell her where they were going. Fifteen minutes later, they were sitting on tall backed stools around a high table.

Mari Sue looked around the crowded bar. She pointed at the empty stool between her son and Tess. "Keep a good grip on that stool, Bobby," she said crisply. "Tuesday is going to need a stool. She probably hasn't eaten yet, and will want to get something here."

"Yes, my Tue Bear will be hungry," Tess said, and sighed. "She can eat."

Bobby was looking at the menu.

"Is this place pretty good?"

"We haven't eaten here a lot, but we always enjoy the food when we do," Tess said. She blushed. "Once we started going to Diane Isis Bar & Girl, that kind of became our go to first place. They have a chef that doesn't let anything come out of her kitchen unless it's perfect."

"What do you think she'll get here?" Bobbi Joe asked.

"Until Diane Isis, she would have gotten the fresh catch sandwich, with cheese, and fries," Tess admitted. "But we got kind of spoiled by the blackened grouper and chips at Diane Isis. She likes the wings here, but I think she's going to be hungry, so that won't do it."

"Those chips, as you call them, *are* 'bout the best I ever had," Mari Sue admitted, and a look of mischievousness came to her face. "What kind of cheese would she get on grouper?"

"Blackened grouper," Tess reminded her. "Provolone, for sure. Tonight, I think she'll probably get their Conch Republic burger, and she'll get pepper jack cheese on it, and fries."

"I think she'll get cheddar," Bobbi Jo said and looked at her brother. He pulled out a five and set it between them.

"I'm thinking the pepper jack sounds pretty likely." He said, and glanced at Tess.

Bobbi Jo snorted and put her own five on top of his.

Tess saw the top of Tuesday's head bobbing between people out near the entrance, and smiled in pleasure.

"She's here," Tess said, and Bobby quickly folded the two bills and put his cap on top of them.

Tuesday eyed everyone warily as she approached, but after getting a good look at Tess, seemed to relax. A smile came to her face, and she hugged her ma and siblings, one by one. Then she gave Tess a big hug, kissed her on the lips quickly, and sat between her and Bobby.

"Need a menu?" Bobbi Jo asked casually, and handed her one.

"Nah, I know what I want," Tuesday said, and watched the waitress coming over. "I'll get a tossed salad," she said and, watching their faces, started laughing.

"Just kidding," she said. "I know Tess would have told you how hungry I'll be, and she's right. I knew none of you would have bet on a salad." She lifted Bobby's cap and looked at the two fives. She glanced at her mother questioningly.

"I know better," she admitted. "I figured you'd know we was bettin', so you wouldn't order what you really want, just to stay hard to figure out."

"Smart call," Tuesday admitted, and smiled at the waitress, who'd been waiting during this entire conversation with patience. She was a well-rounded girl with light-brown hair, and a pink streak through it. She was about Tess's height, and carrying a few extra pounds. But Tess thought she carried them well.

Tuesday grinned as everyone except Tess leaned forward in anticipation. Even the waitress smiled. Tuesday looked at her nametag.

"Wendy, I'll take the Conch Republic burger, with fries." She paused a moment, watching her family members. Tess hid her smile as her girl pretended to hesitate. "I guess I'll make that a cheese burger. You have brie?"

"Uh, no," Wendy answered, wincing.

"Good, that would be gross on a burger," Tuesday said, and handed her the menu. "Could I have pepper jack cheese on that burger? And I'll have a rum and diet coke."

"Okay, I'll be right back with your drink," the waitress said, and flashed the table a smile. "So, who won?"

Everyone in Tuesday's family pointed at Tess, and Bobby picked up the two fives.

"But *I'm* the one that followed her lead," he said pointedly, as he put the money into his wallet. "I think everyone here is ready for another round."

"I'll have it right out," Wendy said, and started to turn away, then swung back around. "Celebrating? What's the occasion?"

"Celebrating a new daughter-in-law to the family," Mari Sue said in a deliberate voice.

"Or a new sis-in-law, in our cases," Bobby said, gesturing at himself and Bobbi Jo.

Tess felt her eyes well up at their clear support, and Tuesday hugged her.

"A fiancé, in my case," she said quietly, and Tess heard the emotion in her girl's voice.

"A second family, in my case," Tess said, her voice quivering with emotion. "One that I love already."

Wendy looked around the table at them, and smiled.

"Y'all are very sweet. I'll get those drinks right out."

"Ma, I'm working through New Year's Day, and then giving my notice," Bobbi Jo said. "One of us should be down here to help Tuesday and Tess see to Chuck, and I'm sick to death of Jacksonville. I've met more nice people in the week we been here, than I *ever* met in twenty-seven years o' living in Jax. Carrie and Carla said they got a lead on someone I could live with."

Tess nudged Tuesday, and her girl looked at her doubtfully.

"You sure?" she asked. "She's a slob."

"Told ya," Mari Sue said blithely to her older daughter.

"Yo, Ho," Tuesday said slowly. "You need a place to stay while you look for a job, we have a couch in the living room. You want to have a job before you sign any leases or anything. You're a good bartender and waitress, but that don't mean there're jobs to be gotten. We'd rather you didn't bring your johns back to the apartment though. There's plenty o' alleys in Key West."

"I'm sure you would know," Bobby Jo said sweetly. "I'm glad to see Tess is going to make an honest lezzie out of you."

"Will you two quit talking so dirty?" Mari Sue exclaimed. "You're both so mean to each other. I'm surprised one of you hasn't killed the other already."

There was a moment's silence, and Tuesday's ma winced.

"Too soon?" she asked, a troubled expression covering her face.

"Too soon," Bobby agreed, and Tuesday and Bobbi Jo both answered in unison.

"Oh, yeah." They looked at each other suspiciously.

Tess became aware, about the same time Tuesday did, that Wendy the waitress was standing behind them, with a tray of drinks. It looked like she was having a hard time keeping from laughing.

"How long you been standing there?" Mari Sue asked in a resigned voice.

"Not that long. I didn't want to interrupt the conversation," she admitted. "You guys are too funny."

She turned to Bobbi Jo, and set a business card down in front of her.

"That's the manager's card," she said. "I think we're losing a couple people after the new year, so there might be some openings."

She hesitated, and then hurried to continue, her face reddening a little.

"I wrote my number down on the back. I *might* know of someone looking for a roommate," she said. "Give me a call when you get back in town." She turned to Tuesday. "I think your burger is coming up now. I'll get it right out to you."

She walked away, and all of them watched her. Mari Sue cleared her throat, and looked at Bobbi Jo.

"I think she kinda likes you, potty-mouth," Mari Sue said, and Bobbi Jo closed her eyes and groaned.

"I *hope* she just needs a roommate, and not a girlfriend," she muttered, and a tittering ran around the table.

◆ ◆ ◆ ◆ ◆ ◆

Lori Lynn led Nico by the hand to the Little tables, and they sat next to Annette and Justin on one side, and Mari and Steve on the other.

"What is this, cop central?" Justin asked, and grinned at Lori Lynn and Nico. "It looks like someone has given up trying to keep a secret." Annette promptly slugged him. "Police brutality," he said, and let his arm droop, as if damaged.

"It's the holidays," Lori Lynn said, and shrugged. "I just don't feel like pretending, or hiding how I feel tonight."

"Ooh, someone's getting lucky tonight," Justin said, and Lori Lynn laughed as she responded, and Annette, Mari, *and* Nico all matched her words and timing perfectly.

"No, he's not."

Laughter broke out around the table.

Lori Lynn nudged Nico. "Get me a whiskey sour tonight. Tomorrow is ladies' night at Diane Isis, and Tuesday is New Year's." She sighed. "After last night, I need to pace myself."

Nico nodded, and watched Melanie make her round of several tables as she worked her way back to them. Lori Lynn followed his eyes, and saw he was looking at all the tables being bunched together down by the elves of Eldamar tables, as Melanie called it.

It looked like they were grouping three different sets of tables in close proximity. There were the three for Eldamar, which made sense. There were already at least six men seated, along with Marilyn and that guy she was seeing regularly. Lori Lynn didn't know much of anything about him. She thought he'd just moved to Key West earlier this year, and it seemed like Marilyn had swooped right in on him.

There was the usual table with Nathan and the girls, and their close circle of friends. Nathan and Yasmin were already seated, as were Nadi and Carlos, the Machado bodyguard she was seeing. Seeing, Lori Lynn thought, amused. That was a euphemism if she'd ever heard one. Sarah, Mariah, and Robbi were also there.

That group of tables made sense, but who was the third group for?

There were three tables, and Lori Lynn saw two women standing next to a fourth, apparently arguing whether they needed it or not. They looked familiar, and Lori Lynn nodded as she placed them. Cindy and Stacey, from Diane Isis, along with a few other women she recognized from that setting, but had never spoken with. The two twins were there, and clearly trolling for men.

Lori Lynn noticed Melanie talking with a table of three, towards the stage, out of the main flow of traffic. It was three women, all wearing hoodies, and in the case of the middle one, a heavy overcoat. Melanie finally headed their way, and Lori Lynn's eyes followed her.

Nico told her what they wanted, Lori Lynn a Wild Turkey sour, he a Makers Mark, straight up. Melanie looked at both of them, and for some reason, looked uncertain. Lori Lynn thought she wanted to say something, but when Steve happened to clear his throat, she headed back to the bar with the drink orders.

Nico looked at Lori Lynn, and she made a "no frickin' clue" expression and shrugged. They had eye contact for a moment and, without a word, turned to look at Steve. He didn't look surprised. He stared back at them, his face a blank slate. Of course, for Lori Lynn, that was a dead giveaway.

Lori Lynn turned back to look for Melanie, but she was at the bar, organizing her trays as Gunther prepared her orders. One tray filled, and she scooted off to deliver them. Lori Lynn let her gaze wander around the room, and could sense Nico doing the same.

"Aw, for Christ's sake," Steve said in disgust. As one, they both turned back to him. He looked at them with grudging admiration. "You two are like synchronized swimmers. Look, it's nothing you need worry about. Ted and I know, we're watching, we got it. But I've been told there will be no problem."

She and Nico exchanged looks, and she could see he was as mystified as she was. Then she cussed herself out as she turned back to the table of three. If it was who she *thought* it was, it wouldn't take long, she thought as she stared at them. Out of the corner of her eye, she saw Carlos glance towards them and wince, then look down quickly.

Damn.

As if her thoughts managed to tap their shoulders, one of the women on the end turned and looked at their table and centered right in on her and Nico. She turned back forward, and the other one waited a moment, and casually turned to look herself.

Those are two hard women, Lori Lynn thought. They're pros.

"Who's between the two guards?" Nico said so quietly, she doubted even Justin and Annette heard him.

Lori Lynn didn't answer, but she wondered where the other one was. He should be here, even if they had new people.

Lori Lynn looked at Nico and spoke, just as quietly as he had.

"Pre-Yasmin," she said, and understanding broke out on his face. "Give her space. Steve knows, it's the end of the year, she's feeling nostalgic. Let her have the privacy."

Nico nodded and settled back in his chair. Lori Lynn turned her own chair to face the table so they were next to each other, facing in the same direction. Her hand snuck over and met his as it was making its own way to her. She drew his back to her so both their hands, firmly held, rested on her leg.

Lori Lynn smiled, and could feel Nico doing the same as they looked towards where Nathan would be playing in a few minutes. She noticed Yasmin had her usual ice bucket full of Dom in front of her. A group of women entered Eddie's from the entrance next to where Nathan played, and began populating the three tables.

Nico stiffened, and sat up straight.

"No way," he muttered. Lori Lynn looked at him curiously, then over at the new arrivals. Izzy and Diane were leading a group that included about half the Amazons softball team, three women she'd never seen before, one of them looking both ancient, and startlingly beautiful, at the same time. Lori Lynn idly wondered how old she was. She was attended by two women that looked like they might be related, and the new hire at Freedom Seas, Aurora. There were also two women, tall, probably six footers, that looked like they could have been personal assistants or bodyguards.

Or both, Lori Lynn realized.

"I have to go say hello to this woman," Nico told her. "I've known her since back when I met Diane and Izzy, and haven't seen her since, well, in a long time. You want to meet her?"

"I don't know, do I?" Lori Lynn asked, half joking, half wondering that she appeared to be a person of importance to Nico.

"I'd like you to," Nico said hesitantly. Lori Lynn looked at him in wonder. She couldn't think of a single time he'd ever asked her to do something for him.

"Well then, of course," Lori Lynn said, and they headed over.

Lori Lynn began to realize how old the woman had to be as they got closer. She was about to sit when she saw him approaching. A smile broke out across her face, and Lori Lynn immediately felt better about, well, everything. The power of the woman's smile was daunting, yet reassuring.

"Detective Skourellos, Nico," she said, and took a step towards him, raising her arms. He automatically hugged her, and they embraced for a moment. She held him out at arm's length, but didn't let go. "You look... well, Nico. And happy." She took in his physical frame and shook her head, tsking. "You still look like you need about a pan of Lamb Ragu, and a full plate of crostata." She looked at Lori Lynn, and the woman's smile made her stand up straighter.

"And who is this, dear Nico?"

"It's *Sergeant* Skourellos, now, Stella," Nico said, smiling at her. "And this would be...Lieutenant Lori Lynn Buffington. Lori Lynn, this is Stella Romano, the absolutely coolest woman in the world."

Stella looked at him, and a knowing smile came to her face. She turned to Lori Lynn and pushed her extended hand away.

"Nico is family, which, I suspect, *Lieutenant* Lori Lynn Buffington, means you are very nearly the same, and will be, when you resolve this annoying rank issue. And family doesn't shake hands, they hug."

Lori Lynn tried to be careful. The woman had to be in her nineties, and she didn't want to bruise her or anything, but the old woman had a very firm, full-bodied hug that began at their heads pressed together, clear down to their toes. "Keep him fed, dear. I always worry about him floating away in the wind," she said, and kissed Lori Lynn's forehead as they released.

"Let's get you seated, mother," the older of the two women said, fussing at her. Stella made a production of sighing as she winked at Lori Lynn.

"I'm ninety-four years young, daughter, not near death," she said, but let herself be seated next to Diane.

"Lori Lynn, this is my daughter, Giovanna, my granddaughter, Giulia, and you may have already met my great-granddaughter, Aurora," Stella said. All three of the women nodded to Lori Lynn.

"Aurora, I didn't realize you were you," Nico said, embarrassed. "You've grown up, from the eight-year old I met fourteen years ago."

"We really haven't had the opportunity to chat," Aurora said, looking embarrassed. "I recognized you when I saw you, and should have taken the time to introduce myself. It's just been such a busy last month or so."

"True," Nico said and, after chatting with Stella a few more minutes, they made their way back to their table. Everyone looked at them curiously, and Lori Lynn couldn't resist.

"Mistaken identity," she said. "Nico thought they were someone else." He nodded with a straight face as they sat down.

"Uh huh," Ted said, and Lori Lynn frowned at him.

"What made you so chatty, all of a sudden?"

There was laughter, and Betsy grinned. "You should hear him talk in his sleep."

"No," Ted said firmly.

"You do, I swear," she said, and everyone was grinning at his discomfort. She changed the subject, more to not get into trouble than anything else, Lori Lynn suspected.

"So, what is Nathan starting off with tonight?"

"Odds are, Elton John," Justin said, looking at the Eldamar tables.

"Maroon 5, I hope," Annette countered.

Betsy said Cat Stevens, Mari said the Beatles, and there were guesses of Chicago, Dan Fogelberg, Jackson Browne, Nico said Hall & Oates. Lori Lynn waited until everyone had guessed. Betsy told her to hurry, he was sitting down at his keyboard.

Lori Lynn made a production of staring thoughtfully into space, and finally answering.

"Steely Dan, 'Do it Again,'" she said, which got thoughtful stares from several people around the table.

Nathan chose that moment to introduce himself, thank everyone for being there, and start playing the introduction to "Do it Again", by Steely Dan.

As one, everyone at the table turned and stared at her. Lori Lynn tried to look innocent, and Ted snorted.

"You asked him."

"I haven't talked with Nathan tonight," she said. "I absolutely did not ask him."

They all knew her well enough to be able to tell when she was making a point of telling it like it was, so they believed her. But some of them still had suspicious stares as he began to sing.

Betsy and Annette began to laugh as Tess and Tuesday danced their way into Captain Eddie's. Tess was doing her usual artful leaps, pirouettes, and prancing steps as she made her way past Nathan, doing an amazingly long spin before sticking a bill into his tip pitcher. Tuesday, on the other hand, was doing some sort of robot walk, with synchronized hand and arm gestures, making her appear very stilted, yet purposeful and powerful jabs and punches. She passed the tip pitcher, pulled out a bill, crumpled it and tossed it over her shoulder. When it disappeared into the pitcher without hitting the side or lip, a cheer went up from nearby tables.

Well behind them, Lori Lynn watched as Nathan and Tess's parents followed, laughing. Suddenly, with no warning to their husbands that

Lori Lynn saw, both mothers stepped faster, doing a soft, jazzy kind of walk, with some corresponding arm motions. They also put bills into the pitcher, but with less pizazz.

Bringing up the rear, Oshba and Phoebe walked hand in hand, both wearing stretch jeans and denim jackets. Phoebe had some sort of headband of material and strands of flowers that was very becoming with her thick, black, wavy hair. Emily and Grace brought up the rear.

"All this and her video has over nine million hits on YouTube," Annette said, shaking her head. "Whoever Frizzy Fuzz is, that posted that complete video of Tuesday in action, has to be making some serious cash on the ads."

Nico happened to be taking a sip and abruptly coughed and started choking. Lori Lynn patted him on the back, and then again, harder, as he struggled to get the coughing under control.

"Went down the wrong pipe," he managed to say between coughing fits. Lori Lynn looked at him suspiciously, and he felt her gaze.

"I'll tell you, if you tell me," he said, and Lori Lynn nodded.

"Later," she said, and he nodded weakly.

Nathan finished the song, and as soon as the clapping began to subside, started playing an old song by Cat Stevens. Lori Lynn recognized the intro and smiled. She loved the song, and when Nathan got to the first verse, she couldn't help jumping right in.

"Well I left my happy home, to see what I could find out…"

◆ ◆ ◆ ◆ ◆

Chapter Nineteen

Nathan finished the song, and let the sound of the last chord die away naturally. "Mad World" by Gary Jules, was a beautiful, haunting song. It was eerie, dark, ethereal even. Going into that after doing Joe Cocker's "High Time We Went", had a very off-balance feel to it.

The crowd had enjoyed it, and it had been fun. He glanced around the tables and the bar area, seeing a fair number of new faces. They seemed to be comfortable with the fact that Nathan's song selection was all over the place. There were nights he played here that he couldn't be so self-indulgent on what he liked to call thought-provoking songs, moody, sometimes dark and depressing, sometimes unabashedly romantic.

Sunday was different though, Nathan liked to think. And that seemed to be the common sentiment, so it was working. His parents were in seventh heaven with the song list, and he'd done three Cat Stevens already, so Yasmin was happy.

He decided to do one more song and take a break. Melanie was giving him those looks. She took a straw off her tray and made a point of bending it until it creased, and the tension of the hard paper snapped.

Ah, break, I get it, he thought, smiling. He nodded to her and started playing an animated introduction to a song he hadn't even known he was going to play. The crowd sat up straighter and waited, as if to see if it was the song they thought it might be.

I forgot I knew this song, Nathan thought, keeping the smile off his face. He focused on the mood and message of the tune, to make the presentation complete.

"Well, you went uptown ridin' in your limousine, with your fine Park Avenue clothes. You had the Dom Perignon in your hand and a spoon up your nose." Nathan grinned and glanced at Yasmin. She was looked at the bottle in the ice bucket in front of her, a bemused expression on her face.

A lot of the room was waiting for the chorus, clearly not knowing the lyrics to the song. But when he got to the chorus the room was rocking.

"Because you had to be a big shot, didn't ya, you had to open up your mouth..."

Nathan let his eyes slide across the tables, looking at Yasmin and the girls, and the parents. The men of Eldamar were enjoying themselves mostly, although he noticed that Tim was significantly subdued. Nathan knew why, of course, but couldn't focus on that now.

The table of women were enjoying themselves as well. He'd played just enough Carole King, Janis Ian, and the Indigo Girls to let them know he was thinking of them. His eyes slowly panned the room as he finished the third verse, and roared into the chorus.

The Little's table was packed, and he thought he recognized everyone sitting at it. He was happy to see a lot of couples at the other tables, and his eyes automatically slid across the faces until he got to one with three women, all with hoodies, watching him intently.

He finished the chorus and went into the brief singing riff, and then the instrumental ending, with him singing "Big shot," over and over again. His hands were on automatic, but his mind ground to a halt as he stared at Amber Machado, sitting bracketed by two very tough-looking women.

He kept playing through the rest of the song, praying his subconscious would get it right. When he hit the last chord and let it ring and resonate, he somehow managed to tear his eyes away.

"I'm going to take a short break. I'll be right back," he said and stood. He walked over to Yasmin's table, and a chair next to her opened up. He didn't sit on it. She watched him closely, and he could tell she knew he was flustered. "Yasmin, I need to talk to someone for a minute."

Yasmin nodded, glancing at Nadezhda, who shrugged, and gave Carlos a dirty look. A wisp of a smile appeared on Yasmin's face.

"Dear Nathan, take the entire break if you need to," she said, and Nathan stared at her in surprise. "I have you for life, I can share you for fifteen minutes. Talk to her. I would like to not be her enemy."

"Thank you for understanding, Yasmin," Nathan said and made his way over to Amber's table. One of the women switched to another chair on the other side so he would be sitting next to her boss. They shifted their seats so they might seem like they wouldn't be listening or watching, even though they sat less than five feet away.

"Hello, Amber," he said, wondering if he should hug her, or just sit down. She helped him with that dilemma by standing and initiating the hug herself. As she stood she pulled her hood down, freeing her long black hair.

"Hello, Nathan."

Their hug was much shorter than it would have been, three or four months ago. But that was understandable. He started to hold her chair, but the closer woman already had it. She saw his automatic gesture and a begrudging nod escaped her.

"How have you been?" Nathan asked, and Amber gave him an ironic stare. He flinched, and tried to think of something else to say.

"My father would tell you I've been fine," Amber said. "As would my brother, and both of their personal advisors. I am focused on work, I am accomplishing great things for our family and the business. I am good at what I do, and I am not distracted by a sweet, silly boy in Key West."

"Hmm," Nathan said, at a loss for words.

"My mother, on the other hand, would say I've been moping around the house far too much. I ignore my friends, bury myself in my work, don't smile or laugh enough, find myself with a much shorter fuse than I used to have."

His face must have given him away, because both of the other women smirked, and Amber had the grace to admit the obvious.

"As you know, my fuse has always been short, so this is not good news for anyone not doing their jobs, or upholding deals we've made," Amber admitted. "I was quite angry at Carlos the last time I saw you, but I found out several assumptions I'd made were wrong. I must admit, apologizing is far harder than I remember."

"There's no shame in admitting you're wrong, or that you've made a mistake," Nathan said, his eyes searching her face, trying to gauge how his next words would be taken. "I didn't know that Yasmin was coming to Key West until she literally walked in that door," he said, nodding with his head at the door.

"Even so, I allowed myself to be inconsiderate of your feelings, as well as ignoring the slap to your pride, when I immediately became involved with her." Nathan sighed, and shook his head. "In Mexico, I kept any attraction I may have felt in check, respected you and did nothing to damage your standing with your employees, or your dignity. When she showed up here, I was shocked."

Nathan felt his face redden.

"When you left that morning, you made it clear we were finished, but I wasn't looking for anything from anyone," Nathan said, and sighed. "She walked in, and somehow, in no time, my gig was over, and she made it clear she planned on coming home with me. I should have told her to slow down, should have not rushed right into something, but somehow, she passively got me to do what she wanted. I guess maybe it was what I wanted too, if it was that easy for her. But I should have been stronger, and not just gone with the flow."

He forced himself to look directly into Amber's eyes.

"I am sorry for the disrespect I showed you," he said firmly. "I'm sorry I wasn't more considerate, and hurt your feelings. I was wrong in how I treated you."

"Did it occur to you I was so angry, that I knew I had to get away from you just so I could calm down?" Amber said softly. "Didn't you consider that I might just need a little time, and that I would come back and suggest we slow things down. That I loved you, and if there was a chance you would grow to care for me, to love me as well, it was worth taking the time?"

"No, it didn't," Nathan admitted. He thought about her words. He glanced at the two women, but they were looking around the room, acting as if they weren't hearing every single word. "I thought that when I told you I wasn't in love with you, it was the nail in the coffin. It didn't occur to me that you would ever willingly even want to talk to me again. And I knew we just weren't on the same page. You had a plan, many plans, really, and I didn't want that kind of structure in my life. And I knew, in my heart, as much fun as we had, as much as I like you, and even love you, in some ways, that it just wasn't that kind of love."

"I miss you, Nathan," Amber said, and he saw the sadness in her eyes. "I miss our nights, our days together. I miss listening to your voice, whether it's when you're singing, or just talking with me. I miss your kindness." She sighed, and it sounded to Nathan like it came from her stomach, it was so deep. "I miss how you affected me, made me a nicer person. Mama says that was one of the things she found most endearing about you. Papa said that was the thing that bothered him most about you."

Nathan chuckled, and she laughed sadly. Nathan looked at the crowd, and sighed.

"You have to get back to work?" Amber asked lightly. "Any chance I could see you later, when you get off?"

"I need to get back up there," Nathan admitted. "Amber, I don't think it would be a good idea, seeing you later tonight. I am in a relationship with Yasmin now, and we've talked a lot, made some longer term plans…"

He sighed. He didn't want to hurt Amber again, but he needed to make her understand.

"Mama told me to ask you to come visit them at Cocoplum," Amber said, and he wondered if she was simply scrambling for anything to say to try and hold him. "She made me promise to tell you that, and that you made a very big impression on her and Papa. She said to tell you that their life changed because of you."

Nathan blinked. He didn't know what she could possibly mean. "Oh?" he asked, and Amber smiled at him, albeit sadly.

"I miss your doing that," she said, and laughed out loud when he looked at her in confusion.

"Doing what?" he asked, and Amber bit her lip.

"It doesn't matter, but Mama blames you for the heat you brought to both of them the night they heard you play here," Amber said, and her eyes were twinkling, even as the sadness clung to them. "That night they created a little brother for me."

"Um, what?" Nathan gasped.

"Mama is in her fifteenth week of pregnancy, Nathan. She blames your voice for making both of them feel so romantic that night when they got back to the hotel."

"Um," Nathan said, and both of the other two women tittered. Amber looked at them, both annoyed and tolerant of their reaction. She sighed and looked back at Nathan.

"By the way, as you can see, my guard has increased, per Papa's orders," Amber said, and her face grew determined. "I told him two was plenty for me, but he insisted. So *I* insisted that if I was to have more bodyguards, they would be women. Nathan, this is Rosa Fuentes and Lucia Perez."

Both women turned and nodded to him guardedly. He resisted the urge to offer his hand.

"Glad to meet you both," he said, and turned back to Amber. "I gotta go."

"I know," she admitted, and gave him a searching look. "Any chance of our getting another chance to work things out? I am supposed to get back tomorrow, but I could stay another couple days, if it meant we were trying to fix us."

"Amber, I love Yasmin," Nathan said slowly, wondering if he was starting a war, or committing a foolish form of suicide. "I am in love with her, and we've talked about long-term plans. She loves me, and we think we're on the same page." He laughed shortly, without humor. "I even introduced her to my parents."

Amber looked shocked. She stared at him for a moment, then off into space, her face struggling with emotions.

"I would like to have met them, but I suppose that would be very awkward," she mused.

"Well, they're here tonight, if you'd still like to." He pointed them out. "And the other couple are Tess's parents."

"Hmm," Amber said, staring at his parents. He could tell she was torn with indecision. She shook her head, and her attention came back to him.

"Nathan, I will occasionally be making business trips here. We have business interests in the area, which is why Carlos has moved to Key West, at least for the moment. I would like to be able to come hear you, and the band, sometimes, without it being an issue. I miss you performing, I miss Tess, I even miss dancing with Tuesday," she admitted, blushing.

"They both miss you, too," Nathan admitted. "They're here. I'm sure they'd love to see you as well. I know Tuesday mentioned how much she missed dancing with you."

"Really?" Amber sounded unsure of herself, and Nathan felt awful.

"Really," he assured her. "But now, I *really* need to get back up there."

He stood and she did as well, and they hugged. It wasn't the body molding hugs of their past, but it was real, and he found it hard to finally let go of her.

"Oh, Nathan, please do me a favor," Amber said and looked depressed. "Could you not make it public knowledge about Mama being pregnant? We have enemies."

"Can I tell the girls?" Nathan asked. "They'll be very happy for your mother. And they can keep a secret."

"And Yasmin?" Amber asked cynically, and Nathan shrugged.

"As far as I know, we aren't keeping any secrets," he admitted. "But she certainly won't share that with anyone else."

Amber nodded, and gestured toward his keyboard.

"Break a leg," she said, and Nathan had to grin at her. She laughed as she read his thoughts, and when he got to his seat and sat down, she was still smiling.

Nathan saw Tess rush over and give Amber a hug. She sat down in the chair Nathan had just vacated, even as Tuesday ambled over to them.

Nathan felt himself smiling, and decided the evening could now be deemed a complete success.

♦ ♦ ♦ ♦ ♦

Tess watched Tuesday closely. She knew her girl often hid her true feelings and reactions, but it appeared that she felt Chuck's first appearance before the judge had gone well. She could feel her parents' eyes on her, watching her and Tuesday talk. She knew her mother worried about Tuesday's family.

Tess wasn't worried about the family, so much as she worried about how Tuesday was handling all the stress of her father's bigotry. And now he was probably somehow blaming Tuesday for Chuck's situation.

"How is Chuck handling being in jail?" Tess asked, and her Tue Bear shook her head with a puzzled expression on her face.

"He seems okay," she admitted. "I got to talk with him right after his first appearance before the judge, and it's like he was calm, and at peace with himself. I just talked with Izzy, and she says he almost seems relieved. She said she was impressed that he wasn't being difficult, but was doing everything she told him to."

"Maybe the closet was closing in on him," Tess said, and looked at Tuesday, worried that her words might be offensive or seem uncaring. But Tuesday nodded thoughtfully.

"You might be on to something there, Tess Mess." She looked at Tess, and a hint of a grin came to her face. "Did you happen to see who Nathan is talking to on his break?"

"No," Tess admitted, a little confused by the ease Tuesday had switched topics. She scanned the bar area, then moved over to the tables. She saw Nathan standing and then a young woman from the table he'd been sitting at, stand and hug him. Nathan's body blocked the view, but Tess knew she recognized the posture and body movement of the woman.

Nathan turned and headed for his keyboard, and Tess got her first look at…Amber!

"Tue Bear, Amber is here, and she doesn't look angry!" Tess turned to her girl, who was also watching.

"She didn't slug him, or have a bodyguard shoot him, so I think you might be right," Tuesday said with a straight face.

Tess slapped her arm lightly.

"C'mon, let's go say hi to our friend," Tess said, and heard Tuesday behind her.

"I thought it was Amber," her girl said, and Tess made a mental note to slug her arm later. Amber was about to sit back down, and saw her coming.

Amber's two bodyguards, both women, also saw her and immediately started to rise. She was about to brake, but Amber said something, and they settled back into their chairs.

Tess enveloped Amber in a big hug, and kissed her on the cheek.

"Amber, it's so good to see you," Tess said, and thought she sounded like she was babbling. Amber returned the embrace, and her lips brushed across Tess's cheek as well.

Tess reluctantly loosened her grip and pulled away enough to be able to see Amber's face without letting go. She looked touched, and more than a little wistful.

Related Matters

"I have missed you, girl," Tess said and was pleased to see her smile.

"I missed you, too, Tess," Amber said, and looked past her. "I guess I even missed Tuesday, a little bit."

"C'mon, you know you miss our dance-off workout regime," Tuesday said, coming around Tess to give Amber a vigorous hug. After a moment's hesitation, Amber returned the hug, and when they broke apart, she was laughing, despite her attempts to look disapproving.

"You running the whole show yet, Amber girl?" Tuesday asked, slipping her arm around Tess's waist.

"Not yet," Amber said dryly and glanced at her two bodyguards, still sitting a few feet away. "You haven't met my new security. Tess Carter, Tuesday Dumarest, this is Rosa Fuentes and Lucia Perez."

Tuesday grabbed Amber by the arms, looking panicked.

"Amber, tell me you didn't cut Hector in half, give him a sex change, to create these two tough babes! Tell me it isn't so!"

Amber looked at Tess and sighed.

"You deal with this, every day?" Amber made a show of grimacing. "I don't know how you keep your positive outlook, and sunny personality."

Nathan struck a chord, and started singing "You May Be Right," by Billy Joel. As one, all three of the girls turned and looked at him.

"Come sit with us," Tess urged her. "We can make room for all three of you. My parents are here, from Atlanta. You can meet them, and Nathan's too. They drove down from Michigan." Tess paused as she realized how awkward that might be. Then she shrugged. She *had* to be curious.

Amber looked uncertain, and was staring at her. She seemed to come to a decision and turned to her two bodyguards.

"You two go ahead and hold this table, in case it gets weird." Amber held up a hand as they both started to argue with her. They subsided, when she gave them the Amber stare. "You *do* remember Carlos, right? He'll be right across the table from me. And you two will be here. Not to mention, I have the human bowling ball, Tuesday. I'll be fine."

"Better to be a bowling ball than a bowling pin," Tuesday confided to the two women. Tess and Amber exchanged glances and grins.

"The more things change, the more they stay the same," Amber muttered loud enough for Tess to hear.

"Damned straight," Tuesday said, and started to continue, but Tess had a finger on her girl's lips, stopping her followup.

"Except..." Tess began and looked at Amber. She got it immediately, and started to laugh.

"…she's not," Amber finished for her, and Tuesday stared at both of them.

"You two rehearse that?"

♦ ♦ ♦ ♦ ♦

Lori Lynn watched Nathan hurry back to his keyboard, look around the room. He apologized for the long break, and said he'd had to deliver a child, not his, and it took longer than he expected.

He went into an upbeat Billy Joel song and she turned back to the table. Steve glanced at her and shook his head.

"Never a dull moment," he said philosophically. "I thought she might slug him again, but that seemed very civilized."

"She has people for that," she said, and there was laughter.

Most of the table watched with fascination as Tess and Tuesday convinced Amber Machado to come join them at their line of tables. The one with Tess's parents, as well as Nathan's. And Nathan's new girlfriend, Yasmin, as well as Nadi and Carlos, who worked for Amber.

Lori Lynn watched them for a while, even as she sang under her breath with almost every song Nathan played. Everyone seemed on their best behavior, even Tuesday.

Nico chuckled and shook his head.

"I guess there won't be any fireworks after all," he said, grinning. "Just when you think you're getting a feel for all the crazy that surrounds them, they surprise you."

"Everyone's acting very…civilized," Annette said in wonder.

"Who wouda thunk it," Lori Lynn said, and secured Nico's hand again. They listened to the rest of Nathan's set, with her leaning comfortably against Nico.

A couple hours later, they were back at her place, courtesy of Uber, and reclining on the loveseat in her living room, holding hands, their feet playing casually with each other. She felt him take a deep breath and wondered what momentous advance in their physical relationship he was about to attempt.

They were holding hands, and he shifted his left over to free up his right arm. It rose and circled around her shoulders, and she sank against him and let her head flop back to rest against the offending arm.

"Aren't you going to fake a yawn to make it seem more happenstance?' she asked, and he chuckled.

"Happenstance? Who the hell uses happenstance in a romantic setting?"

"Is this a romantic moment?" she asked, teasing him.

Nico sighed, and let his head set against hers. "It's a comfortable moment."

"It is," Lori Lynn agreed. "I had a good time tonight. We had an excellent dinner, got to hear Nathan sing for almost four hours, didn't have a shootout with the Machado crime syndicate…"

"That was certainly my favorite part," Nico said dryly, and she snickered. "So, is it later?"

It took Lori Lynn a moment to get it, and then she laughed.

"I texted Tuesday and asked her," Lori Lynn admitted. "They always do some sort of fun entrance that fits the song, so I figured he was telling her in advance."

"Damn, that's premedicated," Nico said, and then laughed at himself. "I mean premeditated."

"Oh boy, you're not driving tonight," Lori Lynn said, and wished there was another reason. She remembered his choking.

"So, who is Frizzy Fuzz?" she asked, and Nico laughed.

"It has to be Latrelle," he said, and Lori Lynn realized he was right. Latrelle had all that footage from the night of the attempt to abduct Tess by the rapist. It would have been a breeze for him to make that video.

"Way to go, Latrelle," Lori Lynn said. "They have that new baby." She looked at Nico in wonder. "She's only four months old. That's twice as long as we've been playing this game we play," she said, sounding shocked.

"Is it a game?" Nico asked softly, and Lori Lynn snuggled a little tighter against him, her head shifting to rest against him.

"Not to me," she admitted. "It only feels like one, because there are all these rules that we've followed meticulously. And it feels like we keep rolling snake eyes, so it takes forever to move across the board."

Nico's hand shifted from her shoulders to cup her head. His fingers played with her hair. She took hold with her right hand and pulled his hand to her lips. He turned his head and kissed the top of her head.

"Lute, what are we doing?" he asked softly. "Don't get me wrong. I can't imagine not being with you, every day. But I don't see the path."

"I know," Lori Lynn said sadly. She tried to lighten the moment. "I also know I haven't put my gun away, in case you're thinking of calling me Lute again."

Nico chuckled, and they sat there, limbs comfortably intertwined.

"I feel the same way, Nico," she said softly. She snuggled a little tighter against him, amazed that such a skinny guy could be so cuddly.

Lori Lynn opened her eyes to see the sun threatening to peek above Cow Key. She realized she and Nico were on the recliner love seat, and they'd slept there all night. Well, all night being about five hours.

She lifted her head to look at Nico. She shifted so she could watch him sleep for a few minutes. Her movement must have disturbed him, because a minute or two later, he sighed deeply, and his eyelids fluttered.

They popped open, and Lori Lynn's face was the first thing he saw. He smiled at her sleepily, then his eyes opened wide in near panic. He glanced down at both of them and looked relieved when he saw they were fully dressed.

"Um, oops?" he said, and Lori Lynn laughed. She stretched, and felt his eyes watch her body as she did so. Oddly enough, that didn't bother her a bit.

"C'mon, sleepyhead, get your ass out of here and get home," she said, and pushed the footrest on her side down with her legs. "Use the bathroom first, if you need to, but you need to get gone."

"Yeah," Nico admitted as he got up as well, and followed her to the front door. "You know, I only live five blocks over. I guess I could have even walked home."

"Don't fret it," she said, and hugged him at the door. He returned her embrace and they stood like that for a while. "Damn, I could get used to that," she said as she reluctantly released him.

"I can't imagine living without it," Nico said in a serious tone, and left. She leaned against the door, and listened as he started his car, and drove away.

"Me neither, Nico. Me neither," she whispered, even though there was no one to eavesdrop.

♦ ♦ ♦ ♦ ♦

"Well?" Yasmin asked, as they walked down Caroline Street, holding hands. Ahead of them, Tess and Tuesday were dancing together as they pranced along the empty street. Sarah, Mariah, Robbi, Phoebe, and Oshba walked a little behind them, as if trying to imply they weren't together.

Nathan sighed, surprised that she'd waited so patiently.

"She wanted another chance to try and make it work, but ended up settling for being friends." Nathan thought about the conversation, trying to decide the points that needed mentioning right now. "She's going to be in town, off and on, and wants to be able to come hear me play without it being some sort of crisis, or problem. I told her that Tess and Tuesday both missed her. I told her I'd like us to be friends. But I was in love with you, and that you loved me." He glanced at her, and Yasmin had an interesting expression. It seemed satisfied, yet guarded.

"I also told her we were trying to make long-term plans, as a couple." Nathan thought about how Amber took that. "I told her I introduced you to my parents, and I think that made the biggest impact." He looked at her. "That's a pretty big deal, usually. Then, ten minutes later, I'm playing and Tess and Tuesday brought her over to sit with everyone. How did that go?"

"It could have been very awkward," Yasmin admitted. "But everyone took it in stride. I think everyone has come to the conclusion that when Tuesday is involved, no matter what the occasion, a certain amount of craziness is certain to be present."

"Well, yeah, there is that," Nathan admitted. "Did they introduce her as my ex, or what?"

"No, actually Tess cleverly introduced her as a dear friend to all three of you, and that she was responsible for your rescue, along with dear Tess and Tuesday, during Hurricane Logan. And that she got a doctor for Nathan when he got all that glass embedded in him. Which is how he got all those little scars, and the one big one on his buttock."

"Did Tuesday want to show her scar, to compete for attention?" Nathan said, only half joking.

"Actually, she did," Yasmin admitted. "Tess was almost unable to stop her, until more than a few people said they'd already seen her scar, poolside."

"Heh, that sounds like Tuesday," Nathan admitted, then got serious. "I was very clear to Amber that you and I are trying to build a long-term relationship, and that we'd told my parents that."

"That both thrills, and absolutely terrifies me," Yasmin admitted, and looked over at him. "I wish the same thing. My only concern is that I may not be able to adhere to the plan. But I want to," she said with determination.

"I love you, Yasmin," Nathan said, and felt his stomach fluttering.

"I love you, too, dear Nathan," she said and stopped walking, turning him to face her. "I have thought much about this, and discussed the situation with several people whose opinions hold value to me. I explained my misgivings, and at least two, as well as Mika and Tuulikki, said it was part of the growing up process." A hint of her usual subtle humor emerged. "Apparently not being selfish and self-centered is part of the maturation process."

"It's not that simple," Nathan protested, but she covered his mouth with her hand, smiling at him, both happy and sad expressions warring on her face.

"Perhaps it is, my love," she said, and melted against him.

♦ ♦ ♦ ♦ ♦

Nathan frowned as Marilyn made the word 'secretion', pluralizing her previous word, 'testicle', even as she crossed another one of her words, 'vaginal', on the 'i'.

"So, my dear boy, secretion changes testicle to testicles, and I used all seven letters," Marilyn said, appearing to be struggling with adding up her score. "I covered a triple word square, and then…"

Nathan tried to block her rambling teasing, even as he heard Robbi whisper to Mariah. "That's the third time this game she used all seven letters."

"You're getting smoked, Nathan," Mariah said, laughing at him.

The crowd seated and standing around, watching the game, was buzzing as everyone discussed Marilyn's latest display of genius.

Nathan didn't know which was worse, the always erotic choice of words she made, or the fact that she was demolishing him. He stared at his letters, knowing he had nothing that would make any kind of dent in her lead.

Or be as impressive, he thought glumly.

"So they weren't kidding," a familiar voice exclaimed. "You and Marilyn really do come up here to the Garden of Eden to play Scrabble in the nude."

"And they have a fan club, Mrs. W," Mariah said, and nudged Robbi. "Would you two like our chairs? We both have to head out pretty soon, and get ready for work."

"Thank you, Mariah," Tess's mother said, and Nathan sighed. "You two have such great tans. I'm very envious."

Nathan tried not to watch as Mariah and Robbi got dressed, all the while chatting with his mother and Kendra. Mostly about him and Tess, he couldn't help but notice.

"Nathan, you're getting pretty racy with your words, this game," his mother said, staring at the board.

"Oh, those aren't Nathan's words," Mariah said as they picked up their towels and prepared to leave. "Those are all Marilyn's."

"Really?" His mother stared at the board, and shook her head. "Usually he's pretty good at this game. How bad are you beating him, Marilyn?"

Related Matters

Marilyn grinned and showed her the score. His mother snorted and pointed it out to Tess's mother. They both turned and looked at Nathan, their faces unreadable.

"You gotta pick up your game, son," his mother said, and Nathan sighed again. "Think dirtier thoughts." Both she and Tess's mother started laughing, as they stripped down and took the two loungers vacated by the two girls. They began spreading sunscreen on themselves. "Oh, and if I forget to, please tell Phoebe her products are brilliant. I haven't burned yet, this trip. And I'm getting the best tan."

The crowd had finally picked up that this was his mother, and he heard some appreciative comments about her looks and general coolness. They were also commenting on Tess's mother in a similar fashion.

"Hey, folks, be cool. This is my mother you're talking about, and we aren't deaf." Nathan didn't have much hope that would stop anyone, but he felt obliged to try. He wasn't wrong.

"Nathan's mom, has got it goin' on," an unidentified male voice said, and there was a murmuring of agreement. Then a girl's voice spoke up, and she sounded not only complimentary, but attracted as well.

"Tess's mom, has got it goin' on!" More than a few voices began singing random segments of the song, always gaining strength as they came to the chorus.

Both women got a little color in their faces, but couldn't quit grinning. Nathan winced as his totally naked mother leaned closer to whisper to him.

"I think I'm beginning to understand the thrill Tess gets out of running the stretching and aerobic classes in the nude," she said, and Tess's mother nodded her agreement.

"So, Nathan, can I ask you something?" Tess's mother asked, and Nathan kept eye contact with her with some difficulty. He nodded, and she looked at him quizzically.

"Is Amber your ex?" She asked, and Nathan winced. "There were some very strange dynamics at those tables last night."

"Well, Mrs. Carter, she sort of is," Nathan began, and she waved a hand at him.

"Please, call me Kendra," she said, and Nathan didn't look at his mother.

"Um, I'll try," he said, and his mother laughed.

"Kendra, the very first lesson he learned as a child, was to always be polite. I don't know how or why," his mother admitted. "God knows we aren't, all that often."

Then Nathan's mother froze him with a stare.

"While you're trying to break twenty-three years of habits, tell us what all has happened around you and the girls since you arrived here in Key West." She smiled sweetly. "I've heard bits and pieces of stories. Stories that include hurricanes, neighbors killed, criminal mercenaries kidnapping princesses, serial killers, more than one. And something about a killer park bench," his mother ended in disbelief. "Now, spill it!"

"Nathan, my lovely boy, are you going to make a word any time soon?" Marilyn asked, and Nathan realized he'd completely forgotten about the game. He looked at his letters and blinked. He rearranged a couple and put 'sex' on the end of 'secretion', pluralizing it, and getting the 'x' onto a triple letter square.

"Now he's getting into the spirit," Marilyn said enthusiastically. "When, where, and in what position, my dear boy? Your place or mine?"

Nathan heard both mothers giggle at his embarrassment and appreciative mutterings from the audience.

He sighed and wondered if he could possibly be more embarrassed.

It took next to no time for Marilyn to answer that unspoken question.

♦ ♦ ♦ ♦ ♦

Related Matters

Chapter Twenty

Felicia sipped her red wine, watching the women mingle around her. Next to her, Kendra did the same. December 30th, this would be their last Monday Night Ladies' Night at Diane Isis, as well as the last of the year, and they were making the most of it.

They were sitting on one of the several new benches that had appeared since last week. Izzy, sitting on her other side, nudged her.

"I like these new benches Diane found," she said. "Traffic on Monday nights has picked up, and we needed more seating. I hate hogging the chairs with the foot stools, and these are probably better for the back, anyway."

"I hate that we have to take that into consideration," Kendra said, and Felicia nodded her agreement.

"Getting old sucks," she said, and Izzy laughed, shaking her head.

"We're not getting old, ladies, we're getting experienced," she said primly, and pointed at Stella, who was making her way slowly over to them. Felicia moved over to make room for her to sit between her and Izzy. As usual, Giovanna was fussing around her. Giulia made a comment to her, and they began to argue. Stella ignored them both and sat in the open spot, sitting upright with excellent posture.

She looked down underneath the bench and nodded.

"You know, dear, an enterprising carpenter could put footrests on extendable arms that fold back under the bench," she told Izzy. "I bet if you mention it, Diane will figure out how to do it to all these benches."

"Would you like a foot stool, Stella?" Izzy asked, and the old woman shook her head.

"No, I find that isn't the best way for me to put my feet up, at this point in my life," she admitted. "But you younger ladies would undoubtedly find it comfortable."

Stella nudged Felicia gently with her shoulder.

Related Matters

"I meant to tell you last night, Felicia, but there were too many things happening, and we didn't get much opportunity to chat." She sighed and winked at her. "I was told your son was a marvelous singer and performer. For once, someone outstripped their reputation. He was inspiring to listen to. His voice is exceptional. He also appears to have an exceptional girlfriend."

They all looked at Yasmin talking with some of the women, the twins in particular.

"Rumor has it, they may be going beyond the boyfriend/girlfriend stage," Felicia said. "He was always so shy, I'm still trying to wrap my head around that."

"Some of us have commented on how he changes when he gets behind the keyboard," Izzy said. "From shy to showman, in one second flat."

"He's gotten so much more polished since he went to college," Felicia admitted. "He was very good, good enough to get a music scholarship at Western Michigan. But he has really stepped it up to another level entirely."

"You are a musician?" Stella asked shrewdly, and Felicia smiled as she nodded.

"I play guitar and tutor, teach high school choir, as well as a fundamental music theory class," she admitted. "Houston teaches history."

"How inspiring, teaching the young, while you can still influence them," the old woman said wistfully. "I did my best with my three generations of children, and would have loved to be a mentor or teacher, but the business always called too shrilly to ignore."

"How long are you here?" Kendra asked, and Stella looked sad.

"We leave tomorrow," she admitted. "We probably should have left today, but I wanted one last trip up these stairs. One last night with the ladies, and my favorite grandchildren," she said, taking Izzy's hand and squeezing it."

"There will be more trips," Izzy said, sounding distressed. "If you find that traveling is too strenuous, we can certainly come visit you, raid your wine cellar."

"Dear, I have heard hints and rumors, and some of my analysts have seen signs, that concern us greatly," she said with a heavy heart. "That is one reason we have sent Aurora to live with you for a while, to get her away from the crush of Europe."

"What kinds of things?" Felicia asked curiously, but the old woman shook her head.

"I can tell you nothing specific," she admitted. "But please, if you have any trips overseas planned, please consider delaying your travels."

"Odd advice from a woman that has controlling interests in several cruise lines, any number of destination resorts, not to mention numerous hotels and hostels, spread across southern Europe," Izzy said, looking thoughtful. "Of course, Aurora is welcome here as long as she wishes. As it is, I think she decided her "aunties" were cramping her style too much, and is living with two other girls, Sarah and Phoebe."

"I met them," Stella admitted. "Sarah will be a very good influence on her, and Phoebe is precious. I *do* hope she and Oshba manage to make their relationship work," she fretted. "I believe they are each other's saviors."

"Speak of the devils," Izzy said, as Sarah, the blonde detective, Lori Lynn, and the busty realtor, Ashley came up the stairs. "Watch out, everyone! Ringers on the roof," she called out.

There was a lot of laughter, Felicia watched as the other ladies enthusiastically greeted them. Lori Lynn came over and gave Stella a hug, grinned at Izzy and did the same.

"Where is Nico this evening?" Stella asked. "I leave tomorrow, and hoped to wish him well."

"He'll be back in a while," Lori Lynn said. "He'll probably have a second dinner downstairs while he waits for me."

"I sense a certain reckless abandon in you, Lori Lynn," Izzy said, and Lori Lynn grimaced.

"You don't know the half of it," she admitted.

Felicia looked at her phone, and elbowed Kendra.

"The girls should be getting here pretty soon," she commented, and heard a ping from Izzy's phone.

"Diane?" she called out, and her wife answered immediately from across the roof.

"Got it."

Tess, Tuesday, and Aurora came hustling up the steps. The moment the girls reached the top step, the Wedding March began to play.

Everybody started clapping and whooping it up.

Tess and Tuesday looked shocked, and their arms instinctively went around each other.

"Don't get ahead of yourselves," Tuesday called out. "We're not getting married until June."

Tess burst into happy tears, and they hugged. Felicia looked at Kendra, and saw her about to mimic her daughter.

Phoebe came hustling up the stairs, watching curiously, and a minute later, Oshba showed up behind her, putting her jacket on as she climbed the steps.

"Our kids are growing up," Kendra managed to say, and looked startled when Izzy handed her a travel pack of tissues. "Thank you, Izzy."

Izzy waved at Lori Lynn to catch her attention, and tossed her another pack. Lori Lynn automatically caught it and looked to see what it was. She burst into laughter as she handed it to Tess.

"Well, they don't have to hurry on our account," Felicia said, and put her arm around her friend's shoulders. Kendra nodded, and leaned against her as she tore the package open. "Now don't be hogging those," Felicia said, taking one of the tissues from the pack, laughing as she dabbed her own eyes.

"The parade of life never stops, dear," Stella said, and reached around to hug both of them. "The trick is not falling behind."

"Damned straight," Izzy said, dabbing her own eyes.

♦ ♦ ♦ ♦ ♦

December 31st, 2019, New Year's Eve afternoon

Lori Lynn looked up from Nico's report as Sheriff Raines came into her office and closed the door behind him.

"Uh, Happy New Year's Eve, Walt?" she said, and looked at his serious expression with misgivings.

"I'll be speaking to Sergeant Skourellos later this afternoon, and I thought you should be aware of the action I'm taking," he said in a serious voice.

Lori Lynn stared at him, her mouth suddenly unnaturally dry.

♦ ♦ ♦ ♦ ♦

Nico glanced surreptitiously at his phone, and saw it was after four. Another hour and he would be able to split for the night. He and Lori Lynn were going to eat dinner at the Hot Tin Roof, listen to Nathan play solo, and then the first set with Dr. Leek and the Prime Rib Veggies.

Their plans after that were vague. Nico thought about Sunday night, and decided that sleeping on a recliner, if Lori Lynn was next to him, would be more than fine. There was only one other choice that was preferable, but he knew that wasn't on the itinerary.

His phone vibrated, and he smiled, thinking she was probably watching the time as well. But when he picked it up, he saw it wasn't from her, but from Sheriff Raines.

My office, now.

Uh oh, he thought. That can't be good. He wondered if he should give

Lori Lynn a heads up, but the word "now" seemed pretty definitive. He hurried to the sheriff's office in the next portable over. As he approached, he saw the door was open.

Nico walked past the personal assistant, holding up his phone, and she nodded, not making eye contact. He knocked on the frame of the door. Sheriff Raines sat at his desk, looking at his computer's monitor screen.

"Close it behind you," he said, his eyes not leaving the screen. "Please sit down."

Nico quietly closed the door, and slid into one of the two chairs facing the sheriff's desk. Sheriff Raines turned to him. He made himself make eye contact and hold it. Raines seemed to be measuring him in some manner, and finally nodded.

"I asked you in here to discuss a few things, current events, and longer developments," the sheriff began, and Nico began to worry. "First, let me say that you did an excellent job on the Renault Case."

"Thank you," Nico said, and waited for the other shoe to drop.

Sheriff Raines nodded.

"I have to admit, I've never seen a case move from accidental death, to possible homicide, to probably manslaughter, to hate crime, to involuntary manslaughter with a possible suspect, to a full confession with no hate crime involved, in thirty-six hours." He stood and reached across the table. "You had to fight off everyone to defend that call, and you handled it well. And, you were right. That was excellent police work, detecting at its best."

Nico sat back down after shaking hands, feeling a little weak. He felt Raines watching him and forced himself to keep eye contact. The sheriff smiled.

"Your interrogation plan and technique were unorthodox, to say the least," he said, his smile widening a little. "But I can't argue with success. You utilized the sister with finesse and kept the focus clear. Maybe we should see if Ms. Dumarest has an interest in law enforcement."

"She's too much a wild card, but she got it done," Nico said, wincing at the vision of Tuesday as a police officer. "And she is a little size challenged."

"Size challenged," Raines repeated, and grinned. "I'll have to remember that. Although, in her case, she doesn't seem to let that be a factor. Her video might go over ten million hits before the year is over tonight."

"She *was* motivated and very efficient in her collar," Nico said diplomatically.

"*And,* she is the only person anyone knows of that took a shot at Mari Little's head, and didn't end up knocked out, in jail, or the hospital,"

Raines said wryly. They both smiled at the memory.

"So, you and Lori Lynn said hello to the Russians," the sheriff said delicately. "I'm curious what your intentions and goals were, insisting on that meet. And did you get anything out of it?"

"Everyone in local law enforcement knew we had a person, fresh from Russia, running their local operations, and his name might be Viktor Medvedev," Nico said slowly, thinking about all the factors involved in that meeting. "We had no face to go with the name, didn't even know for sure if the name was correct. Not to mention, for all we knew, killing Borya might have been an internal cleanup operation."

"So you confirmed the name, and put a face with it," Raines said, and Nico nodded.

"And we confirmed he's definitely the new boss in town, and a very dangerous man," Nico added, then sighed. "We also confirmed he had no idea where Borya was, and wasn't sure he was dead."

"Mmm, you're pretty sure about that last?" Raines asked, watching him intently.

"He has great control over his face, and only shows what he wants to be seen," Nico admitted. "Except, possibly, his eyes. He may have deliberately let me see his thoughts, but I think he slipped. He is pissed, and now he thinks he knows who killed one of his senior enforcers."

"You have your doubts?" the sheriff asked cautiously.

"When Lori Lynn mentioned the second smile, his control slipped. I'm almost certain of it." Nico thought for a moment. "And it may be he doesn't care if we know it. I didn't get the impression American cops were anything he was worried about. More than a little contemptuous, in fact."

"And?" Raines drew him out.

"And, he thinks the slit throat is a giveaway that it's the Columbians," Nico said. "I think it's a giveaway that someone is trying to set them up. Maybe the Machados, maybe another drug faction trying to work its way into the states via the keys, maybe an internal issue, and he has a traitor. But I don't think the Columbians are stupid. And they have plenty to gain, working with the Russians, or coming to some sort of mutual agreement. I don't see this helping them, but I do see it leading to more bodies."

"Damn!" Raines said with feeling. "So he doesn't think we'll be a factor?"

"No, he wasn't taking either of us seriously, or Smith and Smith, across the room," Nico added, and they both grinned. "Very Heller and Catch 22-ish of us, pairing them up."

Sheriff Raines laughed, although there was precious little humor in his tone.

"How about the Neilson Case?" he asked, and Nico shook his head, feeling the frustration that murder generated.

"Sir, we're about where we were last time we spoke," Nico admitted. "Lieutenant Buffington and I have discussed different aspects of the woman in the videos, and I keep thinking there is something right in front of me that I'm missing. But so far, whatever that is isn't giving me a hint."

Raines looked at him intently. When he spoke, he chose his words carefully.

"Both Sergeant Harper and Lori Lynn tell me about how your subconscious will recognize something, and you'll worry it to death until you figure it out." The sheriff's expression changed to a wry one. "Any chance it's mortally wounded?"

Nico laughed ruefully and shook his head.

"At the moment, it's laughing at me, even as it steals beer from my fridge."

Raines smiled at the comment, and his expression changed to a haunted one.

"You know who else used to tell me about your intuitions," he said sadly.

"Richard," Nico said quietly, and the sheriff nodded glumly. "He's never far from my thoughts."

"You couldn't have a better role model or inspirational figure in your life," Raines said and sighed. "I was his boss, but he taught me a lot."

The sheriff's demeanor changed even as Nico watched and he winced inside.

Here it comes. The real reason he called me in.

"That only leaves us one topic left to cover this year," Raines said, his voice heavy with a fatalistic tone. "I've had something of a parade of people that could stand to mind their own business, wanting to make sure I know that we may have a conflict of the rules stemming from the behavior of two senior detectives. I have to take action."

Nico sighed internally. He'd hoped that he and Lori Lynn weren't a topic at this meeting, but it appeared his hopes were about to be dashed.

"Sir, I can promise you we haven't broken any…"

He stopped short as the sheriff raised a hand and waved him to silence.

"Nico, I know. We've spoken about this before, you and Lieutenant Buffington have reassured me, and I trust both of you. But you know that sometimes people's perceptions supersede the truth. I have to take some form of action."

He stared at Nico.

"You did me a remarkable favor, recently, and I remember and appreciate it." He waved a hand to stop Nico's reaction. "I know, you didn't do it as a favor, and I appreciate your attitude more than you can know. You showed practical, intelligent, and considerate attitudes dealing with it. I value that. Your dealing with the Renault case, as well as the Neilson case are exemplary. But I promoted you so recently, that if I try and promote you to lieutenant right now, it will get bounced back by the county automatically. It's just too soon for such a leap in rank. Even if you *do* deserve it."

Sheriff Raines sighed heavily. "I really only see one solution to this matter."

Nico sighed and waited for the shoe to drop.

Nico went to his desk, got his piece, cleaned up the top of his desk, and decided that was good enough. He checked his phone and was surprised to see it was a few minutes after five. As he watched, a text showed up on his screen. It was from Lori Lynn.

I'm home. Get cleaned up and come by. We'll Uber it. I'm wearing a dress, hint, hint.

Nico sighed, and quickly sent a response as he hurried out to his car. *So wear socks and shoes?*

He had one stop, and by the time he got home, she still hadn't responded, which, he decided, was probably her response.

Nico quickly showered, found some decent looking slacks, a pullover collared, short-sleeved shirt that he liked, but almost never wore. He fastened the bottom of the three buttons, hesitated on the second, and decided to leave it open. The weather was moderate, but he decided to bring a light-weight jacket, in case they sat outside.

It only took a minute to drive through the neighborhood to her house. As he walked to her door, he noticed the price was still on the flowers he'd picked up from Publix on the way home. He was trying to get the tag off when she opened the door.

Lori saw what he was doing, and grinned.

"Don't bother," she said. "I shop at Publix too. Best deal for flowers in Key West. No shame in being economical."

Lori Lynn looked at him critically, stepped close, and unfastened the bottom button of his shirt.

She took the vase out of his hands, looked at the bouquet appreciatively.

"They're pretty," she said, and leaned forward and kissed him lightly on the lips. "Thank you."

"You're pretty, too," Nico stammered, feeling stupid. "I mean, you look really great in that dress." And she did, too. It was either light blue or turquoise colored, and was solid material, maybe stone-washed until the last six or eight inches of the uneven hem that barely covered her knees. The bottom panel was translucent, with embroidery interwoven intermittently. It had a corset front from the waist to the neckline, and left her arms bare.

He shook his head.

"What I mean to say is, you look beautiful tonight," he finally got out. He sneered at himself. One kiss shouldn't fluster him like this, but it *was* their first kiss on the lips.

He touched where she'd kissed him and suddenly knew.

"Raines already told you," he stated flatly. "I report directly to him from now on, and you are no longer my boss."

"Raines already told me," Lori Lynn agreed, smiling. "It was after lunch, so no, I wasn't holding out on you."

She put the vase on her bar, and shifted a few of the stems to open the arrangement up a little. She had a waist-length white jacket, and a turquoise purse sitting on a chair, but she didn't pick them up.

Lori Lynn walked straight to him, putting a hand on his chest, lightly pushing at him.

"We're going to do this once, and by then, the Uber will be here." Lori Lynn said. "I am starving, and you were born hungry. So, one kiss, and we're out of here."

Nico smiled and reached for her. She not only didn't deflect him, she reached right back.

Fifteen minutes later, they were sitting in the back seat of a Camry, ignoring the driver's chatter, looking at each other.

"One kiss, five or six, it's all the same," Lori Lynn mused, and Nico grinned.

"I love modern math."

♦ ♦ ♦ ♦ ♦

Related Matters

Chapter Twenty-one

Tess sat next to Yasmin, listening to Nathan sing a ballad by Kenny Loggins, even as she watched her parents chatting with his parents. He reached the chorus, and all four parents sang along with him, as well as the eight or nine men from Eldamar sitting at the next couple tables.

"Please, celebrate, celebrate me home."

Yasmin leaned over and placed her lips to Tess's ear.

"Both you and my dear Nathan are blessed with wonderful, supportive parents," she whispered. "You are very fortunate."

Tess knew she was thinking of her own family, and it was coming up short in comparison. The very idea almost reduced Tess to tears, but she made sure she was in control, and leaned over to whisper back at Yasmin.

"You are family to us, now, Yasmin." She kissed Yasmin's ear gently. "We are your family, and you are loved."

Tess slipped her arm around Yasmin, and rested her head against the Arab girl's. She could feel her parent's eyes on her, but didn't look at them. She just held her friend and gently swayed to the music with her.

Tess could also feel Nadezhda's eyes, on her other side, watching, but she must have been satisfied, because she turned back to Carlos. After a moment, she heard the woman clear her throat.

"Carlos, we finish a year this evening, and it has had its' positive and negative moments." Tess thought she sounded nervous. "I am happy that we met, even under the circumstances, and would be…sad, if you were not a part of my life."

Tess felt Yasmin trying to turn her head enough to watch them without their noticing, and she matched the Arab girl's movements until they had a peripheral view of the two. Yasmin put her hand on Tess's leg and squeezed it twice.

She thought Carlos looked bemused by Nadezhda's sudden bout of sentimentality. But he didn't laugh, and his eyes were for her only.

"I feel the same way." His mouth twitched. "As far as first dates go, I've had worse."

"It ended well," Nadezhda said thoughtfully. "We got to kill mercenaries, help save our employers, *and* had what can only be described as incredible sex. I have not really dated much at all, but I would rank any previous endeavors as inferior to our first date."

"And it was a blind date as well," Carlos said, his mouth turning into a smile.

Nadezhda shook her head. "I could see quite well. Remember? We had night goggles."

"No, I meant..." He abruptly stopped and grinned at her. She gave him a smirk, and as one, they both turned and looked at Tess and Yasmin.

"Please do not let us impede your conversation," Yasmin said, and Tess giggled. "I enjoy finding out new things about my little, older sisters."

Carlos turned back to Nadezhda.

"I think we should continue this conversation later, in a more private setting."

"I will be staying with dear Nathan tonight, Nadi," Yasmin said sweetly. "Oshba will be at Phoebe's, so the house and property are yours for the night. Please do not blow anything up."

Carlos snorted, and Nadezhda looked at him. "Truthfully, I cannot work under these conditions."

They both chuckled and went back to listening to Nathan play a Beatles song.

Yasmin and Tess turned back to do the same, and Tess saw all four parents watching them with grins on their faces. Tess looked at Nathan and saw he was watching them as he did the middle piano riff to "Get Back". She saw him look down at his keyboard, even as Tess felt her phone vibrate.

She read the message, and laughed. She turned to Yasmin.

"My Tue Bear is approaching and wants my assistance for her entrance." Tess had a brainstorm. "Feel like dancin', Yasmin?"

Yasmin looked touched that she asked, and Tess watched her consider the idea. She had a feeling the girl really wanted to do it, but perhaps not tonight. She looked hesitant, and then sighed.

"I am only a princess, not a queen, so therefore, I cannot be your dancing queen tonight, my dear friend Tess." Her eyes twinkled. "I shall observe and learn."

"See you in a minute," Tess said, and tried to look casual as she made her way into the crowd and out the far door.

She got outside and hurried back down Greene Street past the first entrance. She could see Tuesday heading her way, with Phoebe, Oshba, and Aurora following her.

She gave Tuesday a big hug, and they kissed until the other girls caught up to them.

"Anyone dancing with us?" Tuesday asked, and Oshba and Phoebe immediately shied away. Aurora looked interested, and Tess grinned at her.

"Follow our lead, girl," she said, and about jumped out of her shorts when Marilyn spoke from right behind her.

"C'mon girl, I'll let you dance with the grand dame," Marilyn said, and Aurora looked apologetic.

"I am so sorry, but my great grandmother is on her way back to Italy," she said, with fake sorrow in her voice. "I suppose you will have to do."

They laughed and heard Nathan start playing "Every Kinda People" by Robert Palmer, and Tess and Tuesday began their entrance. They went through the usual line dance routine, and when people saw Aurora and Marilyn following their lead, the dance floor quickly filled.

Tess loved that her mother and Felicia both joined them on the floor. The song ended all too quickly. Tess went back and sat next to Yasmin. Tuesday was on her other side, subtly trying to sneak a hand where it did not belong. At least not while they were at Captain Eddie's. And certainly not while her parents were with them.

She saw Nico and Lori Lynn walk in, holding hands, and smiled, very happy for them. She saw them pause as they looked to see if there was a Little family table. Ted was behind the bar, and Steve was over in his office area. Tess saw that the bar was packed, and looked around their line of tables. She decided they had room.

"Hey, could we shift a little closer, so we can fit a couple more people in?" Tess asked, and Yasmin immediately scooched her chair up against Tess's, and leaned against her.

"Feel free to invade my personal space," she said, and there was some laughter from people that heard her. Tess watched her parents manage to squeeze tighter, and get Marilyn and Mitch to shift the other way to make space. Tuesday was already approaching the detectives and pointed to the sudden space.

Nico and Lori Lynn came over to the table, looking uncertain.

"Are you sure you have the space?" she asked. "I don't want to make everyone uncomfortable, just to squeeze us in."

Related Matters

"You've celebrated two holidays with us, Lori Lynn," Tess said warmly. "You and Nico are family. Please sit with us."

"I am surprised you were not here an hour ago," Yasmin said. "I have noticed that both of you, Lieutenant Buffington in particular, are big fans of listening to my Nathan. Usually you are here much earlier."

"Unfortunately, the restaurant we chose for dinner was somewhat slammed, it being New Year's. They dedicated most of the space to people buying tickets for the evening, whereas we just wanted dinner," Lori Lynn said delicately, a hint of a smile ghosting across her lips.

"What she's saying is, I didn't think it through when I chose that restaurant," Nico said ruefully. "We would have probably enjoyed burritos or tacos across the street at Amigos just as much."

"Or, we could have perhaps chosen someplace in between," Lori Lynn said, and winked at them with her left eye, which Nico couldn't see from her right side.

"Okay, tomorrow, *you* choose," Nico said heavily, and Lori Lynn smiled at him with a saccharine smile.

"Oh no, we're not going out tomorrow," she said firmly. "You're grilling something. I don't know or care what, but there must be something in my freezer that we can defrost in time. Or, I'm sure Fausto's and Publix are both open. There's football to watch."

Nico grinned at her last words. He glanced around the table. "She likes football," he said, to no one in particular. Melanie showed up at his side and he glanced at Lori Lynn. She nodded and he told Melanie two Maker's Marks on the rocks.

"Didn't you drink it neat last time?" she asked curiously, and both of them looked at her in surprise.

"Yes, but it's New Year's Eve, and we're pacing ourselves," Lori Lynn said, and shook her head as the woman zipped off to her next stop. "That woman has a good memory."

"Uh oh," Nico said, and Lori Lynn looked at him curiously, and followed his stare. It went about halfway across the room to where a couple sat with a blonde teenage girl.

"Uh oh," Lori Lynn echoed, and hurried to continue. "Please don't everyone turn around and stare. But our boss, the sheriff, is sitting over there with his wife and daughter and is calling us over.

They both stood and walked over to the sheriff's table.

◆ ◆ ◆ ◆ ◆

"It's a trap," Nico said, in the voice of the fish-headed admiral from one of the Star Wars movies. Lori Lynn snickered, and then started giggling as they walked. Nico looked at her with concern, which made her laugh harder.

Sheriff Raines looked at her suspiciously as they approached.

"Lori Lynn, Nico, I'd like you to meet my wife, Sharon, and my daughter, Crystal." His wife smiled warmly at them, and the girl looked indifferent, but not antagonistic. "Girls, this is Lieutenant Lori Lynn Buffington, and Sergeant Nico Skourellos. They each have their own group that together, make up most of my Detective Division."

"Are you two, like, on a date?" Crystal asked, showing Lori Lynn that she had some of her father's smarts and attention to detail. "Isn't that against department policy?"

"Crystal," her mother began, but Lori Lynn didn't give her the chance to shut the girl up.

"If we were in the same chain of command, we would not be able to date," Lori Lynn confirmed. "But both of us report directly to your father, so we're really in parallel divisions and not in violation of any regulations."

"Lucky you," she said, and her father hushed her. He looked at both of them a moment.

"So, who's the designated driver?" he asked, and Lori Lynn grinned at him.

"Some French dude named 'U-bere'," she said brightly. "We're going to get back to our table and listen to Nathan for a bit. Are you staying to hear the first set he's going to play with the band?"

"We heard he was very talented, and he does have a beautiful voice," Sharon Raines said with a smile. "As it turns out, I adore his song selection. So, family night out, listen to some very good music, maybe bond a little."

"Yeah, bonds," Crystal said, holding her hands up with the wrists touching, as if she was tied up.

"Hush, girl," Raines muttered, and gave them an apologetic look.

"Well, you're going to love the band, trust me," Lori Lynn said. "It was a pleasure meeting you, ladies. Walt, Happy New Year."

The Raines family echoed her sentiment and Nico and Lori Lynn walked back to where their drinks were waiting.

"That could have gone worse," Nico said philosophically, and Lori Lynn peered at him.

Related Matters

"He speaks," she said, and he shrugged.

"When you're with three women and your boss, silence is golden," he said, and Lori Lynn couldn't fault his logic.

They sat down and she leaned against him as they turned to watch Nathan play.

♦ ♦ ♦ ♦ ♦

Tess watched Nico and Lori Lynn talk to the sheriff, and noticed Tim sitting next to Lawrence. Tim was withdrawn and sad, and hadn't really even tried to make a pass at Lawrence, which was unusual. She knew he was still upset about Maurice Renault's death.

She saw Lawrence notice her looking, and made a quick decision. "Be right back," she said to both Tuesday and Yasmin, stood, and walked over to Lawrence.

"Dance with me, Lawrence," she asked him with a smile. "I need someone with a solid feel for dance for a few minutes."

He looked at her quizzically, and nodded. It was a slow song by Jackson Browne that always brought her near to tears, so it was good to focus on something else.

"How is Tim doing?" she asked, and was amazed to find he was leading her in a much more traditional slow-dancing style than anyone bothered with anymore. "He was always so hot for Maurice."

"He's so down, he's hardly made a pass at me in the last couple days," Lawrence admitted. "Which is good, because I'm not in the market, but bad, in that I think he's very depressed."

"His old boyfriend, Xavier, is such a good man," Tess said sadly. "He finally told Tim his addiction to Renault was too much for him to ignore, and broke it off. For a while, I thought they were so serious, they might move in together."

"What does he look like?" Lawrence said softly, and Tess started to describe him, but as they slowly circled, she saw Xavier sitting in Lawrence's chair, holding Tim close as he sobbed into the older man's chest.

"Oh, a lot like him," she said, hearing the relief in her voice. Lawrence chuckled. "He seems to have commandeered your chair. Would you like us to make room for you at our table?"

"Thank you, Tess. That is very sweet," Lawrence said, and she could tell he was smiling. "But I suspect the men will make room for me elsewhere at the table."

Tess giggled.

The song ended, and he bowed to her. "Thank you for the dance,

M'lady," he said, and led her back to her chair. Marvin and Mohsen got people to shift to make room for Lawrence.

Nathan played another Sir Elton song, Crocodile Rock, and then said he had time for just a song before he went, and here it was, by Crosby & Nash. Tess and Tuesday nudged each other and grinned. Tess saw Yasmin looking at them curiously.

"This is "Just a Song Before I Go," Tess said, and Yasmin nodded hesitantly.

Nathan played the introduction to the song, and when he began to sing, he had quite a chorus joining in, including Tess and Tuesday.

"Just a song before I go, to whom it may concern..."

Nathan stretched the song a bit, because the audience was enjoying it, but it finally ended, as all things do. Tess and Tuesday hustled up and helped him break down his gear. While Tuesday was carrying the speakers, and then the amplifier to put under the stage, Tess coiled the cords the way he'd shown her, so many months ago.

Nathan had customers come up to talk with him, to put money in his tip jar, in several cases, to slip him cell phone numbers. She smiled as he handled it with confidence that slowly began to wane, the longer he wasn't behind his keyboard. He finally begged off to pack his keyboard and get it to the stage.

Tess had his cords in their flat suitcase and set it on his keyboard after he put it down on the dolly. He headed to the stage, and Tess smiled at the people still milling around, reminding them that Nathan would be playing again in about fifteen minutes, with the band.

She put his tip pitcher in his backpack, and carried it up to him as he got the keyboards and microphones just so. Kris saw her and grinned, nodding. She handed him the backpack and he kept it upright as he slid it behind the keyboard setup.

"Happy New Year, Tess," he said, and she smiled at him.

"Knock 'em dead," Kris," Tess answered, and began whooping as she turned back towards their tables. "Woo, woo, Dr. Leek and the Prime Rib Veggies!"

Tess sat down and saw the parents watching her.

"What?" she said, looking at them.

"You make a good roadie," Houston said, and the rest of them nodded.

"Oh, we just help Nathan get packed up," she said, embarrassed. "And he trusts everyone, and just leaves his tip jar sitting there, where anyone could snatch it. I make sure it gets where it needs to go."

"I should learn to assist," Yasmin said, and Nadezhda and Oshba both began displaying negative reactions. "Oh hush, ladies. In my old country,

I am a princess. Here, I am a girlfriend, maybe future wife and mother. I certainly lose no dignity assisting the man I love."

That brought an immediate silence to the table as everyone, including her two bodyguards, digested her words. She snorted as she saw the reactions.

"Oh please. I have made no secret of my feelings for dear Nathan."

Everyone was still fumbling for a response when they were saved by the band. Kris, the lead guitar player, welcomed everyone to New Year's Eve at Captain Eddie's Saloon, with Dr. Leek and the Prime Rib Veggies, with Nathan Williams. Nathan immediately began playing the introduction to Emerson, Lake and Palmer's Karn Evil 9. Then it was time to sing.

"Welcome back my friends, to the show that never ends…"

♦ ♦ ♦ ♦ ♦

Chapter Twenty-two

Nathan shook hands with Kris and the rest of the guys, and thanked them for the year.

"Don't forget, tomorrow is a new year, and we start at nine p.m.," Kris said, and Nathan grinned at him.

"Oh, the pressure," he moaned. "When will I find time to organize my sock drawer?"

Nathan was still chuckling as he got his backpack and lightly jumped down from the stage. He walked across the dance floor, stopping to chat with fans, some familiar faces, some he'd never seen before tonight.

"Great set, Nathan," a very young blonde girl called out to him.

"Thank you," he said sincerely, glancing at her, but not stopping. He saw she was with an older couple, maybe in their late forties, early fifties. They both were watching the girl with amusement, and he realized she must be their daughter. And extremely young, he thought, and his pace quickened.

He walked straight to Yasmin and she rose and took several steps to meet him. They hugged for a while. He reluctantly let go.

"Let me do the quick rounds, and we'll get out of here," he whispered, and she nodded. He made a point of thanking the men of Eldamar, and there was a lot of hugging, cheery holiday wishes with smiles and, in Marvin's case, big splashy tears.

"At least you have clothes on this time," Nathan said, and Marvin laughed through his tears. He shook hands with Lawrence and some of the others, and gave both Tim and Xavier a big hug together. He nodded at Xavier, and told them to have a safe New Year's Eve.

"I'm taking him back to my place," Xavier confided to him. "He's a mess. Maybe I'm a fool for caring, but I want him to be happy. He had tonight off, but that means he has to work tomorrow, so I'm on damage control."

"You're a saint, Xavier," Nathan said, meaning it, and turned to his own table. Most of them were paying their tabs, and that reminded him he needed to get paid.

Tess hugged him, and Tuesday came bounding over to grab him around the waist.

"We're going to Diane Isis for their New Year's Eve celebration on the roof," Tess said, looking apologetic. "I think most of the girls are. The couples are all doing their own things."

Nathan looked at Yasmin hesitantly. She correctly read his question and shook her head. She glanced at Tuesday, and Nathan wondered what that was about. He found out.

"No, I would prefer to spend the night with my…'honey'," she said, and he laughed, even as he reached for Tuesday. She dodged his grasp easily, and wrapped her arms around him.

"Happy New Year, Nate boy," she said, and stretched up to give him her usual messy kiss on the cheek. "Love ya. Now, go play lesbian with Yasmin."

"Tuesday," Tess said, wiping his cheek with her inevitable tissue, then kissing the same spot softly. "Happy New Year, sweet prince. We'll see you in the morning. We love you."

"I love you both," Nathan said quietly. "Go have fun and tell everyone I said 'Hippo Gnu Eeyore'." He turned to Nico and Lori Lynn. "Thank you for coming by tonight."

He shook hands with Nico, but Lori Lynn hugged him. "You sounded great, Nathan. You make a great date night for us."

"Er, date night?" Nathan said, suddenly knowing why the father of the young blonde girl looked so familiar. Suddenly, he was worrying he might be getting them into trouble. They'd been wonderful friends and very supportive throughout this year, once they were sure he wasn't a murderer. And they'd helped people he loved.

"Don't worry, Nathan," Lori Lynn grinned at him. "We aren't in the same chain of command any more. I'm not his boss. We can date."

"Is that a euphemism?" Tuesday said, suddenly popping up between them. Tess grabbed her by the arm and pulled her along, mouthing "sorry" at Lori Lynn and Nico as she dragged her girl out of the bar. Even Nico was having trouble keeping from laughing, and he never laughed.

Lori Lynn leaned in close and whispered through the side of her mouth. "I hope so." She hooked her arm through Nico's and they left.

Nathan saw that about everyone was gone, except for his and Tess's parents, and Yasmin, who was discussing something with Nadezhda and Carlos. He saw that Carlos was just looking around the furnishings of the bar, while the two women argued. And even Nathan could see that, despite the fact that Nadezhda was undoubtedly armed, she was losing the discussion.

Yasmin pointed at the door, and said something firmly in Arabic. Nadezhda threw up her hands, grabbed Carlos and they left. She called something back over her shoulder.

Nathan was pretty sure he knew what that was about. His mother came over to him and hugged him close. He hesitantly put his arms around her.

"What are you guys going to do now?" Nathan asked. "It's not even eleven yet, so you can probably find a bar or even stay here to celebrate."

"We've seen plenty of New Year's celebrations, Nathan," his father said, and Mr. Carter agreed. They glanced at each other, then back at him. "Bob and I are just waiting to hear what we want to do,"

All three of them grinned, and turned to look at Nathan and Tess's mothers. Yasmin was hugging them, one by one, and looking very shy, which was not usually part of her nature.

"So, are you going bar-hopping? Staying here?" Nathan asked, assuming they were probably going back to their B&B and crashing early.

"Maybe. We haven't decided yet," his mother said, a mischievous expression on her face. "Who knows, maybe we'll go over to your place and use the hot tub and drink wine."

Nathan laughed, pretty sure that wasn't going to be their choice. His father was very shy. He might get in a hot tub with Mother naked, but with another couple? Not a chance.

"Well, just remember the undressed code of the pool and tub," he reminded them. "The other absolutely unbreakable rule is no sharing of body fluids in either."

"Ew," his mother said, and slapped him on the arm. "That is disgusting," she said.

"Right," Tess's mother agreed. "That's what beds are for. Or beaches."

"Or back seats of cars," his mother said thoughtfully. "Living room floors can work in a pinch. Carpeted, of course."

"Those chaise loungers seemed sturdy," Mr. Carter said helpfully, and they all nodded.

"Or canoes," his dad said, and everyone looked at him. He flinched and shrugged. "Or so I'm told."

"That's a story that is going to be fun to get out of Huey," Nathan's mother said, and Nathan threw his hands up.

"I can't be hearing this," he said. "Everyone have fun tonight. Please do not share any details with me tomorrow. I'm going to get paid."

Nathan almost ran over to Steve's office area. He hadn't gotten his pay Sunday night, so the big man had two envelopes for him. He stuffed them into his backpack without looking at it.

"You *do* count those when you get home, right?" Steve asked, shaking his head.

"I trust you, Steve," Nathan said. "I do usually count it, but that's just to make sure I have the deposit right."

"Nice crowd tonight, and Sunday night as well," Steve commented.

"Sorry everyone split after the first set, Steve," Nathan said, feeling bad for the guys in the band, as well. "I guess a lot of them had plans for the midnight hour."

Steve nodded his head at where they'd been sitting. Nathan turned around and saw that the tables were all full, and Melanie was busting her butt taking drink orders.

"Oh, good!" he said, relieved. He blushed. "I guess that was kind of cocky of me to think they needed me to fill the room."

"Well, it certainly doesn't hurt the attendance," Steve said mildly, and frowned at him. "You have a beautiful woman standing alone over there, waiting for you. Don't you have somewhere to be?"

"Oh, right. Thanks Steve." Nathan turned and saw Yasmin waiting for him patiently. "Happy New Year," he called over his shoulder and hurried to her.

"I'm sorry," Nathan apologized to Yasmin. "I can't quit talking to people. Let's get out of here."

"It was no problem, dear Nathan," she said, and let him take her hand and lead her out of the bar. Ted nodded to him as they passed the bar.

"Do you want me to call Uber?" he asked, and she shook her head.

"It is a temperate evening," she said, and he smiled at her formal language. "I enjoy walking with you. I only wish we could forego clothing."

"You want to get an ice cream cone?" Nathan asked, and she looked at him, surprised. He knew he never had suggested that before, but decided he wanted to see if they could function as a semi-normal couple. "We turn on Duval, and Mattheessen's is on the way home."

"That sounds wonderful," Yasmin said happily, and turned thoughtful. "Another evening, I wouldn't mind our having ice cream at home. We could be each other's plates. Or bowls."

She was watching for his reaction, and laughed at his expression.

"I still wonder how you can be such an entertainer, yet so shy and easily embarrassed," she admitted.

Nathan noticed two figures standing in the darkened doorway of the t-shirt shop on the corner. It was the doorway he'd found Sarah, after Steven had broken up with her, just a month ago. He thought the two figures looked familiar, but they were so close together, it was hard to be sure.

He smothered a laugh as he realized who it was, and steered Yasmin right onto Duval. It looked like Nico and Lori Lynn were still waiting for their Uber driver. But it appeared to be time well spent, he thought, nodding in satisfaction.

In no time, they were at Mattheessen's, and looking at the ice cream selection. He was surprised when she chose what he'd intended to get. A minute later, they were both walking down Duval, holding hands, eating their Lime Sorbet waffle cones.

Nathan looked at Yasmin.

"Are you sure you're happy with a low key end of the evening?" Nathan asked worriedly. "Did you want to go with Tess and the rest?"

"I want to be exactly where I am," Yasmin said quietly. "Well, really, in your bed, with you. But we will be there soon enough."

"I don't ever want to take you for granted," Nathan began and she shushed him.

"Nathan, my love, I have been guilty of taking you for granted since we arrived here, and I assumed you would want me in your bed." Yasmin sounded very serious, and Nathan wondered what had brought this on. "By the grace of Allah, I have not given in to any impulse or taken any steps that might have chased you away from me. I think I understand better now, what you were trying to tell me, and I was selfishly resisting. Thankfully, I realized that despite my wanting things, whether they be people or physical belongings, there is one thing I wish more than all of the rest."

"Oh?" Nathan asked, cautiously. She laughed and turned to face him, kissing him deeply, right in front of Fausto's Food Palace. They reluctantly separated and continued to walk down the sidewalk on Fleming street.

"It had never occurred to me that I might find someone, someday, that I actually wished to spend the rest of my life with." Her voice grew a little shakier. "Until I realized I might lose you. And then I knew. I think I shocked your mother and father when I said I would be happy to be your wife and the mother of your children someday."

Nathan almost tripped over a tiny crack in the sidewalk, recovered, and stared at her as they walked. "You told them that?"

"More or less," she admitted. "And it is true. I love you, Nathan Williams."

"I love you too," Nathan said, and tried to remember. "Yasmin Bint Hazza, uh...Bin Zayed Nahyan."

"Zayed Al Nahyan," Yasmin corrected him, and laughed at his expression. "I know, it is long. I will happily shorten it to Yasmin Williams, when it is time."

They looked up, both of them startled to find they were at Eldamar. They walked between the buildings, and Nathan looked at the hot tub.

"Do you want to go in the hot tub for a while?" he asked, and Yasmin considered.

"We could," she allowed. "Or, you could open another bottle of Dom, and we could retire to your room and spend the rest of the night trying to make little Nathans and Yasmins."

She looked at his wide-eyed expression and laughed out loud.

"Well, since I am on birth control, and you have always insisted on using those intrusive little devices called condoms, we would really just be practicing."

Nathan felt himself sag in relief, and looked at her in consternation. He took her into his arms and gently pulled her close.

"When we get married, and you're ready to have children, I will be the happiest man in the world," he said honestly. "But let's put some thought into when you'll be ready to assume the role of mother. It's a big deal, and it will change our lives forever."

"It will probably make my breasts larger," Yasmin said, and slipped the strap of her dress over her shoulder, revealing a perfect, small yet full, breast. "These will hardly provide an adequate meal."

They heard a splash in the pool and turned as Lawrence came out of the water. Nathan looked at him, and then at the pool, in confusion.

"You were there all the time? I didn't hear a splash, and didn't see you when we walked up," he mused.

"I was doing laps underwater," Lawrence admitted. "Never know when you'll be reduced to swimming in pools, looking for pocket change." He pointed with his head slightly. "By the way, your parents, and Tess's, are in the hot tub, in the appropriate dress code. I thought you might want to know before you did anything you don't want your parents to see."

"Thank you, Lawrence, you're a saint," Nathan said, and reached for Yasmin's hand. "Shall we, dear?"

"Good night, Lawrence," Yasmin said, and allowed Nathan to lead her into the apartment. "Would you open a bottle of Dom, dear?"

"Why yes, dear, I will," Nathan answered gallantly, and quickly opened one. He looked at Yasmin. "I need to use the bathroom, very badly. I'll be right back."

He saw her smile impishly, and wondered what that was about. He made a point of closing the door firmly, before sitting down. They had moved past worrying about privacy matters, even in the bathroom, but he really wanted a couple minutes to himself. He'd been holding it for what felt like hours.

When he came out, Yasmin was standing naked in the kitchen, looking at his wine glasses. She chose one that was a little squat for a champagne flute, but that way the center of gravity was lower.

"I find our tradition of sharing our glass in bed to be very endearing, Nathan," she said. "Could you open a bottle of Dom?"

"I already opened one," Nathan said, and stopped, wondering at her impish expression.

"There were beggars at the door, and I have no pockets, so I gave them what I had, which was a bottle of Dom," she said, and Nathan looked at her bemused. Shrugging, he opened another bottle, and she held out the glass. He filled it about two thirds full, and they adjourned to his bedroom.

"I believe you need a shower, dear Nathan," Yasmin said, sniffing. "May I assist?"

"I thought you'd never ask," Nathan said, pulling his clothes off and tossing them into the hamper. They stepped into the shower and he turned the water on. She gasped as it hit them, and instinctively clung to him.

"Happy New Year, dear Nathan," she murmured.

"Happy New Year, Yasmin," He answered. "I love you."

Her response was more physical than verbal in nature.

♦ ♦ ♦ ♦ ♦

Felicia clinked her short plastic glass against Huey's and then Kendra and Bob's, and they all wished each other a happy new year. She took a sip.

"Oh, my God, this is good," she crooned, and Kendra moaned.

"It's so light."

"But tasty," Houston said.

"Like my wife," Bob finished, and Kendra gave him a pretty good whack on the arm. "Ow! That had English on it," he accused her, and Kendra smiled sweetly at him, but didn't answer.

Felicia smiled as she pictured Yasmin walking fully unclothed across the pool deck area, holding a tray with the open bottle and four plastic cups, only a few minutes ago.

"Happy New Year," she said. "Enjoy. I would join you, but I must go wash Nathan's back."

They watched her walk across the pool deck, and Felicia had to admit it was an inspiring vision. She stirred and glanced at Huey and concealed her grin.

"Huey, are you looking at our future daughter-in-law's bare butt?" she asked calmly, and Kendra snickered. Bob muttered a warning to him.

"Trick question, Houston."

"I am," Huey admitted, surprising Felicia. She thought he'd stutter and make up some dumb excuse, but he was owning up to it. Not that she cared, under the circumstances.

"I think when it comes to dealing with our kid's future wife, we should have good hindsight," he said solemnly.

They all groaned.

♦ ♦ ♦ ♦ ♦

Nico and Lori Lynn sat in the back seat, holding hands. He was content, yet mildly terrified. He'd wished for this evening for so long, and here it was. Or was it? Was he reading more into what she intended? Was he misreading her desires, by clouding them with his own?

"So, Nico, did you pack an overnight bag?" Lori Lynn said quietly. They both watched the driver, but he seemed caught up in listening to reggae music on the radio.

"I did," Nico admitted, and hurried to qualify his answer. "With it being New Year's Eve, I thought neither of us should drive, and I could always sleep on the loveseat." He sat waiting for her response, but she didn't say anything. "Or the back seat of my car," he muttered. She tittered.

"We seemed to survive sharing the loveseat two nights ago," Lori Lynn pointed out, and he quickly agreed with her. Her gaze was fixed forward, and her expression was telling him nothing. "On the other hand, there *is* another flat surface in the house that would comfortably fit us both."

Nico's mouth went dry. He wanted what he thought she was saying, so badly it hurt, but he was scared to death he was going to mess things up. "I would be, um, fine with that. If it's what you want," he hurried to add.

"What do *you* want, Nico?" she asked and he opened his mouth and shut it again.

"I want…to tell you I haven't really been dating or anything, for a very, very, *very,* long time," Nico said. "I don't want to mess things up between us by assuming anything."

"Nico," she said, and paused. "Nico?" He turned to look at her. She had an amused smile on her face. "Nico, we want the same thing. You're not going to mess things up by telling me."

"I want to spend the night with you, in your bedroom," Nico said, and swallowed hard.

She saw that and started laughing. "Has it really been that long?" When he nodded, she smiled at him. "Does everything still work right?" she asked, trying to keep a straight face.

"Oh, I think it does, yes," he said, and wondered if his voice sounded as hoarse to her as it did to him. "We might need to practice a bit, to get things just right," he risked saying. Her smile told him it was the right thing to say.

He remembered something, and began to panic.

"Uh, we need to stop at a CVS, or a Walgreen's, or something like that," he said, feeling his face heat up. "Like I said, it's been a very, very, *very* long time."

Lori Lynn grinned, and turned to face him, their lips very close.

"Don't worry, I took care of that yesterday. We're in good supply, in case we don't get out of the house for a day or two."

"Oh," Nico said, and they both leaned forward, their lips meeting.

◆ ◆ ◆ ◆ ◆

Phoebe and Oshba walked in the White Street entrance to Smokin' Tuna Saloon, and saw Sarah hard at work behind a still-crowded bar. As they looked for a table, a group of four got off their bar stools, and went out the other entrance.

They snagged two of the stools and waited for Sarah to finish the fairly extensive drink order she was filling. She saw them and smiled. Phoebe was distressed to see her face looked drawn and she lacked her usual vivaciousness.

"What can I get you ladies," she said, a minute later. "The kitchen is still open if you want menus."

"No, we've been eating nonstop since about eleven," Phoebe groaned, holding her stomach. "I need a ginger ale to settle my stomach. And a Barbie."

Sarah laughed, and Phoebe was happy she'd been able to cheer her roomie up. She really liked Sarah, and wanted her to be happy.

"I too, will have a Barbie," Oshba said, very deliberately. Sarah looked at her closely, then at Phoebe, raising an eyebrow.

"Maybe a little bit," Phoebe confirmed, and Sarah grinned as she quickly made the two frozen drinks, and then pulled a can of ginger ale out of the cooler. She poured it on ice in a tall glass and gave it to Phoebe. "We came to keep my roomie company until she gets off, and then walk her home."

"Oh, that's sweet," Sarah said, and Phoebe could see she was touched. "But I'll be okay walking home alone, if you want to go now. I won't be off for almost an hour yet."

"We will survive without making love that long," Phoebe assured her.

"Hi Phoebe, Oshba," Mariah said as she stepped to the waitress station. "I need six Coronas, and two girls said they wanted whatever the foxes at the bar were drinking."

"Six beers, two Barbies, coming up," Sarah said and quickly filled the order.

Mariah looked at Phoebe and tried to sound casual as she asked, "How is Aurora doing?"

"She's doing well," Phoebe said, knowing Mariah was acting like she wasn't hurt by Aurora breaking up their relationship, short-lived as it was. But she was. And her tone called out the fact that she missed her. "I think she was happy to see her family, but sad when they left and told her to stay here until at least summer."

"Oh? That's new," Mariah said nonchalantly.

About twenty minutes later, Aurora came in the same door they had.

"Hey, ladies," she said, and smiled around at them. She saw Mariah at a table, and a troubled expression came to her face. She looked at Sarah. "Diane Isis is fading fast, so I figured I'd swing by here on my way home, and see how my favorite roomie was doing."

"Fine, thank you," Phoebe said without hesitation, and they all laughed. "And this is so directly on your way home," she joked. It was actually blocks out of Aurora's way, and everyone knew it. She hoped the Italian girl hadn't set her sights on Sarah. The older girl was vulnerable right now, but *that* wasn't happening. Sarah was extremely heterosexual.

Sarah had been cleaning, restocking, doing all the chores she could before closing, so when Smokin' Tuna finally closed, she made quick work of counting her register drawers. One of the managers checked with her.

"How you doin', Sarah?" he asked, and Phoebe thought she intentionally misinterpreted his question.

"Fine, Peter," she said. "I got everything clean, and restocked. The liquor is locked up. I counted my drawer and it balanced."

"Big surprise there," Peter said dryly, and looked at Phoebe and the rest of them. "Your friends are waiting for you. Go on, go home, or whatever you have planned for the night."

"Home, and a good night's sleep," Sarah told him. "Thanks Peter, Happy New Year."

He wished her the same, and Sarah took him at his word. In no time, the four of them were hoofing it down Duval. Phoebe intentionally walked a little slower, making Oshba match her stride.

Sarah and Aurora walked ahead of them a little, but Phoebe could still hear them quite clearly.

"Do you work tomorrow?" Aurora asked Sarah, and she nodded.

"I don't go in until three, though," she said.

They talked about the evening, and Aurora told Sarah about Captain Eddie's, and how busy it was with Nathan and Dr. Leek playing. Then she told Sarah about Diane Isis, and the carefree atmosphere, and all the ladies being there, and just how much fun it had been.

Aurora asked her a lot of questions, and answered when Sarah asked her anything, but Phoebe could tell there was an undercurrent to the conversation. Sarah noticed it too, she saw, and finally brought it up.

"It's fun talking with you, and I feel like we're getting to know each other a lot better," Sarah said, and then plowed on. "But I want you to remember that I'm straight. I think you're sexy as hell, but I'm just not into girls. I've also sworn off any sort of relationship for a while," Sarah said, and Phoebe could hear pain in her voice. "It's too recent, and there's still too much pain."

"I know," Aurora admitted. She seemed hesitant to say more, but did. "We live together, and I am not trying to seduce you, or have a romantic relationship with you. But I *would* like to have you as a friend. Someone that I could talk with about things, who would care about how I was doing, just as I would care about how she was doing."

Sarah looked sideways at her, looking thoughtful.

"I'd like that," Sarah admitted. "I don't think I can handle anything romantic right now. It's too soon after Steven, and too hard, after…" She didn't finish the sentence.

"I understand," Aurora said, and looked at her with sympathy. "He *is* a true friend to you, though. I think he would do anything for you."

"But he's very busy," Sarah said. "They're building a solid relationship, and they both want it to work. I'm happy for them."

"But you only get to see him one evening a week," Aurora said what she left unsaid.

"I miss him," Sarah admitted, and glanced back at Oshba with misgivings. She'd clearly forgot they were walking behind them.

"Do we have the makings for more Barbies at your house?" Oshba asked, and her words sounded a little thick. Phoebe kept her face straight.

"You don't need any more," Phoebe said. "I think you've had enough."

Related Matters

"Oh, okay," Oshba said, and Phoebe wanted to hug her, it was so precious.

Sarah turned forward. Phoebe could see the tension release in her shoulders, and smiled.

When they were in her room, a few minutes later, and they'd heard Sarah and Aurora go upstairs, Phoebe looked at Oshba with a smile.

"That was very good acting, my love," she said, and Oshba looked crestfallen.

"I did not fool you?" she asked plaintively.

"No, and I do not think Aurora fell for it either. But Sarah did, which is all that matters."

"Sarah is a good woman, her heart is open to help others," Oshba said slowly. "It is not her fault she loves a man that loves someone else. It is just unfortunate. She understands and is dealing with it. I think it will take time."

Phoebe pulled her dress off, and then her panties. She sat on Oshba's lap, facing her. Her lover smiled at her, and reached around and unfastened her bra. Phoebe removed it and tossed it onto the chair with the dress.

She kissed Oshba, softly at first, gradually increasing in intensity. After a couple minutes, Oshba cupped Phoebe's buttocks and stood, holding her tight against her. Phoebe wrapped her legs around the love of her life, and let herself be lowered onto the bed, Oshba on top of her.

♦ ♦ ♦ ♦ ♦

Chapter Twenty-Three

Tess and Tuesday walked down the middle of Margaret Street, swinging their held hands high as they walked, or marched, as it seemed to Tess.

"Let's go, Barbie, let's go, Barbie," Tuesday said, and they giggled and without discussion, slowed their pace down to a slightly below manic speed.

"I missed seeing certain people tonight," Tess said, and Tuesday vigorously nodded her head. "Ashley and Wally, first of all."

"They're on a cruise," Tuesday reminded her. "Western Caribbean, I think. Wally has been looking good. I think he's working out, or maybe cutting out Hobbit Elevensies, or both."

"His shirts have been fitting better," Tess agreed. "You can't see his belly that much. He recently told me he was trying to get healthier. I would have loved to have seen Philip and my old mentor, Dr. Meyer."

"It's weird that they were old lovers, and you might have been responsible for them getting back in touch," Tuesday said. "And you were right. If we'd tried to get married now, with Chuck in jail, and everything, it would have been very unpleasant."

"Wait," Tess said, holding up a hand and coming to a halt. "Can we go back to that 'And you were right" comment?"

"Whatever," Tuesday sniffed and kept walking. Tess hurried to catch back up.

"I think June will be perfect, except for the heat," she said, and slapped her girl on the butt. "We can start thinking about invitation lists, venues, flowers, all that kind of stuff."

"Or we could just take Nathan with us and go to city hall," Tuesday mused, and dodged a slap aimed at her arm.

"Is Chuck going to be okay?" Tess asked, suddenly shifting subjects.

"They've got him in his own cell right now, and it's the county jail instead of prison, and so far, still in Key West," Tuesday said. "Hopefully, we can get his sentence served someplace outside of a regular prison. We'll have to wait and see."

They walked into the patio area of their apartment and they both stopped to listen when they got to the kitchen.

"They might be out in the hot tub," Tess said.

"I think they made a beeline for the bed," Tuesday said, and crept across the living room, trying to emulate the Pink Panther. Tess followed her, watching with amusement. They got to Nathan's bedroom door, and Tuesday carefully opened it enough for them both to look in.

Nathan and Yasmin lay naked under the top sheet. It wasn't pulled up high, so they were only covered a little above the waists.

Nathan was lying on his side, facing the middle of the bed, his left arm outstretched under the pillows. Yasmin faced him, her head on his shoulder and outstretched arm. Her left arm was around his waist, his right hand cupping her butt.

"I don't see how that can be comfortable for Yasmin," Tess whispered in Tuesday's ear.

"Yeah, where's her right hand and arm," Tuesday asked, and leaned a little forward, as if that would help her see better. "It isn't detachable, is it?" she asked, and Tess covered her mouth to muffle her giggle.

At that point, Nathan rolled onto his back, and both girls saw where Yasmin's hand was. At that moment, it was gripping a very stiff part of Nathan's body. They both ducked back, and Tuesday carefully pulled the door shut. They scurried to their room and looked at each other, trying to keep from laughing, all the while looking guilty.

"We almost violated the 'No Peeking During Sex Accord," Tess whispered. Tuesday nodded.

"I think it was a set-up," she declared, and they grinned at each other.

"Hot tub?" Tess asked, and Tuesday nodded. They both stripped down, and tiptoed past Nathan's door, then dashed out the back, grabbing towels on their way. They got outside and slowed to a walk, their arms going around each other's waists as they walked.

They were almost to the gazebo with the tub, when they heard a man's cough. Then a very familiar voice greeted them.

"Hi girls, how was Diane Isis?" Tess's mother asked.

Both girls froze, and Tess hurriedly wrapped her towel around herself.

"Hi Mrs. Carter, Hello Mr. Carter," Tuesday said brightly. "Oh, and hello to you too, Mrs. Williams, Mr. Williams."

The four adults laughed, and Tess realized they were all a little snockered. She looked around and saw the clothes her mother had on at Eddie's lying on a chair.

"Have you been in the hot tub since you left Captain Eddie's?" she asked, a little concerned.

"Ooh, bet you're all wrinkly," Tuesday added.

"No, we've been going back and forth between here and the pool," her mother assured her. "Want to join us?"

"No, no, we were just, uh, checking to see if Nathan and Yasmin or we'd left some clothes out here, but they're yours," Tess finished lamely. "So, we'll just be going to bed now. Nite!" she said brightly, and grabbed Tuesday's hand.

They hurried back to the apartment, got inside the back door, and held each other, giggling.

"Well, I guess we should check on Nate boy, and then hit the hay," Tuesday said blithely, and took a step towards the bedrooms.

"No, no, no, Tue Bear," Tess said firmly, taking her hand. "No more checking tonight. C'mon."

She led Tuesday down the hall. As they passed Nathan's door, they heard the sound of the bed creaking a little. Then Yasmin gasped, and Nathan made some sort of moaning sound. Both girls walked quickly down the hall and silently closed their door.

They leaned on it for a moment and looked at each other.

"I think Nathan and Yasmin are onto something," Tuesday said, leering at her.

"I'm going to be onto something too, in a moment," Tess said, and stuck her tongue out at her Tue Bear. "My fiancé."

They both giggled and fell on the bed together.

♦ ♦ ♦ ♦ ♦ ♦

Related Matters

Chapter Twenty-four

Tess saw that her girl had started a pot of coffee, and that most of it was still there, but it also looked like someone had already used Yasmin's coffee maker. Sarah stuck her head in the back door.

"I made myself a cuppa, I hope that was okay," Sarah said, and Tess smiled, happy to see her.

"Of course," she said, and looked at Yasmin's machine with some trepidation. "I guess I need to learn how to use this thing," she said in a quiet voice, aware that Nathan and Yasmin were still in bed, and if looks were to be believed, still asleep.

"C'mere, I'll show you," Sarah said, and a few minutes later, they were sitting at the patio table, sipping their delicious coffee.

Sarah looked pensive, and Tess wondered what she was thinking about.

"Penny for your thoughts," she said, and Sarah laughed, although it was a ragged laugh.

"I don't think you'd get your money's worth," Sarah said. She looked out at the common area of the community. "It's so beautiful here in the morning, and pretty much everyone is nice." She glanced at Tess, and her face colored a little.

"I still have a key, you know," she said, glancing at the door into the pass-through that included the washer and dryer. "I should give it back to you."

"No, Sarah, we want you to have it," Tess insisted. "We need someone besides ourselves to have a key, just in case. And you only live a block away, it makes perfect sense."

"You don't think at some point she's going to realize I have it and ask why?"

"I think she already knows," Tess said, not at all sure about that. "Sarah, you are family, and are always welcome in our home. And you're never alone. You always have us." She tried to think of something to make a joke about it, and grinned as she leaned forward.

"If you didn't have a key to the house, we would probably give one to Marilyn, and then Nathan would have to keep kicking her out of his bed, or find her crawling in with him when he's asleep."

Sarah laughed out loud. She looked at Tess, and her eyes thanked her.

"You ready to swim?"

"I suppose, although sitting here drinking great coffee and talking with my bestie is more fun."

The turnout for the aerobics class turned out to be much greater than Tess expected. And Aurora actually came earlier for the stretching exercises. Tess wasn't surprised to see she could stretch nearly as far as the rest of them. Of course, Sarah couldn't come close, but she accepted that with grace.

Aurora was startled when she saw Lawrence match the rest of them, and her eyes wandered more than once when he was fully extended with a foot pointing straight up. Tess wanted to tell her to give it up, but decided a little humility might do wonders for her.

Tess and Nathan's mothers came for the aerobics, and after the class, the men all wandered back to their apartments, or to put towels out to hold chairs by the pool.

"Sarah, I am going to get cleaned up and go over to my auntie's bar," Aurora said. "They told me there is a New Year's Day breakfast tradition involving something called black-eyed peas, and other foods that bring good luck for the year. Would you like to go?"

"Thanks, Aurora," Sarah said, shaking her head. "But I work at three today, and I've got some things I have to do before then. Thanks for asking, though."

Tess looked at her mother.

"Mother, Tue Bear and I have to work today. New Year's Day is a big one for people going out on the water, one way or another." She looked at her apologetically. "What are you and Father going to do?"

"Your father and Houston are coming over here to watch college football for a while," her mother said, and glanced over at Mrs. Williams. "Felicia and I are going to shop a little, have lunch somewhere, maybe see what is happening at Diane Isis."

"This is our last night here," Nathan's mother said, looking sad. Then she perked up. "We're going to caravan with Bob and Kendra back to Atlanta, maybe stay there a night, before the long drive to the arctic north. We're hoping to have dinner with you kids somewhere, tonight."

"That would be fun," Tess said, thinking about where they could go.

"Tue Bear and I will brainstorm for a good place that you haven't tried yet."

"I got a text from Bobbi Jo a little while ago, and she is definitely planning on packing up her things, putting most of her stuff into storage, and driving down after the weekend," Tuesday shook her head. "I guess she wasn't kidding. She's already given notice to her boss and landlord." She looked at Tess uncertainly. "You sure it's okay if she stays with us a few days until she finds a place? You know what she's like."

"I like her," Tess said, and was surprised to realize that she meant it. "All we have is the couch. Will that be okay for her?"

"The price is right," Tuesday said bluntly. "If she doesn't like it, she can either drop by Diane Isis or call that waitress at the Conch Republic. I'm sure either she or Shanda would put her up for a few days."

"Tue Bear, that's mean. She's your sister," Tess said, smiling to show she didn't mean it.

Nathan and Yasmin came out to the patio area, and Tess listened to him go through the same conversation with his mother about their plans for the day.

"I have to play from about nine to ten thirty," he reminded them. "You might want to go ahead someplace and eat at a civilized time. Especially if you're leaving early in the morning. Yasmin could join you for dinner, and I'll catch up as soon as we finish the set."

"You could eat with them earlier, and we'll catch up when we get off work," Tess suggested. She blinked. "Actually, I'm covering for Aurora today, doing the jet ski tours. I'd be done early enough to meet you wherever. Tuesday would have to catch up."

Tess looked at Tuesday, worried that she would be upset, but her girl winked at her. She held up her phone. "I just texted Aurora, and she said she could work the sunset cruise, so I could get off about the same time as you."

"You think she'll drink much today, before she goes in?" Tess asked, and frowned. "If she looks at all under the influence, I won't let her board the ship."

She looked around the table, and realized her parents were bemused by her firm stance.

"It's a legal thing," Tess explained to them. "The ship is a motorized vehicle, and she can't be under the influence. We could get fined, lose our insurance, lose our license to operate out of Key West, and Captain Jeff could lose his captain's license."

"I'll remind her, and accidentally copy her aunties," Tuesday said, smirking, and Tess laughed.

"That will do it, although Aurora might be a little pissed off," Tess agreed. She winced and looked at her mother with misgivings.

Her mother shook her head, amused.

"Tess dear, you're an adult. Sometimes adults get pissed off."

"I am so glad you and Father made it down here for the holidays," Tess said, and gave her mother a sad look. "I'm going to miss both of you when you leave."

"We'll be back," her mother said, and Nathan's mother nodded.

"Don't we have a wedding to go to in June?"

"Damned straight," Tuesday said, and opened her mouth to continue, but for a change, Tess was too fast for her. She put her hand over her girl's mouth and smiled at everyone.

"But we're not."

♦ ♦ ♦ ♦ ♦

Lori Lynn floated on her back. Her boat, Lori Lynn's Liner, bobbed in the moderate waves about ten yards away, loosely secured by its sea anchor. She also had a cable tied around her left wrist, so currents wouldn't separate her from the boat.

She was a good swimmer, but had no intentions of swimming seven or eight miles back to Key West. Especially since she was naked. Next to her, Nico floated on his back, his eyes closed. She was glad he was a good swimmer as well. But she was sure he was no more eager to drag himself out of the water after swimming so far, in the buff, than she was.

She idly wondered if she'd ever cure him of his modesty and self-consciousness when it came to nudity. She'd been sorely tempted, several times, to sit out at the pool of Eldamar, when invited over by TNT. But she knew there was no way he would. At least not at this point.

And she knew he was right. Somehow, video proof would make its way into the news, either word of mouth at the county, or via social media, with pics to prove it. Despite her joking manner with Walt, someday she *was* going to run for Sheriff. And she was going to win. Being caught naked on film in a public place would not help her.

"You sure the fish won't come for the bait, and decide we look tastier?" Nico asked, and floated a little closer to her.

"Nah, they go for the easy choice, usually," Lori Lynn said, and continued mischievously. "Unless we're dangling parts, they won't pay us any attention."

"Great," Nico muttered, and Lori Lynn smothered a laugh.

"You sure you're okay with our taping the games for later?" she asked, knowing he loved watching football. And college football in particular.

"Yeah, I mean, we both know that Alabama and Ohio State are going to win today," he said in a relaxed tone. He'd managed to drift within arm's reach, and put his left hand on her hip.

Lori Lynn smiled, remembering how hesitant he'd been at first, last night, when they finally made it to where they'd both wanted to be for months. In bed together. Nico wasn't someone that got intimidated by much of anything, but she knew she had a power over him, and getting him to take the initiative had been harder than she'd expected.

But it had been worth the time and effort, she thought with a dreamy smile.

"What are you grinning about?" Nico asked mildly.

She laughed and decided to be totally honest, to see if she could get him to blush.

"I was just rerunning some of the highlight reel from last night in my head," she said. "You know, I *did* grab a couple packets of either catsup or condoms, I don't remember which, when we left the house. I thought there was a chance you might get your strength back."

"What a coincidence," Nico said dryly. "I grabbed a couple myself, and I *know* it wasn't catsup."

"Hmm, all this saltwater has probably washed our sunscreen away," Lori Lynn said, doing a little reaching of her own. "Maybe we should get back on board and help each other put some more on."

She ran her fingertips across his stomach and he gasped.

"Uh, okay," he managed to say as his own hand followed her path, but on *her* stomach. "Good plan."

Lori Lynn laughed and let her hand drag across a lower part of his abdomen, and then was swimming for the boat. She heard him gasp, and then the splashing of him following her. When she reached the ladder, she turned around just in time to greet him by wrapping her legs around his waist.

"You tired from the swimming?" she asked sweetly. "You want to go first?"

"After you, M'lady," Nico said gallantly. "Anyway, the view of you climbing up a ladder, from the bottom, is inspiring."

Lori Lynn laughed and then kissed him very thoroughly, her legs still around him. When they finally came up for air, she laughed again.

"There was a time, not so long ago, that you saying that would have made me very self-conscious." She gave him a last quick smack on the lips, and then turned around and began to climb. Her words drifted down to him.

"At least in *your* case, those times are gone."

♦ ♦ ♦ ♦ ♦

Yasmin yawned and stretched on her lounger. Nathan felt his mouth go dry. It amazed him that although they'd been a couple for two months, and there was no part of either of their bodies the other hadn't explored, examined, and more, that he still felt a rush of his senses watching her, almost every day.

Her eyes were closed, but her lips turned up, and he wondered how she could always tell.

"Nathan, we have the afternoon. Perhaps you should go get the exercise mat, and maybe a sheet or two."

"Uh, yeah, good idea," he managed to croak out the words, and her smile widened.

"Do you need my help?" she asked, and he shook his head. Then he rolled his eyes at himself and answered out loud.

"No, no, you stay there. I'll go get them." He hurried across the deck, glad no one else was here to see the physical evidence of how much her actions turned him on.

He clumsily carried the workout pad and several sheets over near their chairs. Yasmin was watching him now, and made an appreciative sound as she looked at his physical reaction still in an extremely excited state.

"Nathan, I believe you are happy to see me," she said, watching him hurriedly spread a sheet on the pad. He saw her eyes look past him, and react to something. She looked like she was trying to keep from laughing.

"You have to be kidding me," Nathan muttered, and quickly sat down on his lounger, and just happened to put his cap in a strategic place. He felt his reaction subsiding far faster than it had originally manifested.

Yasmin struggled to keep from laughing as she called out.

"Nadi, Carlos, come join us. It is a beautiful winter day with summer temperatures," she said, clearly not concerned with any sense of propriety.

"We do not wish to interrupt anything you were planning to do," Nadi said, looking at the exercise pad. Carlos was looking off into the trees, as if searching for cameras, or perhaps snipers, or...monkeys.

Yasmin looked at Nathan closely, and sadly shook her head.

"I fear that my Nathan is a very private, self-conscious person, and that the odds against there being any use of that pad by us are now astronomical." Yasmin looked at Nathan a moment, then turned back to Nadi. "Perhaps I will take him to my room, and we can…watch American football on my television. Or perhaps play dominos."

"It does not appear that was your original intention," Nadi noted, looking at the pad. Carlos snorted, and glanced at Nathan.

"Lo siento, Nathan," he said, and Nathan sighed.

"No hay problema," Nathan answered, and felt his face get hot. "It's not like either of us have been deprived."

"Then please, get comfortable," Yasmin told Nadi and Carlos. "Truthfully, we are meeting Nathan's parents for dinner, before he plays tonight. They leave tomorrow, along with dear Tess's parents. I certainly would not want to be responsible for draining my Nathan's strength before he sees them. Or plays tonight with Dr. Leek."

"We will be back in a minute," Nadi said, and led Carlos to her room to either switch to swimsuits, or strip. Nathan wasn't quite sure which.

Five minutes later, he knew they were comfortable with sunbathing in the nude, around Yasmin and Nathan, anyway.

Nathan closed his eyes and debated the merits of napping in the sun for a while. He felt Yasmin's hand creep into his and he smiled as he squeezed it.

His smile faltered as he heard Phoebe's voice from across the deck.

"We aren't interrupting anything, are we?" she asked, and he heard Oshba make a strangling sound that was probably her stifling her laughter.

Nathan sighed.

♦ ♦ ♦ ♦ ♦

Phoebe resisted the urge to laugh out loud as she saw Nathan's reaction, partially because she didn't wish to embarrass anyone, and also because her laughing seemed to creep some people out. She and Oshba had gone straight to her room and stripped, without checking to see if there was anyone already poolside. She idly wondered who'd gotten here first and brought the pad out. The sheets were a dead giveaway as far as what at least two people had in mind.

"We came to get some pool time and sun," Oshba said, and looked at Yasmin. "M'lady, if you wish privacy, we could retire to my room." She looked at the pad, and then at Nadi.

"We would not wish to inhibit either of your plans," she said, and Phoebe turned to watch her, recognizing the tone. "Or was this to be a joint effort?"

Phoebe smirked as she put towels down on two of the loungers. She would bet any amount of money that you couldn't get either Carlos or Nathan to take part in what was, for all intents, a two-couple orgy, in broad daylight.

In fact, she doubted witnessing another couple making use of the pad would be at all satisfactory to either of them.

Phoebe blinked as she realized neither of the actions caused her any serious distress. Her viewpoints and comfort levels had definitely expanded since she and Oshba had gotten together. Oshba, on the other hand, wouldn't feel at all comfortable, at least with either of *these* couples.

"I am going to take my Nathan upstairs, so he can get some rest before tonight," Yasmin said, standing up. She didn't bother putting her coverall on, or wrapping a towel around herself. She took Nathans' hand and tugged him to his feet. He automatically reached for his boxer shorts.

Shazam boxers? Really?

Yasmin was too quick for him as she gathered his and her things, as well as their towels, and led him to the house. Phoebe watched them leave, and not for the first time, was impressed by the scar on Nathan's butt.

I bet that hurt, she thought.

She and Oshba got settled on their loungers, and she watched Nadi and Carlos look at each other, then at the pad, and then at them. Oshba started playing a song mix on her phone. She'd played it before, and told Phoebe the songs were from Yemen, Oman, and even Somalia, and were mostly pop songs about killing westerners, or the despots that ruled the various Arab nations, including Yasmin's Abu Dhabi.

Nadi hated that kind of music, and thought Oshba was taking a chance just by having the mix. She thought it was kind of interesting, even though she couldn't understand hardly any of the words. Her lessons in Arabic were going slowly. Every time Oshba tried to give her a lesson, it soon deteriorated into love-making.

As aphrodisiacs go, learning Arabic seemed to be the most effective. Phoebe smiled and nudged Oshba with a finger.

"Oh, I think this is my favorite song on this entire mix," Phoebe said, and Oshba looked at her curiously. Her look changed to admiration as Nadi muttered something, and she and Carlos gathered their things and walked into the house.

"You knew they would do that?"

"I thought they might," Phoebe admitted.

"My little witch is so smart," Oshba said, and looked at her in surprise as Phoebe stood and held her hand out. Oshba rose and let Phoebe lead her to the mat. She spread the sheet over the surface, and then knelt, waiting for Oshba to join her.

"You know, they can look out their windows and see anything we do here?" Oshba asked, and Phoebe shrugged.

"I have no problem with that, my ferocious falcon," Phoebe said, and guided Oshba to a supine position on her back. "You have released my inhibitions, and I wish to love you with abandon, whenever and wherever."

"I recognize that sentence," Oshba said thoughtfully. "Are you reading my romance novels?"

"Maybe," Phoebe admitted, and pushed Oshba back down as she tried to sit up and embrace her.

Phoebe straddled her and leaned over to give her a very passionate kiss. Then she slowly began to slide lower on her lover's body, letting her mouth roam across some of her favorite spots until she reached her goal.

"I believe you helped me attain the heavens of passion, last time," she said, and placed her mouth very strategically. She looked up Oshba's body to stare into her eyes.

"My turn."

♦ ♦ ♦ ♦ ♦

Lawrence sighed, looking around the Eldamar pool area. He didn't see anyone he had any urge to chat with, or even sit with.

Nathan had left with Yasmin, and he was pretty sure that by now, they were either at or in *her* pool, which had none of the restrictions, or audience, that this one did. The girls were at work, Marvin and Simon were visiting with friends 'off campus', as Simon put it, Tim was probably at work or with Xavier.

He sighed. The list went on. He rinsed off by the pool, gathered his things and went up to his apartment. He didn't get lonely or bored, although his current symptoms did seem to indicate one or both states.

He wondered if late this month, or early February was too soon to contact Ronald in Boston, and tell him he would be in town. The doctor had been very nice company and delightful in bed.

Lawrence decided to check the jobs board, and see if there was anything he could tie into a visit. If he was going to travel, he might as well make a little money in the process. He was settled into his chair on his deck, his business iPad on his lap, scotch in a glass at his elbow, before he realized he hadn't bothered putting any clothes on.

Related Matters

He glanced down at the pool, but no one was paying him any attention. He looked to the other side, where he had an excellent view of the street, and anyone passing by didn't have a half-bad view of him as well. He didn't see anyone, and shrugged.

As long as he was out here, he might as well get some sun, he decided.

He saw there was a job on a politician in New York, and he made a note to look at it closer, after he checked all the current choices. There was an open contract on a labor leader in Boston itself, but that was out. As convenient as it would be, he had a standing rule to not work where he played. Odds of anyone connecting Lance Lennon to the death of a local union leader were slim, but odds could be funny. And very quirky.

He saw a job for information only, no action to be taken against the subject. There was a reward for one hundred-thousand dollars for any information that led to discovering where a Yasmin Bint Hazza Bin Zayed Al Nahyan was hiding, probably with two female Arab bodyguards. Some leads pointed to Miami, but she hadn't actually been sighted there.

The listing stressed that no action whatsoever could be made against Yasmin. Any exception to this would result in very harsh consequences.

The very next listing was for a hit on either one of Yasmin's bodyguards, Nadezhda Ahmadi or Oshba Salehi, but only one of them. Yasmin was not to be left unguarded. Any fulfillment of this contract would require location information and details, in advance. Both women were deemed extremely dangerous.

The fee was two million dollars.

Anyone attempting to fulfill this contract was to contact the contractor before taking any action. Due to the abilities of the guards, they wished to have backup support in the immediate area, so that Yasmin and the remaining bodyguard didn't disappear before they could be contacted.

Lawrence sighed, and wondered if he'd ever been handed an easier contract to fill. They were right. Nadi and Oshba were extremely dangerous, and very competent. But they would never see him coming, and it was for only one of them.

Two million would very nearly put him at the cash reserve level he'd deemed necessary for him to retire for life. Not taking the contract, should anyone realize his situation, would almost certainly end his career and put him on someone's list.

The people he did business with didn't like unpredictable assets.

On the other hand, he had a very strict rule regarding working where he lived. Also, no living soul had the slightest idea where he lived, or what he looked like. As far as he knew, everyone in the industry thought the Fox was a female.

Lawrence stared at Nathan's apartment, and the area of pool deck where they and their friends usually gathered.

Clean shot.

He heard a whistle, and through the fog, realized that someone had finally passed by on the street and noticed him. He ignored them.

Lawrence clicked on a file and looked at the hundreds of photos of Nathan in the file, some with him clothed, many of him nude. Some of them distant, some of them very close.

He clicked on one and stared at a closeup of Nathan singing at Captain Tony's Saloon, his eyes staring right at the camera.

Lawrence stared back for a long time.

♦ ♦ ♦ ♦ ♦

Related Matters

Epilogue

The man nodded to the guards, and went into the office, carrying a laptop. A man sat behind an ornate desk, looking at a laptop of his own. He was handsome, in his early thirties, and looked bored. The newcomer wasted no time.

"Prince, I think I may have found something," he said, and the man behind the desk sat up, interested.

"You found the princess?" he asked, and the man shrugged.

He put his laptop in front of the prince and opened it. He clicked on an icon and a picture filled the screen.

It was grainy, and wasn't quite clear. But the picture was good enough to see three figures. They were all nude, two young women and a man perhaps in his late twenties or early thirties. All were attractive, but it was the middle one that both of the men stared at.

She was tall, with long thick, dark hair almost to her ass. She stood at a ballet bar, holding it lightly with one hand. The leg away from the bar was stretched straight up in the air. Her free hand cupped the heel of the raised foot, and she looked graceful. She looked like she was college age.

She also looked very exposed, her genitalia clearly visible from the angle of the camera. The other two in the picture were in the same position.

The man watched the prince lean forward to look at the middle figure's womanhood, and his breathing get heavier.

"Go to the next photo," he said, and the prince finally tore his eyes away and clicked on the arrow on the right side of the photo. It changed to another, with the same girl, and a different man, a young man, only looking a couple years older than her.

They were both naked as well, and had their arms wrapped around each other, kissing. The prince clicked on the arrow again, and it showed the couple just as they were separating after the kiss, both their features easy to see, if a little blurry.

"That is Princess Yasmin," the prince said tightly, his breathing still heavy as his eyes never left her body. "Cousin Yasmin, the perverted, blasphemous whore."

He tore his eyes away to look at the man.

"Where were these pictures taken?" he asked huskily.

"We do not yet know, Prince Rafik," the man admitted. "We found these pictures, as well as a few more, on a laptop that belonged to a merchant that was brought in for questioning. I asked him where these cameras were, and he said he didn't know. He'd frozen images of several videos, and managed to save them."

"What site? Can we find it and view the full videos?" the prince asked, and the man shook his head.

"The site is gone, erased at the source, as far as we can tell," the man admitted. "We are trying to identify the others in the pictures. If we do that, we can find her."

"Do we have any idea where she might be?" the prince asked.

"We know she was in Mexico, and then several places in the Caribbean, before entering the United States in Miami," the man said, rubbing his stubbly chin. "Since then, she made one trip to Finland, but returned two weeks later. We lost her trail then, and are still trying to pick it up again."

"Has she responded to any of the summonses to return home?"

"She has not," the man admitted. "We think she is still in the United States, but she could be anywhere. We are trying to discreetly ask for assistance from the State Department, but at the moment, the United States is not particularly friendly. They are not being helpful."

"I will see what can be done at the family level," the prince said, and sat back down at his desk. He clicked back two shots to show the princess at the ballet bar. He stared at her hungrily.

"Keep me informed of your progress," he said, and pulled his eyes away from the screen. His expression was cold. "Make progress to report."

"Yes, my prince," the man said and left the room.

The end.

Made in the USA
Monee, IL
24 June 2024